PRAISE FOR

'A knockout new talent you

—Lee Child, international ~~bestselling~~ ...or of
the Jack Reacher series

'It really had me gripped.'
   —Marian Keyes, international bestselling author of *Grown Ups*

'The definition of an utterly absorbing page-turner. Richly drawn-out characters, a compelling plot, and a finale that will keep you guessing.'
   —John Marrs, bestselling author of *What Lies Between Us* and
The One

'A real nailbiter of a thriller that gets darker and more twisted with every page. If you liked *What You Did*, you'll love *The Push*.'
—Erin Kelly, *Sunday Times* bestselling author of *He Said/She Said*

'Absorbing, timely, and beautifully written, *What You Did* is a superior psychological thriller from a major talent.'
                    —Mark Edwards, bestselling author of *The Retreat* and
Here To Stay

'I loved this story. The flesh-and-blood characters, dry wit, and brilliant plotting are every bit as enjoyable as *Big Little Lies*.'
                    —Louise Candlish, bestselling author of *Our House* and
The Other Passenger

'A perfectly plotted murder mystery that had me hooked from the first page. Twisty domestic suspense that's perfect for fans of *Big Little Lies*.'

—Lisa Gray, bestselling author of the Jessica Shaw series

'I haven't flown through a book so quickly in a very long time. It delivers on every single level.'

—Caz Frear, bestselling author of the DC Cat Kinsella series

'What a nail-biting, just-one-more-page-I-can't-put-it-down roller coaster of suspense!'

—Steph Broadribb, author of *Deep Down Dead*

'Smart, sassy, and satisfyingly twisty.'

—Sarah Hilary, author of the DI Marnie Rome series

'Huge fun with some very dark moments and brilliantly awful characters. Excellent, twisty plotting.'

—Harriet Tyce, author of *Blood Orange*

'A brilliantly observed and compelling thriller.'

—Anna Mazzola, author of *The Story Keeper*

'A roller-coaster read, full of thrills and one spectacular spill!'

—Liz Nugent, bestselling author of *Skin Deep*

'*What You Did* is a triumph, a gripping story of the secrets and lies that can underpin even the closest friendships. Put some time aside – this is one you'll want to read in a single sitting.'

—Kevin Wignall, bestselling author of *A Death in Sweden* and
The Traitor's Story

'Hitting the rare sweet spot between a satisfying read and a real page-turner, this brilliantly written book deserves to fly high.'
—Cass Green, bestselling author of *In a Cottage in a Wood*

'I absolutely devoured *What You Did*. Claire McGowan has created the ultimate moral dilemma in this timely and gripping psychological thriller. I can't recommend it highly enough.'
—Jenny Blackhurst, bestselling author of *Before I Let You In*

'McGowan writes utterly convincingly in three very different voices and she knows how to tell a cracking story. She will go far.'
—*Daily Mail*

'One of the very best novels I've read in a long while . . . astonishing, powerful, and immensely satisfying.'
—Peter James, bestselling author of the Roy Grace series

'Funny and perfectly paced . . . chills to the bone.'
—*Daily Telegraph*

'Plenty of intrigue makes this a must-read.'
—*Woman & Home*

'A complex, disturbing, resonant novel that remains light on its feet and immensely entertaining.'
—*Irish Times*

'Page-turning.'
—*Guardian*

'Highly satisfying and intelligent.'
—*Bookseller*

'With a great plot and brilliant characters, this is a read-in-one-sitting page-turner.'

—Fabulous

'A brilliant portrait of a fractured society and a mystery full of heart-stopping twists. Compelling, clever, and entertaining.'
—Jane Casey, bestselling author of the Maeve Kerrigan series

'A keeps-you-guessing mystery.'
—Alex Marwood, bestselling author of *The Wicked Girls*

'A brilliant crime novel . . . gripping.'

—Company

'A compelling and flawless thriller . . . there is nothing not to like.'
—Sharon Bolton, bestselling author of *The Buried* and *Now You See Me*

'Ireland's answer to Ruth Rendell.'
—Ken Bruen, author of *The Guards*

TRUTH
TRUTH
LIE

ALSO BY CLAIRE McGOWAN

THRILLERS

The Fall
What You Did
The Other Wife
The Push
I Know You
Are You Awake?
Let Me In

Non-fiction

The Vanishing Triangle

Paula Maguire series

The Lost
The Dead Ground
The Silent Dead
A Savage Hunger
Blood Tide
The Killing House

Literary Fiction

This Could Be Us

Writing as Eva Woods

TRUTH TRUTH LIE

CLAIRE McGOWAN

THOMAS & MERCER

Published by Thomas & Mercer, Seattle

www.apub.com

Amazon, the Amazon logo, and Thomas & Mercer are trademarks of Amazon.com, Inc., or its affiliates.

ISBN-13: 9781662513862
eISBN: 9781662513879

Cover design by The Brewster Project

Cover image: ©Production Perig, Malshak / Shutterstock; ©Michael Prince / Getty Images

Printed in the United States of America

TRUTH
TRUTH
LIE

Mhairi

There were eight of them, that's what she'd been told. Eight adults anyway. Old university friends, who had rented the house and island for a fortieth birthday. The adults were one problem, but there were also kids: a teenage girl, and twin five-year-olds. The kids were what really worried her.

The crossing from the big island to the small took only ten minutes – barely time to start the boat, sit down, and disembark. It looked close enough to swim, but it wasn't, not with the currents and rocks in the narrow channel.

Many people had fallen foul of that over the years.

As the chief police officer for the Scottish island of Tarne, Sergeant Mhairi Douglas didn't have a lot of serious crime to deal with. People on Tarne left their doors unlocked, and children ran free, plus nobody had much to steal in any case. She was kept busy busting drivers pushed over the limit during tasting sessions at the island's distilleries, breaking up fights in the eight pubs on the landmass, and attempting to stop the noise from raucous Airbnb guests who thought nothing of blasting out Beyoncé at five a.m., in a place where most people got up at that hour to fish or farm. She'd not had a single murder since she transferred from Glasgow, five years ago now. And this – she still couldn't take it in really – was potentially more than one.

'Two bodies, you said?' she asked the boatman, Arthur McCann. He'd been hired to take the guests over for the weekend, but had found the dock empty on returning to pick them up that Sunday morning, the island silent and dark. Few things opened Sundays on Tarne, and Mhairi had been asleep when the call came in, her one lie-in of the week.

'That's just what I could see on a quick walk-round.' He had gone ashore at first, thinking they'd slept in, but had quickly become alarmed and retreated. Chances were he'd left traces, which wouldn't please the forensics lot once they eventually shipped them over from the mainland. Still, it couldn't be helped, and nor could it be helped that she would leave her own DNA by going out there now. Just a welfare check, at this stage, but if Arthur was sure he'd seen at least two bodies on the island, it was going to turn into more than that.

'What the hell happened?'

He shrugged. He was a stoical man who'd fought the seas around Tarne for fifty years, and not easily rattled, but she could see it in him, the shake of his hands on the tiller, the pallor of his usually ruddy skin. 'I just took them over Friday. They had all their food and bits, shouldn't have needed anything. They could have called if something was amiss, there's a radio.'

'You should have let someone else take me over, Arthur. You've had a shock.'

He glared stubbornly towards the horizon. 'Need to show you what I saw.'

He'd done the right thing, probably, but she felt fear rising as the small jetty on Mallacht came into view. A desolate lump of rock, nothing but the one house and about two hundred seals, semi-feral sheep, and seabirds. It had once belonged to the Capeman family – the ones who'd hired it this weekend – but had been sold to some foreigner a while back. The Airbnb economy had brought cash to the islands, but also dragged a lot of destruction in its wake. People from the cities, from the South – and that meant anywhere south of Fort William really – had no idea about the islands. How to respect them. How to survive them. To come out here in February, that required a certain level of steel. Or stupidity. Something about it didn't sit right with Mhairi. Why return to a place you had owned, that was no longer yours?

Mhairi wished she had a partner to help her, or at least more backup than Davey Daniels, her part-time deputy, who'd been in Edinburgh on a training course and was hastening back as she sat there in the boat. She had seen death before – of course she had – but she'd never been out to Mallacht. The name was a corruption of the Gaelic for 'cursed', and she'd heard the stories. It was haunted by the ghosts of sharecroppers forcibly evicted in the 1700s. The landlord's daughter had thrown herself off the rocks when her sailor lover abandoned her. Under grey skies, through a haze of light rain, it made Mhairi want to motor back to the relative metropolis of Tarne as fast as she could. What was she going to find out there? She thought again of the kids Arthur had described. Twins who'd been most reluctant to wear life jackets for the short trip over. A teenage girl, horrified to learn the island had no phone reception. Mhairi had never seen a dead child on the job, and she didn't want to start today.

She huddled deeper into her police-issue raincoat, fleece-lined and sturdy. Arthur pulled the boat around to Mallacht's wooden jetty, waves choppy either side, the motor fighting the tide. The water beneath was jet black and freezing. Surely they hadn't tried to swim for it?

The house was on the crown of the tiny island, half-hidden by shrubs and bushes. There were hardly any actual trees on the island – too windy. Glances of windows and a slate roof, smoke rising up from the chimney. No lights on, though the morning was dark and likely to remain so. Arthur had said the electricity was out. A power cut, or something deliberate? Despite the situation, Mhairi was curious to see the mysterious island. The ruins of some older cottages, several sheep silhouetted against the grey sky. The slap of water on jagged black rocks.

Arthur held out a hand to help her disembark but she disdained it, leaping out herself. She might have grown up miles inland, but she was islander enough now to be comfortable around boats. Callum often took their small skiff out on weekends. Not today though; not in this weather. He'd have to wrangle Caitlin by himself, and her endless requests for *Paw Patrol* episodes. Mhairi turned back to Arthur, who was tying the boat up. 'You don't need to come ashore, you know. You've done your bit.'

He shook his head. 'You shouldn't be alone out here.'

She opened her mouth to complain that she might be a woman, but she was still an experienced officer, then shut it again. She'd be glad of his company, because this island was creepy as hell. It was deadly silent, only the moan of the wind in her ears, the buffeting waves. Was everyone dead? Had it been a mistake for Arthur to come back to fetch her, instead of searching the place immediately – but what could he have done by himself? And it was a crime scene, it had to be protected.

But the wee kids. She'd seen a picture on the mother's Instagram. A boy and a girl, bright-blond heads, carrying matching Octonauts backpacks. Not much older than Caitlin. They would be alright, wouldn't they?

She took a deep breath. 'Come on then. Show me what you found.'

They began to trudge up the path to the darkened house.

Amira

Amira was so cold. So, so, so cold. It was meant to be a holiday, for God's sake! Who chose to go to Scotland in February? They could have been in Tenerife or the Caribbean, or at the very least a cosy cabin in Norfolk or Dorset – not a ten-hour drive, then a ferry to an island, then another tiny boat over to a different, uninhabited island. It wasn't her idea of a break, and she knew none of the men would do any housework over the weekend, so she'd probably be cooking and cleaning just like she did at home. Paddy might help, of course, but in a sort of self-congratulatory way that Amira would find hard to bear. He'd already gone off somewhere with Daniel, a bad sign, and she resented being left at the cars with Vicky as they queued for the ferry.

Vicky and Jonathan were obsessed with Scotland. They even referred to themselves as Scottish, despite their gratingly posh English accents, because they'd spent summers at their family's house here, on a private island off the coast of Tarne. A private island! Amira's family hadn't even had a private balcony. Also, they were going to miss the ferry if Jonathan didn't get here soon.

'Where is he?' she risked calling to Vicky, aware that her tone was irritated.

Leaning against her own car, Vicky raised her perfect eyebrows. 'I'm sure he's almost here, Amira.'

'They said check-in closes forty minutes before.'

Vicky waved a hand. Dusty-pink nails. 'Oh, they don't mean that. Look, people are still arriving.'

Amira and Paddy had been there for forty minutes already, the third car in line for the ferry. They had picked up Fiona and Darcy from the nearest train station en route, and Fiona had made one or two comments about it being terribly early. She owned a car too, but Amira guessed she had been too nervous to drive the whole way to Scotland. Jonathan would have done the driving, before the split. Vicky, Daniel, and the twins had roared up in their Range Rover about ten minutes earlier, still somehow getting a spot right beside Amira and Paddy, a new line of cars opening up as if just for them. Now they were only missing Jonathan, and whichever bimbo he was bringing with him – could Fiona really be OK with this? – and of course one other person.

'Louise,' she asked. 'Where's Louise?'

Vicky looked up from her phone, where she was composing an Instagram reel of the ferry port, a picturesque inlet lit by the lowering winter sun. 'She said she'd meet us here.'

Amira bit her lip with anxiety. Hypervigilance, her therapist called it. It was no skin off her nose if they missed the ferry. This wasn't her trip – it was Jonathan and Vicky's joint fortieth, and she was just a plus-one. Just Paddy's wife, though she'd known them all for fifteen years. She felt insecure about the woman Jonathan was bringing, who he'd only been with for six months. What if the Group liked her more than Amira? Surely they wouldn't warm to her, their loyalty lying with Fiona, their old friend – though Jonathan was Vicky's brother, her twin, so she couldn't exactly turn her back on him.

Amira looked round at Fiona, who was in the back of the car, also on her phone. Darcy, Fiona and Jonathan's fifteen-year-old daughter, had gone wandering off to find a coffee, most likely to get away from the grown-ups. 'Are you really OK with all this?' she said, in low tones.

Fiona looked up. 'The influencer girlfriend? I'll be fine, but you are sweet to worry. We have to think of Darcy, and she wanted us both here. It is her dad's birthday, after all.'

It was a hard choice to make, if you were best friends with the wife and the husband was your twin brother, Amira thought, looking over at Vicky as she turned the camera on herself for a shot of her blonde hair flying in the wind. Luckily for Vicky, Fiona and Jonathan had decided their separation would all be terribly amicable and middle-class, up to and including Jonathan bringing some new woman, more than ten years younger than them, on his birthday trip. But of course he would want his girlfriend there, Amira thought. And Vicky would want Fiona, her best friend since university. Maybe it was fine, and Amira was just small-minded.

If Paddy and I break up, I'll be out of the Group like a shot. The thought made her feel even colder. She looked at the clock on the dashboard.

'If Louise doesn't—'

'I'm here,' said a calm voice outside the car, still Welsh-accented despite living all around the world for almost twenty years. 'What's the hassle?'

'Oh! Nothing, hi Louise. Just didn't want you to miss the ferry.'

'I've been here half an hour. I was waiting in the terminal.' Louise had clearly made absolutely zero effort with her appearance, which was annoying in a different way to how Vicky was always so glamorous. Frizzy ginger hair, pale unmade-up skin, dressed in a hiking T-shirt and cargo trousers, a North Face jacket on top, a large rucksack. She had taken the bus here, refusing offers of lifts. Louise lived a car-free life, as she was always reminding them. Also annoying.

'How are you?' Amira tried. 'Long time no see.' Paddy had met up with her a few times since she'd been back, but Amira had not been invited, which smarted a little.

Louise shrugged. 'I'm fine.' She didn't ask the question back. 'No Jonathan?'

Vicky sighed. 'I hoped that once we left home I'd grow out of people always asking me where my brother was. Look, if he misses it, he misses it. We go without him.'

'Really?' Amira was shocked by that idea. A gathering without Jonathan, his jokes, his magnetism? She couldn't imagine it.

At that point, Darcy darted over, slightly breathless, a takeaway cup of coffee in one hand and phone in the other. Amira didn't remember drinking caffeine at all when she was fifteen. 'Dad's here!'

'About bloody time,' mumbled Fiona, then she fixed on a smile. 'Would you like to drive on with him, darling? It's a while since you saw him.'

Darcy shrugged, teenage moodiness falling back like a curtain. 'I don't care.'

'Well, jump in then, they're boarding.'

The cars ahead had begun to roll, after what felt like forever waiting in line. 'Where's Paddy?' Amira panicked suddenly. She'd never driven on to a ferry before. What if she stalled, and the people behind her would get impatient and—

Paddy slid into the driver's seat. 'Sorry. Daniel insisted on getting a drink, even though we'll be on in five minutes.'

'Road beer,' said Daniel, who was getting behind the wheel of the Range Rover, balancing a tin of lager in each hand. 'Come on, Padster, it's a party. Loosen up.'

'Drive,' said Vicky, climbing in beside him. She flashed a tight smile as they passed, getting on first, of course. 'See you in the lounge, try to stake out a big table.' As they drove by, Amira could see the sleeping faces of the twins in their car seats. They were so sickeningly cute, blond cherubs. Of course Vicky's kids were cute. Vicky got everything.

Paddy drove the car on, rumbling on the metal floor. Amira had always been afraid of boats – the claustrophobia, the panic of being far from shore. Ferries sank all the time, didn't they? And the sea looked so choppy. How did the cars not roll about and crash into each other? The deck smelled of petrol and salt water, noisy with the slam of doors and engines idling. Fiona was already getting out, gathering her enormous Mulberry tote. 'Darcy, take your book for the journey.'

'Maybe I don't *want* to read my book.'

Fiona rolled her eyes. 'Well, your phone won't work, so good luck getting on TikTok.'

'There's Wi-Fi, duh.'

'Just you wait and see. It's not strong enough to scroll through ten thousand videos like you do all day.'

Amira avoided Paddy's eyes. This was the hard point of parenthood, when they morphed into teenagers and began to talk back. Not that she would have dared to speak to her mother like that. *My child would never . . .* A small flame of hope flickered under her ribs. The barest flare, like the spark of a match, but it was there. As soon as they banged up the metal stairs and found a table, she would go to the loo.

Vicky had strong opinions on which section of the ferry was optimal to sit in, and when they reached it, Jonathan was already there, papers and maps spread out on the table. 'How did you manage that?' Amira cried. He'd been the last on, surely.

Jonathan leapt up and pulled her into a hug. A proper bear hug, his salt-and-pepper beard scraping the top of her head, his left arm expertly tucked up so you wouldn't even know he couldn't use it. Cerebral palsy at birth, more common with twins. 'I have my ways. Good to see you, Ammy.'

'You too. Happy birthday.' She was still a little shy with Jonathan, despite having known him for years. She saw his image on TV so often, and here he was, large as life, the crackle of his all-weather gear and the faint smell of the whisky he was drinking, smoke and sherry. He must have brought his own, since the bar wasn't open yet.

A woman was coming towards them, phone in hand. She was wearing leather trousers and high-heeled boots. For a trip to a Scottish island! Her hair was long and shiny chestnut, most likely extensions, and she had eyelash extensions too, plus her lips had clearly been filled, unnaturally plump. She was twenty-eight, Amira knew, but could have been any age, with the uncanny gloss of a CGI character.

'Rachel, come and meet everyone,' said Jonathan, beckoning the woman over. So this was the influencer girlfriend. Amira had checked out her feed, which was all fashion shoots and make-up tips, pictures of her on beaches or at glamorous parties, bending into yoga poses. *Namaste* and *grateful* and *blessed*.

'Hi. Good to meet you all.' Her voice had an American vocal fry, though her accent was London, Essex maybe. Amira couldn't help but glance at Fiona, who'd once had jet-black hair as long and glossy as this, but in recent years had been letting herself go grey. Surely Jonathan should have introduced the new woman to her in private first. But Fiona put out her hand, brisk and confident.

'Welcome, Rachel. I hope you don't mind the cold and wet. You've met my daughter?'

'Oh. Yeah.' Rachel glanced distractedly at Darcy, who was on her phone. Darcy didn't look up.

'The Wi-Fi's not working.'

'What?' Rachel's head whipped round, and she unlocked her own phone. 'It did a minute ago.'

As the two of them pressed frantically at their devices, Amira sat down. Paddy had wandered over to the large windows at the front of the ferry, and Daniel was already in line at the bar, which hadn't even opened yet. What had happened to the two beers he'd bought in the port? Louise was sitting down, unpacking some homemade sandwiches, while Vicky was shepherding the twins, who wanted to play with a flashing arcade game bolted to the wall.

'No, come on now, that's not for us.'

'But Mummy, I *want* it!'

My child would never . . .

That reminded her. She stood up again. 'Just going to the loo.' No one had noticed, however. The sign for the ladies was on the other side of the bar, so she made her way over, feeling the engines fire up beneath her, a slight wobble in her legs. It was OK – they'd have time to get off if anything happened, wouldn't they? It was a big boat. Just in case, her eyes sought out the emergency exit, the lifeboats. The water was freezing at this time of year. Most times of year. A burst of anger – why had Paddy made her go to an island, when he knew how afraid she was of water, of heights, even of wildlife? A city girl, she knew she'd be totally out of place on Mallacht.

Amira found a cubicle and locked the door, sitting down, a sense of anticipation building. Nothing, underwear clean and pristine. She counted silently. It should have been two days ago, shouldn't it? And nothing. She was very regular normally. So maybe. *Maybe.* She wouldn't tell Paddy, of course – after ten years of disappointment, it was very far off even being a hopeful sign. Except in her own head, and she smiled at herself in the mirror as she washed her hands, feeling slightly more buoyed for this weekend, for Paddy's difficult university friends, for her constant sense of failure next to rich, blonde, successful, posh, perfect mother Vicky.

When Amira came out, the little girl was standing there, watching her. Genevieve, such a pretty name. 'Hello, sweetheart,' she said.

Genevieve stared at her, sucking her thumb. 'Where did you go?' she mumbled.

'To the loo, darling. Do you need it?'

'No. Mummy won't let me on the machine.'

'Well, she's probably right. Maybe we can get some sweets?' It was risky, offering sweets to someone else's kid, but they were on holiday after all.

'Yes. I want sweets!' Genevieve slid her sticky hand into Amira's, and Amira let herself be led to the bar, now open and doing a brisk trade. It felt so good, that small hand in hers. Maybe this would happen now. Maybe, just maybe.

Vicky made a face when they came back with packets of Fruit Pastilles. 'Oh dear, I do try to not give them too much sugar, Amira.'

'They're on holiday, for God's sake,' said Daniel. He had two miniature whiskies in front of him, almost empty. Jonathan was also most of the way down one. Vicky had a coffee, Fiona a red wine, Rachel a sparkling water, Darcy a Diet Coke, and Louise had clearly brought her own tea in a thermos, ever frugal. Paddy, who was driving, had the large water bottle he'd started lugging about everywhere with him. No one appeared to have got a drink for Amira, but she was used to that, the familiar burn of being left out. Why did they never go on holiday with her friends, frugal and hard-working women, harassed with kids and jobs? Probably because they could only afford camping or basic house-shares, and Paddy, for all his socialist leanings and poorly paid job, had tasted the high life many years ago via Vicky and Jonathan, and didn't want to give it up. At least the house would be luxurious. Amira would try to enjoy the break, and if she couldn't do that, she'd endure it, and count the days until she could do a pregnancy test.

The ferry ride passed pleasantly enough – a calm V of water spreading out behind the boat, glimpses of the wild and rocky coast of the mainland, a steady stream of drinks from the bar. Amira tried to resist the badgering to have one. 'Come on, Ammy, lighten up,' said Daniel, who must have been on his sixth.

'It's early for me,' she protested. 'And someone has to drive at the other end.'

'Well, then, Padster needs to have one.' Daniel squinted at Paddy, who ignored him. It was unfair, when Vicky hadn't had a drink yet either – presumably she would be driving, since Daniel would be way over the limit. Anyway, it was perfectly normal to say no to alcohol at two o'clock in the afternoon. All the same, Amira wondered if they could tell, felt Paddy's eyes seek hers and avoided them. She'd promised him, no more trying for six months. She had lied.

'Alcohol is so dehydrating,' said Rachel, still glued to her phone. 'I more or less gave up last year, never felt better.'

Amira caught the look Daniel shot Fiona, judgemental and amused, and felt included, then ashamed. She had also given up drinking at various points, only to find it made no difference, she still couldn't get pregnant. This group did not take kindly to teetotalism – both Fiona (a GP!) and Vicky regularly declaring it 'wine o'clock' at barely four. Amira's parents didn't drink at all, didn't know she wasn't totally sober herself, and she and Paddy could not have done their jobs perpetually hungover. There was very little leeway in the worlds of a social worker and a teacher. As far as she could tell, Daniel's job involved taking clients to the races or football or fancy restaurants, drinking most nights. And Jonathan was always at award ceremonies or on booze-fuelled shoots.

The voyage went by in chatter and bantering, the usual retelling of old university stories, catch-ups about houses and jobs and other old friends, not part of the group. *The Group*. Always said like that, capitalised. Reminding you that you weren't part of it. Surprisingly, it didn't seem awkward with Fiona and Jonathan and Rachel. He talked about the flat he was renting, in Covent Garden of all places, and how noisy it was for an 'old fogey' like him. Amira knew he was at Soho House every night, drinking and partying.

'And where do you live, Rachel?' she asked, trying to be friendly, ashamed of her earlier glee at the woman being excluded.

There was a short awkward silence. Jonathan said, 'Well. Rach's rental wasn't really working out – damp problems, crappy landlord – so she's in with me for the moment.'

'Goodness!' Fiona's voice was fake-hearty. 'That's fast.'

Rachel said, 'It makes more sense than me trekking in from Essex every night. And I have a lot of meetings in Soho, you know, a lot of brands interested in partnerships.'

Amira was grateful for Paddy then, who would never take up with an influencer in her twenties, and who barely even knew what TikTok was. He'd forgive her for lying, surely, if her secret hope held on. He'd be overwhelmed with happiness. Finally, she could give him this.

Right on cue, Genevieve and Toby came over, clambering on their mother. 'Mummy, we're bored.'

'This boat is SO LONG.'

'We're almost there now,' said Vicky, taking her daughter on her lap and smoothing her long golden hair. 'Did you finish your sweeties that Amira got you? I hope you said thank you.'

They hadn't. 'Oh, that's alright.'

'You know sweeties are only a very special treat, don't you? And you can't ask other grown-ups for them?'

Toby had decided to park himself on Paddy's knee, caught by the map Paddy was looking at. 'What's that?'

'It's the island we're going to. Look, here's the house we'll stay at. Where your mummy and uncle used to go on holiday.' The boy nestled back against him, sucking his thumb, and Amira's heart turned over, even as Vicky reached out to her son to pull his hand from his mouth.

'No thumbs, Tobes, we talked about this. You're a big boy now. Look at the map with Uncle Paddy.'

Uncle Paddy. Exactly the kind of safe, interesting man you wanted around your kids. Yet no one's father. Because of her. And she was never Auntie Amira, was she? Another way she felt left out.

'What is this island?' Toby was, for once, interested in something that wasn't an iPad.

Jonathan leaned in. 'We used to own it. Or Gran-gran and Grandpops did. Then they sold it.'

'But we're going back?'

'We are.' It had seemed a strange idea, returning to the island and house the family had owned for generations. Wouldn't it be weird, hiring it back via a rental website, the new owner someone based overseas? There was a boatman booked to take them over, but then he'd go back across the strait and they'd be alone all weekend, the eight of them plus the kids. Everyone was very excited about that – the isolation, the privacy – but Amira, born and raised in Harrow, found the countryside scary, and the idea gave her the shivers.

'Are there pirates?' said Toby, taking his thumb out of his mouth with a pop. Everyone laughed, except Amira, too strung-out, and Rachel, who was fixated on her phone. 'Or dinosaurs?'

'No, pal,' said Daniel, downing the last dregs of his whisky. 'Nothing scary at all out there.'

◆ ◆ ◆

Two hours later the ferry had docked at the top of Tarne, where most of the island's shops and businesses could be found, and the cars rolled off again. Amira was sad they didn't stay longer in the town, with its pastel-painted houses and snug harbour hung with lights. Vicky had pre-ordered all their groceries for pick-up, but allowed them a quick trip into the Co-op: 'We've got everything we need, but any last-minute requests, go now. There'll be no way to get anything once we're on the island.'

As the others packed the big bags of food into the cars, Amira wandered the aisles of the small shop, panic-buying paracetamol and chocolate and teabags. She found herself staring at a packet of tampons. Would she need them? Superstitiously she felt that if she bought them, it would ruin everything. That made absolutely no sense, but all the same.

Paddy stuck his head in the door. 'Are you coming? Vicky's getting tense, we need to set off again.'

'Just a minute.' She had several tampons knocking about in her bag – that would do in an emergency. She paid for her items at the self-serve till and walked briskly over to the car, trying to ignore the tension in her stomach. They were on holiday! She should be allowed a few minutes to look in a shop, without Vicky staring pointedly at her watch, arms folded in her puffy navy gilet. Why had she ever agreed to go on this trip?

Liam

2007

Most mornings, Liam was the first thing Donna thought of when she woke up. The little boy's picture stood on her bedside table, among the paperbacks and box of tissues and tubes of hand cream. There was another framed picture of Liam on Mike's side, beside his thick non-fiction tomes and alarm clock. She worried about the boy. That new husband of Cathy's, she didn't like him one bit, and nor did Mike, who'd always been a good judge of character. But what could Donna do? She was only the ex-mother-in-law, and since her own son Gareth hadn't been the best dad – working off in Dubai and Saudi for most of the year, never seeing Liam – she knew she hadn't a leg to stand on. She held her tongue in the hope that Cathy would still drop off Liam to stay whenever she needed a break, though it had been a while. And last time Liam had had bruises on his little arms, and wouldn't stop crying the whole time, hadn't wanted his tea.

Donna had mentioned the bruises to Cathy, not wanting her to think he'd got them with his grandparents. 'Maybe a kiddie at nursery or . . .'

Cathy's eyes had shifted away. 'He's fine, Donna, don't fuss.' The tone was clear – *don't interfere*. So she hadn't. But she worried. In fact, she wasn't sleeping, hadn't been since she'd dropped Liam off that day and seen Roman – that was the stepfather, Cathy's husband of four months, though she'd only known him a year even now – backhanding the little boy in the kitchen. He'd been answering back, apparently. Liam was two, he hardly even knew what he was saying half the time. Social services had got involved, and that had been quite a kerfuffle, Cathy ringing up to scream down the phone that she knew it was Donna who'd called them. Donna had convinced her it wasn't, and that was true, she'd have been too afraid to. Afraid of never seeing Liam again. Apparently, it was someone at nursery who'd made the call, so he'd been taken out of that one; and Cathy wasn't working now it seemed, Roman didn't want her to, so that meant no nursery at all and less babysitting time for Grandma Donna. Fewer people seeing Liam, noticing bruises. The social worker on the case had come to interview Donna and Mike, but she'd seemed terribly young, eyes on her phone half the meeting, pushed for time. Donna wasn't sure the girl had heard what she was trying to say without using the actual words.

'Mike,' she said now.

'Ummmm?' Mike was still asleep, it being barely five o'clock. Donna couldn't quite have said what had woken her so early today, except for some vague sense of dread. Of worry. Like something terrible was going to happen. Had already happened.

'I'm worried, Mike.' But he was snoring again and hadn't heard her.

Donna lay awake in the dark before dawn, and her thoughts circled round and round and round. The picture of Liam, smiling at her in the gloom. The dread. The feeling that she'd missed something, had failed to stop something, as if she'd left the stove on or the door unlocked. And no matter what she tried – reading her latest romance, scrolling on Facebook, counting sheep in her head – it just wouldn't leave her.

Vicky

Vicky was annoyed. She had been annoyed ever since they'd left home in London the day before, when she'd had to pack for all four of them and get the kids ready single-handed as Daniel made an endless series of work calls. Before that, really, as she'd had to organise her own fortieth birthday, Daniel pathetically insisting he 'couldn't think of' anything she might like to do. Fielding months of WhatsApps and spreadsheets and grocery orders and travel logistics. Not to mention the shock of Louise saying she'd come, when she hadn't been in the country for a birthday or get-together in years, and Vicky had only invited her out of politeness. The last thing she needed was any of that surfacing again.

She'd become steadily crosser as they drove up through England and Scotland, stopping every hour for wee and snack breaks, Daniel scrolling through his phone at every junction, spending the night at an uncomfortable roadside motel where neither twin slept for more than two hours. Then having to wait for Jonathan, who was always bloody late, and dealing with Amira's usual anxiety, and her irritation with her brother for bringing his side piece on their birthday weekend, for God's sake. The weekend she'd had to organise herself since her husband was useless, and her best friend, Fiona, was preoccupied with the collapse of her marriage. Now they were on Tarne, once her happy place, and Daniel was too drunk to drive.

'So I have to do it, then.'

'It'll be fine.'

'Daniel, you've had, what, seven drinks? I don't fancy being killed in a crash, or my children.'

He rolled his eyes. 'Alright, well, you drive then.'

He knew very well the reason she didn't want to, but she had no choice. The car felt enormous under her, a lethal weapon. Her heart rate spiked as she stepped on the accelerator. *You can do this. Come on, you've driven thousands of times.* At least the roads were quiet on the island, but all the same she didn't want to rush, so it was aggravating when Amira disappeared into the Co-op just as they were ready to set off – what could she possibly want that hadn't been pre-ordered? Vicky had thought of it all. The Google spreadsheet had been in circulation for months, not that anyone had bothered to fill it in. She'd had to do everything, as usual. The thought of Cody rose in her mind like poison gas, and she pushed it away.

The journey across the island, down winding lanes overhung with trees, the glinting silver sea on either side, was beautiful, but Vicky gripped the wheel in terror, afraid every second, riding hard on the brake. Even the twins noticed.

'Go faster, Mummy,' insisted Toby. 'Want to bump on the road!'

She'd never been so relieved to arrive at the smaller town in the south of the island, Port Creggan, where the boatman was waiting for them, booked along with the house. In the old days, they'd kept their own boat in this harbour, their father piloting them across to their private island, black water sloshing on either side. This hired one looked so small – with eight adults and three kids, plus luggage, it would be hard to fit them all on.

Amira quailed on the pier. 'Is it – safe?'

Vicky sniffed. 'We've gone over in much worse. It's quite a calm day.'

'It's just – so cramped.'

Jonathan came behind her, lugging the shiny pink suitcase Rachel had seen fit to bring, his own high-spec rucksack on his back. 'We can shove in. Only takes ten minutes, don't worry.'

The boatman, craggy and reddened, dressed in dark water-proofs, grunted. 'Kiddies need to wear life jackets.'

'Not me,' said Darcy, flushing in horror. She had braided her dark hair in a complicated arrangement on the way over, her pretty face flushed from the wind. Vicky was sure the trip was the last thing her niece wanted to do, at fifteen.

'The little'uns.'

The twins were crammed between Vicky and Daniel, but her hands were full with bags and boxes. Her husband made no move to help. 'Daniel,' she hissed.

Daniel and Jonathan had bought several carrier-bags-worth of booze in the shop, although Vicky had said again and again it was all already ordered. How much were they planning to drink? He sighed. 'Is it really necessary? It's a short trip and they can swim.'

The boatman fixed him with a stare. 'Water's no more than five degrees this time of year. Cold-water shock hits you and you stop breathing. Happens especially to kiddies. Breath knocked right out of their lungs, and they just slip under. I've seen it.'

Jesus Christ. Vicky blinked, then caught hold of Genevieve's arm, rummaged under the seat for a small orange jacket. 'Come on, put it on. Good girl. Daniel, get Toby's.'

Daniel gave an exaggerated sigh and put down his booze bag with a clink. 'Tobes, come here. Toby!'

'No! I don't want to put it on – *nooooo! Nooooo!*'

The boy's wails turned heads in the small port, where various fishermen were tending to their own boats, and locals were walking dogs on the adjoining beach. With all of them and the booze and luggage there was hardly room to move, but then they were off, speeding over the dark water, churned wide in their wake. Vicky's tension eased at the motion of the boat, the spray hitting her face. She had once loved it out on Mallacht. She hadn't been back in years, even before the sale, because the place had taken on so many bad associations. That last summer, when she was nineteen. The reason for the sale. But now it was time to reclaim it, find that girl again, the one she'd been before. In the wildness, with no one to watch her, no one to judge, she had always felt so free. Like she could truly be herself.

Loretta

2008

Loretta could see herself, sitting on the loo, reflected in the bathroom mirror. It was getting light outside, but it was only four a.m. Too early for the kids or Jason to be up, and she was glad, because she'd been able to hide this from them for a long time, and today wasn't the day she wanted to stop.

She knew what Jason would say. Go back to that doctor, demand more tests, don't take no for an answer. But Loretta was very practised at taking no for an answer. The doctor had said it was nothing to worry about, and she had believed it, gone obediently home and continued to suffer pain and bleeding for weeks now. She hardly dared look down. She knew the water would be stained bright red, and she'd have to make sure it was clean before anyone got up. Jason must know. She had avoided his touch for months now, seen his disappointment, while she wanted nothing more than to sink into him, find comfort.

Now, in the clear light of dawn, she forced herself to face up to it. The relief she'd felt when the doctor had said everything was fine – it had been misplaced. The old gnawing fear was back. Something was very wrong with her. And now it might be too late to catch it.

So why not get help? She didn't understand her own inaction. Maybe she didn't want the posh doctor to tell her off again. Maybe she just couldn't bear to acknowledge it. After all, if today was not the day she got bad news, she could go on living her old life. Make porridge for her kids, find their homework and PE kits, send them off to school, kiss Jason on the cheek as he left. Drive to the office, answer emails and fill in forms and drink tea in the peaceful boredom of the place. Not have to be sick.

But denial could only go on for so long. Loretta realised, hands gripping her thighs, that she was bleeding even harder now. She'd have to clear that up, it was on the floor. But suddenly she was feeling so very dizzy.

The bathroom tiles, luckily, were only lino, chosen for practicality and cost. But they hurt all the same as Loretta fainted dead away, hitting her head on the floor, and half an hour later she was found by her youngest child, who was just four, in a pool of blood.

Amira

The small island came into view as they rounded the harbour wall. So close you felt you could almost touch it, but Vicky had warned them it wasn't swimmable. That people had died trying. Amira tried to take deep breaths and not look down at the water – they wouldn't do this if it wasn't safe, would they? All the same they were too close, the black depths, and the ten-minute journey juddering over them, spray on her face, was ten minutes of pure hell for her. Then they were tying up at a small wooden jetty on a rocky shore. Above them on a hill, a whitewashed house with dark-framed windows and a slate roof. Amira wobbled from the soaked wooden pier on to the shingle, wishing she'd worn her walking boots for the journey. Vicky had, of course. She managed to be perfectly outdoorsy and glamorous at the same time, solid-gold hoops in her ears, highlighted blonde hair, subtle make-up. Amira would bet anything that if she asked Paddy, he'd say Vicky never even wore make-up. Didn't need to. Urgh.

The boatman grunted. 'Keep the jackets for the kiddies, case you go in the sea. I'll get them back Sunday.'

Vicky hardly seemed to hear, staring up at the house. 'Alright. Bye.'

Carting her wheelie case up a stony path was not easy, and Amira was quickly out of breath – Paddy storming ahead without checking if she was alright – but at last they were there. The door was not locked, and Vicky pushed it open.

They trooped in, after a sharp injunction from Vicky about no boots in the house. It was beautiful – slate floors, a wood-burning stove waiting to be lit, sheepskin rugs, sofas and armchairs in rich jewel tones. Exposed wooden walls, and the whole back of the house made of glass, looking out over the island towards the churning sea, the same teal as the chair placed in front of it.

'Has it changed much?' asked Amira, to fill the silence of the place.

Vicky looked momentarily wrong-footed. 'Yes . . . it looks very different. The new owner did a complete renovation I suppose. People are so picky now about rentals – Instagram, you know.'

'I can't believe the change,' said Paddy, staring around him.

Amira didn't like that. A reminder that Paddy had come here aged nineteen, when Vicky's parents still owned the island. Of their whole shared history before Amira even came on the scene.

Vicky went to stand with him by the huge window. 'I know. I quite liked the shabby old furniture and the chipped floor tiles.'

'It had character alright. Though this is lovely too. Luxurious.'

Vicky cast him a small, private smile that Amira didn't miss, then raised her voice. 'Twinnies! Stay with Mummy, please.' Toby had already opened a cupboard and was playing with some wine glasses – the havoc they could create in seconds was truly astonishing.

There was a chunky file on the kitchen table which Vicky now opened. 'So a few things to remember. The sewage is on a septic tank, so you can't put just anything down the loo. Paper only. Also there's some instructions here for the wood burner, the fire pit, and the wood-fired hot tubs. Those do take a while to heat up. If we have any issues we can call for help on the radio. There's no phone reception out here of course, but that should work in all weathers. Any problems, the man will come out with the boat.'

Amira couldn't remember when she'd last been without Wi-Fi or 4G. God! She was such a city girl. No wonder Vicky made fun of her flimsy shoes and thin jackets.

'And the food is all sorted?' said Daniel. This was Vicky's birthday, surely he should have done the arranging. Or Fiona, as her best friend. But no, all the emails – many, many emails, plus spreadsheets – had come from Vicky herself. Nothing said 'fun holiday' like an Excel spreadsheet.

'I told you it was, except for Saturday which you said you were organising? Though I don't see any other supplies.'

'I'm organising. Leave it, will you?'

'Fine. Let's put the snacks and breakfast foods in the pantry, and the meals in the fridge. And there's a barbecue and pizza oven also if we feel like that.'

There had been much discussion of who would make what and bring what, which Amira had largely ignored, barely getting time between work and sleep to even read the messages. Paddy, who'd become a keen baker since starting at his current school, had insisted on making a birthday cake, which even Amira hadn't seen, then transporting it with great hassle in a plastic carrier the whole way to Scotland. He didn't seem to be eating many of his creations, however, and his formerly soft middle had tightened in recent months as he cut back on drinking, cycled to work, and measured his calories. He said it was just turning forty that had made him more careful, but Amira wasn't sure.

'Where shall I put this?' he said now, producing the carrier. It was so heavy Amira had hardly been able to lift it, and carrying it flat from south London had been no small undertaking.

Vicky clapped her hands. 'The mysterious cake! Can we see it yet?'

'Nope! I thought we'd have it after dinner tonight. And don't worry, I've factored in Rachel's allergies.'

'You are so good, Pads.' Vicky squeezed his shoulder and Amira gritted her teeth again. There was going to be a lot of that this weekend.

'What room should we take?' she said. 'I'd like to dump my stuff.'

Vicky glanced at her. 'I did the allocations already. You two are down the end upstairs. I'm afraid there's only two en-suites, so you'll have to share the bathroom with the room next door. That's, let me see . . .' She took out her phone. 'Jonathan and Rachel.'

'We're sharing?' said Rachel, who had so far photographed everything in the room. Amira had no idea how she'd made it up from the beach in her high-heeled boots.

'Yes, there are only four bathrooms so some of us will have to.'

'And me?' Louise had come in quietly, with her tiny rucksack. 'I don't mind where I bunk.'

'Yes, I thought you'd say that, if you survived the Sahara! You have the room at the other side of the kitchen there, nice and private. So you can use the bathroom down here, if you don't mind people popping in for the loo.'

Louise gave a faint, superior smile. 'I've been sharing a latrine with fifty other people for months, this is absolute luxury.'

Amira felt guilty, being reluctant to share a bathroom with another room. She was squeamish, and if her period did start, she'd need to deal with it. And why were they the ones who had to share? Vicky and Daniel of course had the best room, with cots for the twins, and the other en-suite had gone to Fiona and Darcy.

'I thought a teenage girl would want some privacy,' said Vicky, stroking her niece's hair.

Darcy shook her off. 'I'm taking my stuff up.'

And what about possibly pregnant possibly not pregnant women who might or might not get their period any second? Didn't they deserve privacy too? At least she wasn't poor Louise, stuck in a narrow single room downstairs, so she'd be kept awake all night by drunken idiots. But Louise never seemed to mind. She was already sitting cross-legged on her bed writing in a journal. Amira was aware that she tried too hard with Louise, as with Vicky, hoping to make them like her, knowing that they never really would. Over the years her invitations to spa weekends or cocktail nights had been met with polite refusals by Vicky and Fiona, while Louise was usually out of the country saving lives. Amira's job was important too, and it was hard, and it helped people, but since she had access to running water and takeaway pizza, she was never going to be as worthy as Louise.

Rachel said, 'Does anyone have the Wi-Fi code?' She was aiming her phone out the window for another shot. 'I can't get reception.'

Paddy had taken the bags upstairs. Jonathan was unpacking cans and bottles, his bad arm folded against his chest. 'Rach, I told you, there isn't Wi-Fi. There's no cables over here, and no reception to run mobile-based internet.'

She frowned. 'Yes, but there has to be *something*.'

'Well no, there doesn't. Lots of parts of the world still have no communications! Ask Lou here.'

Louise called out, 'That's right, we had one dial-up connection for the entire camp I worked in. A few people had mobiles, but there's no reception in the desert.'

Rachel gaped. 'But . . . how will I post?'

'You won't,' said Vicky crisply, taking over the food unpacking. 'That's the idea, to switch off completely. Honestly, Jay, there was no need to buy all this booze, we have enough.'

'It's our birthday!'

29

At that moment Darcy came back downstairs, phone aloft. 'There's really no Wi-Fi?'

Jonathan laughed. 'I can see you and Rachel will get on well.'

Rachel pouted. 'What if something goes wrong? And we're just stuck out here?'

'That's what the radio is for.'

'Yes, but the man said the crossing isn't always possible if the weather's bad. So if someone gets sick, say, or I have a reaction – you know about my allergies? – what happens then?'

Vicky barely disguised her sigh. 'I have all the information about your allergies, and the food's been ordered accordingly. You have an EpiPen?'

'Well yes, but . . .'

'OK then. Everyone should read this folder, it explains the lot. They also ask that we don't disturb the seals.'

Jonathan smiled. 'Seals! Seals are the best. We used to hear their barks at night as kids, remember?'

'Of course I remember. Where the hell is Daniel?' muttered Vicky, as Amira shut the front door to keep out the cold wind. Part of her really wished she was leaving with the boatman. She wouldn't have complained like Rachel, but the lack of phones and Wi-Fi made her uncomfortable too. What if something happened with one of her cases? She didn't trust Martin, who was on call for the weekend – all of twenty-five with a man bun and folding bike.

'Playing with the fire pit,' said Paddy, coming back downstairs. 'I've put our stuff in the room, Am.'

Vicky clapped her hands. She had an irritating 'camp mother' persona on trips like this. 'Right everyone! Get settled in then reassemble in ten for a hike around the island, please! Rachel, you'll need to change your shoes if you're coming, it's very rocky terrain. If you break an ankle we can hardly get you to help now the boat is gone.'

Something about that phrase, *the boat is gone*, made Amira whip her head to the front windows, a cold pit in her stomach. Yes, there was the boat, a dot on the ocean, heading back to the greater mass of Tarne. They were all alone.

◆ ◆ ◆

It was almost dark already as they made their way along the island. It was barely a mile across, moss and shrubs and heather underfoot, just the house on the slight brow of the hill, a few ruined cottages, the jetty they had arrived at, and on the northernmost end, where a beautiful yellow-sand beach was torn by surf, a flimsy wooden hut.

Vicky, who had Genevieve by the hand, had barely broken a sweat on the walk, whereas Amira was huffing and puffing. 'Aw, the surf shed. We used to keep body boards and that in here.' It had a brand-new padlock on it now, Amira noticed, not yet rusted by the elements. There was also a metal box attached to its side that Vicky said was the generator. 'We used to get so many power cuts back then, this thing was a real lifesaver. Looks like they've upgraded it since our time.' It was covered in buttons and levers, emitting a powerful whirring sound. Vicky shielded her eyes. 'Look, Jay, they've put in a wind turbine, up past the house.'

Jonathan spoke with authority. 'That'll be supplying the power. It goes into photovoltaic batteries, and if the turbine's not turning for any reason the generator kicks in. I did a programme about small islands once. If it's not on the mains it kind of has its own electricity grid, pretty cool.'

'The turbine's not turning now,' said Amira, looking to where it soared above the house, the blades perfectly still. 'Even though it's so windy. Is that weird?'

Jonathan glanced at her, and she had that feeling she so often did, that they'd all forgotten she was here and were surprised when she spoke. 'Not really. Sometimes they turn off if the grid's full. Anyway, the lights are on, so it's fine!'

'God, it's like the end of the world,' muttered Rachel. 'So grim.' She had come reluctantly on the walk, still in her leather jacket and high-heeled boots, stumbling over the shingle with her arms folded. Daniel was kicking in the surf, holding Toby with one hand, a can of beer in the other. Seriously, how many drinks was that now? Amira searched for Paddy – there he was, bending down to examine some small yellow plants in the scrubby green grass. No doubt to share with his mates on the botany and geography discussion forums he frequented. Louise had not come for the walk, staying behind at the house instead to sort the fire out, as Daniel had made a mess of it. Amira wondered how it would be to be so self-sufficient. She'd never known Louise to have a partner, male or female, and she had few friends in the UK apart from the group, most of her colleagues usually posted overseas to wherever the latest war or disaster was. Darcy had come on the walk, but only, she said, to see if there was phone reception on the beach. There wasn't.

As it always did in quiet moments, Amira's mind turned to her most pressing cases. So many kids at risk, so many families teetering on the edge, that she sometimes couldn't bear it. Amira's old boss Shelley, a twenty-stone powerhouse of a woman who'd taught her everything she knew, would have said that if the work started to get to you, you needed to step back. But if it didn't get to you at all, you couldn't be fully human. Amira remembered her own little secret, the flame of hope leaping up. No bleeding yet. She was never late, it had to mean something. Through the padding of her coat, she gently pressed her own breast. Was it a bit sore? Annoying that the signs of an incoming period were the same as those of pregnancy.

Fiona tramped over, jaw set in a grimace, dark hair blowing in the wind. 'Christ, it's freezing. Whose idea was it to come to Scotland in February?'

32

Amira winced. 'I know. I can't feel my face.'

Fiona was watching Rachel a few metres away, glowering and brushing sand off her boots. 'I think some people are wholly unprepared for this trip.'

'Mmm. Yes. Are you – it's really OK with you, this?'

Fiona shrugged. Unlike Vicky, she had let herself look her age, relaxing into mumsy florals and shapes. Right now she was wearing an ankle-length padded brown coat that gave her the appearance of a well-upholstered worm. 'It's Jonathan's birthday. And my best friend's birthday. It's complicated. She seems a nice enough girl, if a bit . . . well. Not outdoorsy.'

Amira couldn't believe she was the recipient of confidences like this. She'd always been in awe of Fiona, whose parents had barely spoken English when they came from Hong Kong in the late seventies, and who'd got herself all the way to Oxford and a medical career, a husband on TV, and a beautiful and clever daughter, who was admittedly a little sulky right now. Some of that was gone now, of course. A mutual split, they'd said, when they announced it last summer. But was that ever true?

'Well, you're very good. So poised, I admire you.'

'I just don't believe in unnecessary drama. I'm doing it for Darce. I can't fall out with her father and her aunt now, can I?'

'I suppose not.'

Fiona shivered again. 'I think it's time for a log fire and hot chocolate myself. Laced with whisky if the boys have anything to do with it.'

'They're certainly on it today.'

'Not lovely Paddy of course.' *Lovely Paddy*, that was what the women in the Group called him. Too lovely to date, it seemed, since none of them ever had. But lovely. Dependable. He was coming over now, his face red in the wind, with a sprig of the flower in his hand.

'I think this is purslane – very rare to find it in the UK, I took a little sample. I don't think one bit will matter, do you?'

Ah Paddy. So lovely that he even cared about the picking of a single tiny flower. So why did she feel often, of late, that he didn't care much about her?

'Of course not.' Amira moved over to him, in a way she rarely did now, and snuggled her body into his, trying to close the distance between them. Wondering if Fiona had felt something similar, right before her husband left. Of holding on tight, but still losing grip.

'We should head back,' said Paddy, pulling away. 'I think everyone's getting cold.'

◆　◆　◆

Although it was Vicky's birthday trip, it seemed to go without saying that she would take charge of the evening meal, along with Fiona. They'd always treated the boys in the Group with a sort of eye-rolling nanny-like attitude, even though Paddy for one was a better cook than Amira. Louise never made any fuss on these occasions, quietly laying the table or clearing plates without being asked, melting into the background. She refused a glass of the vintage Moët Daniel popped on returning from the chilly beach walk, as did Amira. 'Wasn't that for tomorrow?' Vicky frowned.

Daniel drained the bottle into his glass. 'I've got something even better for that. Not every day your lovely wife turns forty!'

'Urgh, don't remind me.'

'Come on. You're hotter now than you were at eighteen.'

It was true, Amira thought – she hadn't known Vicky at eighteen, but she'd seen pictures. She was as slim as she'd been then, her hair still glowing fair, with a slick veneer of wealth and taste all over her. Whereas Amira had new greys every day and fought a constant battle with a spreading middle. *She has everything.*

Vicky batted away her husband, drunk and sloppy. 'Yes yes. Now go and stoke up the fire or something. You love setting stuff alight.'

Privately, Amira thought Daniel was too drunk to be let loose near flames, but he ambled off to the wood burner to add more logs. The twins were on one of the big squashy sofas, glued to matching iPads, as was Darcy to her phone. She didn't offer or expect to help with the meal, which Amira was a little shocked by. In her family growing up, everyone had assigned chores. 'Sure I can't do anything?' she said.

Vicky didn't look at her. 'It's all under control, Amira, there's no need. Does everyone have a drink?'

Amira glanced about her. Glasses in the hands of Fiona, Jonathan, who was chatting to Louise about camp life, Daniel of course, and Rachel, who was over by the window trying to capture the final red streaks of the sunset. Even Paddy had one, relaxing his health kick a little, and she was relieved, somehow.

'You don't have one, Ammy,' said Fiona, who was red from the champagne, a genetic trait that didn't stop her putting it away.

'Oh! I was going to wait. Not a big fan of fizzy stuff.'

'This is vintage Moët! It's a crime not to try it.'

'Thank you. Maybe later.'

Fiona cast her a shrewd look and Amira flushed. She couldn't bear it if someone guessed her secret hope, asked her about it even. The chances were so low. She just wanted to enjoy the small private glow of it, of a disappointment that had not yet happened. Of possibility, however delusional.

Dinner was venison stew and a vegetarian one for Louise, fresh crusty bread, salad. Cheese and cooked meats, all of the highest quality. Amira had already started to calculate what she shouldn't eat. Soft cheese, charcuterie, alcohol, coffee, seafood, she'd read game wasn't good either . . . *Oh God, stop it, stop it.* She knew that if she started acting pregnant, she would almost certainly bleed tonight. She cut herself a bit of cheddar, hoping no one noticed she avoided the rest, and began to spoon up the hot, flavourful stew.

'This is top, Vics,' said Jonathan, tearing a hunk of bread with one hand. He was so skilful at that you'd hardly notice his arm. His TV show made a feature of how he coped, roughing it in deserts and mountains. He'd won many awards as a disability advocate and was credited with inspiring thousands, helping children who'd had amputations, donating and raising money for soldiers. Even the split from Fiona had been reported kindly in the press, their statement about 'caring for each other deeply but needing to part' printed verbatim, a nice spread in a magazine about his hot post-divorce body. Even when he met Rachel – extremely soon after, so soon it really made you wonder – that too had been praised in the papers. *TV survivalist and disability advocate Jonathan Capeman, 39, was seen cosying up to influencer Rachel Solenado, 28.*

'It is nice,' agreed Fiona, ladling sour cream on top of her stew. Amira saw Vicky raise her eyebrows a little at that. Both she and Rachel were mostly toying with their food, Rachel photographing every mouthful for her Instagram, although she kept complaining about the lack of internet.

'My followers are going to think something's happened to me! I've never gone a day without posting.' Rachel scowled at her meal. 'Are we sure there's no sesame in this? I'm super-allergic.'

'I was very careful,' said Vicky, sounding bored. 'You'd hardly put sesame in a stew like this anyway.'

'And there's no gluten?'

'I used some flour to thicken it. You didn't mention gluten, did you?'

'Oh.' Rachel's full mouth pursed. 'I just try to avoid it. So fattening.' Amira noticed Darcy take that in, look down at her own stew, and frown. They were so impressionable at that age, especially to influencers like Rachel, peddling pseudo-science and a restricted-calorie mindset. Darcy had been allowed a glass of champagne too, despite being underage.

'You have some terrible gluten allergy?' said Fiona, tearing off more bread. 'Coeliac disease, is that it?'

'Well, no . . .'

'Ulcerative colitis? You poor thing, that's very nasty. Non-stop diarrhoea.'

'I don't have that.'

'What is it then?'

Rachel flushed. 'Nothing diagnosed. I just know I feel better when I avoid gluten, that's all.'

Fiona gave a small snort. 'I'd love to know when wheat became the enemy. Humanity wouldn't exist without it, we've eaten it for millennia with no ill effects.'

Rachel rolled her eyes. 'Clearly you haven't read much about the paleo diet. It's a shame doctors in this country are still giving outdated nutritional advice based on old science. We should be eating beneficial fats and proteins, not grain and stodge.'

'You have to agree with that, Fiona,' said Jonathan, diplomatically.

'Of course. Protein is important. I just can't abide all these fake allergies I see now. Eating processed muck with the idea it's some-how healthier. Like most processed vegan food – it's stuffed full of salt and additives to make it taste of something. And there's no need. Look at Lou here – you manage, don't you? Even in countries where vegetarianism isn't a thing.'

Louise shrugged. 'I never cared much about food, you know that. Just fuel, that's all, and we're lucky we have any at all.'

Rachel didn't let it drop. 'Protein is especially important for women as they get older. It can help stave off menopausal weight gain.' She seemed to look pointedly at Fiona when she said that, a size sixteen in her floral wrap dress, and Amira couldn't bear the awkwardness, and dove in before the comment could land.

'Such lovely food, Vicky. What's for tomorrow, the grand birthday meal?'

Vicky looked unaccountably annoyed at that. 'It was all in the spreadsheet, Amira. And Daniel has some surprises, he says. Though goodness knows how he got them here. I packed all our bags myself.'

Daniel seemed slightly out of it, filling his glass from a bottle of red he'd opened with dinner. Paddy shook his head as Daniel held it out, slopping some on the scrubbed-wood table. Amira had agreed to a glass just for show and was virtuously taking tiny sips. It was so hard with wine, when people like Daniel, Jonathan, and Fiona insisted on filling you up the second your glass dipped below halfway. She had to be careful. A few mouthfuls wouldn't hurt and would hopefully get people off her back.

The twins had eaten only two bites of their stew, spilling the rest all over the table and the lovely slate tiles, where it might stain. They were back on their iPads again. 'Mummy, I want to get down,' whined Toby.

'Say please, darling.'

'Want to get down, please.'

'Alright, off you go.' Vicky let them wander away, with dirty faces and hands. Should they really be having so much screen time? It was something Amira looked for in family visits – a lack of parental engagement.

My child will be different. To dispel such dangerous thoughts, she got up and began to clear the dishes, terrified they would talk about her behind her back and say she hadn't done anything to help. Louise got up too, scraping plates and stacking them in the dishwasher. She said, 'I can hardly get used to these things. In the camp we had these giant plastic bowls we filled with cold water.'

Didn't sound very hygienic. 'It must have been – well, quite the experience.' What a lame way to describe running a refugee camp in a war. 'I couldn't do it. You're so brave.'

Another shrug. 'It's just what I'm used to. I'm sure you have to be brave, in your job.'

'Maybe. Sometimes. The parents can be a little scary to be honest. I've had dads threaten to punch me quite a few times.'

Louise had already stacked the dishwasher and wiped the counter. She was so efficient. Keen to help, Amira took Paddy's cake from the fridge, its box carefully hand-labelled with its ingredients and possible allergens. Gluten, dairy, sugar. Why had Rachel come if she ate so few things? What did she expect on an island off another island off Scotland?

'You're back for good now?' Amira asked Louise, opening a cupboard to look for cake plates. Her return seemed a little mysterious, after so many years.

'I'm not sure yet. I'm at my mum's for a little while, deciding what to do.'

'Oh yes, how is she?' She was vaguely aware Louise's mother had been ill for some years. Louise was an only child and her father had died when she was in her teens – getting into Oxford as a kid from a working-class single-parent family had been a triumph, not that she'd ever have boasted of it.

'About the same. Actually, I'd have liked to check on her this weekend, but she has a neighbour who pops by, so I suppose it's alright.'

Paddy came over then. 'Let me sort the cake, please, Amira.' He sounded irritated. 'I have candles and everything.'

'Sorry. Just trying to help.'

'Well, don't.' Paddy busied himself taking out the candles from their wrapping and sticking them into the cream icing, shielding his creation with his back, even from her. Hurt, Amira returned to her seat as he carried it aloft, a vast four-layer confection of buttercream and sponge, topped with drizzles of caramel, candles glowing. 'Here we are. Salted caramel and popcorn, Vicky's favourite.' His face was in shadow behind the points of light. 'Someone going to start singing?'

'Happy birthday to you, happy birthday to you, happy birthday dear Vicky and Jon-a-than, happy birthday to you!' Amira droned along with their voices – Fiona's rich contralto, Daniel's reedy tenor, Paddy's surprising bass. She'd never had much of an ear for music. The cake was delicious, of course. Soft and moist and sweet. She was trying to think if he'd made a cake for her fortieth last year. He hadn't, had he?

After the meal, Amira did another sweep of the table and living room, collecting glasses and dessert plates, feeling pleasingly martyred. Vicky took the twins up to bed, to great protesting, while everyone else drank port. Amira managed to miss it out by wiping the kitchen counters again, but soon there was no more tidying to do and she had to go and sit down.

Back at the table, Daniel topped up everyone's glasses and motioned for silence. Vicky was coming downstairs, having changed into a clinging white wool jumper with a cowl neck. Her luxury leggings clung to her taut legs and Amira felt so frumpy in her old jeans and bobbly jumper, which she had already spilled stew down. She took a gulp of wine, realised her mistake, had to swallow it anyway.

Daniel said, 'Now, everyone. The real reason we're here. It's twenty-one years since I met my lovely wife, and this crew of reprobates here. Darce?'

Darcy was over at the TV, fiddling with the remote. 'Hang on.' She pressed a button and a picture came up on the screen. It was one Amira had seen before. The six of them – Vicky and Jonathan in the centre, the golden-haired twins. Jonathan had not gone to Oxford, not gone to university at all, but had been there all the time hanging out, so it seemed like he had. Vicky had dated Daniel, the rugby-playing posh boy, and her best friend was Fiona, a hard-drinking medic who had eventually married Vicky's brother. Then there was Louise, an unlikely friend for them, who'd had the next-door room to Vicky, by virtue of their surnames, and had fallen in with Fiona via the college netball team. And Paddy, who'd known Louise from his geography course, and the six of them had become friends. The Group. 'Let's take a trip down memory lane,' said Daniel, as the screen shifted.

Paddy complained, 'This was for tomorrow, Dan.'

'Well, who cares?'

Amira tensed as the TV scrolled through a slideshow of photos, to the groans and claps of the Group. A summer ball, punting, a music festival. Vicky on Paddy's shoulders. A fancy-dress bop. A black-tie dinner. Finishing exams, covered in glitter and silly string. Swigging champagne from bottles. Paddy didn't like people to think it, but his time at Oxford had been just as hedonistic and privileged as anyone's. Even Louise could be seen downing cocktails from plastic cups, dressed up in bin bags at socials for the various sports she'd done – rowing, rugby, netball. Amira's own university pictures looked so tawdry by comparison, rounds of WKDs in tacky Nottingham clubs. Vicky had been insanely beautiful back then, the black and white sub fusc setting off her blonde hair and pale skin. A sepia photo of her was just stunning. Urgh.

Daniel was still talking. 'So since we've all been friends for a long, long time – over twenty years! I thought we could play a few little games to test how well we really know each other. Prizes available!'

'I got the prizes,' said Darcy. 'Uncle Dan gave me his credit card so they're decent.'

Rachel frowned. 'Am I playing this game too?'

There was a looseness to Daniel's movements, oiled by booze. 'Course. We can get to know you as well, Rachel. It'll be fun.'

'I can't concentrate with the TV on,' said Louise.

'Yes, can we turn it off?' said Vicky, grumpily. '*I* can't concentrate with all these reminders of how much collagen my face used to have.'

Darcy switched the TV off with a remote. 'Are we doing it in teams?' said Fiona, who'd never lost her competitive instincts from county-level netball at school. Amira had horrible flashbacks to other instances of organised fun – the round of Articulate that had resulted in Fiona and Jonathan not speaking for the whole weekend because he couldn't guess 'Argentina'; the time Vicky had struck down Amira's own rare victory at Trivial Pursuit because the dice had fallen on its edge. She would obviously lose this game too, having known them all for less time. She sat back, meekly waiting to be the last chosen.

'No need for teams surely,' said Paddy, who didn't agree that competition was good for people.

'One-on-one combat,' said Jonathan, misunderstanding. '*Mano a mano.* Alright then. Bring it on, Danny!'

Darcy explained, 'So here's the rules. Everyone has to get a bit of paper and write down three things about themselves – two of them should be true and one should be a lie.'

Fiona stirred. 'Darce, I think you should go to bed for this.'

'Oh, for God's sake, Mum. I did the prizes! And I've got the paper all cut up, look.'

'I mean it, sweetie. Things could get rude, and you don't need to know scandalous secrets about your parents and your auntie!'

Vicky's mouth pursed. 'I don't think I have any scandalous ones.'

'Dad? I don't have to go to bed, do I?'

Jonathan's gaze flicked between his daughter and ex-wife. 'I think you should, honey-bun. You can keep an eye on the twins, that would be really helpful.'

'We'll slip you a few quid too, Darce,' said Daniel, though Vicky looked annoyed at this also.

'They should be asleep, do try not to wake them.'

'Leave the papers, darling.' Fiona blew her a kiss.

A few moments went by as Darcy gathered her phone and hoody and headphones with bad grace, then clumped upstairs to a chorus of goodbyes she only grunted at.

Daniel spread out his arms. 'Now we can get eighteen-cert.'

'You really think this is a good idea?' said Vicky.

'Why not? It'll be fun. We do it at work sometimes with new hires. Good way to get to know people.'

'So that's the game?' said Amira. 'Two truths and a lie?'

'That's the one. You play it at work too?'

'Um, not exactly.' She got enough lies during her family visits.

Vicky sighed. 'Let me sort it then, Daniel, you haven't explained the rules properly.' She began to pass out the sheets of lined paper. 'Do we have any pens?' Daniel looked blank. Another sigh. 'I have some in my handbag.' A general scrounge-up collected three pens, plus the pencils from a set of Scrabble. 'Now listen carefully. Write down your two truths and one lie, but mix the order up a bit. Don't put your name on it and we'll jumble them all in something, a hat maybe, then we pick them out and we have to guess whose it is. One point for each guess you get right, then we add them up at the end.' God forbid anyone would break the rules of a fun, made-up game.

Taking her slip of paper, Amira thought about it. Did she have any interesting secrets? Not really. *I might be pregnant.* She wasn't going to write that. *I don't like dogs.* That was a scandalous reveal in some circumstances. *I don't really like any of you.* No, not that.

I can't swim. Would they all know that? They'd probably forgotten, and likely no one was observant enough to have noticed her fear on the boat. What about a lie? *I ran the marathon once.* Vicky, Jonathan, and Daniel had all run the marathon at different times, so that would throw some confusion into the mix.

'Do hurry up, if you have one of the pens,' said Vicky, sharply.

Amira passed hers to Paddy. She wondered what he would write, if she would know immediately it was him and vice versa. How well they really knew each other. What the real reason was for his recent changes of habit and lifestyle.

Soon, after much scratching and the occasional quiet chuckle, they were done.

'Does anyone have a hat to put them in?' said Fiona.

Louise said, 'There's a kind of funny wooden box on the side there, that could work.'

'How strange.' Vicky stared at it. 'That was ours. Wasn't it, Jay?'

He glanced over, uninterested. 'Was it? I don't know. Maybe.'

'Mum brought it back from Malaysia. I suppose they forgot to clear it after we . . . after.' She subsided. The sale of the island seemed to be the source of some pain for her. Amira wondered what the story was.

Louise went to fetch the box, removing its lid. The entries were put in and shaken up. Outside, dark had fallen entirely, velvet-thick. From the front windows, the lights of Tarne could be seen, small moving ones indicating cars on the coastal road, the cluster that was the harbour with its pubs and restaurants. A bustling metropolis compared to this island, just the group of them and the sheep. A distant bark now and then that Jonathan had said was seals. Out the back was nothing but darkness, the sea stretching on towards Iceland.

'Who's going to pick?' Daniel shook the box. 'Ammy, you go first.'

Why her? Likely he'd caught scent of her faint cringing fear. Of what, she didn't know. Of people being mean to her. Of being left out, made fun of. It had happened before.

She plucked out a neatly folded piece of paper, written in block capitals in pencil. She'd know Paddy's writing, surely, and this wasn't it. She read: "'My favourite food is prawn cocktail Skips. I voted for Boris Johnson for London mayor. I can't read maps properly.'"

She no idea who that was. Everyone fell to speculating. 'Got to be a man,' said Fiona. 'Admitting to junk food.'

'Not necessarily,' said Jonathan. 'Neither you nor my sister can read a map to save your lives.'

Fiona stuck her tongue out at him, which made Amira tense. Too flirty, for recently separated people? What would Rachel say? She was on her phone again, flicking through her pictures, and perhaps hadn't noticed.

Fiona declared, 'I think it's Daniel. For all your fine restaurants I know you love a good crisp sandwich for dinner.'

'It's true, I do! But I hate prawns.'

'Well, that could be the lie.'

'Yeah, but I'm good with maps too. Orienteering champ at school. It's not me. What about Amira? The quiet one.'

'She'd never have voted for Boris!' cried Fiona. 'No way. Would you?'

'No,' she admitted. And though she wasn't above a crisp sandwich, she was OK with maps too. It wasn't Paddy, she knew. He hated the Tories and these days eschewed all junk food. But it could be Daniel, or Vicky, who she was fairly sure voted that way. Fiona, even, double-bluffing – doctors didn't always have healthy lifestyles.

Vicky said, 'It could be Lou? She's very quiet over here.'

'Yes!' cried Fiona. 'We practically lived off Monster Munch sandwiches at uni.'

Louise just smiled her faint smile, giving nothing away.

'She'd never vote Tory either,' said Daniel. 'And she must have to navigate in the desert all the time. Not her.'

'Rachel?' said Paddy politely, trying to include her. 'Who do you think it is?'

She barely looked up from her phone. 'It's Jonathan, obviously.'

'No way!' cried Amira. 'He's always reading maps on his show.'

'Well, that's the lie then. Don't you get how this game works?'

Jonathan seemed subdued as he took a gulp of port. 'She's right.'

'It's you?' said Fiona, surprised. 'You told me you always voted Labour!'

He winced. 'Don't judge. It was before all the Brexit mess. He seemed funny, you know.'

'Oh my God, Jay! This is all your fault then. His entire career, that's how it started.'

'What, just me personally?'

'If the shoe fits, mate.'

Amira saw Rachel frown, catching the flirty vibe between Jonathan and his ex.

Vicky leaned forward briskly for the box. 'Well, there we go. One point for Rachel. Who's next?' She pulled a piece of paper out, crumpled up carelessly. Amira recognised her own writing and her heart sped up. Stupid. 'Ooh, this is hard to read. Let's see. "I can't swim. I ran the marathon. I don't like dogs."'

'Clearly a monster,' said Fiona, narrowing her eyes round the table. Amira drank some wine to cover her red face, then regretted it.

Jonathan had ideas. 'Dan and Vicky, you've both run the marathon. So Fiona, that could be your lie. But you love dogs. And you're a good swimmer.'

'I'm an excellent swimmer, I'll have you know.'

'So not you. Dan?'

'School champion at the butterfly as well, mate.'

'True, I've seen the pictures of your teeny-weeny Speedos. Harrowing. So the marathon's a lie. Someone really does hate dogs and can't swim!' He looked around at their faces. 'Padster can swim too, so can Vic . . . God, even the kids can swim. Who is it? Not Lou. I remember you jumping off the bridge into the Thames.' His gaze fixed on Amira. 'Bingo.'

She flushed.

Fiona groaned. 'I remember your dog phobia now. One bit you as a kid, right? That makes sense.' Though it didn't stop Fiona letting her two bounce all over Amira any time they visited.

'You can't swim, Amira?' Vicky looked incredulous. 'How is that possible?'

'I never learned. We didn't go swimming as kids, or to the seaside.' It wasn't really that unusual, but everyone looked gobsmacked.

'Padster, why haven't you taught her?' demanded Daniel.

'It's hard to learn as an adult. Anyway, she doesn't want to.'

'I hate getting my face wet. And the changing rooms are always so gross.' Plus she was deeply, irretrievably, afraid of water.

'Well, that's true enough,' said Fiona, kindly.

Louise spoke unexpectedly in Amira's defence. 'It really is hard to learn as an adult. Lots of my colleagues overseas couldn't swim, especially if they didn't grow up near any pools or water.'

Amira felt absurdly grateful. Why had she admitted her shameful secret, given them ammunition to think even less of her?

Jonathan was still going. 'But what if you fall into a river? Or off a boat?'

'I'll just try not to, I suppose,' she said, more tartly than she meant, and everyone laughed.

He chuckled. 'Fair enough, Ammy. Let's do another. Rachel, you pick.'

Rachel reached for the box with a small eye roll. This must be very boring for her. 'Alright. This is . . . oh!' She looked up from the paper, eyes wide with shock. 'Is this meant to be funny? I don't get it.'

'What does it say?' said Jonathan. 'Show me.'

'It's . . . urgh, honestly! This is sick. I may not know you all that well but that doesn't mean you can just, like, haze me. Gross.' She got up, pushing her chair away, and moved to the window, arms folded protectively

'What does it say?' Vicky was frowning.

Jonathan picked up the paper Rachel had thrown down, and his expression also changed.

'She's right, this isn't cool, guys.'

'What *is* it?' Vicky snapped.

He read it out, slowly. 'Well, someone has written – I don't know if . . . God. It says, "Everyone here has killed someone. There is no way off the island." And "You will all either kill or be killed here."'

A short, stunned silence. Amira's mind tried to grab for a reasonable explanation, and failed.

'Whose is this?' Vicky snatched the paper from her brother. 'No one owning up?' Everyone shook their heads, pale shock reflected around the table. 'Well, it's not very funny, is it.'

'Some kind of bad joke?' Fiona's usual confidence had faltered.

Louise took it from Vicky, turned it over in her hands, frowned, but said nothing.

Paddy said, 'It really isn't funny. Dan? Was it one of your surprises?'

'It wasn't me!' he protested, though pranks were admittedly his style.

'Jay?'

'Come on, mate, I'd have owned up if it was me, look how upset Rachel is.'

They all looked round the table. No one admitted to it. So who had done it, then?

Louise had been going through the box, and had a stack of papers in front of her. Now she said, 'It's extra.'

Everyone exclaimed at once.

'What?'

'Extra – what are you talking about?'

'This is messed up.' Voices overlapped.

Louise raised hers to be heard. 'There's eight of us. Two papers opened already, but there are seven in here still. That makes nine. This one – it's from someone else.'

Mhairi

Her first impression was that this was all underwhelming. The door
of the house was open, left ajar, and no one seemed to be inside.
The place was a little untidy, perhaps, and there were candles on
every surface, stuck to plates and inside mugs and bottles. The fire
in the stove was still burning, down to its ashes. There were also a
huge number of empty drinks cans and bottles stacked up by the
door, and some dirty plates and cups left out. Arthur was at her
back, a silent solid presence. 'This is so weird. Where are they all?'

He grunted. 'Don't know.'

Mhairi caught sight of a stuffed Paw Patrol toy on the floor,
and suppressed a shudder. Should she be taking photos? The CSIs
got annoyed if you disturbed anything, even to save a life.

'Hello?' she called out.

The house stood silent around her, chill and empty. They went
upstairs via a dangerous, open-sided staircase, and moved through
the rooms, everything giving the eerie impression that people had
stepped out just a moment before. Cases, toiletry bags, most of the
beds unmade but one or two pulled neat and tight. Two mobile
phones left on dressers. She touched the screens with a gloved hand,
but they stayed dark. Perhaps without power they had run out
of charge. There was nothing that seemed like an obvious clue.
Clothes and books lying round, walking boots lined up by the front

door. She flicked a light switch – nothing. A power cut, or had someone done this on purpose? It was light now, though a typically dreich Scottish day, but at night it would have been pitch-black, only the faint lights of the mainland in the distance.

She asked Arthur, 'Isn't there a generator?'

He shrugged. 'Don't know. I was only hired with the boat.'

He'd done it all over email, because even Scottish boatmen had websites now. Arthur ran wildlife tours in summer, and would have been only too glad of a bit of extra winter work, paid to be on standby if the guests needed anything. He'd shown her the booking email already – something bland from admin@scottishcottagerental.com. When she'd gone to that website, it didn't exist. His instructions had been simply to meet the group at the harbour, then go back for them on the Sunday. It had been a self check-in, with no one there to show them around. Arthur knew nothing more.

She'd had Davey trying to trace the owner and also the caretaker of the cottage. Someone local, surely, but she hadn't immediately known who, like she would for most of the rental properties on Tarne. Mallacht island, cut off as it was, had always been somewhat mysterious, its new owners never seen locally.

Mhairi was on the verge of thinking there'd been some big misunderstanding here, and the missing guests were just out for a walk or a sail or had the checkout day wrong, but then on a circuit of the living room she found it. A huge stain, splashed all over the wood of the walls and floor, ruining one of the white sheepskin throws. As if someone had thrown a dish of food or a cup of coffee, but it wasn't that. It was blood.

Vicky

When things happened that didn't make sense, the mind scrabbled after meaning anyway. She remembered this from the accident, though she had forgotten it in the interim – that sick feeling where the world turned on its side.

She'd felt that way even before the stupid game, as soon as they arrived at the empty house, walking boots echoing on the smart new floors, heat radiating up. It was their house, but not. The furniture all new, a wall taken down to make an open-plan kitchen and living room, full of expensive cloud-like sofas and white sheepskin throws the kids were sure to get sticky. The walls panelled with wood like a ski chalet, instead of the plain whitewash that she was used to. The pantry all fitted out with gadgets and ingredients and a coffee maker that was better than the one they had at home. The hot tubs, the wood burner instead of the draughty open fire, the fire pit outside, the rugs underfoot. It was hers, but not hers. And now this horrible joke, this tedious prank someone thought was funny, ruining her birthday.

'That can't be right,' insisted Vicky, when Louise said there was an extra piece of paper in the box. 'Look, we'll just go through them all and work out who wrote what.' She spread the folded bits of paper out in front of her, separated off the three they had already opened. Amira's, Jonathan's, and the mystery third. She picked up another, folded into a tight square. '"I'm allergic to eight different things. I do fifty push-ups every day. I haven't drunk caffeine in five years."' She suppressed a sigh. 'Rachel, that's you?'

Rachel was stabbing at her phone again, as if willing a signal into being. 'Yes.'

'One was meant to be a lie,' said Jonathan gently.

'I'm allergic to *nine* things, not eight! Did you forget?'

'Ummm, OK, you're right. So that's you. Read another, Vic?'

She opened the next. '"I've slept with two people here. I never wanted kids. I've had a threesome."'

Everyone looked blank. 'No one going to own up?' said Fiona. 'Jay, that wasn't you? Poor taste if so.'

'We had mine.' He scanned the room, frowning. 'I can't think of anyone else with the . . . with two, so that must be the lie. Who's had a threesome then? Padster, the quiet one?'

Vicky glared at Daniel. He'd always claimed to have had one, with two girls in their year at college. But neither of the other statements could be true, surely. He didn't meet her eyes. He seemed absolutely hammered.

Paddy was in the kitchen boiling the kettle, his back turned. 'Look, this is silly. People clearly wrote any old rubbish, it was just a parlour game.'

'That's a yes then,' slurred Daniel. So maybe it wasn't his after all.

Amira was biting her lip. Who else had he slept with then – or was that the lie? He did want kids, didn't he – Vicky got the impression he and Amira had been trying for years? Of course, one of those truths could also be her own, couldn't it? She didn't want people delving too deeply into that so she changed the subject.

'Let's move on. Hmm, weird. This one says, "I've slept with two people in this room. I've thought about how to kill someone and not get caught. I don't believe in the Moon landings."' Vicky blinked. 'Gosh, I don't know who that could be.'

53

'Two of us wrote the same thing, about sleeping with people here?' Jonathan reached for it. 'That's weird. Fi, is that you? You've thought about murder? I imagine most doctors know how to get away with it.'

Fiona was bright red. 'Look, like Paddy says, it's all stupid. We should be focusing on who wrote the extra one.'

Jonathan rested a consoling hand on her shoulder, and Vicky saw Rachel glare at him, looking up from her phone for a moment.

Shrugging him off, Fiona also reached for a slip and read it out. '"I've lost twenty pounds this year. I'm a parent. I once threw up in a wardrobe."' That would have drawn laughs, under different circumstances.

Jonathan frowned. 'Wait. Is *that* yours, Fi?'

'I wish. I've put on twenty pounds, if anything.' She forced a laugh, though Vicky calculated this was probably true.

She picked up another. 'OK, carrying on if no one's owning up. "I haven't seen anyone here for five years. I recently quit my job but didn't tell anyone. I have only ninety pounds left in my bank account."' Everyone looked blank. 'Well, it's not me.' Who had recently given up their job? 'Lou,' she said. 'You just came back. And you haven't seen any of us for years.' Could it have been her who wrote the note? Louise had reason to be angry at Vicky, certainly. More than most.

Louise was stacking the dishwasher with glasses. 'Yes, it's me.'

'So the bank account is a lie. I mean, Christ! Ninety pounds. Imagine.'

Louise said nothing, but she had flushed red too.

'You quit your job, Lou?' said Jonathan.

'Yeah. It was – not really sustainable. And Mum's ill, you know, I can't be overseas all the time.'

Vicky recognised her own paper and pulled it out. 'Well, I'll just admit this one is mine. "I've never had a McDonald's, I'm a mother, and I recently mastered a yoga headstand."'

Amira was sitting at the table with her head in her hands, looking stunned by proceedings. 'What was the lie?'

'McDonald's. I tried one for the first time this year. The twins had a party, someone from nursery, and well, there was nowhere else to get lunch near their house. I had the salad.'

Rachel muttered, 'Their salads can have more calories than the burgers you know,' but no one paid attention. Daniel was opening another bottle of red, almost on autopilot. Vicky had lost count of how many drinks he'd had. Well into double figures.

The papers were all read now. Everyone had owned up except Fiona, Paddy, and Daniel. Daniel had thrown up in every space you could think of, so that must be him, and the weight loss was a red herring to throw suspicion on Paddy, who was of course not a parent and never likely to be as long as he was saddled with Amira. Or maybe that bit was true, and Paddy had never wanted kids anyway. But that would mean he'd slept with two people here – who on earth? Louise? Fiona? Was Fiona's entry the one about the Moon landings – or had she had a threesome Vicky somehow didn't know about, though it was hard to imagine? Or was that a lie? Her head swam.

'So that didn't help at all,' sighed Fiona. 'We've no idea who put the extra note in.'

'But who could it have been?' Amira asked, for at least the third time. 'If it wasn't any of us.'

Vicky narrowed her eyes, staring round at the people she trusted most in the world – her oldest friends, her husband, her brother. Realising she still didn't trust them very much. 'Well, it's obvious. Someone isn't telling the truth.'

Marco

2019

It was a normal day for Luisa, although a little easier than normal, because Marco wasn't there to be hauled out of bed and forced through bathroom, breakfast, and into his uniform, a sleepwalking fourteen-year-old. When she thought of all the years he'd woken her up at five, she had to laugh really. She'd used the extra time to make a nice breakfast for herself and Fabien, fried up some sausage and eggs, eaten it at the table with the radio playing. It had been nice, having the time to chat before they both rushed off to work.

The rest of the day she would hardly remember afterwards. Bus to work at the salon, a cut, a colour, a chat over coffee with the other girls. A nice day. Someone had definitely asked her, 'How's Marco getting on with his school trip?'

'Oh, we've not heard a peep out of him.'

'Typical teenage boy. Probably fine then.'

'Yeah, no news is good news.'

She hoped he would have fun, but also take some inspiration from that nice, steady teacher of his, Mr O'Hagan. He was always so kind, saying that Marco could get into a good university if he'd calm down a little, apply himself, make some friends other than the rowdy boys he hung about with, hopped up on energy drinks like tiny drug addicts. Mr O'Hagan was going to split them up in the dormitories on the school trip, and see if that helped. So thoughtful – how many other teachers understood the cliques of the kids like that? And he'd been to Oxford, everyone said, yet he'd chosen to work in their not-exactly-Eton inner-city school. She appreciated that.

'Lucky him, at the seaside. Devon, is it?'

'Dorset. Looking for fossils and that.'

'Lovely.'

The call came in at 11.07. She would never forget the time because she glanced at the clock as Alice answered the salon phone, wondering if it was her next client ringing to cancel. She didn't have her mobile on her while working, which was why she hadn't seen the dozens of messages and calls from the school.

Alice beckoned her over. 'It's for you.'

'Can't you take a message?' Her hands in their gloves were sticky with chestnut colour, the strong earthy smell of it in her nostrils.

'No, it's – Lu, it's for you.'

Had the dread started then? She stripped off the gloves, tidied her own hair, walked the few steps. Maybe knowing already something was wrong. Trying to delay finding out for just a moment more. 'Hello?'

'Mrs Sanchez? It's Mr O'Hagan here. From Marco's school.'

Something in his voice. A weariness. Suppressed tears.

'Yes?' A tick of panic now at the base of her skull.

'I'm afraid I have some . . . I'm so sorry, Luisa. I'm so, so sorry.'

57

Amira

No one quite knew what to do after that. Rachel had stomped upstairs, stabbing at her phone as if it might magically come to life, still convinced it was all a dig at her. Louise had quietly cleared up the glasses and started the dishwasher. Vicky had gone to check on the twins. Jonathan and Paddy had the slips of paper in front of them at the coffee table, staring at them as if an answer might be forthcoming. Daniel was still drinking steadily, staring into space. Fiona was railing, pacing up and down. 'I hate practical jokes. So silly, scaring everyone like this. What a load of nonsense.'

Vicky came down then, her make-up off and glasses on, but still looking beautiful. Darcy was a few steps behind on the stairs, in her pyjamas with a fluffy hoody over the top. 'I've asked Darcy to join us for a minute.'

'What's going on?' Darcy looked between her parents.

Fiona started. 'You surely don't think she . . . ?'

'She did help to set the game up, Fiona. I just think we should ask her if she knows anything.'

'For goodness' sake! She's a child.'

Darcy bridled. 'I'm not a child! I'm fifteen.'

'There you go,' said Vicky. 'Ask her, at least. If we're asking everyone else.'

'I'm not going to interrogate my own daughter.'

Jonathan spoke up then. 'She's right, Fiona. Darce, sweetheart, someone slipped a nasty note into our game. Any chance you know something about that?'

'What? No!'

'Or did someone give you it and ask you to put it in? Someone here or . . . someone else?'

'Who else could it be?' exclaimed Fiona.

'Well, there's the caretaker of this place. The owner. The boatman. Whoever does the cleaning and makes the beds. Anyone could have left it here.'

'But how would they know we were going to play the game? That doesn't make any sense. It has to be someone here.'

'I didn't do anything,' said Darcy, tearful. 'I only helped with your stupid game to try and join in, like Mum said. I don't even want to be here.' She grabbed handfuls of the papers, left out on the table.

'No, wait—' Fiona started towards her, doubtless thinking that some of them were not for teenage eyes. But Darcy wasn't reading them.

She pointed. 'Look! This is the only one in blue. It's like a Sharpie or something like that. The others are different.' Looked at side by side, she was right. The offending note was the only one written in bold blue, in block capitals. Not with any of the pens they had used for the game.

Vicky said, 'Has anyone seen a pen like this around?' Everyone shook their heads. 'Alright, thank you, Darcy. I'm sorry we had to ask.'

Louise came over then, and put her arm around Darcy's shoulders. 'Come on, will you help me make some hot drinks? Cocoa, maybe? Everyone's had a shock, I think.'

Darcy went with her towards the kitchen, casting bitter glances over her shoulder and muttering, 'I didn't *do* anything.'

'Any other bright ideas?' said Fiona to Jonathan. 'Since it wasn't your teenage daughter.'

'Oh, come on. We had to rule her out, it didn't do any harm.'

'She's fragile enough, Jonathan, without all this! After everything that's happened this year.' The former couple were locked in an intense discussion as if no one else was there.

Vicky said, 'Jonathan's right, we have to look at all possibilities. Obviously, someone is playing a cruel joke.' She retrieved the note, holding it at arm's length. 'Ugh, it's horrible. "Everyone here has killed someone. There is no way off the island. You will all either kill or be killed here."'

Daniel's eyes were half-shut. 'Which one is the lie?'

'What?'

'The game is two truths and a lie. Which one's a lie – that we're all killers? Or we're all going to die?'

Paddy frowned at the papers. 'I've been thinking about this too. Is it true there's no way off the island? No other boats or anything like that?'

Vicky thought about it. 'There used to be a boat. We kept it by the jetty – I don't know if it's still here.'

'Swimming? That must be an option.'

'Nooo,' said Jonathan, half-laughing. 'Mate, you'd drown. There's rip tides, and it's further than it looks. Plus, it's about five degrees right now. You couldn't stay in more than a few minutes.'

Paddy went to push his glasses up his nose, a habit retained even though he'd started wearing contacts. Contacts, exercise, new diet – Amira felt she hardly knew him anymore, a sliding panic as if he was straining away from her. 'So if that's true, one of these other statements must be a lie. Did everyone actually kill someone?'

It wasn't a great choice, Amira thought dully. Either they were all killers, or they were all going to die.

'I don't understand why we're taking this at face value,' tutted Vicky. 'It's just a load of rubbish. Nobody has killed anyone and no one's going to die! For goodness' sake. It's just us out here, no one can get to us.'

'Are we sure about that?' said Paddy, again in his quiet tone. 'Someone could be hiding out here with us.'

Amira shivered, looking out the back window at the dark expanse of the island. Where would someone hide? There was the small shed, but that was the only structure apart from the house and the ruined foundations of old cottages. The outhouse attached to the kitchen, where the wood was stored for the hot tubs and fires. Maybe a cellar, an attic, but that was it.

'The caves,' said Jonathan. 'Remember, Vic? Under the cliffs, you can climb down to them.'

Vicky scowled. 'But why would someone do that? What on earth would they have to gain? I don't understand any of this.'

'We have to go,' declared Fiona. 'Call them on the radio and tell them to come for us. I'm not risking Darcy being upset; it's bad enough her father left us and turned up with some bimbo.'

Jonathan leaned back as if she'd struck him. 'I didn't *leave* you . . .'

'Well, how else would you describe it? You're no longer there. Instead, you're doing coke in the loos at Soho House every night and your girlfriend can barely even be civil to anyone.'

'Hang on now, it's not easy for her, coming into a new group who all know each other.'

'She's right, Jay,' sighed Vicky. 'I don't know what you were thinking, bringing her.'

'Oh really, Vic, you want to go down that road? You want to talk about why we don't even own the island now—'

'Shut up, Jay! It's not the time.'

'You started it.'

Vicky stood up. 'Enough. Stop it now. We can't let this tear us apart. I'm sure there's some perfectly rational explanation. So if there's no way off the island, let's think about this other statement. *Everyone here has killed someone.*'

'Ridiculous,' said Fiona, arms folded. Her reaction to the fear seemed to be impotent rage.

Jonathan's anger had subsided. 'But didn't you have that thing – the malpractice suit?'

She bit her lip. 'That was a long time ago.'

'But it's technically true, isn't it? It could be said that you killed someone.'

'I just – it happens all the time when you're a doctor. People die, and sometimes we miss things. We aren't infallible.'

Amira remembered now. A young mother had gone to Fiona complaining of feeling off, bleeding, pain. Fiona had diagnosed heavy periods, sent her home with paracetamol, and a few months later the woman had collapsed at home, and not long after died of cervical cancer. As a condition it was notoriously easy to miss, and Fiona had been cleared of any wrongdoing, her medical licence upheld. Amira spoke up. 'I suppose it's possible that the family – that they still blame you, Fiona? Even though no one else does.'

Fiona flashed her a furious look. 'Enough to stalk us here to an island? That seems extreme.'

'What do we know about the people we hired it from?' said Jonathan. 'Vics, how did you even get the idea to come back here?' His tone was mollifying, as if sorry for what he'd said to his sister, which Amira did not fully understand, but sensed was something to do with why the family had sold their private island in the first place.

Vicky was quiet, as if in disbelief. 'I got an email.'

'What kind of email?'

'I'd been looking for a while for a venue, sent a few messages and so on, posted on boards, since we'd left it so late to organise.'

She narrowed her eyes at this, and Amira guessed she was wondering why no one else had taken the initiative to actually book a trip they'd been talking about for a year. 'Anyway, then this email came, from something like Scottish rental cottages, and it was Mallacht. It seemed obvious we should come back here.'

'Have you got it still? The email?'

She fumbled her phone from her pocket. 'I think so. Yes.'

Paddy reached for her phone, and she gave it to him, reluctantly. He read the email. 'It's from admin@scottishcottagerental. com. Is there a website you looked on?'

'I think I just . . . emailed them to arrange it all.'

'You didn't use Airbnb or a site like that?'

Vicky shook her head slowly. 'No. We just emailed, organised it direct. There were attached pictures – it wasn't online. There was nothing online.'

'And you didn't think that was weird?'

'Well no, not at the time! It's how things used to be done.'

Amira felt fear rise under her solar plexus. What did it mean? It was bad enough when it was some stupid joke among the Group, but Paddy was saying – what? This had all been planned in advance? They had been lured here?

Paddy still had Vicky's phone. 'Wait, is that the price for the rental?'

'Yeah, why?' She held out her hand for it.

'It's just . . . never mind.' He glared at Daniel, who wasn't looking.

Jonathan sounded impatient. 'What did you think it meant, Vics? Just a coincidence, you get an email and it's our old family home?'

'I don't know! I'd sent a lot of enquiries to find a good place, and she said – well, you can see it. "We saw you were looking and wondered if you'd thought about Mallacht island, it's available for your dates." And it was a good deal, so I took it.'

'Did you tell them we used to own the place?' said Jonathan.

'I can't remember. But look, this is so stupid. It can't be someone external who's planned all this.'

'Who is it then?' said Daniel, his voice thick with alcohol. 'Which of your friends would have done this, on your birthday?'

Vicky seemed to have no answer to that.

After a moment, Louise came back over from the kitchen, carrying a tray of steaming mugs, the comforting smell of chocolate in the air. 'I've sent Darcy up to bed, she's upset. And I've locked all the doors, though they're quite flimsy.'

Of course they were. They had imagined themselves alone on the island, miles across the sea from anywhere.

'We should call on the radio at least. See who answers – if the company's bogus, we'll soon find out.' Fiona seemed to feel better with some concrete plans. She took a mug and blew on it, and Amira did the same. Vicky refused hers, as did Paddy. Jonathan took one awkwardly, his other arm twisted against his chest. Daniel accepted a mug but didn't seem to know what it was, setting it aside and carrying on with his large tumbler of whisky.

'We need a plan,' said Jonathan. 'First, we should try the radio, yes. Then we should search the island and the house, make sure there really isn't anyone out here with us.'

God, Amira couldn't bear that idea. To have come out and hidden for hours, in the freezing cold and rain – that said something about depth of rage. Why would anyone hate them that much? Fiona had caused someone's death, yes, but most doctors would have at some point or another. It surely wasn't enough to have inspired such obsession.

The words burst from her before she realised. 'I was accused of killing someone too. Well, not directly. Of letting them die.'

Everyone stared at her.

'I'm a social worker, it's just part of the job. We make choices every day hoping we aren't wrong, and we either break up a family and traumatise a child for life, or we get the call that they're dead.'

Paddy reached for her hand. He knew about this case.

She swallowed. 'It was a little boy called Liam. His stepdad fractured his skull. There hadn't been signs. Or not enough to remove him, though we were concerned.'

'Was this in the press? I don't think I knew about it.' Vicky frowned.

'I didn't tell anyone. I was ashamed. It was reported in a few local papers.'

'So people could find out about it, if they tried?'

'Yes, it was just after the Baby P stuff so social workers were being vilified in the media.' As if it were her who had punched and kicked the little boy, thrown him down a flight of stairs, allowed him to bleed to death.

Paddy's brow was knitted. 'Anyone else got something like this? A death you could be linked to, something you were accused of?'

'Load of crap,' said Daniel, clearing his throat. 'Mate, why even give this the time of day? Someone's messing about.'

'There was the fall,' Amira blurted. 'I'm sorry but . . . we need to know. Everyone's stories. We need it all out in the open.'

Paddy's voice was tight. 'I think everyone knows about that. There was no suggestion I was involved.'

'It's all in the public domain,' said Fiona, getting up and pacing again. 'There was an inquest, wasn't there? Anyone could find that out too.'

'Yes. But it seems quite tenuous. It's not like I actually caused a death. I mean, we have responsible jobs, you, me, and Amira. It's inevitable that things like this happen. It's not our fault.'

'Anyone else?' said Fiona. 'Fess up. Is everyone happy to share their stories, if they have them?'

'Happy,' snorted Vicky. 'I don't think anyone here is happy, Fiona. And no, I don't see why we should have to respond to these horrible accusations, in fact.'

'Well, I shared mine,' said Fiona impatiently. 'Never mind that I was trying to help people. Doctors get this kind of shit all the time.'

So did social workers, and even teachers. But what could the rest of them have done? Amira tried to think what she knew, any scandal ever hinted at in the past. Wasn't there something about Daniel, the company he'd founded out of university, and the murky reasons it had gone bust? He certainly wasn't volunteering anything. What about Louise, busying herself in the kitchen – she saved lives, surely, fed the hungry and treated the sick. And Vicky, a stay-at-home mum, could hardly have a murderous past. As for Rachel – had anyone ever been killed through the medium of Instagram? Jonathan was famous, so any scandal in his past would surely have leaked out by now. It didn't make any sense.

'Vicky's right,' said Jonathan, after some thought. 'There's no reason we have to respond to damaging slurs like this. That's probably what they want, whoever's doing this. To set us against each other. So, what do we do now?'

Vicky folded her arms. 'Like you said. Search the house at least, then lock down for the night. In the morning we'll search the whole island and make sure no one's here. They can't possibly be, in this weather.'

Amira wished she was so sure.

Jonathan stood up. 'Alright, but let's try the radio first. It'll put our minds at rest. And if someone feels like owning up to this in the meantime, please do. We'll be pissed off, but I'd rather that than clambering down those cliffs.'

Fiona was over at the front door. She called, 'The folder said the radio was here on the wall?'

Vicky glanced at her. 'Yeah, hanging up. It was there earlier.'

'It's gone.'

'What?'

They all rushed over to Fiona, and it was clear – there was the hook for the radio, its charging point, and Amira thought she remembered seeing it when they arrived, a black and yellow hulk of a thing like an old mobile phone. But it was no longer there.

Mhairi

At the back of the house was a seating area with wood and leather chairs covered in sheepskin rugs, a fire pit burned down to its ashes, two tin baths with chimneys attached and lids on top. Wood-fired hot tubs, they called them, which had always seemed ridiculous to Mhairi. It was an outdoor bath was what it was, which took four hours to heat.

The blood in the house had put her on red alert, but even though she'd expected it, it was still a shock to see them stacked in the outhouse. The bodies. The ones Arthur had found on his brief sortie.

The first was tall, over six foot at least, wrapped in a blue tarpaulin and tied about with rope like a terrible burrito. The other was shorter, perhaps five foot five or six, less neatly wrapped. Mhairi could see a flash of white hanging out the side – fingers. Deep-burgundy nail polish. She unwrapped the tarpaulins with gloved hands, and the bodies sprawled out, the first pale and heavy, the second tiny and contracted in death. Her skin was blue and dry already, but her hair was still thick and glossy, her clothes expensive. So at least two people were dead. A man and a woman. Two in one weekend – that could be a coincidence, maybe? No. Not really.

'There should have been a radio, you said? But it's gone?'

Arthur nodded. 'Aye. And the power's out all over.'

Did that mean something sinister had occurred here? Not accidental deaths? 'The kids,' Mhairi burst out. 'Did you see any sign of them, when you arrived?'

Arthur shook his head slowly. 'Not a trace. Two wee twins and a teenage girl, maybe fifteen or so.' It had taken an hour for Arthur to get back to the mainland and wake Mhairi up, and for her to drive to the port and motor over. A lot could have happened in an hour.

Once again Mhairi felt overwhelmed by the scale of this, wished she had a whole team of officers to command, CSIs on hand to comb the island. They would take all day to arrive from Glasgow, and evidence might be lost in the meantime. She bent to feel for pulses on the necks of the corpses, but it was just a formality. They were clearly both long gone.

She stood up, feeling her knees twinge. 'I still don't get where the rest of them are. They can't all be dead, can they?'

Arthur shrugged. 'Did you see that?' He indicated a kitchen knife, abandoned on the ground by the fire pit. Red on its tip. Another thing to document. But neither body appeared to have been stabbed, so what did that mean? Where had the blood come from in the living room?

Mhairi surveyed the island – a small lump of rock, some trees and bushes, lots of sheep. 'I better walk the perimeter. Will you come with me?'

Poor Arthur, this wasn't his job at all. She'd make sure he got compensated for his time, though he likely wouldn't accept it. He nodded grimly. Mhairi paced the back patio, taking note of anything that could be a clue. Ashes in the pizza oven. Blankets left askew over the chairs. Clearly, they'd sat out here for at least one meal. Would they have done that if one of them had died already? On the hewn wooden table, the remains of a pizza. No one had cleaned it up. A child's woolly hat lay on the ground. God, this was like a jigsaw puzzle where she couldn't find the edges.

Mhairi could not immediately identify either of the dead bodies. The man didn't look like Jonathan Capeman, but the face was so red and blistered it was impossible to be sure. She knew him from TV of course – Callum liked his programmes, fancied himself a survivalist too. Mhairi, who'd searched for too many dead hikers in the Cairngorms, preferred a cosy house and a roof over her head. Apart from the celebrity, she didn't have much to go on – it was only luck that one of the Group had posted a selfie of the whole gang on the ferry, before she would have lost mobile reception. Mhairi had screenshotted it on her phone, but even zooming in didn't tell her much. Three men, tagged as Jonathan Capeman, Daniel Franks, and someone called Paddy. Five women. Fiona Capeman – that was Jonathan's wife, or ex-wife maybe by now. Rachel Solenado, an influencer she gathered was Jonathan's new girlfriend, who'd posted the shot to her million-plus followers. That seemed a mind-boggling number to Mhairi. There was also a woman named Amira, whose Instagram contained only a few blurry shots of meals, years old; another tagged as Louise Connolly, who mainly posted about international development issues, and Vicky Franks, née Capeman, whose Instagram was a curated symphony of her cute kids, her beautiful home, her attractive home-cooked meals, her picture-perfect holidays. And the children. The adorable twins, and the pretty if sulky teenage girl, who had a social media footprint larger than China. Darcy Capeman, aged fifteen. Toby and Genevieve Franks, aged five. So who had died? The male body had a wedding ring on the left hand, though the fingers were so maimed and mashed it was hard to see. Mhairi looked round for some kind of answer, eyes coming to rest on the hot tubs.

She approached the one with its top off, immediately wrinkling her nose at the smell. Like spoiled meat. 'Something happened here.'

She noted the smell down, photographed the scene on her phone. The water was cold, ashes in the burner too. She examined the underside of the tub's heavy wooden lid – it was splintered and cracked. Something was floating in the water; Mhairi used a pen to fish it out and stared at it. What was—

'A nail,' said Arthur, coming up behind her. 'Fingernail.'

And so it was. A man's nail, square and bruised, floating there in the cold water.

She shivered, feeling sick and cold and wishing she had chosen another job out of school – law or nursing or accountancy. She bet accountants never found human nails in bathtubs. Carefully, she put it into an evidence bag. 'I'd better check if either body is missing one.'

'Big one is. Noticed when you unwrapped him.'

'Oh. How do you think he—'

'Boiled to death.' Arthur pointed to show her. 'He was in there and someone put the lid on, maybe. They're heavy. He tries to get out, loses a nail scraping at it, but can't manage.'

Someone had boiled a man to death inside a wood-fired hot tub? Who were these people?

'Come on. We'd better check out the rest of the island.' But she couldn't shake the feeling that, apart from these wrapped bodies, they were the only people here, the only living beings apart from the sheep and the seals.

Mhairi set off down the hill towards the north beach. Being winter in Scotland, it would be dark in a few hours, and she needed to be safely on the mainland by then, with lights and electricity and, more importantly, backup. Whoever would cook a man alive likely would not hesitate to take out a slightly overweight detective and a grizzled old fisherman.

Vicky

They all stood staring at the gap where the radio should have been. She could feel the tick of it in the air between them – ramping-up panic. *Something is wrong here.*

'Maybe the kids were playing . . . ?' faltered Jonathan.

'They can't reach that high, for goodness' sake. Someone has done this. I don't understand. I don't *understand*! It's my birthday, it isn't fair.' Vicky was panicking.

Daniel put a clumsy arm around her. 'Look, we'll get to the bottom of this, I promise.'

She glared at him. 'You absolutely swear this isn't some stupid joke of yours? Like an escape room or a prank or something like that? You know I hate pranks.' He'd said he had plans, which had not extended to doing any of the actual organisation of the weekend.

He hesitated.

'*Daniel.*'

'No, no, swear to God. Not this. I swear, Vics.'

She stared at the rest of them. 'There could be a logical reason. Does anyone remember exactly when we last saw the radio?'

Everyone looked blank. Who would have thought to check? You wouldn't imagine you'd need such a thing. That emergencies would actually happen. In the old days, when they'd come to the island, they'd had no phone or radio at all, no means of communicating with the main island. Completely cut-off, the way her parents had preferred. No chance of encountering anyone poor or common that way.

Paddy said, 'Maybe it wasn't even there earlier, maybe it's somewhere else, and we'll find it later. It could all be just some big misunderstanding.'

'I saw it,' said Vicky. 'I looked over when I read about it in the file.'

'Are you sure though? The memory can play tricks.'

'I . . .' Maybe she wasn't sure. And God, she didn't want to be sure, because if she had seen it and now it was gone, then this was much more than a stupid prank which someone here had played and then not owned up to when the joke backfired.

'We should search the house,' said Jonathan, standing up. 'Set our minds at rest a little.'

'The twins are asleep. I don't want to scare them.'

'We'll be quiet. You and Fiona can take the bedrooms, us guys'll do the cellar, outhouse, attic? Look under the beds and in wardrobes and stuff.'

Fiona snapped, 'So the big macho men will do the searching and we'll just mind the kids, is that it?'

Jonathan sounded weary. 'I don't mean it that way. They just might be less scared with their mothers there. I highly doubt Darce isn't awake, listening to every word we're saying.'

Fiona fell silent, looking up at the ceiling. 'I'll go up to her.'

'Rachel's probably asleep too.'

She would be no help at all anyway, thought Vicky, slipping her feet into her Uggs. With her high heels and endless complaining, Vicky couldn't think of anyone less suited to a crisis situation than Rachel. 'Jay, you and I should direct the search, since we know the house. Or we used to. I'll do the attic.'

Daniel was slumped at the table, drinking wine again. 'Don't say "we should split up", Vics. Everyone knows that's when the murders start.'

'Why would you say that?' she exclaimed. 'None of this is funny!'

'Just trying to lighten things up.' God, he was drunk. She felt another surge of fury, molten waves of it hitting her solar plexus. Was this all his fault? She didn't entirely believe his denials.

'Fine, we can all go together. Not you, Daniel, you're hammered.'

'I'll check on the kids,' said Fiona. 'And under the beds like Jay said. I doubt anyone could be up there without us knowing.'

Then who had done this? Either the danger was outside the house or it was inside. One of them. Louise hadn't said anything, just left the room and come back with her coat and two large torches in her hands. 'They were in the pantry.'

'We used to have power cuts all the time out here. I guess they still do.' Jonathan took one, Vicky the other.

Paddy was putting on his coat, a sensible waterproof one with lots of zips. 'I want to check the jetty, see if there is a boat like you said. Then we'll know for sure.'

'You can't go by yourself, it's pitch-black.'

'I'll be fine.'

'I'll go with you,' said Amira quickly. Everyone looked at her.

Paddy said, 'Don't be silly. It's dark out, and freezing.'

'I don't care. I want to be with you.'

He sighed. 'Fine. Let's go now though.'

Amira put her coat on with some reluctance, and Vicky didn't entirely blame her, since rain was peppering the windows and it had been dark for hours, but everyone had to pull their weight. She was still reconfiguring her thoughts on Amira, after that revelation that one of her clients had died on her watch. Poor little kid. As a general rule, Vicky found Amira quite annoying, and she and Fiona were not above the odd cathartic bitch session about her timidity and joylessness. Holding Paddy back, Vicky had always thought. Lovely Paddy, who had been hers before he was Amira's.

'Be careful,' she called, as Paddy opened the door in a swirl of cold air. He glanced back at her and was gone.

Louise said she would search downstairs, so Vicky and Jonathan trooped upstairs where Fiona had already gone.

'There used to be an attic trapdoor,' said Jonathan, gazing above him, as Fiona slipped out of Vicky's own room, padding quietly. Through the closing door she saw that the twins were still asleep, double humps on their camp beds, safe from any knowledge of all this fear and accusation. Vicky's heart eased a little.

'I've done the bedrooms,' said Fiona, in a low voice. 'Nothing.'

'I don't know what you thought you'd find,' said a small cross voice. Darcy was in the doorway of her and Fiona's room, wearing pyjamas with polar bears printed on them. She looked about nine, no longer the sophisticated teen with the manicures and phone glowing hot with TikTok notifications.

'You alright, piglet?' said Jonathan tenderly.

Darcy rolled her eyes. 'DO NOT call me that.'

'Sorry. Fi, did you do my room?'

'No.' Fiona folded her arms. 'Didn't think Rachel would appreciate being disturbed.'

'Alright. I'll check after this. Look, the hatch is in the same place. I think I can . . .' He gave a small leap, good arm extended, and popped the clasp. A ladder slid down, which he manipulated with a series of clanking sounds. Vicky glanced at her door, but there was no peep from the twins. They had to be exhausted after such a long day and missing naptime. She braced a foot on the ladder.

'I'll go, Vic,' said her brother.

'Don't be silly, you can only hold on with one arm.'

Trying to be brave, she climbed towards the square of perfect dark. A musty, dusty smell rolled down, as if the house's true nature lurked underneath the new wood panelling and slate tiles and underfloor heating.

'There should be a light cord on the side there,' called Jonathan.

'I know. I remember.'

Although it was hard to imagine anything like that could be the same, when the house was so altered, giving her the unsettling feeling of waking up in a different body. She found the cord, pulled it, emitting a weak orange light that barely stretched into the dark corners.

'See anything?'

'Just junk.'

Empty boxes, old furniture shrouded in dust sheets. All the items you would shove out of sight if you renovated a house to look shiny, and beautiful. The ugly things that didn't fit the image. But those things could not stay hidden forever, as Vicky knew very well. At least she couldn't see what part of her had feared, the glow of human eyes staring back at her from the gloom.

'No, there's nothing.'

She came back down, pushing the ladder back with difficulty and shutting the hatch, closing off the whistling draught that had come from it. Her brother and Fiona looked a little more relieved, she noticed, and she felt better too. No bogeyman above them.

'Let's just do the cellar and outhouse, to be sure,' said Jonathan.

So they did. They all filed downstairs – except Darcy, who stayed in the bedroom watching them with fearful, scornful eyes.

'Listen out for the twins,' Vicky called behind her. 'Fi, you stay and help Louise look, there's no need for us all to go.'

She and her brother slid into their boots, opening the door to the cold wind. Far away towards the pier, she could see the bob of Amira and Paddy's phone torches. And hadn't he been brave, to volunteer to go out and check? Whereas Daniel was already asleep on the sofa. She'd need Jonathan to help her drag him up to bed.

The outhouse, where they used to store their wood and drip their wet swimsuits, was also now heated, slate-tiled, shiny-clean. A washing machine and dryer, heated boot racks even, like you got for skiing. A pile of neatly hewn logs. Jonathan clicked the light, and opened the few cupboards, but it was clear no one could possibly hide in here.

'The cellar?' he said, and she followed him without speaking.

At the back of the house, above where the hill began to slope down to the beach, was a small hatch that led to what used to be a coal cellar. Jonathan unlatched it and shone his torch in. Sloping sides and no light.

'How did you get the coal out again?' she asked.

He pointed with the light. 'There's a little door back there, see. It used to open into the old kitchen of the house – looks like it's blocked off now, I guess since they got underfloor heating put in. You'd open the door and scoop out coal for the range.'

They'd had an Aga here as children. Vicky could just imagine being trapped in the cellar, struggling to get up the sloped sides. But the place was almost empty, just some broken outdoor armchairs, and a mass of old, smelly fishing net. A junk room.

'Guess they didn't renovate this bit,' said Jonathan. 'Feels more like home, now. The rest of the house is unrecognisable.'

'I know,' she sighed. 'Mum would hate it.' Their mother, aristocratic to her core, preferred the shabby, the authentic, the unshowy. It had been a mistake to come back here, Vicky was realising. You couldn't recapture the past, find what had been lost, not really. 'So – there's no one here, right?'

'I don't see how anyone could be in the house. We can check again in the morning, if you're really worried.'

'Fine.' She huddled into her coat against the wind. 'Look, I'm sorry for what I said about Rachel. She seems nice.'

Jonathan sighed. 'This isn't really her scene. And it wasn't fair to Fiona to bring her, I see that now. Or you. I'm sorry, Vics.'

She reached out to squeeze his good arm, her annoying but dependable brother. 'Come on. I need you to lug my husband up to bed.'

Gabby

2022

The Sudanese sun was beating down on her through the canvas of the tent, and despite having grown up in a warm climate herself, she could already feel her skin burning. It was unavoidable when you worked outside most of the day, but she did worry about melanoma later in life. That would be ironic – to die because she'd tried to help people.

Despite the heat, the flies that gathered on every flat surface, the stench of latrines and sweating bodies, the primitive tent she slept in, life was simple in a camp. There was your tent with a single bed, a folding table with a few toiletries – toothpaste and toothbrush, shampoo, soap, plus her one towel. She wore the same clothes every day, a shirt with the logo of the charity on it, cargo shorts, boots and socks. Underwear plain and practical, five sets washed and rotated. A notebook and pen, a few paperbacks. No phone – there often wasn't any electricity to charge it. When darkness fell it was one dim bulb or a clockwork light that barely illuminated enough to brush your teeth. It made sense to her. She could help people here, provide food and shelter and organise logistics, keep them safe from the roving militias that had emptied out the countryside hereabouts.

The tent flap moved, and she looked up from her inventory of flour sacks and instinctively drew her spine straighter, tried to look busier.

'Louise, hello.'

Not exactly her boss, but definitely more senior, and definitely not someone you wanted to catch you slacking. Louise was much paler than Gabby, who came from Colombia, and had apricot-coloured curly hair, but all the same she never burned, as if even the sun was afraid of her.

Louise spoke briskly. 'Gabby. I need to make a rota swap – would you do a clinic visit for me this afternoon?'

'I was scheduled to build tents, no?'

'Don't worry. This will be good experience for you, to liaise with the clinic staff.'

Gabby hesitated. Normally, field visits were planned days ahead, so you could receive a full safety briefing. She hadn't done one yet, and she had to admit it frightened her. They heard such horror stories of what was happening outside the camp. 'It's not dangerous, out there on the road?'

Louise forced a smile. 'No more so than anything we do. If you aren't up to it . . .'

'No, no, of course I will. No problem.' After all, Gabby was never going to progress if she didn't get experience.

'Thank you. Precious is leaving in half an hour, meet her by the cars.' Louise stooped to leave the tent, a sharp triangle of sun falling on to the ground, and went back out into the bright light. Gabby saw another woman waiting for her outside – tall, slim, with shining dark skin. The locals were always surprised when she spoke with an American accent. Dr Jennifer Abola. Epidemiology specialist, out here saving lives every single day, in a way Gabby could only aspire to. There were rumours about her and Louise, that they spent their free time together down at the river that ran past the back of the camp. There was a small fenced-off area with a bit of grass, where the staff sometimes took a cooler of beers and tried to pretend their lives were in any way normal. Dangled their feet. Tried not to think about what was in the water, with ten thousand people living on its banks. They did their best to get people to drink and wash from the taps, but the queues were lengthy and it didn't always work.

Relationships were not allowed in camp, as things could quickly get dramatic and dangerous, and in a situation like that, people could die. But that didn't stop them happening. Oh well. Not Gabby's place to worry about it. Louise wouldn't be so unprofessional as to send Gabby into a dangerous situation just so she could spend some time with her girlfriend, would she? No. Of course not. Louise was a good person who had dedicated her life to helping others.

Gabby stood up, dusted flour off her hands, and headed out into the sun, ponytail bouncing with every step. Hopefully she'd be back in time for Games Night – it was Twister tonight, her favourite.

Amira

'Well, that was crazy. What do you think happened?'

She had to raise her voice over the howling of the wind, as they crunched down the path to the jetty. They had stepped out into a darkness so complete it took her breath away. The only light on the island was from a string marking the jetty, rattling gently in the wind, and the ones on the gables of the house. Plus their phones, no match for the encroaching black.

Paddy sniffed. 'I think someone's messing about. Daniel probably. He didn't seem all that bothered by what happened, did he?'

'Why wouldn't he confess then, when everyone was upset? Vicky was nearly crying.'

'Some public-school code of honour, who knows. He's always playing jokes. My guess is he'll own up when he's finally sober.'

'Christ, he did put a lot away tonight. Jay too.'

'I don't know how they can function with that much booze in them.'

Amira had never seen Paddy drunk – though the pictures and stories from university suggested he hadn't always been so sensible. She'd never figured out what had made him cut back so drastically. One of the many small dark patches in her husband's character – places where the water ran deep and she couldn't see the bottom.

Paddy said, 'Also, he overcharged us for this bloody trip.'

'What?'

'I saw the actual cost on the email. It was way cheaper than he told us.'

But they had so much less money than Daniel and Vicky. 'What? Why?'

'Because he's an arsehole. Always has been.'

She looked longingly across the strait to the mainland, the distant lights of Port Creggan harbour. If only they could flee right now. But how, without the radio? She'd had no phone reception since they landed here, but maybe there was a patch of it somewhere? If the radio didn't turn up, how could they leave?

There is no way off the island.

If that was true, maybe the other statements were too? But no, it was impossible that all of them had killed people and Amira didn't know about it. But then there was Liam. And Fiona's patient. And the school-trip accident.

It hadn't even crossed her mind when the silly note came up. The thought that Paddy had also, in a way, been responsible for someone's death. It was a few years ago, when Paddy was at his previous, barely functioning school, and had been left to supervise a field trip of thirty kids with only one other teacher, who turned out to have a drink problem and had passed out when they were supposed to be on night duty. Paddy had been in the bathroom with a student who was throwing up, when three others had snuck out and got lost. One of them had fallen off a cliff in the dark. Hardly Paddy's fault, and yet everyone had blamed him, so he'd ended up moving jobs mid-year, taking a cut in salary.

'Do you think the note is right – we all did kill people?'

'Ignore it. Like you said, we just have responsible jobs, and Fiona too. It's not our fault!'

'Someone thinks it is.' Amira shivered inside her coat as Paddy strode off down the path they'd come up earlier. She wished he would take her hand, offer her some comfort. These days he was so lean and closed-off, a sort of bitter shell around him. She wasn't even sure when it had started. She caught up to him. 'This is just so weird. I'm really freaked out.'

He turned to her, her phone reflecting in his eyes. 'Did you notice who *didn't* own up to anything?'

'What do you mean? They can't all have killed someone, surely.'

'Daniel has.'

'What?' He was walking so fast, she was panting to keep up. She wasn't sure where they were even supposed to be looking – the island was basically flat scrubland, nowhere to hide.

'His company. That's the reason it went under. Someone died using one of the products. A kid.'

'Oh my God! How come I never heard this?'

'The family hushed it up, settled out of court. That's why they lost this place. Because of Daniel's fuck-ups.' He sounded so bitter.

'So it could be true that everyone's killed someone? Jonathan? Vicky?'

'It's possible.'

'Vicky would have told you, wouldn't she?'

He had pulled ahead of her again, so she could see the halo of light from his phone, illuminating their feet and the dark uneven path ahead. The outlines of trees and shrubs. 'I don't know.'

'But you're so close.'

'She's one of my best friends, yes. Doesn't mean I know everything about her. No one knows everyone's secrets.'

'That's not all she is though, right?'

He sighed. 'Not this again. You really think an emergency is the best time for your jealousy to rear its ugly head?'

Amira fell silent, dismayed at his tone. This wasn't how she'd imagined the night going. He was supposed to cherish her, care for her, and look after her, sensing somehow the great possibility that might lie inside her. Because her period still hadn't come, and that gave her hope – sustained her in this horrorscape of an evening. 'What are we looking for anyway?' she said huffily. They had almost reached the jetty now, which was at least lit, if faintly. The water looked pitch-black, opaque and choppy in the wind.

'I don't know. Any sign there's a way off.' Paddy knelt down, placing the torch on the rocky ground and peering under the jetty. 'There's something under here!'

'What is it?'

A body, was her first thought. *Oh God, please no.*

'It's a boat.' He lay flat on the wooden slats and fished about, pulling on a rope with a grunt. It was true – a small rowing boat had been moored up under the jetty. Hidden. Or perhaps it had just drifted there. It was empty but for its paddles, the wood worn and sand-blasted. How long had it been there? Was it a clue or just an old boat, long forgotten?

'So there is a way off the island. Potentially. Which means that statement is a lie?'

'Maybe.'

That was the least terrible of the three. She didn't want to think about the implications if so. 'Where would someone be hiding, if they were here? There's nothing, is there? Just that beach hut.'

'Amira, I don't know.'

'What are you doing?' It was so dark she could barely even see Paddy, the faint glow of his phone surrounding him as he lay on the jetty to examine the boat.

'Just seeing if it's safe. Seaworthy.'

'Is it?'

'I don't know. Seems OK.' Paddy stood up, surveyed the island, though it was too dark to see much. The house, a beacon of light on the peak of it. Behind it, down the hill, the beach and the hut. Around the edges were just cliffs, another rocky beach on the island's south side. 'Jonathan mentioned caves also. It's too dangerous to check them now though. Let's go back and tell everyone about the boat.'

They left it there, bobbing quietly in the water.

On the way back, Amira suddenly stopped. 'Can you hear that?'

'What?' Paddy stopped too, irritated. 'Come on, we have to get back.'

'Footsteps.'

'It's probably just the others . . .'

'No, there's no light.'

'Amira—'

'Shh! There's someone here, Paddy!'

God, it was so dark out here. The light of her phone barely nudged the blackness aside, and all around her she felt the island rustle and whisper. They waited, frozen, in the middle of the path, as the steps came towards them. One, two, three, four. A sound like heavy breathing. A flash of eyes in the dark and . . .

'It's a sheep,' said Paddy flatly, as a soft baaaing noise reached Amira's ears, along with a wave of shame. Now she could smell its comforting farmyard stench, grass and lanolin and herbivore poop. Her own breath was loudest in her ears. Such a city girl she was scared of a ewe on a path. 'There's about a hundred of them out here, it's nothing to be afraid of. Let's go.'

The others had already finished their search, Vicky and Jonathan red-cheeked from the cold. No sign of Daniel. Louise was making more hot drinks in the kitchen, and Fiona was at the table, head in her hands, as Paddy explained what he'd found.

Jonathan said, 'You know, that sounds like our old boat. Dad would ferry us over to Tarne in it. Probably not up to the trip now.'

'But it could in a pinch, right?'

'I mean, maybe? Depends on the waves. Not now though.'

'No. Tomorrow.'

No one else voiced Amira's dark thought that if the statement *there is no way off the island* wasn't true, perhaps the other statements were. They didn't even know if any of it was true; it could just be a stupid prank. It most likely was.

'Did you find anything?' She unzipped her coat, gradually warming up.

Louise had lit the wood burner and was bringing over a tray of hot drinks, coffees and hot chocolates and tea. She'd better go for something herbal. Caffeine could harm the baby. And perhaps Paddy shouldn't have made her go tramping over the island in the dark, she thought, in a burst of resentment. Not that he knew or had wanted her to go. But he should have sensed it, somehow. He should take better care of her.

Louise shook her head. 'Attic and cellar both empty. There's nothing else, apart from that little shed, and it was padlocked earlier. There's just nothing. Sheep, fields, rocks.'

'We'll check those caves tomorrow,' said Jonathan. 'But she's right. Nothing.'

Paddy was over with Vicky now, who looked cosy and warm in her soft white jumper and Uggs. 'Are you alright?'

Vicky shrugged. 'Daniel's passed out.' Amira would have liked to warm up by the wood burner, but Vicky was hogging it. 'And I'm scared. I don't like this at all.'

Jonathan gave a deep sigh and ran his hands over his face. 'We should get some sleep, I think. It's impossible to think straight when you're tired. In the morning it'll be light, and we can make a plan, if the radio doesn't turn up. I still think the kids could have it.'

Fiona hugged herself. 'I don't know if I'll feel safe to sleep. The doors don't really lock, do they?'

No, because you'd only come to this island with people you trusted, and knew well. But Jonathan was right, it was pointless to stay up all night worrying about it.

Amira was suddenly swept by a wave of weariness. That could be a sign of pregnancy too, couldn't it? Or being caught up in a terrifying situation, of course. Jonathan checked the doors and windows. Louise shut the door of the wood burner. Amira wondered if she felt afraid. As the only one sleeping on the ground floor, she'd be the first to go. Unless their possible assailant was in the attic after all. Urgh. She wished she hadn't had that thought before bed.

◆　◆　◆

Upstairs, she picked up a towel from the bed, thick and expensive. The room was cosy, with a sheepskin rug on the floor, plaid blankets folded on the bed and armchair, wood-panelled walls. Though she couldn't appreciate any of the beautiful decor; she was too unsettled. She even left the bedroom door ajar as she went out to the bathroom. Paddy was rooting through his neatly packed case, looking for something.

Rachel was in there already. 'Oh, sorry.'

She looked up from the sink where she was washing her hands. Rachel's face seemed pale and featureless – she must have taken her make-up off. 'I'm almost done.' Her toiletries had already crowded out every inch of space in the room. She squeezed something out of a tube and patted it gently over her face. Amira glimpsed what looked like an EpiPen in her washbag. So she really did have allergies after all.

Amira waited awkwardly. 'It's all very weird, isn't it?'

Rachel's voice was tight. 'I don't understand what the hell's going on. Do they often do stuff like this? Stupid jokes?'

'Well – sometimes, yes. The boys anyway. But I don't know if that's what this is.'

'Huh. Well I'm not impressed. It's actually irresponsible to be somewhere with no reception or Wi-Fi, when there are kids. I'm going to make Jonathan leave tomorrow. Call the boat back and sack this off, I'm done.'

How would they do that, with no radio? Rachel likely didn't know it was missing, and Amira wasn't going to be the one to tell her. 'Sure. Well, can I just . . .'

Rachel moved, irritable, and Amira brushed her teeth, washed her face with her own cheap face wash. Why hadn't the woman left? Was she just going to watch as Amira carried out her whole routine?

Rachel said, 'You don't double-cleanse? Did you not have make-up on?'

'A little bit.'

'God, you should really take that off before you wash your face! And those foaming things will just dry your skin right out. I use a cream cleanser and muslin cloth, that's the best way. You've got a good serum and eye cream?'

Amira didn't know much about skincare. 'Um, not really.'

Rachel peered at Amira's face in the mirror. 'Hmm. You want to think about that, at your age.'

At her age! Amira was stung, and suddenly found herself blinking back stupid tears. Today had been a lot. 'Well, OK. I need to shut the door now, alright. Goodnight.'

She closed the door with some relief and heard Rachel thump into her own room. She sat down to wee, experiencing another leap of excitement amid all her fear when she realised there was still no blood. She'd almost forgotten in all the drama. Her breathing slowed. Surely this would all seem better tomorrow.

She washed her hands, realising how meagre her toiletries were compared to Rachel's paraphernalia. Stared at herself critically in the mirror. She did look tired, but then she was forty, it was to be expected.

Going back into the room, she saw that Paddy was dressed for bed, doing his press-ups on the floor. This was a new development, and she could see how he'd got good at them, going all the way down to the floor. His arms rippled with new muscle, and it unsettled her. She knew what the magazines would say it meant, but surely not her Paddy, *Lovely Paddy*.

In her pyjamas, she climbed into bed and waited for him to join her, as she had every night for fifteen years. The bed was smaller than theirs at home, though much more comfortable, and he felt closer, his newly wiry body in the T-shirt and shorts he always slept in. How long since she'd seen him naked? When they had sex it was usually in the dark. It had been a while even for that.

'Goodnight, then.' Her voice sounded forlorn.

'Night.' He turned away, switched off his lamp.

'Can I – I'd like a hug, please? This has all been horrible.'

He turned back over, spooned her from behind. 'I know it has. But it's going to be alright.'

'I don't know. That accusation, that we caused deaths – someone's been researching us, right? Someone has a grudge against us.'

He sighed against her neck. 'You and I know we didn't do anything wrong. If deaths occurred, it was because of other people. You weren't the one who killed that little boy, and you didn't get the proper support you needed to do your job. And me, the school left me in an impossible situation, well below safe supervision levels. I don't blame myself for what happened, and neither should you.'

If only it was so easy. She sometimes felt that, when she died, if they cut her open, they would find the toddler's name etched across her heart. *Liam*. Because she could have saved him, and she hadn't, and maybe that was just as bad as killing him?

'I'd just never thought of it that way. That I killed someone.'

'You didn't.' He turned away again, offering her his hunched back. 'Not everyone here can say the same,' he muttered, before immediately falling asleep in the way he always did.

Listening to his faint snores, Amira knew she would not be able to drop off so easily. Her mind raced, looping back, over and over the events of the day. How could this have happened, someone possibly getting into the house and leaving a sinister note? They'd seen no sign of anyone. Her thoughts turned to Daniel. He did enjoy jokes and tricks, often cruel ones. Had he set all this up to haze his wife and her brother on their fortieth? It seemed too mean even for him. But maybe. And was Paddy right about Daniel killing someone? They'd never got on, those two, which Amira hoped was more to do with the failed business they'd set up out of uni than rivalry over Vicky.

Amira's fortieth had been some drinks in a pub, about fifteen people there, a lacklustre night. Jonathan had come but no one else from the Group – Vicky and Daniel in Barbados, Fiona on call, Louise overseas of course. No luxury cabin for her, no weekend away, no fuss. But then, no horrible accusations of murder either, and no threats of death. The thought comforted her slightly, and she managed to fall into an uneasy sleep, full of dark dreams.

Kira

2022

'Can anyone smell fish?'

The laughter rippled out like a stone had been dropped into a pond, through the classroom, washing up against the girl now fighting tears, her face flushing red. Kira Lonzo. Scholarship girl, in a second-hand uniform, on free school dinners, never coming on the annual ski trip. Her parents ran a fishmonger. She was top in every subject, which didn't make people like her any more.

The comment about the smell – in fact Kira did not smell at all, except of cheap shampoo and body wash – was from Autumn De Ville, the stereotypical bitch of year ten. Kira had seen enough high-school films and sat through enough talks about bullying to know that it wasn't nice or cool to pick on the poor kid. Worse than that, it was incredibly basic to bully her just because her family did normal jobs and weren't famous. However, knowing this did not make it any easier, and unkind daily comments, hiding her water bottle, spilling expensive seltzers on her sports kit, the barely anonymous messages on social media – they were all starting to grind.

'Quiet, girls,' scolded the history teacher, Miss Batts, who was somewhat deaf and tended not to notice the whispered comments. Autumn seemed to have a bet on as to what horrible things she could say in the middle of a lesson without getting caught. Finally, the lunch bell rang and Kira went to the cloakroom to get her sad little lunchbox that smelled of cheap tuna. The others were going to Pret today, like they did every Wednesday. Friday was sushi. Often the bill came to twenty quid each, she knew. A whole week's groceries for her family.

As Kira lurked, Darcy Capeman came in to get her designer jacket. Darcy, with her dad on telly, was accepted into the group, although her mother was a bit overweight and Kira had seen some raised eyebrows from Autumn at parents' evening. Her parents' recent split, the coverage in the papers, had also caused some murmuring. But Darcy would never be like Kira, because she was wealthy, because her parents had paid for her teeth to be straightened and her acne treated, and she had long shiny hair inherited from her mother, treated in a proper salon. Kira was sure Darcy knew she should stand up to bullying where she saw it. Ask Kira to sit with her at lunch, or go for a coffee or hang out after school. But she never did.

'Darcy,' said Kira.

'Um?'

'Why do you go along with it?'

'What?'

'You know. You're not like that, are you? You're not a bully?'

'Of course I'm not a bully!' Darcy was stung. 'I've never said anything mean to you, have I?'

'If you go along with it, you're just as bad as they are.'

'I don't know what you mean, Kira.' She flipped her hair over the collar of her jacket, and Kira saw how light and shiny it was, compared to her own greasy frizz. She desperately needed a good hairdryer, some nicer glasses, a dermatologist. But those things cost money. If she could only have a friend, a proper friend – something that was free but seemingly so hard to find – it would make all the difference.

'Yes, you do.'

Darcy flounced. 'Look, I'm just getting my coat, I don't need you attacking me. I didn't do anything to you!'

'You didn't do anything to help either. Tell her not to say those things, tell a teacher.'

'Why don't *you* tell a teacher? That's what they always say to do.'

'It would only make it worse.' Kira knew this was true. For all their anti-bullying policies, the school didn't like to rock the boat or upset pupils with rich parents, and snitches still tended to get stitches.

'Well, what can I do about it? They'll only turn on me.'

'Be brave. Like those people who stood up to the Nazis we just learned about.'

Darcy snorted. 'Autumn might be a bitch but she's hardly Hitler. Come on.'

'Just have lunch with me. Or walk into class with me this afternoon. Sit beside me in art. Or the next time they say something, call it out. Say that's not nice. Because it isn't, it's twatty. And you know' – here her voice wavered – 'I might seem like it rolls off me, but it doesn't. I just can't let my parents see. They've worked so hard for me to get here, I can't leave.'

'I'm sorry,' muttered Darcy. 'I didn't know it was that bad.'

'So go on then. Sit in the canteen and eat a sandwich with me. You'll only have to listen to Autumn going on and on about *Love Island* otherwise. Don't tell me you enjoy that.'

'I'm going out for lunch.'

'They do sell food in the canteen.'

'Urgh.' But Darcy hesitated.

Kira felt a surge of hope. It wouldn't cost her much, would it? It would be a nice thing to do. But then Kira moved her lunchbox, letting out a whiff of the tuna, and Darcy's eyes travelled over the sad bruised apple packed in with it, the packet of multi-buy crisps, and took a step back. 'I . . . Maybe some other day.'

'Sure.' Kira's head drooped again, as if she carried the world on her fifteen-year-old shoulders. 'Whatever.'

Vicky

She lay awake long after the sounds of the house had died down, people finally settling to sleep after such a scare. Daniel was sprawled on his back beside her, snoring loud enough to shake her glass of water. Well, screw him. Screw him for making her organise her own birthday and for getting so drunk and insisting on the stupid game and for Cody and the business and the island and, well, all of it.

She looked at his sleeping face, mouth half-open, breath sour, hair rumpled, and felt not a hint of tenderness. The only thing about him she liked was the fact he had the same nose as the twins, who were asleep on camp beds just metres away. Genevieve hugged her Paw Patrol dog, and Toby had his iPad on his chest, like the funeral marker of a king. What a morbid thought that was. All this fear was getting to her.

It wasn't *fair*. Yes, she knew there were more pressing concerns, such as the fact that they were trapped on an island with someone who perhaps wanted to kill them, who was perhaps also one of her closest friends, and her children might be in danger, but all the same the uppermost thought in her mind was that. It wasn't fair. It was her fortieth. She deserved a lovely party, to be showered in gifts and affection and champagne. This wasn't exactly what she'd hoped for. She hadn't even had any presents at all yet. There was supposed to be some big surprise planned for tomorrow, but she'd seen no evidence of it, and she didn't know what they were going to do for dinner, since Daniel had said he'd sort it.

It had been bad enough before the strange note and then traipsing round the house in the dark and the cold. She'd had to find the cottage, organise everyone, wrangle their various date changes and refusal to answer messages, their dietary and sleeping preferences, basically a one-woman travel agency for her own bloody birthday. Daniel's only contribution had been to collect the money and organise that stupid games night, which had ended so badly. But as irritating as that had been, at first she'd thought it was only a bad-taste joke. But now the radio was missing. Or was that part of the prank?

Moving silently, though she could have blown a trumpet near his ear and he wouldn't have woken, she manoeuvred Daniel's phone in front of his face so it unlocked. She tried not to do this too often, because she knew that every time she went through his messages the chances of getting their marriage back on track went down, but she had found she couldn't stop. There was a squirming dirty pleasure in waiting for his breath to go heavy, picking up his smeary-screened phone and trawling through it, looking for suspicious texts, new apps that might be concealing something, clues that Daniel was still the dirtbag he'd always been. Not quite knowing if she wanted to find proof or she didn't.

Immediately, she saw her own name. On WhatsApp – *Vic and Jay's 40th secret group*. Everyone in it but her and Jonathan – even Rachel was there. So Daniel actually had tried to plan things for her. Just not the food or transport or accommodation or anything actually useful. Daniel saw himself as being responsible for the fun of any situation, rather than the boring everyday arrangements of what they would eat and where they would sleep. The group chat was just a thread of games ideas, suggestions for sports and activities, not that there was much to do on the small island.

Paddleboarding, boating, swimming though it was February and three degrees outside. A wine-tasting evening, as if he needed any help to drink more. She saw that it was Fiona who had suggested Two Truths and a Lie, leading to this horror show. She'd always been keen on games and competitions, which sounded completely exhausting to Vicky, the mother of twin five-year-olds. She just wanted to relax, talk to her friends, maybe drink a glass of champagne without being interrupted. She wanted Daniel to take some responsibility, to live in the real world, but apparently that was too much to ask for. Vicky did not like surprises. She'd had enough of those over the years.

There was no sign of messages from Cody or anyone else. Of course, that didn't mean there wasn't a new Cody on the scene. He could just be better at hiding it than she thought. After all, she hadn't seen it when it was right under her nose.

She looked over at her children again. The warm weight of them on the beds, their heavy breaths rising and falling in unison. Their matching silky blond hair, exactly the same as her own. Outside it was starting to rain again, pattering against the windows. They had to find a way off here. In the morning she would send Daniel and Jonathan out in the rowboat, see if they could make it over or flag down another craft. But that note, that horrible note. Fiona, Paddy, and Amira had all owned up to being involved in deaths, though that was not surprising given what they each did for a living. Who else could be accused of killing someone?

She could, of course. But that had been an accident, a horrible accident, and no one here knew about it. She'd made sure of that.

But maybe someone did. Because there was the note.

Vicky did her best not to think about it, but all the same the light was turning grey outside, and dawn was almost breaking, before she finally fell asleep.

Melissa

2018

She was going to look absolutely banging when it was over. That's what she had to keep reminding herself. But it was hard – now she was stripped down to just a raggedy gown and hairnet and those tight socks – not to be afraid. She wished her mum or bestie Ali could have come with her, but the flights were too expensive on top of the clinic fees. She just had to get through it, recover for a few days, and then she could fly home, with her new perky butt carefully cushioned for travel. She was a bit worried about how much it would hurt, and if she'd be able to sit on a plane for four hours, but the clinic had just waved away her questions. She wasn't actually sure that they'd understood her questions, but surely it would be fine. After all, it was a proper clinic, wasn't it? They must do this kind of thing all the time.

Hearing footsteps outside, Melissa clutched her phone so tight it left marks on her sweaty hand. She stared at the feed of Rachy Rach, the one who'd started her on her self-care journey by posting a ten-per-cent-off deal with this clinic in Turkey. It must be OK if Rachy had recommended it – she was so careful about health and nutrition and allergens. It was through Rachy that Melissa had realised she was intolerant to gluten, although she had eaten about three pittas last night out of nerves. Her stomach gurgled – she'd been fasting for hours and was bloody starving. The sooner this was over, the better. She took one last look at Rachy in her profile pic, pouting and staring back over her shoulder, a hand on her own perfect, round, thicc bottom. That's what Melissa would look like when she woke up.

The footsteps were louder now. The door opened and two nurses came in, speaking to her in a language she didn't understand. One of them snatched impatiently at her phone, and set it on the bedside cabinet. Melissa looked back at it longingly as they started to wheel her bed away. Would it be safe? She didn't know how she'd cope without it. She couldn't wait to post a message to Rachy Rach and tell her she'd had the surgery. Maybe Rach would even showcase her in a guest post, and all that praise and admiration would shower down on Melissa too.

Too late, she remembered she hadn't sent a message to her mum to say she was going in. Oh well. She'd be awake again in a few hours and she'd do it then.

Her bed was shoved through plastic doors and into a startlingly bright, bleach-smelling space. She had the impression of various doctors and nurses doing things, speaking in low voices that she couldn't understand. It was time.

Amira

The world came into focus, and a wave of fear and horror flooded her, like a bucket of cold water dumped over her head. Amira groaned, stretched out her feet in the smooth sheets.

'Oh God. I didn't dream all of that, did I?'

Paddy was awake and fully dressed, sitting in the armchair with his laptop. Marking didn't stop over a small death threat. 'Finally. I've been up for hours. And no, you didn't.'

She could hear the chatter of voices downstairs, and more fear swamped her. They had probably missed breakfast, and Vicky would no doubt be snippy about that, and they would maybe all be talking about embarrassing Amira and how she could barely cope outside of the M25. Urgh.

Paddy shut his laptop. 'You should get up now. Everyone else has been down there for hours, we're wasting the daylight.' A cardinal sin in Paddy's book.

'I need to shower first.'

'Rachel's in there, and Jonathan's next.'

She sighed. Why couldn't they have gone to a hotel and had their own bathroom, instead of paying a grand to share with a total stranger? Or why could they not have had an en-suite like everyone else? She was a little resentful they'd even been asked to split the cost of the rental, to be honest. Daniel was loaded, and so was Jonathan, but she and Paddy – and of course Louise – didn't earn much. Yet they were still expected to chip in for vintage champagne and private islands. And Paddy had said Daniel had even overcharged them for it – was that really true? Unable to brush her teeth or wash away the sticky fear of the night, she put on her dressing gown and followed Paddy downstairs, bracing against the wall on the stupid dangerous stairs that had no banister. Who'd thought that was a good idea? It would be so easy to fall and break your neck.

'Morning, Ammy.'

Daniel seemed disgustingly fresh for someone who'd been drinking most of the day before, eating a sausage sandwich and dripping ketchup on the table. Open bottles of champagne and orange juice sat out – they were drinking again, already? Amira sat down at the table, which was covered in egg-smeared plates. Paddy had already poured himself cereal, left her to sort herself out. Vicky's face was judgemental.

'I'm afraid there isn't much left, Amira, it's so late. You could fry up some bacon maybe.'

Amira had never eaten pork in her life, which Vicky had been told approximately one thousand times. 'Oh, that's OK. Is there tea?'

Darcy was in the kitchen, boiling the kettle. 'I'll make you one, Amira.'

'Thank you, sweetheart. Oh, and happy birthday, Vicky. The present's upstairs.' A barely acknowledged nod. She had put a lot of effort into selecting some nice toiletries for Vicky and whisky for Jonathan, but already knew they wouldn't look impressive next to the haul sitting unwrapped on the table – champagne, perfume, new Beats headphones, a small fortune in luxury goods.

Unlike Daniel, Fiona looked grey, and was chewing her way through a stack of toast. 'Christ, we never learn, do we? Always go too hard on the first night, then we're a wreck.'

'I feel fine,' said Vicky, chopping a banana for the twins, who were both playing with loudly beeping devices, making Amira wince. 'You just need to learn when to stop, that's all. You could have come to bed when the rest of us did.'

Fiona rolled her eyes at Amira, which cheered her up, to feel included. No one was mentioning the events of the night before, the strange note and its sinister implications. Amira noticed that the carved box was back in its place on the sideboard. Rachel came downstairs then, in a silk dressing gown with a towel around her hair, saying good morning to no one, heading straight to the kitchen.

'Where's Lou?' Amira asked.

Daniel spoke through his sandwich. 'Went out early to walk round the island. She can't sleep past seven now, she says.'

'Neither can I,' said Vicky. 'Welcome to twindom.'

'I can still sleep anytime,' said Fiona, pouring more coffee. 'Legacy of being on call. And Jay always could too. Naps can really help a marriage, believe me.'

Except it hadn't, not long-term. Rachel, who was now eating a plain yoghurt and on her phone despite the lack of reception, looked up at Fiona's comment and frowned even more deeply. She must be regretting that she'd come; but then what had she expected, going on a weekend with her boyfriend, his ex, and all their friends?

As Amira sipped the tea Darcy had made – too much milk, but welcome – she gradually began to feel more human. She wished she could shower though. Everyone else was dressed in expensive knitwear and various tweedy outdoorsy items. Like a Scandi crime drama: beautiful scenery, log fires, and simmering tension.

'So what's going to happen?' said Rachel. 'We're leaving, I assume?'

Everyone looked at each other. 'Seems a bit hasty,' said Daniel. 'No need to ruin the whole weekend over a stupid joke gone wrong.'

'Hello? Someone threatened to kill us! Of course we're leaving.'

'Right, but how? There's no radio.'

'*What?*'

'The radio's not where it's meant to be.'

'Oh my God! Well, we have to look for it. Search everywhere. Get in people's bags!'

'This isn't Nazi Germany,' said Fiona crisply. 'And we have a plan. We're going to search the island.'

Rachel folded her arms. 'I thought Jay said there was a boat?'

'We should go and check it in the light,' said Paddy, standing up and clearing his bowl away. 'If it's seaworthy, maybe someone should try to make it over.'

Daniel stretched. 'In the meantime, why don't we do our best to carry on as normal? We've all come a long way and paid a lot to be here, we should at least get some use out of it.'

Vicky looked sceptical, but Fiona was nodding. It seemed crazy, but maybe he was right. With no radio and no phone reception, there was little they could do but stay put.

'What was the original plan today?' said Fiona. 'Organised fun all round?'

Vicky pushed her breakfast plate away, hardly touched. 'I thought people might like some time at the house, using the hot tubs, even swimming in the sea if we can brave it. I had planned board games and such, but . . .'

'No more games,' said Fiona heavily. 'Let's just take it easy, until we figure out what to do.'

'Alright. Daniel can get the hot tubs and fire going.'

'Already done it, boss. Been up since seven, I have, with the kiddos.' Amira saw Vicky frown at the term *boss*. 'Aren't there paddleboards somewhere also?'

'I think so. We can check for those after the boat.'

Paddleboards could be a way off the island, Amira thought, her mind returning to the conundrums of the night before. So maybe it wasn't true that there was no way to leave? And that meant the other statements were true? Likely it was all just a stupid joke, as others had suggested. In the pure grey light of morning, the waves licking the shore and boats coming and going in the strait, it seemed ridiculous.

Daniel stood up, leaving his dirty plate and cup for someone else to clear. 'I'll go and start the tubs. I imagine you ladies will all want a go?'

'Why just ladies?' said Jonathan, coming downstairs with shower-wet hair to a chorus of *happy birthday*. 'I've done them in Norway, it's great. No chemicals, just really cleansing.'

Hot tubs had been on the doctor's list to avoid, as well as cycling, if you wanted to get your sperm count up. Not that it had stopped Paddy taking his bike into school every day, citing the environment and the cost and his overall health. Would he go in the tubs too? Amira glanced at her husband, but he didn't appear to be listening to the chat, finishing his coffee and staring out of the window at the sea. Her heart sank. If she really was pregnant – if the crazy hope was somehow true – it might turn things around between them. Stop this spiralling fear she kept feeling when she looked at him, for months now, that he wasn't quite the person he'd been, but in some subtle way she couldn't put her finger on.

'Alright then, let's get going.' Vicky stood up, starting to clear dishes, though Amira hadn't eaten a bite yet. 'Jay, we're going to check the boat and paddleboards, search again for the radio. If it doesn't work, people should just try to enjoy themselves, I guess. If that's even remotely possible after last night.'

'Well, alright. That seems the best plan. No sense in wasting the holiday if it's all nothing. After all, we get picked up in the morning.'

Daniel clapped Jonathan on the shoulder. 'That's what I said, bro.'

'Well, then, who's going to check the boat?' said Vicky. 'Amira, you could look for the radio.'

'I still need to grab a shower,' Amira said. Vicky gave a small sigh. Amira burned with rage. Why did she have to be like this? Vicky had just said there were no concrete plans, so what did it matter if Amira took twenty minutes to wash herself? Of course, when she went up and turned the shower on, she discovered the hot water had run out. She felt filthy, sweaty, caked in the dirt of travel and fear and tramping round the island in the dark and the damp. She remembered Rachel's thundering shower with hatred in her heart. It wasn't fair. Why had she come away with these people? They weren't her friends. Even her own husband seemed indifferent to her. She'd just get through the weekend, then they'd have a serious talk once they got home.

After her lukewarm shower, she rubbed steam from the bathroom window, which looked out over the back of the house. Smoke was already rising up from the fire pit, pizza oven, and hot tubs, Daniel piling wood into them, seemingly happy and hangover-free. Did someone like him ever feel shame, or guilt, or self-doubt? She thought of what Paddy had said the night before – that Daniel had killed someone. How, and when? The whole thing seemed so mad in the light of day.

Amira was rooting through her case for something to wear – everything looked wrong – when Fiona knocked on the door. She too seemed strangely upbeat, after everything that had happened. 'Hey Amira. Just checking all the rooms again. Mind if I have a look?'

She didn't really want Fiona going through her things. 'Um. OK.' The two of them looked under the bed and in the wardrobe, which held a hairdryer and spare blankets, nothing else. The drawers of the wooden dresser were empty.

Fiona's eyes then strayed to Amira's wheelie case, and Paddy's rucksack. She'd hardly insist Amira turn them out for her, would she? 'OK. Just . . . keep an eye out, I suppose.'

Alone again, Amira dressed and slapped on make-up to hide her hungover skin, went downstairs. No sign of anyone now.

They've left you behind.

She pushed down her stupid, pathetic thoughts, and went to look for them.

Fiona was now out the back in her swimsuit, wrestling herself into a giant canvas dryrobe. 'I knew this would come in handy. I think I'll brave the waves, if you fancy it? Since there's no sign of the radio.' Everyone seemed to have decided they might as well actually enjoy the trip, if there was no way off until tomorrow.

The boatman had said it was below five degrees in the sea. Amira looked at Fiona, incredulous. 'Without wetsuits?'

'Best thing for a hangover. Just a quick dip does no harm, if you're careful. You'll feel amazing afterwards.'

Darcy came out of the house in a black bikini, a dressing gown over the top, hair tucked into a rubber hat. 'I'm ready, Mum.'

'That's my brave girl. Jay? You always liked to get wet.' Her tone was provoking, almost but not quite flirtatious.

Jonathan was hauling an armful of wood over to the tubs, every inch the caveman. Daniel was nowhere to be seen, but the tubs were clearly heating up, steam rising already. 'I could be persuaded. Can't be colder than Iceland.'

'Oh God, with actual ice on the water? How could I forget?' Fiona's laugh trilled, and Amira wondered if this was the reason for her new high spirits. Had she and Jonathan had some kind of reconciliation last night?

Rachel came out then too, in leather trousers and a thin Nordic-style jumper, her hair blow-dried shiny. 'What's going on?'

Jonathan said, 'We're headed for a swim. Would you like to come?'

'In the sea!' she screeched. 'Are you insane?'

'Studies show multiple health benefits,' said Fiona, pulling up her zip. 'We're off now, don't feel you have to come.'

She set off walking, her arm around Darcy. Jonathan looked torn between his girlfriend and his family. 'I won't be long. You could come and watch, take pictures?'

'Not much point when I can't post them.'

'Well, do a what-do-you-call-it? Latergram.'

'No thanks. I'll just stay here I suppose. By myself.'

Rachel turned back to the house, picking her way over the gravel. She was in a different pair of heeled boots, and Amira was starting to understand how she had so much luggage with her. By contrast, she wished she had something nicer than the same jeans from yesterday, stained where she'd spilled some of her stew, and an old much-washed jumper. And where was Paddy – and Vicky? With nothing else to do, Amira trailed after the Capemans down to the north beach.

Despite the perfect yellow sand, compacted under her feet, the shore was swept with a stiff breeze that stirred the waves to meringue-white points. All the same, Fiona was already stripping off her robe and rushing to the sea with every sign of enjoyment.

Darcy looked more unsure. 'Is it cold?'

Fiona called back, 'It will be cold, of course, but just for a moment. You'll be alright.'

Jonathan too was sweeping off his jumper and jeans, and Amira couldn't help but notice what good shape he was in, the lines of muscle along his chest and abdomen, the fine striations of his arms. He took care of his health, pushed himself to be the best he could. No wonder people found him such an inspiration. Part of her regretted not bringing a bathing suit, even though the water looked choppy and freezing. And of course, she couldn't swim, which no one ever seemed to remember either.

Fiona was in now, yelping. 'Christ!' She submerged, came up like a seal, laughing and breathless. 'It's so clear and beautiful!'

Jonathan was hopping in, bellowing at the temperature. 'Ahhhh! You're insane, woman!'

'Oh come on, don't be a wuss, Capeman.'

Darcy still stood at the edge, shivering in her bikini. Her limbs were skinny and pale, just a kid really. 'Urgh, it's so cold!'

'You'll feel great after, darling.'

Amira thought the girl wasn't going to do it, but then she set her shoulders, threw back her head, and dove straight in after her parents.

And didn't come back up.

Amira counted. *One, two, three, four, five.* Where was she? Hard to make out heads in the churn of grey sea.

'Darcy?' she called. Jonathan and Fiona, battling with the waves themselves, had not noticed their daughter vanish. 'She's – she's gone under.' Her voice was torn away by the wind. A ripple of panic went through her. There was no sign of Darcy.

Hadn't the boatman mentioned this? Cold-water shock, often affecting children and teenagers, a strange phenomenon where your body simply stopped breathing because of the temperature. You drowned with no water in your lungs. Oh God, she was going to have to wade in and she couldn't swim herself, and the water was so cold around her ankles already, so rough and tearing.

She looked around desperately. Where had Darcy even gone? There – white limbs tossed in the grey. Tumbling over in the rough surf. Oh God. She had no choice. She started pulling off her boots, then splashed right in, gasping as the cold bit her feet and soaked into her jeans. Shouting to anyone who might hear. 'Darcy! She's under – she . . .'

There was a long moment where a wave broke over Amira's head, and the world turned heavy and dark, and she felt her hands scrape along the bottom, and she was drowning too, because she couldn't swim. A second of absolute terror, sure that she was going to die and she could not breathe, she could not get air in, and . . . Then Jonathan was there, pulling his daughter up, and Darcy was spluttering and crying, coughing up water, and Amira was somehow on her feet, sloshing as fast as she could out of the waves. Fiona had finally noticed and was swimming to them with strong sure strokes.

'Darling! Are you OK?'

Between them, they got Darcy out and she collapsed on the sand. 'Mum, I couldn't breathe! It was so cold.'

Fiona wrapped her own robe around Darcy. 'You're OK. I'm sorry, sweetheart, I shouldn't have encouraged you.'

No one looked at Amira, wet through and gasping, her nose and ears filled with salt water. She took in big shuddering breaths. Filled with horror at what had almost happened. Of how it would have been to drown, and the baby that might be growing inside her, how Paddy would have only found out when it was already too late. Her mind turned to the note. *You will all either kill or be killed here.* And look, Darcy had almost drowned, and Amira too, perhaps. If you couldn't swim you could drown in a foot of water.

Finally, someone had noticed her. Jonathan patted her shoulder. 'You OK, Ammy?'

'Yes, I just . . . I saw she went under and—'

Did no one even know she'd plunged in to try to find Darcy?

'Well, don't worry, I got her.'

He squelched off to find his pool slides. Amira felt tears prick her eyes, that so-familiar feeling that she didn't matter here, she was the least of this group. She watched Jonathan kneeling with his ex-wife. Both of them rubbing Darcy's shoulders, soothing her, their daughter, helping her up and supporting her back to the house.

Amira trailed after them, dripping water and plagued by childish, destructive feelings. No one, not even Paddy, would notice if she didn't go back to the house. If she sat in the cold all day, if she drowned in the sea. No one really cared. God, she wished she was anywhere but here.

She was almost at the back door when she heard the screams start up. A symphony of them, from the highest female soprano – Darcy? – to the deepest bass.

'She's dead!' Amira heard Jonathan shout, as she broke into a run. 'Oh my God, she's dead!'

Mhairi

Thank God for the radio, her only contact with the mainland. Mhairi crouched against the house, blasted by the wind, straining to listen to her constable's voice all the way across the strait. He'd made it back to Tarne despite Sunday services on the ferries.

'How's the scene over there, boss?'

'Weird. Two bodies so far, wrapped up like sandwiches for us. No sign of anyone else.'

'We'll need the CSIs then?'

'Yep. Send the message now, I doubt they'll make it today even.'

Always a problem on the remote island. With bad weather and intermittent transport, you couldn't guarantee that even a multiple murder would get people there on time – the ones who catalogued and photographed and roped off and protected. For now it was just Mhairi, and she knew that bringing Arthur ashore with her was already going to cause some headaches.

'Any idea who's dead?'

'Well, it's a man and a woman. I'm pretty sure the woman is Rachel Solenado – you know, the Instagram one.' An influencer who seemed to spend her life making posts and videos of herself dancing, words appearing in bubbles above her head. 'Anaphylactic shock, I'd say. An allergic reaction.' Rachel posted a lot about food safety, and had a number of allergies and intolerances, including to gluten, nuts, and sesame. Wouldn't she have had an EpiPen in that case? Could she not get to it in time? That was going to be a real pain, proving if it was an accident or murder. Mhairi would have to ascertain if Rachel normally carried an EpiPen, if it was where it should have been or someone had moved it, and who had made the food and if they were aware of her allergies. 'Anything your end?'

'Well yes, actually!' Bless Davey, he was so eager to please her, bringing his discoveries like a cat with a mouse. 'We managed to get in touch with the owner of the island – lives in Denver, that's in America, like.'

'Yes, thank you, Davey, I'm aware.'

'Right. Well, he has this property company called SunStyle – just an umbrella thing. Like when you see the wee picture on Airbnb, your host or whatever, that's someone who's likely never set foot in the place, they just buy up places all over the world. Shocking it is.'

She agreed, but now wasn't the time for one of Davey's socialist rants. 'They must have someone local making the arrangements?'

'Aye, it's Maggie Andersen, you know.'

That made sense. Maggie had set up a company to clean and manage the growing number of rental properties on the island, most not local-owned. She was making a fortune out of it, fair play to her.

'But get this – they both say there was no one staying this weekend. It wasn't rented out.'

Mhairi frowned, wondering if she had misheard in the wind. 'What?'

'Yeah. Not much demand in February, and it's an expensive place to heat with the generator and that, so they don't bother.'

'But – people were out there! Someone must have got it ready for them, made the beds and that.'

Davey sounded baffled. 'I know. Doesn't make any sense. I mean, they used to own the place, right? So maybe they had some

112

arrangement. Place is never locked, after all. You could just sail right up and go in.'

Mhairi shook her head. She didn't understand any of this. Who then had told the group to come, booked Arthur for the pick-up? What was going on?

'Maggie's fit to be tied, thinks someone's trying to undercut her and get Mallacht for their own cleaning business. And the owner's none too happy they weren't getting paid.'

'It's very strange alright. Maybe we can get into their emails and find out what was going on.'

'I'll try. Over, boss.'

'Aye.'

She hung up the radio with a sigh, wishing with all her might she was away from this freezing, hostile island, which refused to give up its many secrets.

Arthur was coming up the hill towards her, holding something in his hands. A flash of orange. 'What's that?'

He was shaking, she saw. This stoical man, unruffled by most of life's ups and downs. He was actually shaking now. 'I – it was floating in the water.' She saw now that it was a life jacket. A small one.

'Is it . . .'

'The kiddies had them on. The little ones. I told them to hang on to them.' He met her eyes, and Mhairi felt a large stone lodge in her stomach.

Vicky

Rachel lay on the rug by the bed, limbs sprawled in a heap. Her face was blue and lifeless, her microbladed eyebrows up, as if death had taken her by surprise. On the bed was her pink case, ransacked, clothes scattered about the place. Jonathan sat on his heels beside her, rocking to and fro.

'I came in and found her like this. She must have been looking for her EpiPen, she . . . I wasn't here to help her. God. She must have been terrified.'

Vicky could only imagine it, the building panic, your throat closing up, hands burrowing through silk and wool, desperate for the salvation you had been sure was there. And finding nothing. She had been with Paddy, walking the island to look for possible ways off. They'd heard the screams when they were almost at the jetty and run straight back. Paddy was fit these days, surprisingly so, but Vicky had easily outpaced him as she pounded up the path, fuelled by sheer terror. Where were the kids? And Daniel? Oh God, how could this be real?

Fiona knelt beside Rachel, pressing futile fingers to the woman's neck. Her voice shook. 'She's gone. I'm sorry, Jay.'

Vicky had her hands clamped to her face, feeling her own heart hammering, her breath panting in her throat. 'What could have done this?'

'Sesame,' said Jonathan, bleakly. 'I know she claimed a lot of intolerances, but she really was allergic to that. She always made sure she had the pen.'

'She definitely had one?' asked Fiona.

'I saw her pack it. She usually showed me where it was, just in case.'

'I saw it too,' said Amira, who was in the corridor, breathless and dripping for some reason. 'In her washbag, last night. Is she really gone? She can't be. Did you try CPR, Fiona?'

No one answered her. 'But she couldn't find it in time?' asked Vicky. 'I don't understand.' The world seemed to have stopped, a weird buzzing in her ears. She was dead. *Dead.*

Amira said again, 'We should try to revive her! Why won't you try?'

'She's dead, Amira,' snapped Fiona, suddenly covering her mouth. 'I'm sorry. God, it's just such a shock.'

Jonathan's voice was hollow. 'The pen's not there. Look, she's tipped her washbag everywhere.' He pointed out the door to the bathroom, where expensive toiletries had rolled across the floor. One glass bottle had smashed and Vicky had the distant thought that she should clear it up before the twins came near. They were nowhere to be seen, luckily, and hopefully would not realise this was happening. Unfortunately, Darcy had already witnessed it, before being ordered to her room, where she could be heard crying.

'So . . . what are you saying, Jay?' asked Vicky, trying to marshal her thoughts.

'Someone took it out, maybe. Someone did this on purpose. What could it have been in – did she eat anything or drink or . . . ?'

'There's a plate,' said Fiona, picking it up. For God's sake, Vicky had already told them all no eating in the rooms. *Oh God, stop it, Vicky!* That didn't matter now. The plate had remnants of birthday cake on it, the portion Rachel had ostentatiously not eaten the night before, complaining about sugar and gluten. She could imagine Rachel grabbing it from the fridge, to comfort herself if Jonathan had been swimming with Fiona and Darcy, the realisation that perhaps he was still more enmeshed with Fiona than she had imagined.

'The cake had sesame in it?' said Jonathan, bewildered. 'Where's Paddy?'

Paddy was coming up now, feet creaking on the stairs, breathing hard. 'Oh my God! What happened? Christ!' Amira fell into him, weeping hard. He put his arm round her distractedly, never taking his eyes off the scene in the bedroom. 'What's happened? Is she *dead*?'

'Did you put sesame in the cake?' Jonathan's voice was heavy. He stood up from where he had crouched down by the body, rising to his full height.

Paddy was still staring at Rachel, aghast. 'God, no. I was very careful. I knew she was allergic.'

But sesame oil could have been added to her portion after, hidden in the rich caramel sauce, the same brown colour. So maybe someone had killed her deliberately – not just hidden the EpiPen but poisoned her as well. A murder.

Vicky shuddered. The nightmarish feelings, dismissed in the light of day and bustle of plans and swimming and breakfast, were back. This was real. Maybe someone actually had followed them here and was picking them off. Rachel was dead. Actually, really dead. Vicky made a sudden movement. 'We have to get off here. We can't stay – we have to get the kids away.'

Fiona was still kneeling down, as if winded. 'We'll need to try the paddleboards. Or the boat Paddy found. We can flag another boat down, maybe.'

Jonathan nodded slowly. His eyes were riveted on the body, blue-lipped and pale, which only half an hour ago had been a beautiful, breathing woman. Her chestnut hair trailed over the wood of the floor, matching its tones.

Vicky said, 'I just can't believe this. I was so careful, ordering the food.'

'There's no way it was an accident?' said Fiona, voice shaking. 'I don't know, cross-contamination? An ingredient mislabelled, so Paddy didn't realise?'

Paddy looked close to tears. 'But it can't have – no, that can't be. I was so careful.'

Jonathan said, 'And where's her pen if it's an accident? Why couldn't she find it?'

Fiona bit her lip. 'Oh, I don't know, maybe it fell out on the way, or maybe the kids or—'

'My children don't go rooting around in people's luggage!' exclaimed Vicky. 'Can we stop blaming them for taking things they couldn't even have reached? Someone is *dead*.'

It was beginning. The predictions were coming true.

And yet, Rachel did have terrible allergies, clearly, and it could just have been an ill-timed accident. Nuts and sesame could creep into so many things. But now, here, after the sinister warnings of the game? It was too much of a coincidence, surely.

'Mummy?'

A little voice came from the corridor. Genevieve was in the doorway of their room, clutching her stuffed dog. Had Daniel left them alone in there? She'd specifically told him to watch them while she went with Paddy. He'd been fiddling about with the fires outside at the time. Maybe he hadn't heard her.

'What's wrong, Mummy?'

'Nothing, darling. Come on, let's go back in there.'

She walked the little girl away, careful not to let her see anything. Bloody Daniel hadn't bothered to make the bed or pick his clothes up off the floor that morning. Where the hell was he?

Never there when she needed him, when someone had died and she was scared that the horrible note was coming true. Toby was in the room too, sitting on the double bed with tousled hair, on the iPad as always.

'What's happening, Mummy? Someone was shouting.'

'Nothing. Nothing!'

'Where's Daddy?' Genevieve climbed on to the bed, thumb in mouth.

God only knew. Drinking somewhere, most likely. Or calling Cody. But no, she wasn't going to think about that. His phone wouldn't work, anyway – it was one of the reasons she'd chosen to come back here. She'd thought without his phone he might actually have to pay attention to his family for the weekend. But apparently not.

'Did Daddy bring you up here?'

'He said he'd make us pizza. Then said we can go on the iPads, Mummy. Where is he? We're hungry.'

It was past time for their lunch, almost one. Had Daniel forgotten all about the kids? 'He's planning a lovely surprise for Mummy's birthday, I think.'

'I'll make you a card, Mummy. Can I have my crayons?' Toby clambered towards her.

'Of course. But let's just stay here for a little while.'

She crawled on to the bed with them, took them in her arms. The thought of anything happening to them sent fireworks through her nerves, actual shudders running over her skin.

Rachel was dead. *Dead.*

They had to find a way off here. She would send Daniel and Jonathan in the boat, see if they could make it over to Tarne or flag down another craft. At least no one could be accused of killing Rachel if it was just a horrible accident. But why would her EpiPen be missing then?

Maybe the note was real, and this was just the first death. Why Rachel though – had she too been responsible for a life lost? Like Vicky herself was?

She heard footsteps outside. Jonathan, pale underneath his year-round tan. 'We have to move her. She can't stay here.'

Vicky hadn't even thought of that. They couldn't leave a dead body in the house, especially if they were stuck on the island for another day. But there was no one they could call; no one who would come to help them. Police, ambulance, civilisation – all just a few miles away, but as inaccessible as another planet. 'Where though?'

'The outhouse I guess. Paddy and I are going to lift her, then try the boat. You're right, we need to get out of here immediately.'

'Where the hell is Daniel?'

'No idea, but I think something's burning in the pizza oven.'

Vicky stayed with the twins while the others moved the body, doing her best to distract them, though it was impossible not to hear the bangs and scrapes of a heavy object being carried down the precarious stairs, the occasional soft curse and exclamation. Glancing out of the window, she saw Paddy and Jonathan carrying Rachel into the outhouse, one white hand flopping down, her hair over her face. It seemed impossible to take in. How someone could go from breathing, moving, irritating life, to just – nothing, in only a few seconds. Poor Rachel. She might have been a pain, but she didn't deserve this.

There was a knock on the door. Jonathan again, his face grim and set. 'It's done. We're going down to the boat now.'

'No sign of Daniel?'

'Not yet. Or Lou.'

'I'm so sorry, Jay. For you – for her.'

He said nothing to that. 'Come on. Let's try to get out of here.'

Fiona said she'd stay behind with the kids, feed them the charred pizzas that had been left in the oven outside, if she could scrape some of it off. Darcy could still be heard crying in her room, a jagged wailing noise of pure shock. She'd had such a sheltered life up till now, that finding a dead body must have floored her. Vicky kissed the twins on their heads and left them in the living room with their iPads. They were having far too much screen time this weekend, but at least it distracted them. Then she followed Paddy, Jonathan, and Amira down to the jetty.

The boat was where Paddy had said, floating in the choppy surf, tied to the jetty, only one oar in the bottom. Would it get them across? It looked so flimsy.

Jonathan had already waded out to it, sloshing water. 'Will it float?' Vicky called. Amira was standing beside her, wringing her hands in distress, no help at all.

'I'll give it a try,' said Jonathan decisively, running his hand over the barnacled hull. 'It's a risk worth taking.' That was a catch-phrase from his show, wasn't it? If she was honest, Vicky rarely watched it. All that self-congratulation and manufactured peril was a bit hard to stomach from her brother.

'Shouldn't someone else go?' she had to ask. Saw him frown. 'I'm sorry, Jay, but – you know.'

He clenched the fist of his non-usable arm. 'No one else knows about boats, unless you want to go.'

She couldn't leave the twins here, not with their father MIA. 'Well, OK. If you're sure.'

In the absence of adult life jackets, Jonathan had taken the child-sized ones the boatman had left, and clipped them around himself, though she couldn't imagine that would do much good in the water. But there was nothing else to try. Why had she let herself sleep last night, instead of trying everything she could to get away? It hadn't seemed real, that was why. Even though the moment she'd heard the words *everyone here has killed someone*, she had immediately thought of him. Tomasz. His white shoe in the middle of the road. The sheen of his bike lights in the rain.

It wasn't *fair*. The same thought rising up in her mind, filling her chest with rage. This had been her island, belonging to her family for generations, and now some stranger had bought it and changed it and now they were trapped here. Last night she'd gone through all the messages she'd sent about the booking, looking for clues. The first email, from someone called Jane: *Hi Vicky, I see you put in an enquiry about holiday cottages. I have one here that may interest you.* And she'd clicked and it had been her own island. She hadn't thought it strange, as she'd sent enquiries to lots of sites when it became clear no one else was going to organise her birthday. She'd written back, *I've actually been to that island, as a child. Who owns it now?*

An investor based overseas. Since you have a special connection to the place, I can offer you an exclusive deal. And she'd taken it, walked right into the trap. She wasn't entirely sure why – being back at the island brought up all kinds of painful emotions. Maybe she had wanted to feel like that girl again: pretty, bubbly, confident, rich. Before the accident, before kids. Before Daniel. Back when it was just her, Jonathan, Louise, and Paddy. Lovely Paddy.

She glanced at him now, realising again how his body had changed since she'd last seen him, become lean and compact. It was easier to notice differences when you didn't live with someone every day. He and Jonathan were calling instructions to each other, pushing the boat out into the waves.

'Is it OK?' she shouted.

'There's some water in the bottom,' yelled Jonathan. 'Might be a leak, but I can't see where from. I can bail out.'

And still, where was bloody Daniel? Why had he left her in danger, on her fortieth birthday of all days? She hadn't seen him since walking away from the house earlier, with Paddy. Only an hour or so ago, but things had seemed calm then, the fears of the night before forgotten, settling down. Now Rachel was dead and they were in a totally different story. Now someone was perhaps trying to kill them.

'Are you sure, Jay?'

'We've been in this boat hundreds of times, Vics. It's fine.'

Was this really the same one, with its peeling paint and rusted rivets? She hadn't paid much attention back then was the truth, thinking they would always have the island. And it was Daniel's fault too, wasn't it, that they'd lost all this? Perhaps she had made the wrong decision all those years ago. Missed out, maybe, on a better man who was right in front of her all along. But it was dangerous, thinking that way.

Paddy splashed back over to her, his face inscrutable. He would never panic or go to pieces or drink so much he passed out.

'Are you going with Jay?' she asked.

She didn't want that. She wanted to be near him, because that made her feel safest.

'I think it's best with one person, test it out, in case it is leaking. Where's Danny?'

'God, who knows? Nowhere helpful. He was doing the fires, but when we came back up, after we heard the screaming, he wasn't there, was he?'

'I don't think so. He went to look for phone reception, maybe. Were the kids alone in the house?'

'Yeah. In our room.'

She had left them too long again, and who could she really trust to stay with them? Surely Fiona, her best friend, her sister-in-law. Former sister-in-law, soon. But that didn't matter, did it?

Whatever beef Fiona had with Jonathan, she was still loyal to Vicky. Even if Vicky had sided with her brother, invited Rachel on this weekend? She'd had little choice – it was Jonathan's birthday too, after all.

A worm ate away at Vicky's stomach. She could trust no one, was the truth. Not her husband, not her best friend, not her brother, even. They'd always been so close, but she had no idea what was going on with him the last year or so. He'd stopped answering her messages, hadn't come to the twins' last birthday, had moved in with a twenty-eight-year-old Instagram influencer, for God's sake. In fact, they hadn't been as close since the loss of the island. Maybe she didn't know him any more either.

She watched as Jonathan rowed the boat out into the shining waves, alternating sides with the one oar he could handle. The rickety little thing stayed afloat for now.

'Hey.' Louise materialised behind her, unobtrusive as ever. She was red-faced from the exertion of walking and had mud on her boots. 'Did you get the boat working? I've been all round the island, looked everywhere. Nothing to see.'

Louise didn't even know about Rachel. 'Lou – did you go to the house already?'

'Not yet. I saw you all down here. Why?'

'Um, well—'

Paddy cut in, harshly. 'Rachel's dead, Lou.'

Louise's pale eyebrows almost disappeared into her hair. '*What?*'

'It looks like she had a reaction of some kind. To the cake, maybe. Though I'm sure it was safe.'

Louise's mouth was working like a goldfish. 'But how . . . I don't get it. Just an accident?'

Amira shuddered. 'Her EpiPen was gone too.'

'But . . .'

'We don't know anything,' said Paddy quickly. 'We just need to not panic. It could have been an accident. We put her in the outhouse.'

'But – what are we going to do?'

'Jay's trying the boat, maybe he'll make it across.'

'But – that doesn't . . . Oh my God.'

'Right now I have to get back to the kids,' said Vicky. As long as she could keep them safe, that was all that mattered.

Louise shook herself. 'Yes, we need to get back to the house. Come on.'

She was so practical. Louise had likely seen dozens of dead bodies, from famine and war and disease, the kind of suffering that was everyday in many parts of the world. Vicky would like to have said she'd never seen a body before, and she could almost claim that, except for that one searing memory. The shoe in the road, the huddle of clothes and bike nearby.

The four of them turned from the beach, towards the house. Smoke was rising from the hot tubs – perhaps Daniel was up there waiting for her, with no idea what had happened to Rachel. Perhaps she was being too harsh on him, and he'd been busy all this time, trying to help. She seemed to have simply no tolerance left for him, like a maxed-out bank account.

Amira clung to Paddy, holding him back, so Louise and Vicky strode on. It was a long time since they had been alone together. Years, probably. The silence between them thickened, took on an awkward, feverish quality. Louise was walking fast, pulling ahead.

'What do you make of all this?' Vicky asked her old friend, gasping for breath as she tried to keep up. Louise had always been something of an enigma, never one to open up or get drunk or cry over someone unsuitable. In fact, had she ever had a relationship? 'I mean, who wrote the note?'

'Hmm?' Louise glanced back. 'I thought at first it must be Rachel. She was a stranger, and she seemed angry about something, and her whole Instagram thing – well, people do all kinds of stupid pranks for the internet, don't they. I thought the note was just part of that. But if she's dead . . .'

So that meant it had to be one of them who'd written it. Unless it had been Rachel after all and she'd died accidentally, coincidentally. Vicky glanced back at Amira, another outsider, long part of the Group and yet not part of it. Vicky had often longed for a weekend of just the Group – Daniel being part of that of course – and had even suggested 'no partners' at times. Fiona had pointed out that was hardly fair, since both she and Vicky had married within the Group. Jonathan had not been at uni with them, yet he was so often there, hanging about, it had felt as if he was.

'What about what it said – that we all killed people?' Vicky could hear her voice was unsteady. Louise was walking so fast. 'Totally crazy, right?'

Louise's boots crunched hard on the gravel. 'Is it though?'

'What?'

'Well, Fiona said she'd missed something and a patient died. And Amira's case and Paddy's school-trip kid. And me, I had something like that too.'

Vicky's eyes went round. 'You did?'

'Vic, I work in life-and-death situations. People come into the camps and they're so malnourished and weak they drop like flies.'

'But how could that be your fault?'

'I had a colleague. Quite junior, hadn't done the right training, but with Covid we were short-staffed, people had gone home and not come back. We had to do a site visit to a village out in the desert. I'd received reports of rebels in the area, but usually . . . well, usually they leave us alone. I mean, who targets aid workers? We're trying to save people. The Jeeps are clearly marked.'

'Did something happen?'

'They ambushed her. She was found – her and a local staff member – they'd had their throats cut. Burned at the side of the road, the Jeep nicked. Raped too, we think anyway.' Louise's voice was flat, dispassionate. 'It's why I came home. When the locals start to turn on you – well, it's time to get out. There's nothing more we can do. I had to call her family and tell them what happened.'

'What . . . what was her name?'

Why hadn't she heard about this? Didn't such terrible stories merit the news any more? Not that Vicky really watched the news.

'Gabrielle Perez. Gabby.'

'But Lou, it wasn't your fault! She was attacked.'

Louise had her hands deep in the pockets of her down jacket. 'I was meant to go that day, but I switched the rotas. I sent her to her death, and Precious too – she was the local nurse travelling with her.'

Vicky had barely even noted the death of the local woman. That was terrible, it really was.

'OK, but it's still not your fault. It's not like you . . . Well. There was no way you could have avoided it. It could have been you instead of her. You can't blame yourself.'

Louise looked at her sideways. 'You think you can cause someone's death and just get over it? Anything *you* want to own up to?'

She thought of lying, denying it outright, then realised the time for that was long past. 'I . . . had a car accident. A few years ago.'

Louise nodded. 'So that's why you don't drive any more. I wondered why you were so upset yesterday.'

'I lost my licence for a year, and since then I just – I can't. It was an accident but I . . . It was still my fault.'

'Haunts you, doesn't it? That is, if you aren't a sociopath.'

'Surely everyone would be traumatised by something like that. I mean, it's a human life. Gone because of you. And their family, never the same again – so much suffering and pain. No one could cope with that guilt, could they?'

Louise laughed, deep in her throat, startling Vicky. 'You would think. But there are people who cope with it absolutely fine.'

Her mind leapt back to the note. It had seemed ridiculous, but so far she, Louise, Fiona, Amira, and Paddy had all confessed to being involved in people's deaths. Even if accidental or not their fault at all, they had been implicated, they carried the guilt from it. Lives had been lost. So maybe everyone really was a killer.

What about her brother? Her husband? Had Rachel harboured secrets – she'd certainly had an extreme reaction to the contents of the note? Even Darcy, at her age, could she be guilty of something like that? At least the twins had to be safe. At just five, they were totally innocent. But if something happened to her, or to Daniel, where would they be? And if that part of the note was true, what about the other bit – the horrible threat? *You will all either kill or be killed here.* And Rachel was already dead.

'Who do you mean, Lou? I think we all need to be honest with each other now.'

She shook her head. 'Not my story to tell.'

'But . . .'

'Not now. Look, we need to make the place safe, sort things out. Put out all the fires for a start, stay together. I'm going to stamp out the hot tubs.'

Louise strode on ahead, and Vicky saw her heave off the heavy wooden lid of the first tub. She stumbled. Fell back on to the ground. And let out a long howl, like an animal in pain.

Lola

2009

It was uncool, and he would never have admitted it to anyone, but Steve had once really loved arriving to work at the office. The big glass box of reception, the water feature and tropical plants, the ping-pong tables and artisan coffee bar, he'd loved it all. The name on the wall in a trendy font, *Button and Ball*. Research had shown that people trusted brands with double names, that it appealed to the kind of bougie housewife who was their main customer. It all cost an absolute fortune, but he knew it was worth it. Investors were impressed when they saw it. They thought the company must be doing well, which wasn't entirely true, but appearance was every-thing. Money flowed to money.

But today Steve Ballantine, head of product for Button and Ball, did not notice any of the features he'd once enjoyed so much. Because he could only think about one thing. And thank God, the boss was coming in at last, almost an hour late. Steve had been hovering by his office since nine.

'Morning Steve, mate.'

'Good morning, Daniel.'

He'd told all his staff to call him Daniel, and he hosted them all the time for office beers and ping-pong tournaments, but he was the boss, and everyone knew it. No one to answer to but himself. His friend Paddy O'Hagan was technically a co-director, thanks to some money he'd inherited from the sale of his grandmother's farm in Ireland, but he stayed hands-off. The world of business wasn't for him, he'd told Steve at the Christmas party. He was busy with a law conversion course anyway.

'What's up?'

'Did you read my email?'

'Not yet.' Daniel liked to decompress on the way in, listen to music.

'It's a product issue – the Sleepy Baby wooden crib? The manufacturer has folded and we have a thousand units from them. And they didn't send over the safety certs.'

'So? Did we pay them already for the stock?'

'Not all of it.'

Daniel clapped him on the shoulder. 'That's good then. Keep selling and we'll make a profit.'

'But – there's a potential safety issue. They never sent the compliance forms, and I've now learned they failed their last inspection.'

Daniel went to his desk, leafed through his letters. 'I still don't see how this is our problem, mate.'

Steve couldn't believe it. 'You must do! If the cots are faulty, a child could be injured. And we wouldn't be insured since we never received the safety documents.'

Daniel switched on his computer. It had been a cold hard decision, starting this company, he always said, after seeing how much his brother and his sister-in-law had spent on their new baby. Parents would spunk any amount of cash on their little darlings. The cot, a simple wooden crib, was on sale for over three hundred pounds. 'What could actually be faulty? It's just wood, isn't it?'

'So many things. The paint could be contaminated, the screws badly put in so it doesn't stay up, the bars too wide . . . It's not worth the risk. We need to pull it from sale, issue a recall notice for any already shipped.'

'God, really? People are so cautious nowadays. Bit of rough and tumble never hurt me – you know, when I was a kid, our dog climbed into my crib and bit me! Look, still have the scar.'

'Yes, yes, but Daniel – the lawsuits if we don't . . .'

Daniel sighed heavily. 'It'll cost a fortune to pull it.'

'I know.' And not to mention the bad publicity. The brand rested on being totally reliable for your precious little bundles. You'd put them down to sleep and they'd be cradled safely. That was what people were buying, rather than sanded cedarwood and hand-crafted carvings. But a recall was infinitely better than an accident. 'I don't think we have a choice, Daniel.'

Daniel sighed again. 'Alright.'

'You'll get that done?'

'Of course. I'll talk to Distribution.'

'Good.' Steve's shoulders sagged in relief. 'Thank God we caught this in time. They shouldn't have been put on sale in the first place, not without the certificates. We need to look into how that happened.'

'Sure, sure. Sorry, I have a ten o'clock.'

Daniel turned round to look out the window at St Katharine Docks below, dotted with boats. He had been talking about getting his own – his wife's family had one on some island they owned. Once, Steve had drunk in details like this, imagining a time when he'd live the high life too. Probably there'd be no bonus this year if they did this recall. But there really was no other way.

It was less than a week before it happened. Steve arrived at the office in a chipper mood, smiling at the pretty receptionist, hardly registering the gaggle of workers standing outside their offices in little worried knots.

'Steve.'

'Mmm?'

The receptionist, he saw now, was grey-faced above her pink silk blouse. 'He wants you,' she said. No need to ask who *he* was.

Daniel was never in this early, but there he was standing by his windows looking over the dock.

Steve knew instantly. Funny how that happened. 'The cot?'

Daniel just nodded.

'A kid?'

'Eight-month-old.'

Steve's body continued on autopilot, pulling out a chair, sitting down. But his mind had short-circuited. It had happened. It had bloody happened.

Daniel was still talking. 'She got her head stuck in the bars – they were too wide like you said – and she suffocated. Lola, that was her name. Lola Carlisle. Steve, there's going to be a court case. And a shitstorm of publicity. What are we going to do? Someone could go to prison, even.'

'*We?*' Steve had once been annoyed not to be a director, when he'd helped to build the company from the ground up. But he suddenly saw now that this could be a good thing. 'I'm sorry, Daniel. I've got it on record that I told you about the cot – so it won't be me. Also, I'm resigning. Effective now.'

He stood up, walked downstairs and out past the sunlit glass.

A baby was dead, and that was horrific. But at least, unlike Daniel Franks, he knew that it was not his fault. Because how could someone live with something like that?

Amira

Daniel. It was like a nightmare. First Rachel, blue-lipped, horror on her face, cuts on her hands from where she must have scrabbled among her smashed toiletries, searching for her EpiPen, not finding it. Now Daniel.

His arm bobbed over the side of the hot tub, fingers almost brushing the ground as they hung loose. His skin was pink, puckered. The bath had been bubbling for hours under its lid, and he must have been dying the whole time they were messing about with boats and pointless discussions. How long? Was he in there when they'd come back from the beach earlier? Perhaps still alive and desperate for help, unable to call out?

Amira bent over. She thought she might be sick. She choked it back. That would help no one. Paddy was standing a few metres away, not coming to comfort her. He looked dazed, stricken. Like she felt. And Rachel was dead too. She couldn't take that in yet, and now here was another death. Surely this was all a horrible nightmare she'd soon wake up from, a fever dream of wine and cheese.

Fiona sat back on the ground, fighting tears after letting go of the wrist where she'd been searching fruitlessly for a pulse. 'He . . . Vic, he's been dead a while. I'm sorry.'

'How?' Vicky said dully. Fiona and the kids had come out of the house on hearing Louise's screams, but she'd quickly sent Darcy back inside with the twins, to keep them from seeing their father like this. Poor Darcy was in hysterics. 'How did he die?'

And when? Amira wondered again. Had he been here during all the drama with Rachel? Dying and they'd not even noticed?

Fiona's voice was small. 'I think he – sort of boiled. Severe scalding can kill a person fast. We usually see it with small children, if they're put in too-hot baths. Rarely an adult.'

Because they'd be able to get out, wouldn't they? The hot tub was just a tin bath with a fire burning under it, now extinguished by Paddy, though the water was still too hot to go near. Daniel's body was floating in it, feet knocking against the wooden lid, eyes staring up at the sky. Pink all over, like the world's worst sunburn. His jeans and jumper waterlogged. Amira felt panic rise in her throat.

'Who did this?' she heard herself shout, half-hysterical. 'Who?'

Fiona mumbled something about an accident, but she was still on the ground, as if frozen in horror, and didn't sound convinced.

Paddy kept saying, 'But I don't understand. We've all been together. No one could have . . . I don't see how.' Louise was also sitting down on the grass, her head pressed into her knees, as if winded.

Vicky seemed frozen too, expressionless. She stood over her husband's body without touching him. Getting him out of the bath would be quite a feat, heavy and soaked as he was. Paddy went over to her, tried to put his arm round her.

'Vic, I'm so sorry—'

She shook him off like an irritation. 'But I don't understand – how did he end up in there? He's dressed, so he wasn't using the tub. Why didn't he climb out?' Amira didn't understand either. The water would have taken hours to heat up. He couldn't have been in there all that time, ever since this morning – could he? She'd seen him from the bathroom window after her shower, lighting the fires – that was two or three hours ago now.

'He could have been unconscious,' Fiona said. 'Maybe he hit his head. Or someone whacked him with something. Or drugged him?'

But how? Unless someone had brought a syringe with them, or a bottle of chloroform. No, it was ridiculous.

Amira suddenly remembered. 'The lids. They were off earlier, when we went to the beach. I remember seeing the steam, and Jonathan was stoking them up. They were on when we came up just now.' Louise had lifted the lid of the one Daniel was in, slid it half-off before seeing what was in there.

They all looked at each other. Tentatively, Fiona said, 'So – you think someone put it over him deliberately? That's mad.'

'They would have to be strong,' said Amira, shakily. Daniel was six foot three. Not easy to knock down.

Louise raised her head, her voice hoarse. 'You don't think – I mean, he could have just banged his head. Slipped in there. If he'd been drinking . . .' Another terrible accident. And it was true he had cracked open the champagne with breakfast, to make mimosas supposedly for Vicky, though she hadn't touched a drop.

Vicky shook her head slowly. 'The lid was on. He couldn't have pulled it down on himself, could he? And then there was the note.'

It was just possible Daniel had slipped in, and the lid had fallen down on top of him. If Daniel had fought to get out before the heat overpowered him, that would explain why his hands were mangled, pulpy. But if someone had done this, then who? Just six of them alive here now, plus Darcy and the twins, and Jonathan had left so that meant only five. Who could be trusted? Someone had to be doing this, and that left a selection of close friends, husbands, wives, siblings.

'We need to move him,' said Paddy dully. 'I suppose we . . . put him in with Rachel. Oh God. This is mad.'

'Who can lift him?' said Vicky, her voice still like that of a robot's. 'He'll weigh a ton. I doubt any of us women will be much help.'

'Where's Jay?' Fiona stood up, with difficulty. The front of her jumper was soaking wet.

'He took the boat out,' said Louise.

'By himself? Is that safe?'

Maybe safer than this island, Amira thought. 'We don't know,' said Paddy. 'He wanted to try.'

Amira tried to pull herself together. This wasn't about her – she hadn't lost anyone close, and Vicky had lost her husband, the father of her children. She went over and tried to touch Vicky's arm. 'I'm so sorry – do you want to come inside? Sit down maybe?'

Vicky turned to her, eyes glassy. Her voice sounded like someone else's. 'I think it's time we all laid our cards on the table, don't you? Because this isn't an accident. Someone is picking us off one by one.'

Amira was going to be sick. She turned and bolted for the house, thundering up the dangerous stairs past Darcy and the twins in the living room, running into the shared bathroom, pushing aside the toiletries that still littered the floor. All too easy to picture Rachel's body lying on the bedroom rug next door. On her knees she stared into the loo, feeling nausea ripple through her. Was she going to throw up? Did that mean she really was pregnant, now of all times?

She could hear Paddy next door, perhaps changing his own wet clothes. Moving around in their room. She hoped he would come in to check on her, but he didn't, and after a few minutes she heard him go back downstairs.

Her nausea subsided, slowly, and she got to her knees with a deep breath and went into their room, sitting down on the bed Paddy had carefully made that morning. What was going to happen now? It would probably involve trying to get to shore with either the boat, if Jonathan came back, or the paddleboards. Reporting not one but two deaths. Somehow getting Daniel's body out of the tub. Mechanically, she took off her jeans, which she hadn't got round to changing after plunging into the sea, and put on some leggings that would at least dry easily. She'd had some idea she might do yoga this weekend, perhaps to impress Vicky. Clearly, that was something that could never happen. The woman's husband had just been boiled alive and she was still beautiful, composed. Not a hair out of place.

Amira realised her jumper was also wet through and stinking of seawater, and the one from last night had stains on it. Why had she only brought two? Paddy was right, she knew nothing of the countryside. She stepped over to open his rucksack, packed to military precision, thinking she could borrow something wicking and sensible.

Paddy was a very neat and minimalist packer, so she saw it immediately when she unzipped the bag. A bulky item, yellow and plastic, with buttons and a receiver on it, tucked in under his washbag. Amira stared down at it in great puzzlement. Could she really be looking at the missing radio, and if so, what on earth was it doing in Paddy's bag?

From downstairs, an impatient voice. 'Amira! Come down, will you. We need to make a plan.'

Paddy. Would she confront him about this? How could she, in front of everyone? She had absolutely no idea who she could trust. What the hell was going on?

'Amira.'

'Coming,' she shouted, and went.

Elizabeth

2020

It started small. A sore throat, bit of a sniffle, tired enough to go to bed after the *Channel 4 News*. Then the cough set in. She had to cancel looking after Andrew the next day, which she hated to do, as it meant Julia would miss work. But no sense giving everyone her bug, especially in these days of Covid.

Two days in it was clear this was something nasty, and a test confirmed it. She was down with the dreaded lurgy, after being so careful, isolating all through the first outbreak. Likely she had picked up something at Andrew's third birthday, all those little ones running about, runny noses and sticky hands, but she wouldn't have missed it even so. She'd already lost so many months of her beloved only grandson thanks to lockdown. Anyway, everyone said it didn't affect you too much if you were fit and healthy. Elizabeth was sixty-two but did Pilates three times a week and walked the dog every day. She hoped to tough it out, banned Julia from coming to nurse her in case she passed something on. It was sad to be alone and ill, but she'd grown used to it after she'd split with Julia's father in her fifties. She was independent. She'd be fine.

After two more days, Elizabeth could barely climb out of bed to reach the loo. She had to admit this was getting to her. And it was a little bit frightening, to feel so tired, to find the room swimming even though she was lying down. She hadn't been able to eat anything for days, and even water was hard to swallow when her throat hurt so much. But she'd be fine. Wouldn't she?

The next day, when Julia called her on FaceTime, Elizabeth put out her hand for her phone and found she could not pick it up. She simply didn't have the strength, and she couldn't draw in breath; she felt like she'd just climbed a steep hill even though she'd only been lying there. With great difficulty, she stretched out a finger and pressed the answer button. Julia's face appeared.

'Mum? Are you OK?'

I'm fine, she tried to say, but a storm of coughing overtook her. Oh dear. She really couldn't catch her breath. 'I . . .' More coughing.

'Mum, you aren't well. I'm coming over.'

'No . . . no . . .'

'No arguments, Mum. You can't breathe properly! I'm calling an ambulance too.'

She rang off, and Elizabeth sank back against the pillows. Such a terrible fuss. But actually she did feel quite awful, and maybe it wouldn't be so bad to go to hospital. Just to get checked out. A puff of oxygen, perhaps. After all, there would be something very terrible about losing consciousness and having no one with her.

Vicky

Daniel. She had been so annoyed at him, wondering where the hell he'd been all day, and now she knew. He was dead.

She couldn't think beyond the next few seconds, because this just couldn't be true. It was just like at the police station after the accident, when they told her Tomasz was dead. Her mind had slipped and slid over it, desperate for a way out. For it not to be true, because it didn't make sense. It wasn't fair. None of this was.

The remaining adults, minus Jonathan, sat around the table. Vicky had hugged the twins tight, told them they needed to be good, then corralled them into the living room with their head-phones and iPads. It comforted her to see them, the tops of their matching blond heads. How much had they witnessed? How was she going to explain this? She hadn't told them about Daddy yet. Luckily, they were used to him not being around much, and hadn't asked where he was once they'd been fed on half-burnt pizzas.

Darcy had joined them at the table, pale and shaking. She was only fifteen, this wasn't fair on her. Fiona was holding her hand. Beside her sat Paddy, still damp from launching the boat, then Louise, and then Vicky. Amira, who had changed her clothes – nice to have that luxury – was behind them in the kitchen, boiling the kettle, staring mindlessly into its clear sides. As if hot drinks could fix any of this. And did Vicky feel safe to accept food or drink from anyone now? Someone had perhaps given Rachel sesame. And maybe Daniel had been drugged to get him into the tub.

'Amira, sit down,' she said impatiently. 'No one wants coffee. We need to sort this.'

Amira slid into a seat, face creased in anxiety. Could it be her doing, all this – she was an outsider too, after all? And she'd never liked Vicky, probably because she was jealous of her closeness to Paddy. But ruining someone's fortieth wasn't quite in the same league as murdering their husband.

Vicky's breath caught ragged in her throat. It couldn't be true. Any minute now she would wake up and the world would make sense again, Daniel snoring beside her. She inhaled. 'Alright. It's time to stop playing games and being coy. We need to be honest.' Vicky looked round at them all, her best friends of so many years, her beloved niece. 'I think we should level with each other. Have we all actually killed someone? I know I have.'

It hurt, even after all these years, to see the look on Paddy's face. A flash of censure. Like she wasn't who he'd thought she was.

'It was an accident,' she said quickly. 'I really didn't . . . It was awful but it could have happened to anyone. I knocked him off his bike in the rain, someone else ran over him. Horrible.'

'That's why you stopped driving,' said Paddy. 'You didn't tell me.'

Amira looked up at his tone. Intimate – accusing.

Vicky hurried to move past it. 'Well, no, I was so ashamed. Hardly anyone knows. And Lou just told me one of her co-workers died in Sudan, after she sent her out on a mission. Not her fault either, but you know, technically.' She couldn't read Louise's expression at all. Only blankness. Shock, perhaps. Vicky certainly felt that way herself, numb around the edges. As if a great pain was coming but had not yet hit. 'So who else? Fiona, Amira, Paddy, you told us yours. Do we know about Rachel?'

Fiona shuddered slightly. 'OK, look, I'm really ashamed of this, but I googled Rachel before we came here. She was linked to a death, yes.'

'Who?'

'Oh, she gave some stupid advice on her Instagram. Some controversial beauty treatment she was paid to advertise, and a young woman died from it. Her family tried to sue Rachel, but of course you can't legislate for people listening to rubbish on the internet. God knows I see enough of the aftermath.'

'So that's another one. What about Jonathan?'

Fiona frowned, remembering. 'One of his crew died last year, remember? On the hills in Scotland, during a storm. I wonder if he might have been involved in some way. He never told me the full story, and well – we separated not long after.' She glanced at Darcy, squeezed her hand tight.

Vicky wished her brother were here now so she could ask him about it. He'd never spoken to her about the death, just said it was an accident, the kind of tragedy that happened when you worked in dangerous surroundings. Was he alright, out in that leaky boat? He'd been in worse situations for sure, much more dangerous. But someone was trying to kill them now. She wouldn't rest until she could see his face, feel his arm about her, hear his bluff loud voice telling her it would be alright. He would be devastated about Daniel too, but he would support her. They'd always closed ranks when it mattered. And yet she hadn't told him about Tomasz.

Darcy let out a sob. 'Auntie Vicky, even I did something bad.'

'What? Sweetheart, I'm sure you didn't.'

'Yes, I did. Someone died because of me too.' Darcy gulped. 'It was something that happened at school. Last year. It – it was kind of my fault.'

Fiona said, 'Don't make her talk about it. A girl died, it was very sad. She took her own life, so it could hardly be anyone's fault. Darcy, you know that's true.'

Vicky said, 'I think we need to work out if we can reasonably say everyone here is responsible for a death. Daniel, Jonathan too.'

'But Darcy didn't—'

She cut in. 'No matter how stretched it is. We need to know if that statement from the note, that everyone here has killed someone, could possibly be real.' She looked up. 'Because if it's true – well, then, there's still that third one.'

You will all either kill or be killed here.

Which of the three statements was true and which the lie? Either they had all killed someone and they couldn't escape, or they couldn't escape and they would all be killed, or they'd all killed someone and they'd all be killed too. That meant there was a way off. But there didn't seem to be. Her head was spinning.

'She killed herself,' Darcy gulped. 'In her room. With her school tie. She left a note. It said she just couldn't cope with the bullying. And the loneliness. That she was so lonely. And she . . . she mentioned me in it. By name. They said at the inquest thingy that's what made her do it.'

'Oh darling.' Fiona put a hand over her daughter's. 'It wasn't your fault. She must have been unhappy. People never take their lives for one simple reason.'

'But she asked me for help, and I ignored her! That basically is my fault. And Uncle Daniel's dead! And Rachel! It's really true!' Darcy burst into noisy tears. 'I don't want to die!'

Neither do I, thought Vicky. She had felt old turning forty, but now she realised how stupid that was. There was so much life ahead and she wanted all of it. Daniel and Rachel's had been snuffed out. 'So everyone did kill someone in some way. It's true, that statement.'

'It seems that way,' said Fiona dully. 'We don't know for sure about Daniel or Jay.'

'Daniel killed someone alright.' Paddy's voice was so cold as he said it. Cracked about the edges.

'What?' said Vicky. 'What are you talking about?'

'Come on, Vic. You know perfectly well. The company? The reason it collapsed?'

'But – that was just an accident!' She hadn't even thought of that, it was so long ago and all so unfortunate.

'And you think ours were deliberate? At least we just made mistakes, or failed to stop something happening. Daniel was warned the product wasn't safe and he didn't recall it. He had blood on his hands.'

She stared at him, horrified by his tone. Paddy had never spoken to her like that. 'But—'

'I think the time for lies is past, don't you? Never mind about the stupid note – who knows what it means, if anything. People are dying.'

Vicky's hands were trembling. Wasn't it bad enough her husband was dead, without his name being slandered, gross accusations being thrown around? 'It's not true.'

'Yes it is. That's why you lost this island in the first place, isn't it?'

'How dare you, Paddy! You know nothing about it. You don't know what Daniel went through.' She heard her mouth frame his name, her husband all these years. So close he was like a part of her body, albeit one that she'd hated much of the time. How could he be gone?

'Oh, don't I? I wasn't a director of the company, then? I didn't lose everything because of him? After he convinced me to sink my whole inheritance into it?'

'I didn't – you weren't really involved, you don't know how hard it was . . .'

143

'Harder for that family who lost their little girl. And you just paid them off, got away with it, while I lost the lot.'

'So what are you saying – whoever wrote the note really thinks we all killed people? And they're killing us?'

Louise cleared her throat. 'You said Rachel's death was an accident. And Daniel . . . maybe he fell, I don't know . . . It doesn't mean anyone's doing it, does it?'

'Well, we don't know either way, do we? Two accidents in a row?'

Fiona slapped her hands on the table. 'Stop it, everyone. This is stupid. It doesn't matter who did what. Just that we can get out of here safely. There must be a way. We can see the mainland, for God's sake. What about, I don't know, is there a farmer who comes to feed the sheep?'

Paddy had his head in his hands. 'I think they're wild sheep. Actually, there are some breeds that eat seaweed in winter, it's interesting . . .' He stopped himself. 'Not important now. Sorry.'

Fiona sighed. 'Well, what about Daniel's big surprise then?'

Vicky hadn't thought of that. Some of the plans had been in his email, but there were hints in the group chat of another thing, a big thing. 'Does anyone know what it was?'

They all exchanged glances. Fiona shrugged. 'No point keeping it secret now. Look, Vic, it totally slipped my mind before, with everything, but Daniel asked me to help because, well, you know he's hopeless at organising things.' She paused, and the unsaid *was* seemed to float in the air between them.

'Well? What was it?'

'A private chef,' muttered Louise. 'Crazy expensive. Two Michelin stars.'

'Bobby Landford – you know, the one off that TV show? He was going to come out from a cruise ship a few miles away,' said

Fiona. 'It wasn't easy to arrange. Dan spent hours on the phone. I think Jay pulled a few strings too.'

'Oh. That certainly would have been a surprise.' It would have been amazing, actually. Vicky could have made a big splash on Instagram about it. She might even have forgiven him temporarily, if he'd pulled it off. Too late for that now, and it hit her that she would never make up with him this time, never find a way back. 'Did you – was he going to cover the cost of that?' Surely Daniel wouldn't have asked their friends in poorly paid jobs to chip in for such a thing. And why hadn't he just paid for the whole rental, as Vicky had suggested? They could afford it and it wasn't even expensive, far less than she'd expected for such a place. She didn't understand.

'Of course not,' scoffed Paddy. 'There was no suggestion that we wouldn't pay for all this. Such extravagance.'

'So Bobby will still be coming? He didn't cancel?'

'I don't think so,' said Fiona. 'He messaged yesterday to double-check Rachel's allergies. I remember because – well, it seemed annoying, causing that much of a fuss.'

'So if he wasn't cancelled, he'll come here and rescue us?' As long as he made it over. Vicky wasn't sure she believed in the idea of magical salvation. 'I suppose that explains why Daniel didn't order food for tonight. I had no idea.'

Vicky wondered if she would have liked it, or if like every other time she would have found a reason to be annoyed at some thoughtlessness of Daniel's, or swing wildly between finding it a waste of money and being miffed that he hadn't spent enough. She would never get a meal personally cooked by Bobby Landford now. Her mind edged into the future, where she no longer had Daniel's salary to cushion her from life, and she shied away from it like a sting. Too soon to think about anything. She could only think about the next few hours, keeping her kids safe. Then later, it would all have to be faced. Daniel, still outside in the tub. Impossible to take in.

Fiona nodded. 'I think so. He can take someone back to the ship and we can radio.'

A visceral relief flooded Vicky's bloodstream, despite her husband being dead, despite someone perhaps trying to kill them. They could get off the island. She could get the kids away, and then she'd deal with the wreckage of her life.

She caught Paddy's eye over the table. His brow creased but he looked away, as if ashamed of berating her. 'What time is he coming, does anyone know? Bobby Landford?'

'Dinner was at eight,' said Fiona. 'So he'd need at least two hours to cook? I'd imagine about five, six.'

It was now almost three. Only two or three hours to survive, and they could be back on shore by nightfall, telling their story to the police. With any luck the twins wouldn't even remember this horrible twenty-four hours, would recover from the loss of their father.

Vicky stood up. 'Alright. Just in case that doesn't pan out, we still need to get the paddleboards and keep looking for the radio. It has to be here somewhere. Let's get organised.'

Daniel's body proved harder to move than Rachel's, water-logged and a dead weight to heft over the side of the bath. She watched out of the window, keeping the twins well away, while Fiona, Paddy, Amira, and Louise wrestled him out and on to one of the tarpaulins they'd found, which covered up the barbecue and fire pit when there were no guests. Soon, both bodies, one large and one small, were bundled up and secured away in the outhouse.

Vicky took a deep shaky breath. That was done, at least. Now she just had to get Jonathan back. She scanned the sea but could see nothing, just a cluster of boats in the distance near the port at Tarne. They could try signalling with lights maybe, once it got dark.

Wasn't SOS three long, three short, three long again? She thought she remembered that from the sailing courses their dad had sent them on, determined that Jonathan would not be held back by his arm. Forcing him to use it anyway until he cried with pain. Her poor brother. Where the hell was he?

The bodies dealt with, the five remaining adults assembled by the fire pit. Vicky had left Darcy with the little ones, under strict instructions to lock the doors to the house. Not that it was secure even with locks – it had been designed as a private family retreat, not the kind of place you'd ever need to shut people out. But it made Vicky feel a little better.

'What now?' said Fiona, panting with effort. She had a sheen of sweat on her forehead from all the exercise.

'We should check the caves. Lou, you can climb, yes?'

Louise blinked. 'Um – I used to, yeah.'

'There's rope in the outhouse. Someone should go out and look for Jay also, if we get the paddleboards from the shed. Anyone got experience with them?'

To her surprise, Amira raised a sheepish hand. 'I did it on a hen-do a few years back. I could probably handle one.'

'I thought you couldn't swim.'

'I can't. But you don't have to go in the water, do you?'

That was true, if a little surprising that she would volunteer.

'Paddy will come with me,' she said. 'Won't you? The booklet said there were two boards.'

Paddy looked wrong-footed. 'I thought I could check the caves with Lou.'

'The paddleboards are a better bet,' said Vicky. 'If we can actually get away, we'll be safe. OK?'

They barely nodded. Louise was pale, as was Fiona, who hadn't stopped shaking since they found Daniel. Amira was crying on and off, and Paddy too was frozen somehow, eyes wide. Everyone was going to pieces, and here was Vicky rising to the challenge even after losing her husband. A surge of determination went through her. Their father had always instilled in her and Jonathan the need to be calm in a crisis, to take action instead of panicking, and she was going to do her best. Even if her husband's killer might be here with her, among her group of friends. Because that was the possibility no one had said out loud yet — either someone had stalked them here and was hunting them, or one of them was doing all this.

Mhairi

Mhairi and Arthur had arrived now at the north beach, working their way round the island systematically from the jetty where they'd arrived. The house was in the centre, elevated on a small hill but with trees behind it. There had been nothing at the jetty, just the wooden platform on stilts. Following the overgrown gravel path around the island, she'd seen several impassive sheep and some tumbledown ruins, but nothing else. Then they'd arrived at the top of the land mass, where the beach was, facing north to Islay. This actually had a structure – something like a boatshed with the door open, a padlock lying on the ground beside it.

Mhairi poked her head in. It was neat and dry, with rows of cut logs, boxes of firelighters, generator fuel, and bottles of water and dried food such as cereal. Everything you would need to survive bad weather and power cuts. On the ground were some damp clothes and a rumpled picnic blanket, as if someone had slept here the night before. Hooks on the wall hung empty, leaving the dusty outlines of something large. She looked askance at Arthur.

'Paddleboards,' he grunted.

Of course – the new obsession with SUP, or stand-up paddleboarding. She didn't see the appeal at all – her core had never been the same since pregnancy. Did this mean the missing guests had taken the boards out? Mhairi clicked the light switch a few times.

Like the ones in the house, it was dead. 'There's fuel here. Is the generator nearby?'

'Aye. That wee box there.'

She looked out – there was a large metal box attached to the shed, with various buttons and levers on it. She pressed her ear to it and heard nothing. 'It should have come on if the storage batteries dipped?'

'Aye. Unless someone turned it off.'

She looked all around the area but could see nothing suspicious. No signs of struggle or foul play. The beach itself was wide and beautiful, with wet yellow sand, perfectly clean but bleakly cold. The water was clear, but she knew it was freezing cold too.

'What's that?' She had seen something bobbing around in the surf and began to walk towards it. 'There's something in the water!' She thought immediately of the tiny, empty life jacket, but it wasn't that. Not a person. Something flat and light.

'Wait, wait, would you, lassie!' Arthur pushed past her, wading into the sea in his thick fisherman's overalls, waterproof. Clad only in polyester trousers, Mhairi was grateful. He towed the object back to shore, lashed by seaweed and missing a chunk from the side.

'Is that . . .'

'Aye. One of the paddleboards.'

So if the board was being tossed around in the surf, where then was the person who'd been on it? Mhairi shivered again, the cold whistling through her jacket. This place was so unnerving. Where was everyone? They couldn't have all disappeared, eight adults and three children. God, she hoped the kids were alright.

'Is there a chance someone else picked them up, took them to shore?'

Arthur scratched his head, looking back to the mainland. 'Maybe. They'd have put it out on the radio though.'

'Someone just passing, an amateur sailor who doesn't know to radio?'

Arthur shrugged. 'They'd have made it back by now.'

Was there a possibility she was going to find the rest of them on land, sipping whisky safe and sound in the Tarne harbour pub? No, surely they wouldn't have left the bodies here and not even called it in. It seemed so unlikely, and she could see no boats on the strait today. It was too cold and wet for pleasure-sailing. So where the hell were they?

Amira

Amira was flooded with nausea again as the board bobbed beneath her, and her brain registered the utter imbecility of trying to stay afloat on a flimsy piece of fibreglass on choppy seas. The note had said it: *There is no way off the island.* Except, perhaps, the narrow strip that she was currently trying to balance on.

Part of her had hoped they wouldn't be able to get the shed open, but the code in the booklet had worked on the padlock, revealing a space full of extra fuel and supplies, neatly stacked. Plus the two boards and their paddles hanging on the wall, along with two life jackets, so she'd had no choice but to go through with her foolish offer to take one out. Trying to look brave and grown-up and strong. Not a pathetic idiot who was scared of heights, and water, and everything in between.

This was hell, she decided. Actual freezing, icy, soaked, miserable, terrifying hell. She had been on a paddleboard once before in her life, at a tranquil shallow lake on a summer's day. Being on the open sea was an entirely different matter.

Paddy had forged ahead of her, in his usual determined way, ploughing his paddle through the waves and soon disappearing round the side of the island. She had tried to follow, wobbly on her knees, and had watched the small figures of Fiona and Vicky recede into pinpoints on the beach, then vanish as she turned around the island. It looked totally different from the water. Forbidding rocks on that side, with small clear coves where birds floated. The water slapping white against the cliffs, each smack threatening to pull her board in with it. She could see birds nesting in the hollows of the rocks, fluffy and adorable, and might have been interested on any other day.

Alone with just her own heavy breath and the wind in her ears, her mind ran over the events of the past twenty-four hours. The weird note, that had been one thing. Rachel dying, her EpiPen gone. Daniel dying, the closed lid of the hot tub. Could it really be the case that someone had followed them here, tracked all their previous transgressions, and planned to kill them for it?

Amira knew she was not to blame for the loss of Liam. Ultimately the people who were supposed to care for him had caused his death. Yes, she could have done more – taken him into care, placed him with a foster family, got a court injunction – but only in the most technical sense. She was under pressure to keep children with their families, and some of the foster carers were barely better than the parents, doing it only for the cash, shouting at toddlers when they cried or made a mess. It made her heart hurt to see it, but what could she do? She had a hundred other cases. No one could have known Liam's stepfather would choose that day to throw him down the stairs and fracture his little skull.

Poor baby. Tears came to her eyes, partly at the memory, partly at the salt water and wind whipping around her so she could barely see. Where was Paddy? Why couldn't he have waited for her? She remembered the days when he had always matched her pace as they walked, holding out his hand to carry her bag, jogging in slow circles so they could talk on runs, even when he was twice as fast as her. Now he had basically abandoned her on the high seas. When had this rot set into him? After the school-trip death? But no, it had happened before that, hadn't it? After he'd been barred

153

from the law, because he was technically a bankrupt, something that had plagued them ever since. It was why they had such a small flat, because only Amira's salary could go on the mortgage. It was why he'd had to choose a career he had never really wanted, had no vocation for, because he couldn't work in most industries that made serious money. And whose fault was that?

Daniel's. Daniel, who had persuaded Paddy to come on board with the company he was starting out of uni, promised such great returns on Paddy's inheritance, then lost it all through his own hubris and recklessness. And why had Paddy been so stupid as to give Daniel his inheritance? Vicky, most likely. He would have wanted to impress her, show her he could make as much money as her then-fiancé. Maybe he'd even hoped to win her for himself.

Was it possible – could it really be possible – that Paddy had killed Daniel? Her upright, law-abiding, sometimes annoyingly self-righteous husband? She just couldn't see it. But he certainly had motive, and if she could recognise that then so could the police. He'd certainly been out of her sight for several hours after breakfast – plenty of opportunity. And then there was the radio, hidden in his bag, which she was putting off asking him about. That gave her a precipitous drop in her stomach. Of course, Paddy could have no reason to kill Rachel, who he'd only just met. Using all the hot water, while annoying, was not a murdering offence. Maybe her death had simply been an accident. Maybe Paddy had found the radio and hidden it from the others, in case someone else destroyed it. But if so, why hadn't he told her?

It was such a mess. But there was still hope. She might be pregnant, she hadn't bled yet, and if she was, that changed everything. Paddy would return to her, be his old loving self. All she could do was try to survive, find Jonathan, keep her husband out of prison, and get off this bloody island. Bury Rachel and Daniel, deal with the fallout.

Rounding the corner of the island was difficult, and she dropped to sit on the board, feet trailing in the freezing water. The current was so strong she could hardly keep the board's nose steady. Paddy was barely visible, an upright figure in the mizzle. How was he staying up? To her knowledge he had never done this before, but now he was sporty, skilled, muscled, disciplined. A cyclist, almost a teetotaller. He wasn't the man she'd married, who got breathless climbing the stairs with their nightly mugs of Ovaltine, a selection of chocolate bars tucked into his hoody pocket. He was a stranger.

'I've found the caves.' She could barely hear his voice, snatched by the wind.

'What?'

'Just come here, will you?'

Impatience. Heart sinking, she paddled desperately on, straining against the pull of the water.

'I'm doing my best!' She realised she was crying. What a disaster. An absolute miserable failure.

Finally, she turned the corner and saw the west coast of the island. Paddy had taken his board over to the rocks and pulled it up, and was carefully disembarking on to the black, spiky shore. 'What are you doing?' she shouted. That was madness. He'd be stranded on a metre of inhospitable rock, which would vanish when the tide rose.

'I think I can get up to the caves. Check if anyone's hiding there.'

'But that's crazy!' She looked up at the sheer rock face. 'Anyway, we're meant to be searching for Jonathan.'

'Look, the old path is still partly there. Lou might need help if she manages to climb down.'

Privately, Amira could not imagine Louise ever needing help with anything. 'What about me?' she burst out. 'I need you too.'

Paddy's face was coated in rain, his hair slicked to his forehead. 'Come on, Amira, don't be pathetic. You can survive on your own for ten minutes.'

It all boiled up in her then. The weekend, every time Vicky had touched his arm or they'd laughed together over an old memory. The fact he hadn't even noticed she wasn't drinking, hadn't even considered she might think she was pregnant. The fact that she never was, while Vicky had those two rosy-cheeked cherubs. A boy *and* a girl! Spoiled. Even if Vicky had just lost her husband, it was the first bad thing that had ever happened to her. The way he hadn't asked her once if she was OK, when two people had just been killed, when there was likely a murderer out here with them.

'Fine then!' she screamed, into the wind. 'I'm not going with you.'

And without waiting to see if her husband fell to his death or not, she paddled furiously off, continuing around the island. Everything was falling apart. Maybe her marriage was over. Paddy could move on to someone else, someone not infertile, maybe even Vicky since she was now a tragic widow. Amira would be left on the scrapheap, a single forty-something making a huge deal of godchildren and outings to the theatre once a month. She'd have to get a cat or something.

She had known this weekend would be a trial, but this was the absolute worst day of her life. Worse than her failed IVF. Worse than hearing Liam was dead.

She had gone only a few metres when she saw the old rowboat. For a moment her mind couldn't process what she was seeing, but then she realised it was upside down. Capsized. Fearful, she began to paddle hard against the current.

'Jonathan. Jonathan!'

Pete

2022

'I'm sorry, Jay. We just can't do it today. Forecast is for gale-force winds.'

Jonathan exhaled deeply, making a growling sound in his throat. Pete saw the producer, a twenty-five-year-old named Arabella, quail at the sound. 'Well, what do you suggest we do? We're three days behind and going over budget by the minute.'

Arabella winced. 'I know, but it just isn't safe, yah? The network won't sign off on it.'

'Look, this is a survivalist show, right? And you're telling me we can't go up a mountain in a bit of weather? It's perfectly fine out.'

Jonathan indicated the scene out of the window of the B&B the crew had commandeered, all seventies bedspreads and tiny cakes of plastic-wrapped soap. Fort William was not a place you went to for the culture or nightlife, but the lake was tranquil and shining in a bolt of spring sun.

'Yah, but it's snowing on Ben Nevis.'

'We can hardly do survivalism in bright sunshine, now can we, Arabella?'

She looked miserable, fiddling with her clipboard. 'So what do you want me to do?'

Jonathan stood up from the table where he'd just finished a breakfast of charred bacon and hard eggs. 'I'll sort it, since you're clearly not capable. All I need is a cameraman and sound guy to come up with me. If everyone else is too afraid.'

'But – the network has said that—'

'Trust me, they'll be happy if we get the shots. This happens all the time.' It was the reason Jonathan was so successful, his shows so in-demand. He was a man who looked at limitations – his arm, for example – and overcame them. That was what people responded to, what inspired them. Jonathan signalled to Pete, who was finishing off his coffee at the next table. 'Pete, Sean, a word?'

Pete Anderson was one of the most respected camera operators in the business. He and Jonathan had been everywhere, from the Amazon jungle to a base camp in Antarctica. Sean Madden was younger, in his twenties, but getting a name for himself as the sound guy to use in bad weather. He was a genius at capturing dialogue even in the windiest or noisiest environments. His footage from behind Iguazu Falls had won him an award.

The two got up and followed Jonathan outside to the van, both of them rugged guys, rangy with muscle, decked out in snoods and carabiners and heavy canvas trousers.

'You two will come up with me, right? None of this nonsense about a bit of weather.'

Sean was laconic. 'Network sign it off?'

'You know what that lot are like. Soft Londoners, sat behind a desk. We can do it with the three of us, what do you think?'

They exchanged a look. Sean said, 'I go by insurance recommendations, Jonathan. They say it's OK I'll try.'

'Pete? I know you're up for anything, mate.'

He paused longer than he usually would. 'Miranda's in her seventh month now, you know. I promised her I'd be extra careful this time.'

'And I get that. I do get that. My missus was the same when we had Darcy. But the thing is, women, civilians, they don't always know how it is in the field, right? I bet you didn't tell her about the time with those loggers in Brazil.'

He hadn't. And what good TV it had made, running from the men with guns through the jungle, his body singing with adrenaline and energy. Pete nodded cautiously. 'I don't tell her all of it, no. But we don't wanna be stuck up there if it's blowing a gale.'

'Look, if I clear it with the insurance, you'll do it? I'll call them now.'

Pete shrugged. The insurance wouldn't let them do anything unsafe. 'Sure. Not afraid, just being sensible.'

'That's great. I totally support that, mate, but we do have a job to do, end of the day. Give me a minute.'

Jonathan took his phone to the opposite side of the car park, and Pete watched him talk into it, walking up and down. After a few moments he gave them the thumbs-up. Pete nodded. It was probably for the best. If they didn't get the footage today, they'd be into weekend hours, and that would push them over budget. Being over budget was the excuse the network needed to cancel the show, and that was the jobs of hundreds of people. Pete glanced up at the mountain, lit by sunshine, a white cap of snow at the top. How bad could it be, really? They'd be up and down in a few hours, film in the can, drinking beers in the pub and relaxing.

Five minutes later they were in the van and driving to the car park at Ben Nevis. No cable car or café here like on Aonach Mòr. Just the mountain.

The snow set in as they were halfway up the north face, lugging cameras and sound equipment. 'We should try to film, Jay,' said Pete, watching the sky, yelling over the wind that had picked up. 'The light's gonna go.'

'Just a bit further. It'll look better from the next lookout.'

Jonathan prided himself that nothing on the show was faked. But in reality, there was always a crew behind the camera, with food and coats and sunscreen at the ready. This was intense for him, a bitter shower of hail that felt like pebbles on your face, howling wind, biting cold. It was hard to believe that just an hour away downhill, the team were out in light jackets. Such was the Scottish weather system. It would pass. What was the thing he said on the show? It had even started cropping up on T-shirts and mugs. *There's no such thing as bad weather, just the wrong clothes.*

After a few more minutes, Sean spoke up. His voice was high and nervous, reminding Pete how young he was. 'Eh, boss, I do think maybe we should stop. We won't get any sound in this anyway.'

Jonathan sighed inside his hood. 'Alright. We'll hunker down and wait.'

They found a boulder and tucked in beneath it, as the snow and wind swirled around them. Hellish, but Pete had always loved it – the wildness, the freshness of salt and peat. Like the finest whisky. He'd never been afraid before, but somehow the thought of that baby coming, of his wife at home, had spooked him, and he was seeing danger everywhere.

After a few long minutes, the wind died down, as it always did. Jonathan shouted, 'Let's try and get some shots, Pete? Show how bad it is up here. People always like that.'

'Hmm, OK.'

'Why don't you go up there – film me from above? I'll look great.'

Pete looked doubtfully up the mountain, barely visible in the white-out. But this was his job. He took his smaller camera and trekked up as best he could, the wind like a giant hand pushing him down.

Pete took a few steps back, holding his camera. It would look good, Jonathan battling with the elements. Jonathan motioned him to get a wider angle, show how high they were. Pete stepped back again. Held up his camera to frame the shot. Then suddenly the ground was no longer there, and the world vanished, and everything was white, and so cold, and he couldn't breathe, and that was all he knew.

Vicky

She and Fiona had watched as Amira struggled to control the paddleboard in the choppy waves. Paddy had gone on ahead, pushing out to sea.

'She'll never stay up,' said Fiona. 'It's too rough.'

Trying to sound hopeful, Vicky said, 'Maybe Jay capsized or something – he could be treading water out there. We need to at least look for him. Or maybe he made it over to Tarne.'

It was strange now, talking to Fiona, her best friend, about her twin brother. He had become a shadow between them. Someone who would cheat, and leave his wife and daughter for an influencer twelve years younger who didn't believe in 'Western medicine'.

'If anyone can, he can. He's strong, he'll know how to stay safe.'

'You speak so kindly of him still,' marvelled Vicky. 'Fi, you're a class act. I'm sorry if I didn't say that before.'

Fiona looked out to sea, her dark hair whipping round her face. 'Huh. I wasn't at first. When I found the messages between them and looked at her profile. She was so young. So . . . thin.'

'But you came for a weekend with her!'

'Well, what's the point in being bitter? It's not good for Darcy to hate her father. And maybe – well, it wouldn't have lasted, I don't think. Rachel was . . . I hate to speak ill, but she wasn't a very serious person. And Jay might think he likes that glitz and glamour, the social media and the admiration, but deep down he isn't like that. Before he got famous, he was so steady. Held us all together in our mad Oxford bubble, didn't he. Grounded us.'

She still loves him, Vicky realised, in a sad moment of clarity. Was it too much to hope? They were so good together, swapping jokes, caring for Darcy above all else, sharing so many interests. Whereas Rachel – well, the woman was dead, but she had ruined the party long before that. Vicky suddenly saw it. 'You're very shrewd.'

'What do you mean?'

'Well. If she comes here, and you're all kind and welcoming, and she's whiny and self-centred – the contrast is pretty clear.'

Fiona gave a rueful laugh in her throat. 'That obvious, was it?'

'Not at all. I only just twigged. God, you always were three steps ahead of the rest of us.'

'It was working, too. Last night we had kind of a – well, a nice moment. Just before bed. But it backfired, didn't it. She's only bloody gone and died. I'm glad I wasn't a bitch to her, at least not openly. Because everyone seems perfect in death.'

Vicky took her friend's arm, warm and solid. 'He'll get over it. Honestly, I think she was starting to grate.'

'But she's dead, Vic. How do you get over something like that? Christ, what a mess. And Daniel. I'm so sorry. I just can't believe it, really.'

'Neither can I.'

'You managed to hide it pretty well too. The bitterness.'

Vicky shot her sister-in-law a sideways glance. 'What . . . ?'

'Oh, I guessed. He's all friendly with the young pretty nanny, then one day she's gone with no replacement? Oldest story in the book. And I bet she wasn't the first. Honestly, what a cliché.'

Vicky let out a deep sigh. 'I really liked Cody too. Poor girl, I think she felt coerced. She was in bits, I couldn't even be angry at her.' The burn of rage rose up in her throat. Daniel, aged forty, hitting on – sleeping with – twenty-one-year-old Cody, his children's nanny, a bright bubbly Australian who they'd all loved. Leaving her so broken, so guilty, weeping till her eyes were red. Such a fucking stereotype. 'It's strange being angry with someone who just died. I honestly don't know what to do with it. It won't sink in.' She was still rehearsing all the things she would say to Daniel when she next saw him.

Fiona walked on a few more steps towards the hill. 'Vic. Have you thought about what you'll tell the police? Eventually we're going to have to explain all this.'

Vicky could hardly think that far ahead. Being rescued seemed an impossible dream. 'What do you mean?'

'Think about it. Rachel dies, and she's my husband's new girlfriend, who he left me for, paraded in front of me. And you – Daniel's been cheating on you with your nanny. And he's the reason you lost your island in the first place. Right?'

She hadn't wanted to think about that either. Had long ago pushed down the anger and resentment, the memory of her father's expression as he'd passed her the papers to sign, the ones that transferred the island to some American buyer. Her island, her birthright and inheritance. And it would have been hers alone, because her father had already made it over to her. Not Jonathan. Why – Vicky had never wanted to dwell on too closely. Their father had made some strange decisions in his time, but she was getting an island out of it, one she had always loved. Jonathan had never known – would not have needed to find out until one of their parents died. And now it was gone anyway, because Daniel had been arrogant, and refused to listen to advice, and invalidated the company's insurance. And the horror of the child's death! She'd been haunted by it all through her own pregnancy, and it was one reason she'd never left the twins alone until after the accident, could hardly even sleep when they were small. How stupid she'd been to come back here. It was tainted now, with the dark legacy of what Daniel had done. 'You don't think they'll suspect me?'

'Always the husband or wife, isn't it. And you had plenty of motive.'

'Not to kill!'

'I know you didn't. But it looks bad. Did you ever talk to him about it? The lawsuit – the death?'

'I – honestly, I try to never think about it. It was so awful.' The worst thing being that Daniel, her husband, who she'd pledged her life to, had refused to take any responsibility for it. When she'd had the twins and held them in her arms, two squirming, healthy, living bundles, all she could think about was that baby. Lola. Eight months old. The agony of her mother at the press conference they'd shown on the news. Yet somehow it had all been hushed up, Daniel's name kept out of it for the most part. He had been declared bankrupt, her father's extremely good lawyers had got the Carlisle family to settle rather than pursue criminal charges, and six months later Daniel had a new job. He was barred from being a company director ever again, but he was doing very nicely, earning high six figures a year, and she was pretty sure he never even thought about baby Lola.

Then, of course, she'd hit a cyclist because she was so tired, because she couldn't bear to leave her children with someone else, and she'd lost all the moral high ground of staying with him, defending him. Agreeing that the baby's death was also a terrible accident, when she didn't think that at all. If you'd been careless and selfish and arrogant, and someone died, then maybe you were as good as a murderer.

'Paddy's never forgiven him, has he,' said Fiona. 'For losing all his money too.'

'You don't think he . . .'

Fiona shrugged against the wind, out of breath from just the small slope of the beach. She really was unfit. 'It seems crazy. Paddy's so straight. But – someone killed Daniel.'

'You don't think it was an accident?' Vicky was still clinging to this hope, despite all evidence otherwise.

'Unless he was absolutely hammered, and he fell in and couldn't get back out. But someone must have put that lid on. Then there's the note of course.'

Fiona shivered. 'God, I hope they find Jay. It's just you and me on dry land right now. Although, where the hell is Lou?'

Just then Louise appeared on the brow of the hill, a coil of rope over her shoulder. Eight adults, two dead, one missing, two setting out on uncertain seas. They seemed to be dropping like flies.

'I'd better go and spot her,' Vicky said. 'You'll stay with the kids?'

'Of course. I don't think the twins know what's happening, luckily.'

Vicky caught up with Louise as she turned to the west coast of the island, while Fiona made for the house. Louise strode forward in her heavy boots, and Vicky realised she felt comforted by her presence, as she would be by a man's. God, she really was a terrible feminist.

'I wish Jay were back,' she said, uneasily.

'Mmm. Maybe he made it all the way over.'

Wouldn't someone have come by now then? Wouldn't they have heard the *thwick* of helicopter blades or the roar of a boat engine, coming to rescue them?

'I just don't get all this. I mean, yes, most of us have some connection to a death. All of them were accidents. You didn't even cause yours, it was just a shift change, right?'

Louise sighed. 'That's not true, Vic. I switched the rota because I wanted to spend the day with Jennifer.'

'Jennifer?'

'My – a woman I was . . . involved with.'

Vicky blinked. Louise had never addressed this with her directly, the matter of her sexuality. The rules seemed to have shifted on this trip, as if the ground were moving under her feet. 'Oh. I didn't realise . . .'

Louise rolled her eyes slightly. 'Oh, come on, Vic. You knew. If anyone knew, you did.'

No, no, this couldn't all come out now. She stammered, 'I—'

Louise snorted. 'Oh, don't worry, your secret's safe. That one, anyway. I've kept it all these years, I won't tell now.' She looked over her shoulder. 'My point is, we're all guilty in some way. Some more than others. It was over there, wasn't it. Off the beach. Where it happened. The boat.'

Vicky flinched. 'Look, we can't keep dragging up everything that's ever happened in the past. It's not helpful.'

Louise said nothing. Then, 'The past isn't past for everyone, Vicky. And someone died that day too. Didn't they?'

She'd been doing her best not to think about that. 'Stop it, Lou.'

'Vic. You know what I'm talking about. I can't believe no one has even mentioned it yet. Don't you think it's kind of a coincidence, that we're back here and this is happening?'

'It was an accident. All of these things are accidents!'

'Daniel? He was only lucky not to be held criminally liable for that baby's death. Now he's dead.'

Vicky was trembling. 'Look, can we not? My husband's just died. And my kids might be in danger.'

Another brief pause. When she spoke again, Louise's voice was softer. 'I know you cared for him. But he hurt you. Didn't he?' She placed her free hand on Vicky's arm, and Vicky shied away, remembering other things. So many memories, rising up from the depth like sea monsters. She couldn't bear it. 'Even that stupid game – which paper was his, do you think?'

'The threesome one, I guess. You remember he always boasted about that.'

'Oh yeah.' Louise's mouth twisted. 'Thing is, I'm pretty sure that never happened. Susie Philips told me he actually passed out that night. She and what's her name – Gina? – they just carried on without him. Susie's married to a woman now. Her and me had a little thing, second year. Before I . . . left. So, that was Daniel's lie, I'd say.'

This was too much to take in right now. 'Let's just try and get into the caves.'

Soon, they had reached the west cliffs. There had once been a path along the side, but it was now so eroded you could barely put a foot down. There were three caves in the side of the cliff, the lowest washed by the sea, but the others big enough to hide a person. What would they do if they found someone there? She hadn't thought that far ahead. Down below, the sea slapped the rocks. 'Just be careful.'

'You ever been in these?' Louise was tying the rope to the base of a sturdy bush.

'A few times. The path used to be safer, so Jay and I would climb down and have picnics, play smugglers. We had to stop when a giant chunk of the cliff fell into the sea, and Mum said we weren't allowed.'

She wondered what her mother would say about all this, pictured her in the house in Holland Park, on her way back from Pilates perhaps, with a mat slung over her bony shoulder, or at the hairdressers' getting her ash-blonde hair tinted. Something like, *Oh Victoria, how could you let this happen? And on your birthday?* Or her father, looking disapprovingly from behind his newspaper.

He'd barely spoken to her since they lost the island. It wasn't *fair*. None of this was her fault.

Louise had now tied the other end of the rope around her waist, and was advancing towards the edge of the cliff.

'You're just going over?'

'It's safe enough with the rope. The path should hold me, so this is just in case of rock fall.'

She was so brave, so sure of herself. Vicky remembered how much she had been drawn to that at university, though everyone had always been surprised they were friends – polished law student Vicky, and carabiners-and-cargo-shorts geographer Louise. Lezzie Louise, as she had imaginatively been nicknamed, not that she'd ever come out back then. Why would you, when it was still so homophobic?

'Be careful,' Vicky called again, as Louise scrambled down the head of the narrow path, her red hair soon disappearing. Vicky ran to the edge to watch, but vertigo soon pushed her back. She had a memory of university, going on an activity weekend somewhere in the Cotswolds, Louise's strong fingers helping her into the harness. She bit her lip – she couldn't think about that now. Her head was a mess.

'Anything?' she called.

No answer. She risked looking over – no sign of Louise. She must have already gone into the first cave. Vicky could remember little about it, a damp and unpleasant space full of seabird droppings. She'd been afraid of getting bats in her hair and Jonathan had made fun of her.

Oh Jonathan, where are you? Fear was choking her.

'I can't see really,' came a muffled voice. 'I'd better check the other one.' It was harder to get to, the path largely non-existent at that point. She watched Louise clamber down, intensely focused, holding on to rocky outcrops and tufts of springy grass. 'Damn. The rope doesn't stretch far enough. I'll just untie myself.'

'Are you sure?'

'Yeah. It's safe enough in the mouth of the cave here.' Vicky looked over but could only see the sheer cliff face and the drop to the dark, restless sea, dizzying. A good place to hide, since you couldn't be seen from the top. Quiet fell, the only noise the waves and the sad cry of birds soaring on air currents. From here she couldn't even see the house, tucked away behind the brow of the hill. She could make out the roof of the shed, on the north end of the island by the beach. The east coast held the jetty, but what about the south? They hadn't looked there yet. A large grassy area grazed by sheep, ending in a rocky beach, which they'd hardly ever used back in the day, since the sandy one was much nicer. There were no structures, nowhere to hide, unless something had been built that she didn't know about. After all, this wasn't her island any more.

Her mind turned it over for a few moments, before she realised she hadn't heard from Lou in a while. 'Louise? You OK?'

No answer. She shook the rope, which flopped freely, untied at the other end. The second cave was smaller than the first, as far as Vicky remembered. Where could she have gone?

'Louise? Lou?'

She called and called, but there was no response. She might have been totally alone up there.

Frightened, Vicky ran back up the hill towards the house. As she approached, huffing on the gravel path, she was relieved to see light in the windows, and smoke from the wood burner. As long as they could keep the children safe, the worst would not have happened.

'Look!' Fiona waved to her as she went into the warmth. 'I brought up some more wood for the fire, keep us cosy at least.' She seemed a bit brighter.

'Louise climbed down to the caves,' Vicky panted. 'But then she went quiet.'

'She didn't come up?'

'No. She untied herself to get inside and then – nothing.'

'She didn't fall?'

'I'd have heard. She just kind of . . . disappeared.'

'Maybe she got into the caves. They go far back, right?'

'Yeah. I suppose.'

They looked at each other, trying to hide their worry. 'And Jay hasn't come back either,' said Fiona. 'And Paddy and Amira out at sea. Maybe they'll all be back soon.'

Vicky bit her lip. Would Paddy, at five foot eight, be any protection against someone that wanted to kill them? And the thought of Louise crawling in the caves, deeper and deeper under the island, was horrifying too. Why couldn't she just have gone to a spa or something for her fortieth? She hadn't anticipated potholing and paddleboarding and getting drenched in freezing water.

And another thing. If it wasn't true that there was no way off the island – there were the paddleboards, and a boat – then the other two statements on the note must be true. That they had all killed someone, and that they would all kill or be killed here. Unnerved, she slipped out of her boots, needing to hold her children. Whatever happened, they would be alright, wouldn't they? But if she was attacked, the kids would be on their own. Leaving two five-year-olds alone on an island was as good as killing them anyway. She hoped to God Bobby Landford would come, or that Jonathan had made it to the mainland and someone would arrive to rescue them soon.

Darcy and the kids were huddled on the sofa, iPads out. Darcy looked up, fearful, as Vicky came over, but they were all safe and whole. Vicky pulled both children close, kissing their heads, but they leaned away, transfixed by the cartoons she'd downloaded for the trip, unable to bear the idea of entertaining them alone all weekend. She should have been grateful for every second spent with them. She stroked her niece's arm. 'Are you OK, darling?'

'I think so. Where's Louise?' said Darcy.

'Um, she – she's checking out the caves.'

'And Dad?'

'Amira and Paddy went to get him.' Vicky said it confidently, as if there could be no other outcome. 'They'll just go round the island and look for him and then they'll all be back. He can't have got far. Maybe he even made it to Tarne.'

Unless he'd gone all the way to the bottom of the sea, of course, but she couldn't think that. She had to stay hopeful for the children.

Mhairi

They followed the path around, skirting the island's edge and heading west, where the land sheered into steep cliffs. That was when she found the next piece of evidence to be documented – a snapped-off branch, and obvious damage to the nearby bushes and grass. Fibres tangled in the shrubs and on the ground.

'What do you think – there was something tied here? A rope?'

'Aye. Someone climbed down.'

'Then where's the rope?' Mhairi peered over as far as she dared. The ground nearby was churned up, as if the rope had dug into it. Or as if someone had fallen over. 'Look, I think I see it down there.' There was something coiled on the rocks, like a dead snake. A blue climbing rope. 'You think they went down there?' But why, unless a boat was waiting for them? And who had been left to untie it? She looked over again. 'Looks like there could be a cave?' She lay on her stomach to get a better look, trying to ignore the sheer drop and the sea raging below her.

'Aye, there's caves.' Arthur's voice came from behind her. 'All through this island.'

'You never said.'

'Didn't think anyone could get into them. You'd need climbing experience, and why would you? Nothing in there but bird shite and seaweed.'

But it could be a shelter, perhaps, if you were hiding from someone. She called over, 'Hello? Police, is anyone there?'

Her voice was quickly swallowed up by the wind and the waves. No answer, except from the birds that cawed to each other, hidden among every crevice and cranny of the cliff face. No sign of human life at all.

Arthur was above her on the bluff, silhouetted against the low winter sky. It would be dark soon, and she was no nearer to finding survivors. Assuming there were any. Mhairi stood up, brushing soil from her trousers. 'Nothing. Come on.'

The rope bothered her, though. If someone had used it to go down for a look, why had they not come back up the same way? And if the rope had fallen – or been detached by someone – then had they become trapped down there?

Heading on, they made their way round the island to the south beach, the stonier one. Arthur nodded ahead when they reached it. 'That's your other paddleboard there, I reckon.' And so it was. Pulled up on the shingle, as if someone had simply come ashore and hopped off, safe and sound. So where were they then?

Arthur made a sudden movement, the rustle of his coat startling her for a second. He was so quiet it was sometimes easy to believe she was out here alone.

'What?'

'There's something else on the shore there.'

She peered out where he was pointing, further along the beach, near the waves. Something was lying there alright. A huddled mass of some kind.

'We should check it out.'

He seemed to hesitate a second. 'Reckon we have to. Come on.'

They made their way, hopping over the rocks, huffing with effort. But when they reached the edge of the water, Mhairi was not at all prepared for what she saw.

Amira

The boat was drifting, half its hull under the water already. Sinking.

'Jonathan!' she shouted again. Hoping he could hear her over the wind. If he was still able to hear.

'Here!' A faint voice, croaky and weak.

She paddled round the boat and there he was, clinging to the side, treading water, hair soaked and plastered to his head. He had one child's life jacket over his bad arm for some help floating, and was holding on with the other hand, though the slimy barnacled wood gave little grip.

'Thank God, Ammy. I can't do this much longer. I lost the other life jacket.'

'What happened?' she called, trying to manoeuvre beside him. Could they both fit on her board? It was only a flimsy thing, light.

'There was a hole in the boat.'

'What, because it's old?'

'I don't know. It could have been drilled in there.'

A cold pit in her stomach. Someone had perhaps done this on purpose, left the boat there so it looked seaworthy but would gradually take on water and sink before you reached land. Someone who was trying to kill them, one by one.

'Why? Who would do that?' She thought of Paddy, examining the boat last night, and pushed it down. He wouldn't.

'I have no idea. Christ, this is just a nightmare. I keep thinking of Rachel, all alone and cold up there. I brought her here and now she's dead.'

'Daniel's dead too,' she blurted. 'I'm sorry. He was . . . in the hot tub.'

'*What?* You mean he fell in?'

'The lid was on. So it must have been – I don't know! I think someone is doing this.'

'Oh my God. This is a nightmare. Please, help me! My arm – it's seizing . . .' He cried out as the arm floating on the life jacket spasmed and flopped into the water. The small orange jacket drifted off, into the sea.

'I don't know if it will hold us both.'

'I'll paddle and you can lie down to stabilise it. Or you might have to swim behind, push it a bit.'

Amira looked doubtfully at the icy water around her. Even just her foot going in had sent cold needles through her body, making her gasp and swear. 'But I can't swim, Jonathan, you know that.'

'Well, not swim, just hold and kick then. Come on, Ammy! It's not far round to the south beach. I don't have the strength to do it. Please. Don't let me drown, Ammy!'

How could she say no to that? Having heard the litany of deaths they were all responsible for already, including her, according to someone unknown, who felt that her mistake with Liam – not even a mistake, a judgement that had proved wrong – condemned her to die on this island. 'Come on.'

He transferred his weight from the boat to the paddleboard, splashing hard as she braced down with her knees and arms, hoping it didn't turn over as well. Then they'd both be in the freezing water. She saw that he was shaking, as if hypothermia was already setting in, which it easily could be in a sea this cold. To get him on, Amira had to slide right to the back of the board, while he tried to hump himself up, like an ungainly seal. 'Bugger!' Jonathan had missed, slipped off into the water again. The paddleboard rocked, and Amira almost fell off herself, managing to brace with all the core strength she could muster. If only she did Pilates like Vicky.

'Be careful! Or we'll both be in.'

God, where was Paddy? Had he really climbed up a cliff face while she paddled out to sea by herself? This was insane. She had never really taken in how large Jonathan was. A tall, powerful man, heavily built. Trying to get on to a board that was only six feet long and already contained her. He tried again, slipped off again, and the board rocked. She fell to her stomach with a cry, managed to stay on. Her legs dipped into the water, and it was so cold that she gasped.

'I'm sorry, Jay, this isn't going to work! You should stay here, and I'll get help.' She could come back with Paddy's board, towing it behind her. Yes, that could work. And then go back for Paddy, or maybe he'd even found a way through the caves and would pop up somewhere else on the island. 'I'll get the other board!' She gestured round the island. Jonathan looked up at her, both arms on the board, treading water.

'What?'

'We can't both fit! I'll go and get Paddy's board and come back, OK? You just hang on.'

'No! I can't, I've been here for hours, it's so cold! And my arm isn't working! It's seized up. This happens when I'm cold. Please, Amira! I always liked you. Please don't leave me.'

But what could she do? If they wouldn't both fit she could stay with him, which would do no good as he'd still freeze and maybe so would she. Or she could give him her board, cling to the sinking boat, hope he came back for her. Did she believe that? Amira bit her lip, tasted salt and blood. Thought of her baby, her possible baby, growing more real to her every second. 'On your shows, I've seen you do harder—'

'The bloody shows are all faked!' he yelled. 'I always have a crew nearby with blankets and heaters. Did you think I filmed it all by myself, for God's sake?'

'No, I —'

'Let me on!' He splashed at the board, rocking it from side to side.

'*No*,' she hissed. 'No, this is the best way. Just stay here and I promise I—'

With a guttural cry, Jonathan heaved himself out of the water, putting all his weight on his working arm.

'No. NO!' He was going to tip her off. Tip her off and steal the board. Jay, who'd always been so kind to her.

But he'd done this before, hadn't he? He'd perhaps killed his cameraman. She knew what Jonathan was like – obsessive, driven, determined to let nothing hold him back. It was quite possible he'd sent his crew into a dangerous situation. So who was to say he wouldn't leave her to die as well? After all, she wasn't his sister or daughter or ex-wife or even a close friend. She was expendable. And Amira was tired of being expendable.

She didn't even think about it. She rammed the paddle hard into his fingers where they gripped the board, hearing him shriek as it broke flesh. And before she could reach out to steady him, he had sunk, wide-eyed, below the waves, swallowed up by the depths. Jonathan was gone.

Amira froze for a second. She could hear water striking the board, and the sides of the floundering boat, which had sunk even lower since she'd been there. She could hear the cry of the gulls and the moan of the wind. She could feel her clothes clinging to her, wet and cold, her hands raw from the rough surface of the board, her own heart pounding in her chest. She sucked in a breath of damp air. She was still on the board. She was stable, she was alive. She could save herself. She looked into the water where Jonathan had vanished, dipped the paddle in, wondering if he might grab on to it like in *Jaws*. Nothing. Just silence. Her mind blank and ringing, Amira began to steer off, round to the rocky south beach.

Tomasz

2019

He'd been having a good week up until then. His boss had all but promised him a promotion soon, with an increase of £200 a month in pay. He'd set a personal best at the gym that morning running on the treadmill, which boded well for his entry to the London Marathon in April. And he was seeing his new girlfriend, Lucy, that night, for tapas near her flat, then the night in her cosy double bed, then brunch in the morning since it would be Saturday. British girls were all so enthusiastic about brunch, it was funny.

Coming out of his small but clean flat, he unlocked his bike and clipped on his bike lights, as the morning was gloomy. He put on his helmet and reflective tabard and mounted his bike. As he set off towards work, he had that familiar surge of glee, the same feeling as being a little boy in Warsaw and zooming down a big hill near his house. Like flying, like freedom. He was determined to get Lucy cycling, though she said she was too scared. He'd get her a second-hand bike for her birthday, if they were still together then, and he hoped they would be.

Tomasz was a careful cyclist. He followed the flow, he stopped at lights and never ran them, he gave vehicles a wide berth. In this part of London, you had to watch out for those enormous

Jeep-style cars, usually driven by very tiny women who could hardly see you through their tinted windows.

He had done everything right. He had been so careful, taken so many precautions, looked both ways before moving. But all the same, he stopped at a light, and when it turned green again, a beautiful emerald shade reflected on the wet road, he had just kicked off when one of those large cars went past him, too close, and clipped him, pushed him into the incoming traffic.

Tomasz spun off his bike, bracing for impact. Hit, skidded over the wet road, stopped. On the ground, he assessed himself. Skinned hands, sore knees, hopefully nothing too bad. But before he could push himself up, the rainwater soaking through his waterproofs, another car had come, and it was not able to stop in time before it went right over him, and in that instant Tomasz's mind, with all its thoughts of Lucy and dinner and the future and the present moment, was silenced forever.

Vicky

Darkness fell early in Scotland in winter, and the sky was already dull, with no sign of Paddy, Amira, Louise, or Jonathan. All the same, the house was comforting, glowing with light and warmth from the wood burner. She had even opened the fridge and stared inside. The twins had eaten pizza earlier, but they'd be getting hungry again soon and there was no evening meal planned. Daniel was supposed to be sorting that. But then maybe the chef would turn up in the next hour or so and they would be saved. The fridge held the remnants of her birthday cake, but Rachel had died after eating that, so Vicky couldn't bring herself to have any. In the meantime, she plied the kids with some of the organic snacks she'd brought over, which they declared 'yucky'. The two of them ran about, playing, fighting, causing a mess, while Darcy sat on the sofa with her big pink earphones, not that she could be finding anything to watch on her phone without Wi-Fi.

Was this how life would be now? On her own with the kids, forever? She'd have to hire a new nanny. At least she wouldn't have to worry that Daniel would sleep with them. She silenced the thought, shockingly disloyal when her husband lay dead in the outhouse next door. But it was true, wasn't it? She'd have to go back to work also, though that was no bad thing. And there'd be a big life insurance settlement – she remembered signing the papers when Daniel got his current job. They could stay in the house at least, and in time the twins would likely get over the loss, since they were only five and barely saw their father anyway most days. And what about her? Would she ever be able to move on? She'd been with Daniel since she was nineteen, and that brief window where life might have held other prospects, other paths, had seemed long shut. But maybe.

She turned to Fiona, who was wiping furiously at the already clean counters, keeping her voice low. 'What was that thing Darcy said earlier? About the girl at school who died?'

Fiona sighed. 'That was a bad business. But honestly, teen suicide has rocketed since social media got its hooks into them. Darcy might think she had a significant conversation with the girl right before she did it, but it's never just one thing that pushes a person over the edge. It's more – a small accumulation. Like a pile of tiny pebbles you add to every day, then one day it breaks the roof.'

'Could someone blame her for it, conceivably?'

Fiona scowled, swiping at the counters. 'She's a kid! Anyway, I still think the note is just some nasty game.'

'You don't think someone's out here with us?'

'How could they be? I think one of us has been doing it.'

'But – who?' And did that mean they had taken the EpiPen, put the lid on the hot tub? Stolen the radio?

'Paddy, maybe? He was absolutely furious with Daniel, probably even more so now he'd been cheating on you.'

Vicky winced. 'How would Paddy know about that?' She hadn't told anyone. She'd been too ashamed.

'Oh, Daniel talks. You know that. *In vino veritas*. And the three of them have those boys' nights sometimes, steak and whisky and all that crap.' Although Paddy seemed to have quit meat and alcohol too, so maybe not recently.

'But Rachel? What possible motive would he have for that – he's never even met her before!'

'Maybe that was an accident. Or have you thought about Louise as a suspect? She's always had a ruthless streak, hasn't she?'

'But what would her motive be? She's our friend!'

'We've not seen her in years, Vic. The life she's been living machete attacks in the bush, for goodness' sake, cholera outbreaks – it's not the same as ours. We don't know her any more. Plus she never liked Daniel, did she? Wanted you all to herself.'

Vicky's head flicked round at the tone. Did Fiona know what had happened that night more than twenty years ago, the night before the accident? No one should know. She'd lived in fear for years, that Louise would talk, that someone would guess based on how they acted round each other. Louise leaving like that, dropping out of college before finals. 'I don't know. She wasn't his biggest fan, I suppose.' Who was? Even Jonathan had never quite forgiven Daniel for the loss of the island. 'But again, Rachel. She'd never met her before.'

'I think that was an accident, Vic. Honestly. A serious sesame allergy is so dangerous. I've lost patients to it before.'

'But her pen. She couldn't find it.'

'Look, there's any number of explanations for that. Someone moved it by mistake, or it was there after all and she just couldn't find it in her panic. We never actually checked, did we? Anyway, there's Bobby Landford due to come soon. We just need to stay safe until then, and watch carefully for the boat. What about the others?'

Vicky sighed. 'I have no idea where Jay is. Amira, Paddy . . . I don't know their agenda. Lou – I can't imagine her hurting any-one, but like you said it's been a long time. I don't trust anyone but you and the kids, to be honest. We have to take care of them now. Right?'

Fiona glanced around. 'Where are they?'

Vicky looked for the twins, didn't see them, then turned to find Darcy shepherding them both out of Louise's small room off the hallway. 'Oh, sorry, Darce. I didn't even see them go in there.' They were impossible to watch at this age, twin dynamos determined to destroy everything in their path. 'Did they make a mess?'

Darcy's face was stricken.

'What's wrong, love?' said Fiona, concerned.

'Mum, Aunty Vic, the twins got all into Louise's stuff, so I was just tidying up and I found – well. I found something.'

With shaking hands, she held out a sheaf of papers, folded neatly. News clippings, print-outs, one or two from magazines. Vicky grabbed for them, spread them on the table. There was the name that rarely left her mind. Tomasz Kazinsky. *Cyclist killed by dangerous driver.* Her own death. And there was Daniel's also. *Company goes into receivership after product-related death.* She leafed faster and faster, catching only names and phrases. *Mother dies of missed cancer* – that was Fiona's patient. *School trip tragedy* – Paddy. *Tragic tot found dead* – Amira's little boy, that must be. *Questions raised around cameraman's fatal fall.* That was Jonathan's colleague. And look, *Aid worker slain*, that was Louise's story. *Influencer linked to surgery death*, that was Rachel. All of them, all eight of them. Someone had tracked these stories down, printed them, brought them here. Someone who really did think they were all killers, and that they should be punished for it.

Numbly, she looked at her niece. 'It's OK, darling, it's just, I don't know, a bad joke, a game for the adults, and—'

Darcy gave a sob, then reached into her jeans pocket and took out a folded piece of paper. 'That's not true, is it?'

It was a news story about the inquest into a girl's suicide, asking whether bullying on- and offline had contributed to it. A mention that one factor was 'rejection by a school friend whose help Kira sought in her last hours', and who was referred to by name in her suicide note. 'This story, it's the girl at my school. And the school friend – that's me. She put me in her note. So that means – they included me as well. In the game. They meant that I killed someone too, and so . . .'

Darcy didn't need to finish. She meant that, even at just fifteen, she was included in this sick game of revenge.

Vicky sat staring at the clippings, absorbing the horrors she'd known and the ones she hadn't. She couldn't believe it. Jonathan had been responsible for his cameraman's death, morally if not legally, and he'd never even told her. She had met Pete several times, a nice quiet guy with a dazzling talent, and remembered commiserating with Jonathan on his friend's loss. Now she found he had actually caused it, by lying that the insurance company had authorised the trip up the mountain in terrible weather. It was only a small story from the internet, so it must have been kept out of the wider press. Likely Jonathan, or the TV company, had paid a PR agency to hush things up. Vicky knew her brother. His way of getting people to do what he wanted, even if it included lying. After all, it wasn't the first time a person had died because he'd persuaded them to do something they knew wasn't safe. Was it?

Then there was Rachel's story.

INFLUENCER LINKED TO SURGERY DEATH

Rachel Solenado, 28, best known as 'Rachy Rach' to her vast collection of followers on TikTok and Instagram, has been linked to the tragic death of a beauty tourist in Turkey. Melissa Hunt, 19, had travelled to a plastic surgery clinic in Turkey to undergo weight-loss surgery as well as a bottom lift, which Solenado had promoted on her channels. She even offered a 10% discount to followers who used the clinic, which has now been shut down after a string of safety failures.

Melissa failed to wake up after her surgery, prompting mum Colette to fly out to find out why her daughter hadn't got in touch, after phone calls to the clinic went unanswered. But Colette says staff ignored her plight. 'They couldn't understand anything we asked them. The room was dirty and her dressings weren't being changed enough. I pleaded and pleaded but they just did nothing. She just never came round from whatever it was they gave her.'

After three days in a coma, Melissa suffered a cardiac arrest and died of what was later determined to be sepsis, caused by poor wound hygiene procedures. Because of disclaimers Melissa signed, the Hunt family received no compensation and no assistance in repatriating their daughter's body. 'It cost us thousands,' says a tearful Colette. 'We reached out to Rachel for help, since she made a bomb off that advertising deal, but she never even responded.'

So Rachel's stupid little videos had led someone to their death. But could that really be said to be her fault? Vicky pushed the article over to Fiona, who was also reading the clippings, wordless.

Darcy paced in the kitchen, clutching her elbows anxiously. The twins, seemingly oblivious to what they'd unleashed, were back on the sofa, iPads beeping with some infernal game.

'Would you blame Rachel for that?' she asked Fiona.

'No. It's irresponsible, but she was hardly giving medical advice. Just being greedy. Really, who would take medical advice off social media in any case?'

'But someone did blame her, if this article's here.'

Fiona glanced at her. Vicky could see her friend was looking her age, silver strands in her dark hair, lines around her eyes. Maybe Vicky looked old too. Forty had hit and it was all downhill from there. 'I still think it's just a coincidence.'

'Mum, it can't be!' said Darcy. 'Hello – the notes, and Rachel's dead, and Uncle Dan is . . .' She gulped down tears.

Vicky looked through the rest, a litany of guilt: Daniel's laziness and greed, her own carelessness, Louise's selfish choice, Darcy's cruelty. And her brother's horrible error, his arrogance thinking he could take on the mountain and win. Wasn't that him all over? Yes, it was inspiring that he battled against the odds, but sometimes he trampled on other people to do it.

Like Fergus.

She swallowed hard. She hadn't thought of Fergus in years, had done her best not to. Even coming across yesterday her mind had simply skipped over the memories of that day, as if it was nothing to do with her. But it was the same boat, wasn't it? The one Jonathan had taken out. Of course it was.

Fiona was still going through the clippings, frowning now. 'There's another one.'

'What?'

She snatched it up. She had missed it, adhering through static to the back of another page. It was printed off Facebook, a death announcement. Posted by someone called Julia Casey.

RIP to the best Mum ever. Elizabeth Mary Dennings caught Covid last week and went rapidly downhill. She was put on a ventilator and the staff really did their best but she never woke up. We weren't allowed in to say goodbye, so the nurse held up a phone and we told her we loved her. It breaks my heart to think of her dying alone but this is the reality of 2020. PLEASE PLEASE PLEASE do not take your kids out if they have symptoms, they may be fine but it could kill a vulnerable person! I'll never know for sure but there were definitely people coughing and sniffling at Andrew's party and Mum got sick after that.

Underneath, the comments offered sympathy, condemned people for their selfishness. The date of the post was from November of that year. The name Julia Casey was familiar. She peered at the tiny profile picture. Yes. Her stomach turned over.

'I think I know her,' said Vicky. 'Her kid's at school with the twins.' Andrew. Timid little boy. She dimly remembered now that Julia's mum had died of Covid in the middle of the pandemic, a fit and healthy sixty-two. Hadn't she actually met the mum in fact? That was right. Andrew's third birthday. The twins had gone, held in the garden during the brief window where such things were allowed, between lockdowns. She remembered a kindly grey-haired woman taking the twins by the hands when she dropped them off. *What poppets. Hello, I'm Julia's mum.* And hadn't Vicky felt a little jealous, because her own mother would never deign to even visit her at home, let alone help with a children's party? She had never really forgiven Daniel, or Vicky, for the island.

Vicky was trying to piece the timeline together. She'd been dimly aware that Julia's mother had died, but she'd been really busy because – yes, that was right. 'The twins had Covid too,' she said slowly. 'Just – well, just after that.' They'd had symptoms that day in fact, sniffles and a slight temperature, but she'd let them go to the party anyway. Just for a break. Reasoning that it was outside, and they were little kids so they'd hardly get ill even if they did catch something. Then Vicky herself had got it, and by the time they'd all recovered Elizabeth had been buried and she'd scarcely remembered to send Julia a card. But did that mean that Elizabeth had caught it—

Vicky felt all the blood drain from her body, as if replaced by the cold, churning sea outside. 'Oh God. Oh my God.'

'What?' said Fiona.

'This woman – I think maybe the twins gave her Covid, and she died. Or that someone's saying they did. I mean, how could you ever prove a thing like that, it could have been anyone . . . But that means . . .'

She looked over at her children. 'Fiona, I think – they're part of this. That this means they killed someone too.' She turned to her niece suddenly. 'Darcy, where exactly did you find these? You said in Louise's room?' Darcy looked between her mother and her aunt. 'You won't get in trouble,' said Vicky impatiently. 'I just need to know where.'

'They were in her bag,' said Darcy nervously. 'I saw them sticking out after the twins made a mess, and I – well, I wondered.'

Vicky felt as if she'd been hit by a wave. Not Lou! The one person she'd always known adored her, would never betray her, who had never breathed a word of their secret to anyone.

But.

Fiona was saying, 'I mean, it makes sense, Vic. She hates us. The look she gave me when I opened champagne at breakfast. She sees us all as out-of-touch elitists, and if she thinks we killed people too . . . You know her dad was hit by a careless driver also, and he died. Louise was only thirteen.'

'Oh my God,' whispered Vicky. 'I'd forgotten all about that.' Because Louise never talked about it, never looked for pity. But wouldn't she want revenge on someone who'd killed a man in the same way?

'And she loathes Daniel, always has. Me, she can take or leave, I guess.'

'Paddy? They were always close.'

'And he's fine. Think about who's dead.'

Vicky couldn't take it in. 'Rachel? She didn't know her.'

Fiona shrugged. 'Camouflage. Revenge against the shallow world of social media, telling everyone to spend money they can't afford on plastic surgery and designer labels. Or like I keep saying, an accident.'

God, it made sense. 'And Louise has gone missing. She's disappeared!'

Vicky had been worried something had happened to her. But what if it was the opposite – she'd hidden so she could pop up later and harm them all?

In her horror, Vicky had almost forgotten her niece was there, until Darcy gave a strangled sob. 'But I like Louise. Why would she want to hurt me? Or the twins? They're only little.'

Fiona put her arm around her daughter. 'Come on now. We don't know anything for sure. This might all be . . . a misunderstanding.'

'Then where's Dad, Mum? Why haven't they found him yet?'

'Maybe they have, love. It can take a while to paddle back, you know that.'

'I've been watching out the window! There's no sign of anyone on the sea. I'm frightened, Mum.'

Oh God. Her world was spinning. Vicky crossed the room to the twins, desperate to hear their heartbeats up close. She knelt on the floor between them, holding on to one small socked foot of each child, as they ignored her in favour of their game. She would do anything to protect them. Daniel was gone, too late to save, and even her twin brother she could live without if she had to. But not the kids. They were innocent. It had been Vicky's choice to take them to a party when they had Covid symptoms, and she should have known better, after causing one death already. This one had not even been on her radar. Everyone went out with symptoms after the first wave. They were barely three then, it wasn't fair they should spend their lives cooped up meeting no other children. So she'd reasoned at the time. And there was no way to prove who'd given Elizabeth the disease. Could have been the other way round—

No, Vicky, stop self-justifying. This was her fault, and she had to live with that.

'What's that?' said Darcy sharply, head whipping round.

Vicky could hear it too. A loud banging.

'It's coming from the pantry.' Fiona got to her feet. Vicky followed her into the small room off the kitchen, heart hammering. Bang, bang, bang.

Darcy pointed. 'It's behind there! The dresser.' She was right. The noise seemed to come from behind the heavy wooden item.

Fiona stepped forward. 'Come on, help me move it, Darce.'

Vicky protested, 'No, wait . . .' It could be the person they feared, some mysterious onlooker, if one existed. Hiding in the very walls.

Fiona and Darcy shifted the dresser, grunting with effort, making the dishes on it rattle, and there in the wall was a small latched door, like the one into the attic.

'It's the coal cellar,' she said. 'The old hatch. I suppose they just blocked it up. But are you sure we should . . . ?'

Too late. Darcy was stooping to open it, and then someone was climbing out, dripping water on to the floor. Louise.

Fiona's eyes went wide. 'How did you . . .'

'There's a way through the caves.' Louise's hair was soaked, moisture clinging to her coat, and she took off her boots, which were covered in dirt. 'There's a tunnel of some sort, comes up into the coal cellar, and then you can crawl out, if you pile up some of the junk down there. It wasn't easy.' She caught sight of the newspaper clippings spread out on the table behind them. 'What's all this?'

Amira

Left, right, left, right. Breathe in, breathe out. She was doing it. She, who couldn't swim or climb a medium hill, certainly could not sail or ski or dive like Vicky and Jonathan and Daniel, had even managed to stand up on her paddleboard, buoyed by adrenaline, surging from a squat to her feet. It was easier to steer this way and she was making good progress, as the waves were calmer now. Past some more cliffs, more seabirds, back to where she'd left her husband. If she could get his board, tow it back with her, there was still a chance she'd find Jonathan alive, wasn't there?

She thought of how the dark waters had closed over his head, and let out a moan of panic. It wasn't her fault, was it? There was nothing she could have done for him.

She had reached the caves now, their gaping mouths more visible from the water. Above, you'd have no idea this was even here.

'Hello?' Her voice was torn away by the wind. 'Paddy?'

Then she noticed something else, peering in the failing light. His board was gone. It had been there, dragged up on the rocks, but she saw now that the tide had risen already, lapping around the tops of the boulders Paddy had been able to stand on earlier. So his board had washed away, perhaps. One way off the island, gone.

'Paddy! Paddy!'

She could only hear her own voice echoing back to her. Where was he? Was it possible he'd climbed down and taken his board, gone back to the beach? That he was safe and dry in the house right now, with Vicky, while she risked her life at sea? She couldn't swim and he knew better than anyone how scared she was of water. Squinting with all her might, Amira could make out a rope tied on at the top of the cliff. Maybe he had climbed up that? She had no idea, and clearly he hadn't given her a second thought.

It was getting dark now and Amira realised there was nothing she could do but paddle back to shore. She let the tide carry her round the other direction, past where Jonathan had been, just in case he was still there, and towards the stony beach that lay to the south of the jetty. She was giving up. She paddled and paddled with all her might, ignoring the screaming in her arms and ache in her legs, and soon the beach was in sight. It was bleaker than the north one, stony and grey.

And . . . there was something in the water with her.

Amira stifled a scream, as a large body coiled through the sea beneath her. Flashes of mottled skin, ripples all around her. Oh God. Oh God. There weren't any sharks in Scotland were there? Oh God! Something had nudged her!

Amira let out a shaky half-scream, half-laugh, as a snout popped up and a pair of dark curious eyes regarded her. A seal. It was a seal. Large, sinewy, brindled like a dog, with the same whiskers and air of playful curiosity. It hung there, body straight down in the water and head up, watching her.

'Hello,' she whispered. 'I'm sorry we came here and disturbed you.'

A feeling of great peace spread over her, and she stretched out a hand, as if she could almost pet it. It let out a honking noise like a sneeze, and vanished below, the backwash nearly knocking her off the board. As she righted herself, she laughed in shock, and then she was crying. Oh God. It had been so beautiful, so innocent. And everything else was so rotten. Rachel was dead, Daniel was dead. Maybe Jonathan now too.

Amira let herself sit on the board, her legs dangling in the water on either side. As she hunkered down, she felt a wetness underneath her. Seawater? No, the crotch of her leggings was dark with a spreading stain. Metallic. Dark red.

Amira blinked. Not wanting to believe what she was seeing.

Blood. She was bleeding. And that meant she wasn't pregnant after all.

Amira leaned over, closed her eyes against the wave of disappointment and anger. It wasn't *fair*. Why could everyone else – Fiona, Vicky with twins FFS – do this, and she couldn't? What was wrong with her? The doctors hadn't been able to find anything. The first round of IVF had failed, and they weren't eligible for another free one. She'd thought this was it, her miracle. But no. She was bleeding. It was over.

Her mind tried to scrabble for a few shreds of hope. You could be pregnant and bleed a little, couldn't you? People sometimes didn't know that they were, for months and months. But no, this was too heavy for spotting, and she now had to admit to herself she'd had period symptoms all day – grouchiness, heavy breasts, nausea. She wasn't pregnant. With that patch of blood, with that knowledge, the future shifted and rearranged itself. She had allowed herself to believe in it, picture a child with Paddy's smile, hoisted up on his shoulders. The three of them under a Christmas tree, or celebrating Eid. The first day of school, taking them to Disneyworld. And now, nothing. Paddy had abandoned her, and she was alone out here on the sea.

Mhairi

She understood at last the splashes and splotches in the living room, as if someone had smashed a bottle of ketchup. The third body had not been neatly bundled up like the others, but was instead sprawled out on the stony southern beach, a blood-stiffened tarpaulin loosely tucked around it. She hunkered down, her hair and the hair of the corpse both blowing in the wind. But the eyes looked straight up at the bruised sky, unbothered by the sand that flew into them. A woman. Sensible outdoor outfit, shoes missing, thick woollen socks.

The cause of death was pretty clear. Her jumper had a gaping slit in it, crusted with dried blood, which had spilled all down her trousers and splashed on her socks. She had been stabbed indoors, Mhairi guessed, automatically parsing the clues the body left her.

'Someone attacked her in the house, then dragged her down here. Why?'

Maybe she had still been alive – you could survive a stomach wound, if you were lucky and near a hospital. Maybe she'd died as they'd pulled her over the bumps and stones. Who was 'they' though? One strong person could have done it. Or two smaller ones. She thought back to the knife she'd found up the hill, the disarray of the house, the blood on the wall. This death had been chaotic, unplanned. So this woman must have died third, when things were starting to fall apart. When panic had set in.

She wasn't supposed to touch the body, but with gloved hands, she bent and gently closed the open eyes. Three dead, five to locate, plus the teenage girl and the little children. Mhairi could not entertain the idea that she wasn't going to find them safe. She straightened up and turned in a circle. They had looked over every inch of the island. Hadn't they? Except the caves, and she wasn't going in there by herself when it was only a few hours from being dark. So what to do next? She was stumped.

Mhairi crunched across the shingle, and looked over towards the jetty on the west coast, with its string of dead light bulbs. 'I'm going to radio in again. This is really starting to creep me out.'

Vicky

Vicky advanced, buoyed up by sheer rage, facing off to Louise. 'As if you don't know what these are.' She picked up a handful of clippings and clutched them in her friend's face.

'I'm sorry?'

'As if you didn't plan all of this! Well, we know about it now. So come on, tell us. What's your grand plan?'

'Darcy, go upstairs,' warned Fiona.

'But—'

'Now! Go!'

Darcy ran, padding upstairs in her socks. Fiona came to stand behind Vicky, as she confronted Louise.

The rage was building in Vicky, filling her, popping like exploding candy in her bloodstream. 'What's going on, Louise? We don't see you for years and then you're suddenly keen to come for my fortieth? Weird, isn't it?'

'I – I've been overseas all that time. I happened to be back. You know why, for God's sake! I got someone killed. That sort of thing changes you. I couldn't keep doing the job.'

Vicky had never seen Louise so rattled.

'Why was this in your bag? All these clippings?'

Louise dropped her gaze to the table, shaking her head. 'But that wasn't meant to – those aren't mine!' She was lying. Lou had always been a bad liar.

'Darcy saw them sticking out. They must be yours.' Louise was backing away, towards the living room. Vicky followed her. 'What were you planning to do with them, put them in our rooms to give us a fright? Look, we're all in here. Even one for the twins! They're only babies, Louise!'

Louise's face was slick with sweat. 'Vicky, you have to believe me, I would never hurt the kids. I would never hurt any of you! It wasn't supposed to be—'

'What?' Vicky pounced on that. 'So you do know something about all this.'

'I . . . Look, it's complicated and—'

'My babies! They're only five years old! And there's no way to prove they gave Covid to that woman, and even if they did, how could they possibly have known what they were doing? If it was anyone's fault it was mine.'

At that, Louise's face changed. Her fear boiled down into solid anger. 'No surprise there. All of this is your fault, you know. You were always the smug little centre of everything.'

'I don't know what the hell you mean.'

'Don't you? Think about it. Would anyone of us be here if not for you? Paddy, you led him on for all of first year, treated him like your boyfriend, then next thing we know you turn up in second year with bloody Daniel on your arm. Daniel, who made our lives miserable! Who called me a dyke to my face, made Famine jokes to Paddy, did racist impressions at Fiona! Not to mention that horrible trick he played on me.'

'That was just . . . a joke.'

'Some bloody joke. I ruined my degree over it, I was so broken! And you still married him. You pushed Fiona into marrying your brother, so she's been cheated on for years, abandoned for a younger model.'

'Come on,' muttered Fiona, whose eyes were swivelling wildly round the kitchen as if looking for backup that wasn't coming.

'Isn't it true?'

'Well, yes, but it's hardly Vicky's fault.'

Louise said, 'Let's be honest, Vic. If you hadn't lied for him, Jonathan would have gone to prison when he was nineteen. He's a liar and he's careless with people's lives.'

Vicky gasped. Not this, not now. 'That's not true! It was an accident, everyone knew that.'

'Was it though? That poor boy, left to drown. How do you think his family would feel, watching you swan around on this island, the same place he died? Using the same boat, for Christ's sake? The one you wouldn't let him back on?'

'That's not what—'

'I was there, Vicky. Remember? I know what I saw.'

Vicky was shaking. Her hands groped at the table for balance. 'Well, we lost the island in the end, didn't we.'

'Because Daniel killed someone too! And so did you! You just don't care, do you. You're so careless, you smash up people's lives, regardless of whether they live or die, and you just carry on, rich and polished and perfect.'

'I'm not perfect. I never claimed to be.'

'And Darcy has learned from you, and from her dad.'

'Don't you talk about my daughter!' snapped Fiona. 'Come on, Lou, I'm not saying some of this isn't right, but she's a child.'

'A child who's turning out as shallow and callous as her father. You're not like that, Fiona. You're just . . . complacent is all. You've spent too much time around this family, got used to the money and the luxuries. I mean, look at this stuff.' Louise spun round the kitchen, pointing out delicacies. 'Champagne on tap, because God forbid Princess Vicky should drink prosecco. Chateaubriand steak, Ladurée macarons. Designer outdoor gear, Range Rover replaced every two years, hundred-pound T-shirts for five-year-olds. A private bloody Michelin chef for the evening! Christ, you thought it was a joke I had ninety quid in my bank account. Well, that was true, Vicky! I have no job and I'm supporting my sick mum, we're all on our own, and yet you still asked me to cover the cost of your private-island birthday. It's disgusting, to be honest.'

It wasn't fair. It wasn't *fair*! 'We work hard! Why shouldn't we have nice things? You could too if you didn't insist on living in a refugee camp. Saint Louise, helping the downtrodden, unimpeachable. Well, you were there too that summer. It was as much your fault as ours. Not so saintly then.'

'Do you remember *everything* about that summer?' said Louise quietly.

Oh no. It was happening.

Louise's blue eyes locked on to Vicky's, and she took a step closer, and it was all coming back. That night, a rare summer heat on the island, cotton dress brushing her bare legs. The pills Jonathan had brought with him coursing in her blood, wanting to touch everyone and everything. Then Louise was there, her arms slipping around Vicky's waist.

Are you feeling it?

God yes. You?

Yes. So much.

The feeling that everything could be said now, everything could be done. Frightening, in its way.

Vicky's voice was shaky. She could feel the grain of the table under her sweaty palms. 'Look, it was just – I was high.'

Louise laughed. 'I'd believe you, if that was the only time it happened. Never told hubby that, did you? Or big bro?'

'What's she talking about, Vic?' Fiona was at the bottom of the stairs now, backing away from Vicky herself, probably without realising.

Louise sneered. 'Didn't tell the BFF either? It's nothing to be ashamed of, Vic. Sexual fluidity is very in right now.' Vicky saw Fiona's face as understanding hit. Surprise. Judgement. A hint of disgust? And she couldn't bear it. Louise went on. 'Of course, Fiona hasn't told *you* everything either, has she?'

'Shut up, Lou!' yelled Fiona.

Vicky had no idea what this all meant. 'So that's what this is about? You're jealous I chose Daniel over you? Grow up, Lou. It was one druggy night, I'm not gay, for God's sake.'

'And Daniel did it for you, did he? Made you happy? Made you feel sexy and loved and safe? Put you first always?'

'Shut up. You jealous bitch.'

Louise looked down, and her face turned suddenly white. Vicky was walking towards her. Fiona shouted, 'Vic, no! Put it down!'

Put what down? She looked down and the knife was in her hand, the one they'd been using to cut the cake, which Fiona had washed up earlier. She must have picked it up without realising. It was angled at Louise.

'Say it's not true,' Vicky insisted. 'Tell Fiona it was just a stupid drugged-up experiment. You took advantage of me, I was high.'

Louise was moving back into the living room again. Towards the twins, still engrossed in their iPads despite the raised voices around them. Was that a twitch of Genevieve's head?

'But Vic, I can't do that. It wasn't the only time.'

Fiona was trying to get around the table and chairs. 'Vic, no, don't do this. It's not worth it.'

'She did this. Scared us all like that. Killed Rachel. Killed my husband!' It all made sense now. Louise had always hated Daniel, probably because she'd been nursing a long obsession with Vicky herself. 'Didn't you?'

'No! I've never even met Rachel before. I swear, I would never hurt anyone on purpose. I've spent the last twenty years trying to save lives!'

There were only inches between them now. 'Tell the truth. Why do you have these clippings? What have you done?'

Louise was crying. 'I didn't want anyone hurt. I was just – the greed of it all, it made me sick. I work with people who haven't eaten in three days, who've walked a hundred miles with all their belongings on their backs, dying for want of a glass of water or a hunk of bread. And you and Daniel, you spend money like it's going out of fashion! You pour away two-hundred-pound bottles of champagne. You eat two bites of premium steak and throw it out, you hire a private chef and a private island for your birthday. Your kids leave their designer clothes and iPads out in the rain and you don't even tell them off! It's disgusting, Vicky, is the truth. Daniel caused that little girl's death, and a few years later he's back on top with a six-figure job. He fucks your nanny and she's the one who gets fired.'

How did Louise know about that? No one was supposed to know about Cody.

Louise turned to Fiona. 'And you and Jonathan, you're just as bad. Look, you're still wearing your diamond engagement ring even though he left you, humiliated you. Dropping a casual grand on whisky. And Vicky, you killed that poor boy on his bike and you only paid a small fine. Jonathan sent that cameraman to his death and no one even cared! He won an award and he pretended to cry over his dead friend on live TV! Meanwhile, did you know this, the man's family didn't get a penny in compensation, because he was self-employed? His wife is on her own with the baby and Jonathan didn't even send a card.'

She hadn't known this. How did Louise know? She was supposed to have been in Sudan for years, she shouldn't know any of this.

'How did you find all this out? The twins, Darcy?'

Fiona exclaimed, 'Yes, how did you know that? Darcy didn't give evidence at the inquest – under-eighteens don't usually – and she wasn't named in any of the news stories, we made sure of it.'

Louise gave the ghost of a smile. 'Not had much else to do since I came back from Sudan, have I? There's Google Alerts. Press services. Social media, of course. I always said it was a bad idea, and you have no idea how much you all put up there. Pretty easy to glean from Darcy's hand-wringing posts about Kira that she was the one named in the note – plus the papers picked up that Jonathan went to the inquest, Mr Super-Famous TV Star. Why would he do that if Darcy wasn't implicated? And anyone could see that the twins had Covid at the same time as that woman died, thanks to all your moaning posts, Vic. It's the talk of the local mums' Facebook group, let me tell you. The one you *aren't* in. They all think it was your fault, poor Julia's mum.'

'They're children, Louise. Babies.'

Louise was almost at the wall of the living room now, her hands raised to ward Vicky off. 'I would never have hurt them.'

'But you wrote the note.'

'Well – yes.'

'So what was your plan then – bring us here and kill us one by one, to punish us for being successful? That's insane.'

'No, no, I didn't want anyone to die! I don't know what happened to Rachel, just an accident I thought, a coincidence – and Daniel, I don't know how it happened, I swear, it shouldn't have . . .' She was crying hard now. Louise never cried. 'Look, I'm sorry for my part in this. But it wasn't all me. Put the knife down and I'll explain.'

Vicky might have done that. She was so confused, swirling with anger and guilt, painful memories attacking her like birds with sharp beaks. But then a little voice said, 'Mummy?' and she saw the twins were watching, taking their headphones off.

'Fiona, take them away!'

'I—'

'Now!'

Fiona rushed past her peripheral vision, hustling the twins towards the kitchen. Louise's head turned to them. And Vicky thought of the clippings, the fact that Louise had included her babies in that horrible list of guilt, accused them of causing a death too, and she gasped with the unfairness of it all. Her parents had never protected her, and she wasn't going to let that happen to her kids.

Louise moved slightly. Vicky raised the knife.

'Get away from them.'

'I'm not – I would never touch them!'

She could hear Fiona saying, 'Come on, twinnies, let's see what's in Louise's room, come on!'

Louise was against the wall, nowhere else to go. 'Vic, please put the knife down. Your kids are here! This is mad.'

She didn't care. Maybe it would be good for them, to see their mother wasn't going to be pushed around any more. She was all they had left, she had to fight for them. 'Not until you tell me who else is involved in this plan.' She couldn't rest for a moment until she knew who to trust. What if Fiona was in on it too, angry with their family after Jonathan's betrayals? Or Amira? She'd never liked Vicky either. Someone she'd considered a friend – or multiple someones – had lured her here to kill her on her birthday. She wasn't going to stand for it.

'I – can't do that.' Louise gulped. 'I made a promise.'

'You'd better.'

Louise's eyes went from side to side. She was trapped against the wood-panelled wall, scrabbling behind her for a door. Not finding one. 'I—'

'Tell me. Who did this?'

Louise tried to rally some courage. 'You did it. It's all your fault and you know it . . . Get off! Get off me!' She put up her arms, strong from years in the field, and for a moment they fought, both of her hands pushing against Vicky's where she held the knife. 'Stop it, Vic! I . . . Aaaaaah!'

Her shriek was piercing. Vicky hadn't really meant to do it. Had she? But she looked down and the knife was now embedded in Louise's stomach and her own hand was running over with blood.

Fiona was still hustling the kids out. 'Don't look, darlings, look at Auntie Fiona! That's right, in here!'

Louise put her hands to her middle, eyes dark with shock.

'*Vicky*,' she said, her voice a croak. And her body slumped slowly to the floor, leaving a bloodied trail along the wood of the wall.

Amira

Almost at the shore now. Her legs were cramping with exhaustion and shock, and she was wet through, damp and chafing. But there was the beach, and the water shallow enough to see all the way to the bottom through the clear, cold grey. Fronds of seaweed, large rocks. She steered the board into the shallows, and as she did she saw two figures struggling down the path from the house in the gloom. They were dragging something on a blue sheet. Some big object. What could it be?

When it was shallow enough she jumped off, wincing in the cold water. It was Fiona and Vicky on the shore, she could see now, as she splashed towards them. Dragging each end of another of the tarpaulins, and now they had stopped at the head of the beach. One was kneeling down – Fiona, she thought. Amira ran over the stones, feeling the chafe of her wet clothes. She was soaked to the skin, despite not having gone into the water. She was still a few metres away when she saw that it was Louise on the tarpaulin, sprawled out, a pool of red collected about her body, like rainwater. Eyes open and staring up. Dead. There was no question about it.

Amira let out a whimper. 'What happened? Is she . . . ?'

It was Fiona who was on her knees, yes. The front of her jumper was saturated with blood, and there was some on her face too, as if she had tried to give CPR. She looked stunned. 'She's dead. I tried but I – I couldn't.'

Amira looked down at the mess of Louise's stomach, bile lurching in her throat. 'Who did this?'

'I did,' said Vicky dully. She was standing up, arms hugging herself. She wasn't wearing a coat or shoes, and her socks were splattered with blood. 'I stabbed her. She did this, Amira. She was going to hurt all of us. Even the twins. I had to stop her.'

Amira felt entirely off-kilter, lurching as if still on the water. 'I don't understand. Why did you bring her here?'

'We were trying to find Jay, or one of you with a board,' said Fiona. 'We thought – I don't know, maybe we could get her to the mainland. She would have needed urgent surgery, after a stomach perforation. I couldn't do anything.' That explained why they were out here hardly dressed, no shoes on – Vicky had stabbed Louise in the house.

'But why? What did she *do*?'

Vicky seemed curiously flat and expressionless. 'Darcy found things in her bag. Articles about each of us. That proved all of this was her. She wanted to get back at us because she thought we'd all killed a person and gotten away with it. I can show you the clippings she had. There's one for you too.'

Louise? She was the one behind all this? Well, she had always been odd, and she clearly judged them for their expensive lifestyles, the waste and commercialism of their lives. If she was now dead, that meant they were safe. The children were safe, and Paddy was probably alright in the caves, and Jonathan . . .

How could she tell Vicky she'd left her brother to die? Darcy's father, Fiona's husband, who she obviously still loved? A small cold thought entered Amira's head. Nobody had to know. Only she and Jonathan knew what had happened out there, and he was most likely gone.

'What do we do?' Fiona, always so practical, sounded broken. 'What's happening? Is someone else out here with us? Daniel . . . I don't understand.'

Amira didn't know. Daniel and Rachel, they could just about have been accidents, but now this revelation that Louise was behind the note, and the fact that Vicky had *stabbed* her, for God's sake. Killed her. She screwed her eyes together, as if she might wake up and find none of this real. But it was. Louise lay on the blue tarpaulin. Jonathan was in the water, and she had pushed him down there. The grey sea lapped the shore. She was wet through and shivering and there was no sign of Paddy. And she was not pregnant.

'Come on,' she said. 'It's almost dark. Let's go back to the house at least. We're only getting frozen out here.' She looked down at the body. Such an expression of shock on Louise's face. 'I think . . . maybe we should leave her here for now. I know it's horrible, but dragging her back up the hill will only tire us out. And – she won't know the difference.'

She was thinking so clearly, as if her mind had also been rinsed in salty water. They just had to survive this, figure out if someone was targeting them, and if it was one of them – Louise maybe, so the danger had passed now? Or someone else altogether?

Vicky stirred from her trance. 'Look, I had to do it, didn't I? To protect my children.'

'I don't know. If you really thought she'd hurt them, maybe.'

'She was going to. She moved towards them. Right, Fiona?'

Fiona was still kneeling down, in a kind of daze too. 'I—'

'Fiona, I had to! What if she killed Rachel, and Daniel too?'

'Vic, why would she do that?'

'There was a hole in the boat,' blurted Amira. 'I'm so sorry but I found it out there floating, half-sunk. No sign of Jonathan.'

Fiona frowned. 'You mean – someone did it on purpose? Put a hole in it?'

'I don't know. Maybe.'

'Christ.' Fiona let out a sob. 'Where was he?'

'I don't know. I didn't see him.'

Vicky blinked hard at this new blow. 'I had to do it,' she repeated. She began to rub at the blood on her hands, as if she hardly knew it was there.

Fiona gave another torn sob, and Amira stooped down to help her up, feeling for once like the one in control of the situation. 'Come on. Let's get warm.'

Back at the house, Amira went upstairs to take off her life jacket and change her wet, bloodstained clothes yet again, having no choice but to put on the dirty ones from earlier. She scrounged up some loose tampons from her handbag. When she came out of the bathroom, Darcy was in the corridor. She looked like she'd been crying. 'What's happening, Amira?'

How to even begin to explain? 'It's alright, sweetheart.'

'But it's not, is it? I heard noises earlier. Someone screamed downstairs – was it Louise? Mum brought the twins up but she wouldn't tell me anything.'

'I – I don't know.'

'And where's my dad? Did you find him?'

'No, I didn't. But that doesn't mean anything.' How could she lie to a teenage girl like this? But the alternative was telling her that her aunt had stabbed Louise, and that her father was most likely dead too, pushed under by Amira herself. 'Just stay here, OK? We'll come get you in a minute. Look after the twins.'

'But I want to know what's happening! I'm not a kid.'

'I know. Let me – I'll tell your mum to get you in a minute.' Once she had figured out what, if anything, to do.

When she went down, Vicky and Fiona were sitting at the table in silence. Amira boiled the kettle, made drinks, glad of something to do. Vicky wrapped her hands around the mug of cocoa Amira passed her, and she must have been in shock because Amira had never seen her eat sugar before. Even her own birthday cake had been barely touched.

Vicky said, for the third time: 'I don't understand. Where was Jay?'

'The boat was sinking, Vicky. Like I said.'

She clearly hadn't processed it, so full of the horrors of the last few hours, and who could blame her. First Rachel, cold and frozen, terror on her face. Daniel, his body pink and boiled, suffocating in hot water. Then Louise going missing in the caves and reappearing, Jonathan vanishing in the boat; herself and Paddy setting out on the rickety paddleboards. Paddy going missing too.

Then, the most horrific. Vicky stabbing Louise in the stomach, right there in the kitchen. The blood had splashed up the wall, which Amira could see herself, still wet and running down. Fiona had tried to save Louise, clearly, getting up to her elbows in blood too, but it was too late, she'd said. A stomach wound was too messy. Even if you survived the blood loss, infection would likely get you. And the nearest proper hospital was miles away, all the way back in Glasgow. Covered in blood still and blank with shock, Fiona was sitting at the kitchen table with a shivering, damp Amira, and an even more bloodstained, horror-stricken Vicky. At least the children were safe upstairs. But where was Paddy?

'I don't understand, Amira,' Vicky said again. 'You found the boat – so where was Jay?'

'It had capsized. He . . . he wasn't there.'

'But he must have been.'

'I couldn't see him.'

Was there any hope for him? Where could he have gone? He'd swum to shore, perhaps, though it wasn't easy one-handed. Crawled up on to a rock or outcrop to wait for rescue. But he'd hardly been able to hang on when she'd seen him. Vicky made an impatient movement. 'We have to look for him. He'll be wet through, freezing.'

'You don't understand,' said Amira, tears in her voice. 'I think he – Vicky, he must have gone under.'

'Under what? The boat? You mean there was an air pocket?'

'Under the water. Look, I think he's gone. The water is so cold – if he went in he couldn't have lasted long. I'm so sorry.'

'But he's used to the cold. He swims all the time.'

'She isn't hearing me,' Amira said to Fiona. 'I think she's in shock.'

'I think we all are,' said Fiona, her voice shaking. 'Look, is there any chance he's OK? There must be, right?'

'I . . . maybe.'

'If anyone can survive it, Jay can.' Fiona looked between them as if seeking reassurance, but none was given.

Amira said, 'What are we going to do? Is there any chance that chef is still coming?' She'd been so star-struck when she'd heard Bobby Landford was booked for them. She'd watched him on that reality show he'd won, and she was going to actually meet him. But it seemed crazy now, a pipe dream.

Fiona had her head in her hands. 'I thought he'd be here by now.'

Amira looked at the kitchen clock – close to six. Wouldn't he have arrived already, if he had to prepare dinner for eleven people? 'Why would he not come though, if he was booked?'

Fiona shrugged. 'Someone could have radioed to cancel it.'

'But we lost the radio.' Although it was upstairs, in her husband's bag. He wouldn't have had time to call. Would he? He hadn't been back to the house since they'd found Daniel.

Vicky looked at her with bleary resignation. 'Haven't you figured it out, Amira? Someone did all this. They took the radio, they cancelled the chef, they pushed Daniel into the tub, slipped something in his drink maybe. Poisoned Rachel, took her EpiPen. Put the note in the box. Sank the boat, probably. One of our friends is behind all this.'

'But who?'

'Isn't it obvious?' Vicky nodded to the slick of blood on the wall.

'You really think Louise planned it all?'

'She as good as admitted it. Before I . . . before she died.'

'But could she really have got Daniel into that bath?' said Amira. 'Sorry, Vic. But he was a big man, she would have struggled.'

'Maybe she gave him something.'

Amira shot a quick glance at Fiona, who looked sceptical. When someone was as heavy a drinker as Daniel, you didn't have to give them anything, they would gladly swallow it themselves. A drunk man might be easier to topple into a bath.

Fiona gave a juddering sigh. 'She was trying to tell us something else. About it not being the plan for anyone to die. And she said it wasn't just her.'

'Who could it be then?'

Paddy.

Amira could almost see Fiona have the same thought. There was no one else. A lack of trust seemed to have come up between the three of them like panes of glass.

Fiona faltered. 'I don't know. Someone outside the Group, maybe.'

Vicky said, 'Where's Paddy?'

The suspicion lay between them, a tangible thing. 'I don't know,' said Amira. 'He left me at the caves.'

'Is there any chance he's found Jay?'

Amira shrugged helplessly. 'He just went into the caves. He didn't come back down.' Though his board was gone, so maybe he had. She had no idea.

'That's how Louise ended up in here,' said Vicky. 'I left her at the caves too – there's a tunnel all the way through to the coal cellar. Dad always said there was, but we were forbidden from going into it. I didn't mind, I'm claustrophobic anyway. But Jay was always interested.'

She didn't seem to have absorbed the news that her brother might be dead. And they didn't know that for sure, did they? Amira had only seen the scuppered boat. Not his body. He could still come back and accuse her. She had to be careful.

Vicky had pushed back her chair and was walking into the pantry. Fiona and Amira followed, and Amira saw the remains of the birthday cake on the side. The one Rachel had died after eating. That Paddy had baked. She didn't want to think about that.

The big wooden dresser was pushed to one side, and the hatch Louise had come out of was still open, a wooden latched one that had previously been hidden. There was a slope leading down into the dark of the coal cellar, where a trapdoor stood open in the ground, a damp smell rising out of it. The passageway was small – someone as tall as Daniel would not have been able to stand up in there.

'It really goes all the way through to the cliffs?' said Amira, doubtfully.

'Of course it does,' said Vicky impatiently. 'How else could Louise have got here? Daddy said smugglers built it, so they could make a quick getaway if the coastguard came. Maybe the new owner had it cleaned up and fixed.'

Amira could see that it would be a good tourist draw, a real-life smugglers' tunnel. But where was Paddy then? Why hadn't he come back up too? She called down it. 'Hello?' Her voice bounced around and she shivered. Maths was not on their side. Rachel, Daniel, Louise, all dead; Jonathan missing, maybe Paddy too. Just the three of them left.

But no. There was a scraping noise coming up from the dark. The women looked at each other fearfully. What was this?

Footsteps, heavy, echoing.

Vicky leaned over, shining the torch she'd taken from the dresser. 'Is someone there?' Who else could it be? There was no one left on the island.

Paddy's face emerged in the coal cellar, white in the gloom. His hair was wet and dripping. He stood below the hatch and looked up at them.

'There's a tunnel,' he said, breathing hard. 'Through to the caves.'

Amira sat back on her heels. She felt so very tired. 'We know,' she said.

'God, it's so dark down there. I kept getting lost, my phone torch hardly did a thing.' Paddy stretched out an arm. 'Here, can you help me up?'

Vicky and Fiona had frozen, but what could Amira do? This was her husband. She grasped his hand and helped him haul himself up the slope, into the pantry, where he stood shedding water on the floor. 'Thank God. I was crawling about in there for ages, they go on forever. Did Lou appear? I couldn't find her.'

Vicky was standing in the doorway between the pantry and the living room. 'We know, Paddy.'

'What are you talking about? Amira, did you find Jonathan out there?'

'No. The boat had capsized. He . . . I didn't see him.'

'Oh.' He looked between the three of them, counting. 'Where's the kids?'

Fiona said, 'The kids are upstairs, they're fine.' Though all of them had seen terrible things today, and they'd most likely lost a parent each as well.

'And Lou? I could see she'd come up in the tunnel ahead of me, the footprints of her boots. I must have got branched off.'

Vicky said again, 'Paddy, we know what she did. She told us.'

He frowned. 'Told you what?'

Fiona said, 'We found clippings in her bag. Newspaper stories. About all of us. The people that we – the deaths that occurred. It was her who wrote the note. Did you know?'

'What are you talking about?' Paddy caught sight of the wall in the living room and froze. 'What's that? What's happened?' His eyes travelled to the blood on Fiona, on Vicky. 'Why do you have – where is she?'

'You must have helped her.' Vicky was swaying slightly, and Amira knew the feeling – the shock percolating through your blood, leaving you shaky and light-headed, as if drunk.

Paddy pushed past them into the living room, and they parted to let him by. Leaving muddy drips on the tiles, he stopped in front of the bloodstained wall. His voice was tight with fear. 'Is someone going to tell me what's going on? What did you do to her?'

'She's dead,' said Amira, her tone hollow. 'I'm sorry. She was stabbed and she just – well, she's on the beach down there.'

Paddy stared at her. His eyes moved to Vicky, the blood on her jumper. 'What did you *do*?'

'She threatened me! She threatened my kids! I didn't mean to, I just – we fought, she attacked me. Have you seen what's in those clippings? Stuff about Darcy, about the twins! Even they were part of her sick little game!'

'So you fucking *stabbed* her? Jesus Christ. What's the matter with you?'

'What's the matter with me? My husband has been *murdered*, Paddy, that's what. Rachel is dead – and you made the cake. My brother is missing, and it was you who checked the boat, wasn't it? Maybe you did something to it. Maybe Louise did. Maybe she

217

killed Daniel too. I don't know what the hell is going on, but I know she was behind it.'

'I promise I did nothing to Rachel. And we don't know Daniel was murdered – it could have been an accident!'

'With the lid on top of him? Get real. And she always hated Daniel, didn't she.'

Paddy sank on to a chair, fingers raking his face. 'Vic, I know he was your husband, and I'm sorry he died, but you must realise that a lot of people hated him. Not just for the collapse of his company, but other things he did during his life. Think about uni. He was such a dick to all of us, to everyone really, except the popular rich kids. Remember what he did to Lou? She had every reason to hate him. That doesn't mean she killed him.'

'Oh, for God's sake!' cried Vicky. 'Not this again. It was just a bit of fun. A prank.'

'Come on. She dropped out of uni over it. She never got over it. He ruined her life and you know it.'

'He just – he was warning her off, that's all. She was obsessed with me, I was starting to get uncomfortable.'

Paddy gave her a pitying look. 'She told me what happened. The fake note saying you wanted to meet her in the boathouse. Then it was him and he locked her in, left her there all night. She wet herself, and then the first crew found her that way and told everyone. She missed one of her exams, even! She was terrified of him, Vic. And Daniel told you she'd done it herself, for attention, and you believed him. No wonder she dropped out.'

So that was the story. Amira had heard hints, but never actually known. How horrible Daniel had been, though it was wrong to think ill of the dead.

'I did believe him! Do you not remember how Lou was that year? Going off the rails! Not sleeping, wanting to spend every waking hour with me – and yeah, like you say, she dropped out! Normal people don't do that!' But Amira didn't blame her for it, knowing what she did now. Vicky went on, 'She was totally obsessed with me. She was jealous, that's the truth, so she made up lies to try and split up me and Daniel. Well, it didn't work.'

Paddy laughed bitterly. 'And you never stopped to think how it was for her, after everything we went through together on this island, to see you drop her for a guy who never stopped screwing half the college? She was in love with you, Vic. So was I.'

Amira jerked with a kind of automatic pain. Had he even remembered she was there? It was all coming out now. The secrets and resentments of the past twenty years. All those times she'd asked if he'd ever slept with Vicky and he'd said no, never, was that a lie? She thought of someone's answers in the game. *I've slept with two people here.* She'd thought it was Jonathan, probably, but he'd said it wasn't. Maybe it was Paddy and he'd lied to her all this time.

Ineffectually, Fiona said, 'Come on, people—'

'I can't help that!' Vicky snapped at Paddy. 'I never encouraged it. You – we were friends. I was very clear.'

'A friend that you flirted with when it suited you. And Louise? Wasn't she exactly the same? And more?'

A sharp silence fell. Amira's mind reeled. Was it true? Vicky and Louise? They'd spent a lot of time together at uni, Paddy had told her. Slept in each other's beds, even. Yes, it was possible. And it would explain a lot. So maybe it was *Vicky* who'd slept with two people here, and she'd lied about her game entry before. But not with Paddy. Louise.

'She loved you,' said Paddy. 'And you flaunted Daniel in front of her. In front of me too. Getting off on the validation of everyone wanting you, isn't that it?'

Vicky glared at him. 'So I was right then. The two of you teamed up. You planned this together. She couldn't have done it by herself.'

Without thinking, Amira said, 'You've been meeting with her. For months now. Just the two of you.' She hadn't thought much of it at the time – they'd always been good friends, Louise and Paddy, and they were the only ones without kids, the flexible ones. The main surprising thing was Louise being back at all. But had they used it to plan such a horrible trick?

Paddy shot her a furious look, and she was sorry, but she really didn't know what or who to believe.

Fiona said, weakly, 'So that was her lie, in the game. That she hadn't seen any of us in five years. The two of you met up and planned this.'

Paddy had his head in his hands. 'It wasn't supposed to be like this. We were just . . . at the end of our tether. Lou was the only one who got it. She could see how I'd been festering all these years. Losing all my money, ending up in this job that just sucks the life from me, watching the rest of you earn so much. Always being Lovely Paddy, the one that got screwed over, and no one even cared. The school trip, the way I got blamed for something that wasn't even my fault, while Daniel just walked away from what he did, killing a kid too, a baby. And then Lou told me what you did, Vicky – the cyclist – and I knew Daniel had screwed your nanny and all that happened was the poor girl got fired. So Lou said, why do they always get away with it? Let's do something. Let's show them what it's like to be scared. And then you started going on about your birthday and it seemed kind of obvious. I felt so much better once we had a plan. I got fit, I stopped drinking, I had a *purpose* again. Maybe I shouldn't have got drawn in. But Jesus Christ, didn't we have some provocation?'

Vicky blinked at his fury. 'See? They were planning it. How to lure us here and . . . kill us.'

'No. No! No one was meant to get hurt. I don't know what happened to the others. And it was you who killed Lou! You killed her! Your own friend!'

Fiona said, 'Look, let's just calm down and think this through. Lou was trying to say the same. She said something like, "it wasn't supposed to be" . . . What does that mean?'

Vicky snapped, 'Isn't it obvious? She and Paddy planned the whole thing, and he's trying to throw suspicion off himself.'

Paddy ran his hands through his wet hair. When he spoke, his voice was lower, as if trying to calm the situation. 'Look, you've got this all wrong. I'll admit Lou and I planned to add the note during the game. Daniel wanted activity ideas and someone suggested Two Truths and a Lie. In fact, wasn't it you, Fiona?'

She looked stricken. 'I thought it would be fun.'

'Or you liked the idea of secrets coming out. We wanted to jolt you all, I suppose. Even Jonathan, he's got so arrogant since he became famous. Leaving Fiona and Darcy for some bimbo! And he basically killed his cameraman, someone who was supposed to be his friend, just to get a boost in ratings. Fiona, Amira, me, Lou – we blamed ourselves for deaths that weren't actually our fault, but not Vicky and Daniel and Jay. They really were your fault and you got away with it. Lou was absolutely broken by what happened to her colleague, and she knew I never got over the school trip, and poor Marco. He was just a kid. Amira's never forgiven herself for little Liam.' He was talking about her like she wasn't there, not even looking at her. 'But you lot didn't seem to give a damn who you'd hurt. Same with Rachel, though we didn't really care about her. It didn't take much research to find out she was guilty of something too.'

Vicky gaped. 'So you *killed* her? Jesus Christ, Paddy. You've gone mad.'

'Will you listen? That's what I'm trying to tell you! No one was supposed to die, for God's sake. It was just to scare you. Spoil your birthday that you were so obsessed with making perfect.' Could

Amira believe him? God, she wanted to. But he had the radio in his bag and so far he hadn't offered any explanation for that.

Vicky cried, 'So you murdered people? Terrified us all? Because I wanted to celebrate my fortieth? You're psychotic.'

'I swear on my life, I didn't hurt anyone. Rachel? Honestly, I don't know, I think that could have been an accident? Like maybe she was distracted because of the note and she ate the wrong thing? I don't know. There definitely wasn't any sesame in the cake.'

'And Daniel? Don't tell me that was an accident.'

Paddy faltered. 'I – I don't know either. He was pretty blasted and leaning over hot water. It could have been.'

'I don't believe you,' said Vicky, but there was a waver in her voice.

Fiona leapt in. 'I agree Rachel could have been an accident, yeah. But what about my daughter? You included her in this sick plan – how could you do that?'

Paddy squirmed. 'I . . . didn't think that was fair. But Lou was adamant that Darcy was old enough to be blamed for the bullying. Lou was bullied herself a lot, I suppose. At school and even Oxford. By us, sometimes, when we weren't much older than Darcy is now.'

'And the twins?' said Vicky. 'These clippings seem to say they gave someone Covid. How could you even know something like that for sure?'

At that Paddy looked even more guilty. 'It wasn't their fault, if it's true. But you remember how Daniel was about Covid – never wearing his mask, moaning on and on about how it was just like a cold, breaking the rules to go on supposed "business trips" that were really holidays. We wanted him to see the consequences of that.'

Vicky was flushed with anger. 'I don't believe a word of this. Of course you're behind it all. You've always been obsessed with me. Both of you.'

'And didn't you encourage that? Louise told me something went on between you. That summer. You know when. That was why she helped to cover up . . . what you did. And you just turned your back on her after, pretended it never happened.'

'*What* happened?' said Amira. 'Is someone going to tell me?'

No one answered. They kept hinting at something on this island, the summer they'd stayed here, the four of them. Paddy, Louise, Vicky, Jonathan.

Fiona's eyes were flickering between them, confused and wary. Amira felt the same. 'So wait, you were going to hurt Darcy? She's a child!'

Paddy made a noise of frustration in his throat. 'I keep saying. No one was meant to get hurt at all, just a scare. A bit of a lesson.'

Fiona said, 'That's horrible, Paddy. We're your friends.'

'Are you?' He rounded on her. 'You all sided with Daniel, didn't you, when he lost my money, ruined my future? Even when he killed someone? Even when he fucked the nanny? Though I suppose he had *you* over a barrel, didn't he, Fiona?'

'Shut up!' Fiona cried, her eyes glittering with tears.

What did that mean?

Vicky was frowning, as if also confused. 'Why are you doing this, Paddy?'

'I'm sick of this lot always getting away with it. And your precious Jay too. He left you, humiliated you, and you're still here batting your eyelashes at him, hoping he'll come back. It's pathetic, Fiona. You used to have more backbone.'

Fiona was weeping now. 'He's my husband. He's Darcy's father! I had to try.'

'Yeah well, he's a killer. And Daniel was too. I don't mourn him. But I swear I didn't do anything to either of them, or Rachel. So we need to work out who did, before it's too late. Because there might be someone else out here with us.'

Amira shuddered. Which was worse, the idea that her husband had done all this? Or that some anonymous person was here with them, hiding?

'I don't believe you. You both hated Daniel,' said Vicky. 'You, because of the business. And even before. Because of me.'

Paddy's face twisted into a snarl. 'That's what you have to expect, Vic, if you use your friends to cover up your own crimes.'

'What are you talking about?' said Fiona, massaging her temples. 'I don't know what you mean. So Vic hooked up with Lou that summer, big deal? Everyone slept with everyone back then. Maybe you're jealous, Paddy, because it wasn't you.'

Amira winced again. She might as well not be here, watching the rapid implosion of this twenty-year friend group. But her own marriage was also imploding too, though no one seemed to notice. She did not recognise this Paddy, so angry, so cold.

Paddy sneered, 'That's not what I mean. Go on, Fiona, ask her. Ask Vicky what else happened that summer we were here. Ask her who died.'

'Don't be stupid. I'd know if something like that happened.'

'Would you? Tells you everything, your best friend? Did you know about her and Lou? About the dead cyclist and her driving ban? And for that matter, does she know about—'

'Christ, shut up, shut up!' Fiona threw herself at him, slapping at his chest.

Amira had never seen Fiona so upset, though Paddy seemed barely to notice it, continuing to talk over her, raising his voice.

'That summer,' Paddy said. 'End of first year. When we visited the island, the four of us. You didn't come, right? Daniel wasn't on the scene yet.'

Fiona stopped. Blinked. 'I was working in my parents' restaurant. Had too many labs on to earn cash in term time.'

'Right. I worked too that summer, and Lou, but we took the week off as holiday. That's how Oxford is, isn't it? You have to pretend you don't even need to earn money. But we didn't have that luxury.'

'So what did happen?' Fiona asked. 'The four of you were weird after that summer. Jonathan would never tell me the full story.'

Vicky licked her dry lips. 'Look, none of it was my fault. I was nineteen, for God's sake!'

Amira had had enough. Her voice shook. 'Someone better tell me what you're all talking about. I may not be in your precious "Group", but I'm here too. I'm not just . . . nothing.'

Paddy barely glanced at her. 'Well, what happened is Vicky here killed someone. Her and Jonathan – that summer was the first time they took a life.'

Fergus

2002

There wasn't much to do as a teenager on Tarne in 2002. Messing about on boats, and drinking tinnies on the beach in the howling wind, or going round people's houses to watch TV and snog on the sofa. The lack of entertainment did mean they had to make their own fun, meaning that at eighteen Fergus had already slept with six girls – two locals, four tourists. But he'd always wanted to have a crack at that girl whose parents owned the small island off Tarne. They were sometimes spotted in Port Creggan loading up with food, or they might come over to have lunch in one of the restaurants. Otherwise he hadn't seen her about much, always spirited over the waves in the boat their dad kept in the harbour, blonde hair flying in the breeze. There was a brother too, big guy with something wrong with his arm, but Fergus didn't pay him much heed. What he needed was to make contact with the girl somehow. Even her name was posh, exciting – Victoria Capeman. No one on the island was called Victoria, it was all Mhairis and Morags.

Fergus had a cheap mobile he'd been given for his last birthday, so that his da could summon him to help out on the boat whenever he needed, but it also let Fergus text his vast army of mates and girls all night and day. So he was pleased when, while slumped in front of rubbish summer TV one lunchtime, he got a text off his friend Nash, who worked at the island's one petrol station, just by the ferry dock.

Heads up – Princess V on the lunchtime boat.

Result! She was coming over, and she'd be bored and in need of fun. Enter Fergus. He also had the vague idea that posh kids like them probably had access to better stimulants than Buckfast or Benson and Hedges. He'd never even tried E.

Another text. *She's got some mates with her. One lass.*

Hot?

Dykey. Other is fella.

Brother?

Nah another one.

He was tearing through his credit with all these messages, but it would be worth it.

Threat level?

Weedy.

That was OK then. Maybe she'd just brought over a group of posh friends, and even if this other guy was her boyfriend, which Fergus doubted, he was confident in his own abilities. He stopped to spray himself all over with Lynx, lifting up his Celtic shirt to spritz his pits, and slicked his hair down with gel before dashing down to the docks.

His da was waiting there, winding up rope. 'What are you doing here?' he grunted.

'Thought I'd give you a hand. Are you no' taking that family over to the island today?' As they were bringing extra guests, they weren't going to all fit in the usual boat.

His da looked suspicious. 'First time for it. After some cash, are you?'

'If it's going spare.'

'This lot are rolling in it, not that they'd ever put their hand in their pocket to tip you. Look, here they are.'

Sure enough, there was the giant Jeep rolling into the harbour now, manoeuvring into the little parking space set aside for them. There was no way to get a car to Mallacht, and no need for one anyway. The Jeep was piled high with belongings, even pulling a trailer, and stuffed with extra people, more than was legal, but nobody bothered too much on the island. Fergus sussed out the new boy. Maybe a friend of the brother. He couldn't see Princess Victoria going for some nerd like that.

He sprang across to help them unload, getting there in time to open the door for Victoria. She was wearing cargo pants like the birds from All Saints, and a little vest top, her skin tanned from warmer suns than Tarne's, her hair all shiny and blonde.

She shot him a look. 'Thanks.'

'All part of the service.'

The father was locking the car. 'You're the young lad, are you?'

'That's me. Giving me da a hand today.'

'That's good, since we're extra.'

There was the mother, thin and disapproving, in jeans and a heavy wool jumper. The brother in a rugby shirt, nodding warily to Fergus. There was also the nerdy boy, who was carrying a backpack with books bulging out, and some red-haired girl with freckles dressed like Sporty Spice. Dykey, like Nash had said.

'You're the boat boy?' said Vicky, looking down her pretty nose.

She could call him that if she wanted. 'Me da owns the boat that'll take you over, aye. I drive it sometimes.' Not that his da actually let him near it much.

'That's cool. Dad wants us to take some sailing lessons this summer.'

'I could come over one day, teach you. I'm an instructor.' He wasn't, actually, but he could show them the basics, mess about in the water near shore, without any harm.

Vicky tossed her hair. 'Cool. Come on over and find us then.'

Fergus felt a surge of excitement. This was going to be an OK summer after all.

Vicky

This couldn't be happening. All her secrets spilling out one by one, splashing their filth over everything, like Louise's blood on the wall.

Fergus. That day on the water in the small boat, Jonathan egging them further and further out, Paddy and Louise terrified, wanting to go back to shore. The waves, the boat tipping, Jonathan and Fergus suddenly in the water. The decision so clear and cold in her mind. Save her brother. He had a bad arm. And by the time they'd dragged him into the boat, over six foot and already weighing fifteen stone at nineteen, the slight local boy had vanished under the water.

They had tried. Hadn't they? But they couldn't find him in the dark water. A terrible accident, more Jay's fault if anyone's, certainly not hers, and her father had whisked them away the next day, made it very clear his children were not to blame. Vicky had felt terrible for a time, then pushed the feeling down as deep as she could. She had hardly even thought of it since. Done her best not to. Just a bad thing that had happened, nothing to do with her.

But the rest. Tomasz. The day she could barely bear to remember, because that really had been her fault.

◆ ◆ ◆

It was one of those days where nothing had gone to plan. Daniel had come in close to midnight from a client dinner, reeking of expensive brandy then snoring all night long, even when she nudged him, her nudges getting less gentle as the hours wore on. The twins, still babies then, woke up at four thirty, dark outside.

Daniel grumbled as the wails came through the video monitor. 'Can you get them? I need to catch another hour, I have a big meeting.'

She'd stood in the pale dawn coaxing porridge into them, as blueberries were squashed on the hardwood floor and oats ground into her hair and clothes. 'Darlings, please. Eat a little for Mummy.'

She'd been thrilled when the scan showed twins – it ran in the family, and she and Jonathan had always been close. She was having a boy and a girl too, best friends for life. But she'd had no idea how all-consuming it would be with two of them, every single breathing space between mothering swallowed up into nothing. She hadn't wanted a nanny, which meant she wouldn't be able to go back to work until they were at school. God, she missed it. The scalpel-neat intricacies of the law, where she could work hard and get it right almost all the time. Not like being a mother, which was a game where no one had told her the rules, and they changed on an hourly basis anyway.

Daniel would have happily hired a nanny if Vicky wanted to work. What he didn't want was to have to look after the twins himself, ever, even for an evening – to give up the endless rounds of corporate dinners and drinks, concerts at the O2, football matches, days at the races, all of it apparently essential to his job at the hedge fund. Head of client relations. Not what he'd dreamed of when he set up his own business out of college, but the least said about that the better.

By seven Daniel had showered and dressed, ruffling the twins' hair – too rough, Genevieve starting to cry – and left, gym bag over his shoulder. He still had time for the gym! Vicky could feel the fat depositing on her hips and loathed it. Impossible to get through the day without injections of sugar for energy, and she felt old and frumpy. Fiona had been so wise, having her child years ago, though even then the experience had put her off ever having another.

'No way,' she'd confided, one Sauvignon-drenched night. 'It set me back five years in medicine, I'm not joking. What a bloody swizz.'

Eight a.m. A whole day and night alone with two tiny children who fought constantly and cried in rotation. Genevieve would only eat Pom-Bears, Toby was afraid of his own shoes. She had to get them out of the house, or she was going to go insane. But the weather was foul – endless dripping rain, a grey haze over everything, barely light at all. Soft play. Thank God for soft play, although her own mother frowned on it, called it a health hazard, mixing with all those common children. It took twenty minutes to leave the house, both twins howling over their rainsuits and wellies and her cruel refusal to let them bring half their toy collection in the car with them. She just had to get them there, and then she could sit for maybe ten whole minutes and drink a cup of bad coffee, and not have anyone touching her. That feeling was like some intangible heaven. She got them into their car seats and started the car, a huge Range Rover Daniel had wanted but which she felt sheepish driving around the streets of Wandsworth. It was so bad for the environment, and it wasn't as if they had a second home in the countryside that required it. Not since the island had gone, anyway.

She nudged the car out into heavy morning traffic.

'Mummy, want songs! Songs, Mummy!'

This meant a CD of nursery rhymes they loved, sung in eerie childlike voices. She pressed play and 'Mary Had a Little Lamb' filled the car.

Genevieve was crying. Vicky tried to look at her in the mirror while watching traffic. 'What is it, darling?'

She sucked in a huge gulp of air, ready to rain down a storm of howling tears. 'MY SNACK! BAD TOBY!'

'Toby, give your sister back her snack.'

'Noooo Mummy, no snack!'

'Well where is it then?'

'On FLOOR, Mummy.'

She craned her neck around, catching the edge of the raisin packet out of the corner of her eye. 'Alright, Gen, you'll have to wait, Mummy can't stop.'

The light had gone green, the colour neon-bright on the wet road. Someone beeped behind her. She had the vague impression of a cyclist on her left side.

'Alright!' she shouted, as if the beeping car could hear. Genevieve's howling went up a notch.

Toby started clamouring for a different song. 'Humpty Dumpty, Mummy! Humpty DUMP-ty.'

The cyclist had sped ahead of her but something had happened, his pedals were slippery with water perhaps, and he hadn't moved off fast enough. Or Vicky hadn't fully registered him at the side of her enormous car, and as the person behind her beeped again, longer this time, she threw the car into gear and moved off with a lurch. She felt the bump, the ricochet of the bike against the side – oh God, she'd hit him, it would scrape, oh God.

She was barely doing ten miles an hour. On another day, not raining, in another car, it would have been an angry altercation, maybe a few dents on car and bike. But somehow, on this day, the bump from Vicky's car sent the bike spinning and slipping, and the cyclist off it and into the road, right into the path of oncoming traffic.

◆ ◆ ◆

It had been an accident. A combination of rain and a too-big car and an exhausted mother distracted by twins, a tricky junction. Tomasz Kazinsky. That was the name of the young man she'd killed. Twenty-five, commuting to his IT job by bike. He'd been wearing his helmet and reflectives, doing everything right, but Vicky had hit him and pushed him into oncoming traffic and his lungs had been crushed when another car went over him, unable to stop in time. He'd died in the rain less than a minute later, gasping his last – terrified and confused, no doubt.

She had caused that. She'd never told any of her friends, not even her brother. The shame was too great. She had appeared at the magistrates' court, accepted her conviction for driving without due care and attention. Her negative breathalyser, the bad weather, her previous spotless record, her obvious contrition – she had cried the whole time in the witness box – all meant she served no time in prison. She'd paid the fine and accepted her suspended licence for a year. To other people she had simply made the excuse that she was trying to do her bit for climate change, then later she'd insisted they hire a nanny with a driving licence. When she needed things she got them delivered. It was surprisingly easy not to drive at all in London, and no one had needed to know, bar a tiny item in the local paper.

Vicky knew she had not meant to kill Tomasz, that it could have happened to anyone. It wasn't as if she'd been speeding or looked at her phone. She was just tired, so very tired and distracted, and it had been dark and the visibility poor. She was by no means a killer – the courts hadn't even given her one day in jail. But all the same she would never forget him, his mother crying in court, his younger sisters (Liliana, Krista). His girlfriend, Lucy. His white Adidas trainer lying in the middle of the road. The sound of the car that ran over him, helpless to stop, and that driver's life ruined forever too. She would never forgive herself for it. And certainly she had not meant to harm Fergus, a young good-looking local she'd barely given a second glance to before that day. It was just unfortunate, rough seas coupled with youthful high spirits and a disregard for danger. She had hardly even thought of him in all this time, but deep down, she must have known she was capable of causing someone's death and carrying on with her life as if nothing had happened. And now it had happened for a third time, in a way she could not explain or rationalise or mitigate. She had pushed a knife into Louise, once her best friend or even possibly more, felt the give of skin and muscle and the thunk of bone on blade. Seen the shock in her friend's eyes as the blood bubbled up. She had killed Louise and even the most lenient court would see that as a crime.

In some ways it was almost a relief that someone else had seen what she'd known in her bones ever since Fergus: she deserved to be punished for what she had done.

Amira

Amira had felt on the verge of passing out for the past hour. Not just from the cold and wet seeping into her bones, or the fact that she was bleeding, or the series of deaths that just kept coming, but the sheer unbelievability of what she was hearing and seeing. Her mild-mannered husband – Lovely Paddy – swearing and turning on his oldest friends. Accusing Vicky of terrible things. Saying he, along with Louise, had planned this horrible prank and carried it out without his wife even knowing. Had held hate in his heart for over twenty years. Had been in love with Vicky. And now he was saying Vicky and Jonathan might have killed someone?

Someone else?

'I don't understand,' she said weakly.

Paddy was still dripping muddy water on to the flagstones of the kitchen, but since they were already spattered with Louise's blood, it hardly mattered. Normal life just seemed to have stopped. No one appeared to have even heard what she said. The four of them, her and Fiona and Vicky and Paddy, were standing about like people in an awkward play.

'We didn't kill Fergus,' said Vicky in a stony voice. 'It was an accident. You were there, Paddy, you know that.'

'I know Jonathan pushed him to take the boat too far. I know we didn't go in after him when he fell. I know you made us pull Jay out first, then row away.'

'But it wasn't safe – we could have drowned too!' Vicky's voice broke. 'It was terrible, what happened. I never got over it.'

'You certainly seemed to, when a month later you got together with Daniel.'

'Because I couldn't bear to look at you! Any of you! You all knew what had happened, what I'd – what we did. Daniel didn't know. He still saw me as . . . good. You all knew that I wasn't.'

'That's what you got wrong, Vic. We knew and we still loved you.' But there was no softness in his voice now, no love.

'I didn't see you stopping me,' she said, trembling. 'Or Louise, for that matter. Why should I take all the blame?'

Paddy gave a deep sigh. 'Lou and I had no clue, Vic. Working-class kids, poor kids. We didn't know it wasn't safe to take the boat out that far. Well, I certainly didn't. I hadn't even been on a boat before the ferry to Tarne, do you know that? Not so much as a pedalo. I was too embarrassed to say, and I was terrified when we drifted out that far and the waves were so high, coming over the side. I was so afraid it would capsize, and then, well – there was Jonathan. Horsing about. Competing with . . . the poor boy. And they both fell in, and we chose to save one. You made us complicit.'

Fiona had her eyes closed, as if she were about to cry. 'He wouldn't tell me. I knew there was something.'

'He's my brother,' shouted Vicky. 'He can only use one arm, of course we pulled him out first! Fergus was always bragging about how good he was at swimming. I didn't even notice he'd gone under until – well . . .'

'Will someone please explain to me what you're talking about?' Amira forced her voice out through chattering teeth, and finally they turned to look at her.

'We all came here for the summer,' Paddy said finally. 'We took the boat out, with this local kid – his dad was one of the harbour boatmen. He fancied Vicky, he was showing off, him and Jay goading each other on, we went out too far . . . well, the truth is, they both went in, we didn't get him out in time, and he drowned.'

'But – how? If he could swim?'

'The water's barely ten degrees even in high summer. And the waves are much stronger than you can tell from here. Plus, what the boatman was saying yesterday about cold-water shock. It was too late. We lost him in the water, and he washed up onshore the next day.' Paddy closed his eyes briefly. 'He had a hold of Jay's arm and Jay . . . pulled his fingers off. Let him go under.'

Just as she had done to Jonathan. She shivered. 'That's awful.'

Vicky said, 'Yes, but it was an accident. We all felt terrible, but what could we do? It was right to pull Jay out first, with his arm. But of course it looked bad. The rich kids, saving their own, letting the local boy die.'

'Could all of this be something to do with the boy?' Amira asked. 'It just seems a big coincidence, another death on the island. What happened after?'

'We left. Daddy drove us back to the mainland that day. Then later the island was sold. So yeah, the last time I came here was that summer. But I'm sure everyone's long forgotten about it. It was over twenty years ago!'

Amira wasn't so sure. 'But his family—'

'Look, who cares about some stupid accident from years ago! People are dying now. And Paddy and Louise planned it all.'

'No, no! I keep telling you, no one was supposed to—'

'Yeah, you keep on saying that, Paddy, but the thing is people *are* dead. Three of them!'

'And you killed one of them, Vicky!'

She was shaking. 'I had to. It was self-defence, protecting my kids.' But she no longer sounded convinced.

'Funny how none of these deaths are ever your fault, Vic. The cyclist, or Lou, or—'

She screamed at him. 'Don't say that! Go on then, if you didn't do all this, who did? If there's someone else out here watching us, then where are they? Hiding in the caves, ready to come out once it gets dark? Was it them who sent me the cottage in the first place? Or was it you?'

Vicky had suddenly moved into the kitchen, and Amira was very aware of the block of knives behind her. Missing one, but there were another five just sitting there. Waiting to be used.

'It wasn't me!' said Paddy. 'I swear.'

'Then who? How did we end up here?' The knives were inches from her hand now.

'I don't know! The cottage was nothing to do with me. It was just supposed to be the note. The clippings. Some scares, that's all. To make you think about all the damage you do, you and Daniel and Jonathan. The stuff with the kids – that was just to show you what you're passing on, what you're turning them into, before it's too late. Fiona, I've nothing against you, not really. Rachel, just collateral damage. And Lou – that was on you, Vicky. You killed her. Christ, you've no idea how hard her life has been, and you just . . . snuffed her out. Jesus, Vic. You're a murderer.'

'It was self-defence! And I'll do it again if I have to.'

'Oh what, you're going to stab me too?' Paddy sneered.

'Don't push her,' Amira cried. 'Paddy, come on. Things are way out of hand.'

'She's right,' said Fiona shakily. 'Please, everyone, calm down. If Paddy swears he didn't hurt anyone, maybe we should believe him.'

'After that stunt with the note? Why would I believe anything he says?'

239

'I'm not the one covered in blood,' Paddy said quietly, and Amira clenched her fists in fear.

Things hung in the balance for a moment. Vicky's gaze seemed to turn over her shoulder, to the knives. Amira was poised, ready to run forward and . . . what? Wrestle her down? Throw herself on the blade to save Paddy?'

Then Vicky shook herself and held up her hands. 'I'm done with this. It's dark now, and we're clearly not going to be rescued by some Michelin chef anytime soon. We need to secure the house before night – my kids and my niece are in here and I'll do what I have to. So you . . . need to get out.'

Paddy frowned. 'What do you mean?'

'Get out of this house. Get as far as you can away. Go to the shed.'

'But it's freezing!'

'I don't care. You're lucky I don't gut you where you stand. No court would convict me, after what you've done. Not with my babies here.'

Fiona said, 'Vic—'

'Shut up! Your daughter is here too, and she was on their disgusting list! Don't you care what they do to her?'

'But – it's Paddy!'

'Yeah, Paddy who planned all this . . . horror. He's not who we thought he was.'

Amira could not help but agree. The man standing there, hair damp, in the jumper she had bought for him, was a total stranger.

'What about Amira?' said Paddy, as if finally remembering she existed.

'What about her?'

'I didn't know about any of this,' Amira said. 'I promise. I just – I'm in as much shock as you are.'

Vicky narrowed her eyes. 'How do I know that? You've never liked me.'

Amira protested. 'You've never liked *me*. I tried and I tried. Fiona, you were usually nice to me, but in general I've always been made to feel like the cleaner or something. Always an outsider, though I've been around for fifteen years now.'

Fiona had the grace to look ashamed. 'You aren't going to make her sleep outside, Vicky? It's so cold.'

'I don't trust her. She's his wife, not my friend. And she's just discovered her husband's been in love with me for twenty years. She's always been jealous of me.'

'Amira?' said Paddy. He was holding out his hand. 'Stay with me. I don't trust Vicky – she's already killed one person today.'

'Well, I don't trust you!' retorted Vicky. 'For all I know you have too.'

'I haven't,' said Paddy irritably. 'But you're right, it makes more sense if we spend the night apart. In the morning the boatman should come back for us and we can sort this whole mess out.'

Amira was still hesitating. Yes, he was her husband, who she'd slept beside almost every night for fifteen years. But he had planned all this and not even told her. And then there was the radio in his case.

'It was just a prank?' she said. 'The note?'

'Yes, I told you. Turning the tables on Daniel, showing Vic and Jay they can't just trample over people. It was only supposed to scare them a bit. Daniel being Daniel, he couldn't even think of games of his own accord, so we'd already agreed we were going to play Two Truths and a Lie. I wrote the note on the ferry, and Lou slipped it into the box.'

'But – were you going to own up?'

'Of course, at some point. We were going to put the clippings in people's rooms before dinner – that's why we had ones for us too, to cover it up, keep it going as long as possible. Spoil the whole stupid extravagant meal.'

'And then what?'

'Confront them all. Say our piece – then we hoped the chef would let us come back with him, so we wouldn't need to spend a second night. That was our plan, anyway. Then Rachel died and it all kind of . . . unravelled. We couldn't own up in case you turned on us – I didn't even get a chance to speak to Lou after the deaths. We were going to meet in the caves but I couldn't find her. I don't know what she was thinking. I guess I never will.' His voice was bitter as he looked over to where Louise's blood stained the wall.

'No one was meant to get hurt?' Amira repeated.

'No one. I'd never hurt someone on purpose, you know that. Now, are you coming with me or not?'

But he had hurt her, in so many small ways. And someone had killed Daniel, and Rachel. Someone had damaged the boat, perhaps. Who should she trust – Vicky, who she'd always hated, standing there covered in Louise's blood, or her own husband? She sought Fiona's eyes and saw that the other woman was conflicted too. But she had her daughter to protect, a clear course of action. Staying here was the right choice, as Vicky would surely never hurt Darcy, her own niece.

'Alright,' she said, though her heart sank at the idea of going out into the howling gale. 'The shed will be a bit sheltered, I suppose?'

'Come on, we'll be OK.' He took her hand, pulling her to him, as she had longed for all day. He turned to Vicky. 'Promise me you'll leave us alone if we go now.'

'I'm not setting foot outside this house tonight. Stick to the beach and there's no need for us to have contact.'

Very reluctantly, Amira put her coat on. She had never properly warmed up from the water, and the shed couldn't have much heat in its thin wooden walls. Here, the stove was down to glowing embers, but it gave out a comforting warmth still, and the underfloor heating was drying out her socks. And there was food – even if nothing for dinner thanks to Daniel's strange plan – and booze, and a comfortable bed. 'We'll need a torch,' said Paddy, stiffly.

'Just one,' warned Vicky.

Amira asked, 'Can I just get something from upstairs?'

Vicky frowned. 'It's not a hotel, Amira. I said I want you out.'

'It's just I – I'm bleeding.' She could hear the shame in her voice. Fiona caught her eye, a world of apology in her expression. They were all afraid of Vicky now, because she was the one who'd shown how far she was willing to go. And there was still a block of knives on the counter.

Vicky snapped, 'Be quick.'

Amira dashed upstairs, quickly fumbling the radio out of Paddy's rucksack and stuffing it into her small backpack. She added some dry clothes of his, a towel. Her phone was beside the bed, but checking it, she saw that it was out of battery. It wouldn't be much use anyway. She didn't think Vicky would give her time to charge it, so with a last regretful look at the warm soft bed, she left.

'Come on, Amira.' Paddy was impatient. He opened the door into the dark, stormy night, and she stepped out alongside him. 'We have to get away from her. She's out of control. And I need to see for myself where Lou is.'

'But are you sure you want to—'

He was moving at a rapid clip down towards the south beach, the beam of the torch bouncing around, feet crunching on the stones. It was the first time they'd been alone since the crazy events of the day. She scurried after him.

'Are you OK? About Lou I mean.' He glanced at her but didn't answer. 'What's happened, Paddy? You can tell me whatever it is you didn't tell them.'

'I've told you everything. We planned the stupid note and the clippings, just to force them to think about all the horrible things they've done to people, and we were going to reveal the truth and get out of here. Lou said we should have nothing more to do with these selfish, shallow people, and I eventually agreed with her.'

A day before, she would have been elated to hear that. But now at least three people were dead. Rachel, a stranger, but still a human being, with her whole life ahead of her. Daniel, who she'd never liked that much, but had at least spent a lot of time with over the years. Louise, who she'd never got to know well, but who had clearly been a good person, dedicating her life to others. Paddy's friend. How would he get past this?

She said, 'Is that why you took the radio?'

Paddy was silent in the dark. His crunching footsteps came to a halt, and Amira held her breath. 'Ah.'

'I saw it in the bag.' She shook her backpack. 'It's in here.'

His voice was mechanical. 'Oh. That was smart of you. So maybe we can call for help from the beach.'

She sucked in breath. 'So Louise is dead because of you. Because you took it.'

'Louise took it. I was just hiding it.' His voice broke. 'How could I know Vicky would stab her, for God's sake? The whole thing was Lou's idea.'

'And you joined in. Quite willingly, it seems.'

A pause. 'I suppose you want to know why I did it.'

'I can't even begin to imagine, Paddy. I can't follow any of this.'

'Well, with the radio, Lou was worried they'd want to go back right after the game. And she needed them to – well, stew a little more, I suppose. She took it when she was downstairs alone. Honestly, I was afraid she might smash it, so I persuaded her to give me it to hide. In case someone went into her room, I said – well, that did happen in the end.'

'But we could have called for help already! Why didn't you own up?'

'I tried earlier. I couldn't get it to work. And you can't think it was a good idea to confess to having had it this whole time – Vicky just put a knife in Louise, she could easily do the same to me.'

Amira felt hopeless. 'What's going on, Paddy? Do you actually think there's someone out here with us?'

'There could be. It wasn't me who hurt Rachel or Daniel.'

'But – how could they have got here? We'd have seen them if they took a boat over. I've been watching the strait all day.'

He started walking again. 'I don't know, do I? Clearly there's a cave network on the island. Who's to say someone didn't pull up at the cliffs, say, then go through the tunnel, come up and kill them, go back down again?'

Amira mulled it over. 'Why kill Daniel and Rachel, then? Why not the others?'

'I have no idea.' Paddy sounded irritated, like when she failed to grasp how time zones or currency conversion worked. 'We have to protect ourselves while we find out what's going on. Vicky's completely unhinged. She stabbed Lou. I still can't believe it. Is this where they left her?' He shone the torch over the beach, light reflecting off the dark lapping water.

It had been Amira's idea to leave the body here. 'Yes, she should be just – oh. There.'

Louise's body lay on the shingle, sprawled out on the tarpaulin in a pool of her own blood. Eyes open and staring.

'Oh, Lou.' She heard Paddy's voice crack as he knelt down beside her. 'There was really nothing they could do?'

'Fiona tried. You saw, she was covered in blood too. Vicky just – went for her.'

He ran a hand over Louise's ginger curls, tangled by the wind. Her eyes gleamed in the dark. 'Someone will have to tell her mum.

She has no one else – she can barely leave the house any more. What's she going to do without Lou? Christ, it's a disaster.'

'You really think Vicky would hurt us too?'

'I think she's capable of anything if it protects her own interests. And her husband's dead – she's completely unstable. All that grief and guilt too. Despite what she says I know she blames herself for that cyclist, and Fergus. And now Lou as well. She's not a monster, deep down.'

'You always seemed to think so highly of her,' Amira marvelled. 'I was jealous, you know.'

He looked up. 'I know. But sometimes it takes a while to see the truth of people.'

'So what now – we just hide from her all night? It's hardly secure in the shed.'

Maybe they could move the padlock to the inside, would that work? She didn't know. The wind was so loud it was howling past her ears, and they were starting to ache from the inside out. Would Vicky leave them alone or come after them in the night? She was just protecting her children, something Amira would maybe never know. The loss hit her again, somewhere beneath her navel.

'I suppose.' He stood up, stooping to wrap the tarpaulin roughly around Louise, like a blanket. 'I wish I could do more for her.'

'There's nothing we can do now. Come on.'

They trekked back up to the path, skirting round the coast of the island to the other beach. It was so dark Amira could barely see a foot in front of her, the torch's beam faltering against the great black.

'What was that?' said Paddy, freezing suddenly.

The light of his torch slid over the surrounding landscape, casting crazy shadows. On either side, the mossy grass, twisted trees, and shrubs.

'I don't hear anything.'

'Shhh.'

She listened hard. A rustle, maybe. Her heart quickened. 'Is someone here?'

'*Shhhh*. I'm trying to hear.'

Another rustle, like the movement of outdoors clothes, perhaps. A great weariness overtook her. 'Look, it's probably just a sheep again. Come on, we're almost there.'

She wished he would reach for her hand as they picked their way down the rocky hill, but he didn't. She could see a little more as she got used to the dark, the white sand of the beach and occasional gleam of the moon on the water. The waves were unsettled, choppy, and she thought again of Jonathan. The hand seizing her ankle, how she had fought him off, gouging his skin with the paddle. The slick of blood in the water. The lie she had told. She was a killer now too, even if she hadn't been before.

She thought of the note. *You will all either kill or be killed.* 'Paddy? What did it mean, the note?'

'What?' His voice was muffled by the hood of his coat.

'What was true, and what was a lie?'

'Amira, it was all nonsense. We just wanted to freak them out.'

'So there might be a way off the island?'

'We didn't know. I'll admit, I saw the boat had a small hole in it, but Jonathan seemed to think it was safe, so . . .'

'You let him take it out when you knew it might sink?'

Paddy snapped, 'He's so bloody arrogant! Mr Know-It-All about boats and mountains and deserts and you name it, as if he doesn't have a full crew helping him behind the camera. If he was willing to try, I wasn't going to stop him. He was quick to point out I knew nothing about sailing.'

He sounded so bitter again. But she could hardly judge, when she had literally left Jonathan to drown. She had killed, perhaps, like the note had warned, and Jonathan had been killed. So had

Rachel and Daniel and Louise. But it had meant nothing, Paddy said. Just a way to spook them, although now it seemed to be coming true. And could she trust Paddy? She had no choice, because Vicky was clearly prepared to kill anyone she saw as a threat.

The shed looked even smaller than she remembered, just a salt-stained shack on the shore. At least it had a light, which Amira could see was on, the door ajar.

'Did we leave it like that?'

'I don't know.'

She could feel the fear rise in her throat – what if someone was in there already?

Paddy pushed on the door, and the wind noise died down as they stepped inside. It was an area maybe eight foot by eight, just about big enough for two to huddle up in. The smell of diesel and neoprene. No one could be hiding inside; there wasn't anywhere to hide. Paddy had found a picnic blanket and was spreading it out. It was cold inside but not freezing.

'Here. Will this do?' He unclipped his life jacket, which he was still wearing from the paddleboard, and laid it down too.

'Yeah.' Amira found she was so tired that she began to droop almost as soon as she lay down on the makeshift bed, the smell of old salt water so prevalent she had almost stopped noticing it. 'What time is it?'

Paddy held his phone up. 'Almost seven.'

'Your phone still works? Mine was dead.'

'Mine almost is. They lose a lot trying to find signal.'

'We should try the radio.'

Amira realised she had no idea how they even worked – did you tune it into a particular frequency, like the one she had in her kitchen at home, or was it more like a walkie-talkie, needing a twin? Paddy took it out, a bulky item, and pressed the buttons on it. It switched on, emitting white static. He turned the dial slowly.

'Well?'

'Um. I'm not sure it's picking up on anything.'

'No sign of that chef, then. Bobby Landford.'

It had seemed nonsensical, the idea of a Michelin-starred chef coming all the way out to this desolate place. But Daniel had a way of not accepting the limitations of the world, and Bobby Landford had really apparently been booked. Did that mean someone had radioed to cancel him? That someone was watching them out here?

'What does it matter? Are you hungry?'

'Not really. It's just strange he didn't show.'

This wasn't such a bad place to hunker down – there were various tins and cans, bottled water and soft drinks, even some dried cereal. Overspill from the cellar storage, perhaps, or provisions for taking on a boat, so you didn't have to carry them down the hill.

'Does the door lock?'

Paddy was fiddling with the padlock. 'No – it only attaches to the loops on the outside.'

'Oh well. I'm sure we'll hear anyone walking about.' And what could they do, if Vicky came and she had a knife? Fight her off with a paddle? That made her think of Jonathan again, and she shivered. She felt like she'd been cold all day. 'I should put on more layers – I can't get warm still.'

'You fell off the board?'

His hand, clasping her ankle, the water splashing as she almost went under. 'Almost. I got soaked.'

'That must have been scary.'

'It was. It's much choppier than you can tell from the shore.'

She waited for him to say he'd been badgering her for years to learn to swim, but he didn't. Instead, he rummaged in the rucksack for a waterproof top with long sleeves, and Amira rolled it on. She took off her jeans, which had never dried properly from earlier, and wriggled into a spare pair of his. It felt strange to undress in front of him, somehow, despite all their years of marriage.

'Better?'

'A little. Thank you.'

Paddy's clothes were wet too, so he took off his coat and waterproof trousers. Underneath he wore jeans and a jumper, both slightly wet. Amira heard him scuffle about, lying down beside her.

'What do we do now?'

'I don't know. Try to rest, I suppose.' She did feel very tired, despite the early hour. It was so dark outside it felt like midnight.

She thought of telling Paddy. *I did see Jonathan. He tried to get on the board, and we would both have gone in, so I pushed him off. I pushed him into the sea.*

Did that count as killing someone? Unlike her, Jonathan could swim, but it had been cold and choppy and the strength in his arms had gone. *Go on, say it.* She could be close to Paddy again, now that their secrets were out in the open. Now she knew the reasons for his new direction in life, his changed attitude. *Paddy, I have to tell you something.*

No. She couldn't bring herself to do it, completely shatter any remaining illusions he might have about her. He turned over beside her on the hard floor.

'Not exactly the luxury retreat we were sold,' he said drily. 'And I can't believe he overcharged us too. Bloody Daniel.'

'We shouldn't speak badly of him. He's dead.'

'I know.' Paddy sighed. 'I never imagined it would be like this.'

'How did you think it would go? After the game?'

'Honestly, it was just supposed to unsettle them. So they'd have to face up to what they did. Then we'd plant the clippings and really freak them out.'

'You included us. Me.'

250

'We had to make it less obvious who did it. Come on, Ammy, you're no killer. You just have a difficult job. You, me, Fiona even – we tried to help people, and maybe we got it wrong, but at least we tried.'

But I've killed now.

She took in a breath that was almost a sob. 'I'm so tired and scared. What if someone's out there, Paddy? Whoever set us up, brought us out here? I feel like the note is coming true somehow, even if you just made it up. We're being killed. Or . . .' She had almost told him about Jonathan, and gulped the truth back down in fear.

'God, I have no idea what's going on. It was Vicky who killed Louise. Jay – well, he might be alright, but if not it was the sea. His own arrogance, again. Rachel, that could have been an accident, just bad luck . . .'

'And Daniel? Do you really not know what happened?' He paused. Her heart dropped. 'Oh Paddy. Please, no . . .'

'It wasn't me! Amira, I'm not a *killer*. You know me.'

But did she? 'So?'

'It's possible the lid just fell down. He was so drunk earlier, you saw that. So, you see, there could be an explanation for all of this.'

'But what about the booking? How did we end up here in the first place?'

'I don't know. Really, I've told you everything now.'

'What are we going to do if we get out of this?' Her voice was very small.

'God, it's going to be a nightmare. Endless police statements. All over the papers probably. I might lose my job, if they can prove I was involved in the note thing.'

Was it a crime – malicious communications, something like that? Either way they'd probably have to move again. A secondary-school teacher wrapped up in multiple murders would never do.

And they'd probably have to eat into the money they were slowly saving up for more IVF. If she could even imagine having a child with this man now, this stranger with cold hands and wet socks. She could feel his breath on her face, steaming in the icy air. And she was so overwhelmed with grief and fear and guilt, for the loss of her possible baby, her lovely husband, her own sense of herself as a good person, that she sucked in a deep breath and let one out that was close to a scream.

'Jesus, Amira! Do you want them to find us?'

'Who? You told Vicky where we were, and according to you there's a rational explanation for all of this.'

'I don't know, I said! I don't know if someone else is out there!' She heard the frustration in his voice. She tried to tell herself it was OK, that she knew the truth of everything now.

But it was only a few moments later when they heard the crunch outside. A sound like someone walking on sand.

Vicky

The children were asleep again, one on each sofa. Vicky wanted to gather them in her arms and squeeze them tight, but it was better that they slept through as much as possible of this terrible night, so she'd carried them downstairs as quietly as she could to keep them in her sight. Now she was pacing up and down, restless. Fiona was over on the armchair, huddled against Darcy, both of them staring miserably into space.

'But where is Dad?' Darcy kept saying. 'Is he dead, is that it?'

'We don't know, darling,' said Fiona. 'He went out in the boat.'

'So maybe he made it all the way over? Maybe they're going to come for us?'

Fiona met Vicky's eyes over her daughter's dark head. Amira had found the boat drifting, so Jonathan had not made it over in that at least. And he could hardly have swum it, with his arm. But by tacit agreement neither of them had said this to Darcy, not yet. Maybe Vicky just couldn't face the loss of her brother on top of her husband, on top of having just stabbed an old friend in the stomach until blood came out of her mouth. Maybe the need to shield the children allowed them to shield themselves.

Darcy clutched her phone on her chest, despite its uselessness. Holding on to it like the kids held on to their soft toys. Louise's body lay on the shore in the dark. Daniel and Rachel's were in the outhouse, hidden from the kids. Vicky's brother was missing somewhere out there. But Jonathan was used to the cold, she told herself, used to being in freezing water. He made shows about it. He'd be alright. He'd come back any minute, soaking wet and dripping and grinning with the sheer life of it all, adrenaline singing through his veins. God, she hoped so.

Fiona couldn't settle either, now jumping up and walking about, testing the doors and locks. 'Is there any chance he's still coming? Bobby Landford? I know it's late but . . . he could be, right?'

'I don't know. I didn't know a thing about it.'

'Five or six o'clock, Daniel said. I'm sure of it.'

Vicky looked at the clock above the fire. Five past seven. She wished she could get back into Daniel's phone, but that would mean holding it to his dead face, and she certainly could not stomach such a thing. But the waiting was killing her.

She picked up the binoculars and peered out. 'You know, I think there is a cruise ship out there.' She could see the rows of lights, far away in the distance. It was hard to believe there were thousands of people, drinking and dancing and eating, unaware that just a few miles away across the water, their group was being stalked and murdered. 'Look!' Her heart leapt up in a way she wouldn't have thought possible before. 'Is that a boat?' Fiona came beside her and reached for the binoculars, snatching at them in a way that would have irritated Vicky if she hadn't been flooded with hope, the strangest sensation. 'You see, the little light moving away from the big ship?'

'Yes. I see it! You think it's Bobby?'

'It must be. Oh, thank God. We need to intercept him! Get down to the jetty, I assume that's where he'll land. Who knows what Paddy might do otherwise.'

'Will it just be him? The chef?'

'I suppose he might have an assistant. I mean, how would he carry all the food up the path otherwise?'

But what if Paddy really did waylay him? Or if someone else was stalking them out here – what lengths would they go to, to chase off intruders? Was she perhaps luring more innocent people here to their deaths? But there was no way to get in touch with Bobby. Then she remembered her previous idea. 'The lights. We can try to signal.'

'You think they'd see them, all the way out there?'

'I think so. Light carries far across the water.'

'It's worth a try. What would we say?'

'I guess the standard SOS. I know how to do that, at least.' Her father had made her learn maritime signals as a bored teen, and she wished she had paid more attention now.

'Sure. Let's try it. I'll watch. Darcy, get the ones over there.'

Darcy ran to the other wall, while Vicky went to the light switch by the door and began to turn it off and on. Three long blasts, three shorts, three long. Repeated. 'Anything?'

Fiona peered out into the dark. 'It's still moving, as far as I can tell.'

'Keep trying, Darce.'

The light flashing had disturbed Genevieve, who stirred and yawned. Vicky saw the confusion dawn on her daughter as she saw where she was, and a fresh burst of anger popped in her. It wasn't fair. Yes, she and Daniel and even Jay might have made mistakes in life, but not the kids. They had to be protected, at all costs.

Darcy exclaimed suddenly. 'Oh no!'

'What?'

'It's turning!'

Fiona squinted. 'She's right, Vic, it's turning away! They're going back! No, no, don't go back, don't go back!' She banged on the window, as if the boat could hear her, leaving dirty smears.

SOS. SOS. Vicky started slamming the switch back and forward, desperate, so that both twins stirred. 'No. No! What happened?'

Darcy was crying. Fiona looked stunned. 'I don't know. Maybe you signalled something that means go back?'

'Of course I didn't.' But she wasn't sure. If only she'd listened during all those lessons her father had tried to give her. 'Argh. I don't know what happened!'

She joined her sister-in-law at the window and watched as the small point of light and life, their only salvation, sailed back towards the cruise ship.

'Mummy,' said Genevieve, sitting up. 'What's going on?'

'Where's Daddy?' said Toby, rubbing his eyes.

'I'm hungry.'

'Where's *Daddy*?'

Vicky sucked in a breath. What were they going to do? Even if they made it through the night, fought off Paddy and whoever else might be hunting them, how could they be sure the boatman would come back for them in the morning? If he'd managed to cancel the chef, Paddy could have got to the boatman too, told them they were staying longer – or worse, that they'd already left. They could be stuck here for weeks! But then Paddy and Amira couldn't get off either. Trapped on this small island, with three dead bodies and at least one person who wanted to kill her. What would she do?

Fiona sounded broken, mechanically rubbing her daughter's back as she wept. 'I don't understand how any of this happened.'

It could easily have been their signal that made the boat turn around, some maritime convention Vicky didn't understand. But what was more likely – that the other group on this island had signalled first? Who knew, maybe they even had the radio hidden away. Amira had been carting what looked like a hefty backpack when she'd sent them off. They could have called the ship and told them not to come, and scuppered all of Vicky's plans of rescue. Assuming it was just them. Could someone else be involved too? Could it be *all* of them? Everyone she loved and trusted, out to get her? She felt like she was going mad.

Each twin came up beside her, winding their arms around her, and she hugged them tight, knowing that as long as she was alive she would fight to save them. 'Darlings, will you go up to bed with your cousin? I think you should all try to get some sleep.'

'It's nowhere near my bedtime.' Darcy sniffed, wiping her eyes with the heel of her hand. 'Urgh. OK.' She stood up and held out a hand for each twin. 'Come on then, rugrats.'

Vicky watched them climb the stairs, her heart aching with how carefully the little ones had to place their feet, then went over to the sideboard, opened the carved box that still contained the original notes from the game.

'What are you doing?' said Fiona.

'That stupid game. There has to be some clue in all this. About why it's happening.'

'But we know why. It was Paddy and Louise who wrote the note, but it didn't mean anything.'

'Then why is all this happening – the radio, Bobby Landford not coming, the boat sinking? Rachel, Daniel? Did you believe Paddy, that it's not him doing it?'

'I – I can't imagine him killing someone, no. Or Lou.'

'Right, so who then?'

'I . . . don't know.'

'Exactly. I have to do something, Fiona. I can't just sit here waiting to be attacked.'

Vicky spread the notes out. All of them had been claimed except three. One of the three said, *I've lost twenty pounds this year. I'm a parent. I once threw up in a wardrobe.* She'd thought that was

Daniel's, with the weight loss being the lie. But maybe not. 'Fi, did Paddy ever throw up in a wardrobe?'

'What? I don't—'

'He did, right? At the start of second year. Just after we came here. It's why he cut down on booze so much.'

She remembered it now, helping him to bed, how drunk he'd been, and how he'd mumbled on and on about boats and the sea and the thing that they did. It was not long after that she'd let herself sleep with Daniel. Daniel, who didn't know what they'd done to Fergus, and likely wouldn't have cared if he did.

'I – maybe, yeah.'

'So this is Paddy's answer, I think. The parent bit is the lie. He's lost weight since we last saw him, could easily be as much as twenty pounds.'

Fiona threw her hands up. 'OK. So what? What could these possibly tell us?'

'So that means one of these two is yours.' She pushed them over to her friend.

> *I've slept with two people here. I never wanted kids. I've had a threesome.*

And the other.

> *I've slept with two people in this room. I've thought about how to kill someone and not get caught. I don't believe in the Moon landings.*

'Weird, isn't it, that two people wrote the same thing? The only person who'd done that, as far we all knew, was Jay. But it wasn't his. We had his first. And it isn't mine. So which of these is yours, Fiona?'

'Vicky, I—'

'I know you always wanted kids, since you were little, and you certainly haven't had a threesome. Have you?'

'Well, no, but—'

'I think the first one is Daniel's. He was kind of obsessed with threesomes. He always boasted he'd had one at uni, but Louise told me it wasn't true.' She thought about it, pieces clicking into place. 'He probably thought it was funny to put that in, given I'd believe it was true, but it never actually was. So if it was a lie – if that was just another one of his tall stories – then the other two must be true. He didn't want kids. I think I always knew that, deep down. He hardly even looked at them. And he slept with someone else in the Group.'

'But we don't—'

'And you. I imagine most doctors have at least thought about how to kill someone and get away with it, and you can't stand people who believe in conspiracy theories, you think they're all morons, so that's the lie. You see what I'm saying? Either way, it's true that two people here have slept together. It could have been you and Jonathan, it could have been me and Lou, or Jonathan and Rachel, even, but it wasn't. Right? It was you and Daniel.'

In the firelight, Fiona's face had drained of blood. 'Vic . . .'

'It was Daniel, right? You slept with him. And I know when, too. While I was in having the twins and you stayed over to be on hand. I remember noticing the spare room hadn't been slept in and I wasn't sure why. You fucked him, in my bed.'

Fiona hissed, 'Keep your voice down! The kids will hear.'

She didn't care. 'Why shouldn't they know what you're really like? That you betrayed me? Betrayed my brother? My God, Fiona. How could you do it?'

'I – I was just so sick of Jonathan cheating on me. It never stopped, especially once he got on TV. I wanted to get my own

259

back. And you were so bloody smug about it – *oh Fiona, my marriage is so happy, oh Fiona maybe if you just took better care of yourself, just lost two stone and fixed your hair and your nails and your entire personality, then maybe he wouldn't cheat.* Well, it turns out Daniel was exactly the same.'

It was as if she'd always known it. Even Fiona had turned against her. 'I don't understand why you'd put it in the note last night. Why risk it all coming out now?'

'I didn't think anyone would realise. Or if Jonathan figured it out, then it served him right. But then, last night, we had a kind of moment, after Rachel went to bed, and I didn't want to own up to it. I thought, maybe, once we got off here . . .' Fiona was staring at her hands, eyes hollow. 'I'm so sorry, Vic. I just wanted him back. And now he's . . . lost out there.'

Rage surged up through Vicky like a wave, unstoppable. 'So even you can't be trusted. You slept with my husband, while I was in labour.'

'I'm sorry!'

'Oh, screw your sorry. I trusted you – you were the only one! – and now I find out you've been lying to me for five years. Laughing at me behind my back.'

'No, Vic, I haven't – Vic, stop.'

Vicky looked down. Without fully realising, she had pushed back her chair and stood up. Fiona leaped up from the sofa now too, and her eyes darted to the kitchen. Vicky saw what she was looking at. The knife block, with one still missing. The one she had used to kill Louise.

Amira

Amira stood looking out to sea, peering into the darkness of the night. 'I'm sure that boat was headed for here.' She'd been so full of hope when she saw it, and then it had inexplicably appeared to turn away, swinging towards Tarne. The Michelin-star chef they'd all thought might magically rescue them, but there was no sign of him. God, she wished she was on the cruise ship she could see in the far distance, sipping a martini and eating a prawn cocktail. Listening to lounge piano. Gently bored and drunk, not freezing and terrified for her life.

They had opened the door after hearing what sounded like footsteps on the sand round the shed. Paddy was prowling around, shining the torch with its meagre light.

'I definitely heard something,' she insisted.

'So did I, but it could have been another sheep. Or one of those seals.'

She wouldn't fancy meeting one of those in the dark, despite how friendly the one had seemed in the sea. Some of them were twice her size. 'Come on, let's go back in.' It was at least marginally warmer in the shed.

Paddy nodded reluctantly, and then went in, getting back under the makeshift covers. Amira had no idea how they'd get through the hours until dawn, and then there was no guarantee the boatman would come back anyway. She wished Paddy would hold her, but she was glad of his presence all the same, not to be totally alone out here. It was hard to believe that just across the strait, the pubs would be busy and the restaurants full, with light and laughter and clinking crockery and music. They had wanted to get away from it all, to be totally private, but look – when you turned your back on civilisation, it wasn't always there when you decided you needed it after all. No police, no ambulance, no boat. No one coming to help them, and at least three dead bodies on the island with them. How were they going to explain all this? Would she go to prison for her role in it?

They had just settled down when she heard the crunch from outside again, and sat bolt upright. 'Paddy!'

'I heard it. Ssssh.' He stood up and yanked the light switch, plunging them into brightness again. Amira held her breath. Another footstep. Whoever it was, they were right outside the shed. The other side of the thin layer of wood. She heard a clanking sound, a loud whirr, and then the light went out.

Amira screamed. She couldn't help it, an atavistic response as if she'd found a spider on her arm. 'The power!'

'I know, I know!' Paddy was speaking in a harsh whisper. 'Be quiet. Someone's out there.'

'See who!'

'For God's sake, what if they attack me? People have died, Amira!'

But she couldn't bear it. Waiting for the unlocked door to open with a creak, as the footsteps crunched once, twice, three times – and then she realised they were turning away. Whoever it was had gone. Paddy lunged for the door, shining the torch again. Surely it would not last much longer. 'Amira, the generator. It's stopped!'

Sure enough, she could see that the entire island was now in darkness. No ambient light from the jetty or from the house, reaching over the hill. And the comforting background hum of the machinery had also stopped. Total silence. Someone had cut the power.

Vicky

'Christ!' snapped Fiona, her back almost up against the sink, blocking Vicky from the knives. 'What was that?'

A buzzing noise had started up. Vicky swung her head around and saw that the TV had turned itself on. At first she'd thought it was the kids, but they were upstairs, and anyway, they wouldn't have understood how to make it work without touchscreen like they had at home. 'Did you do that?'

'Of course I didn't,' snapped Fiona. 'Did you?'

'Don't be ridiculous. Look!'

It wasn't just the TV. The microwave in the kitchen had also started whirring, and the coffee maker had blinked to life. A blast of music came from the stereo system. Fiona dived to turn it off.

Vicky felt the hairs on her neck rise again. She thought that if she could manage to detach herself from all this, it would almost be interesting, this experience of being so very afraid over a sustained period. 'Is someone else doing this?'

'How?'

'I don't know. It could be on a timer or . . .' Their TV at home was controlled remotely, and once or twice one of the twins had given her an almighty scare by switching it on from their iPads. But that wouldn't work out here, surely, with no Wi-Fi. As she watched, the screen began to display an image.

She knew that picture. It was from the summer ball, before they'd come to the island. Just before the accident. Her, Jonathan, Fiona, Paddy, Louise, Daniel. She was smiling, lit by sunshine, arms around Paddy and Fiona. Daniel off to one side as if he'd photobombed the shot, wearing an askew bow tie. Jonathan with his arm round Fiona, Fiona's gaze on him not the camera, adoring. Louise beside him, but awkward, not quite making contact, as if she didn't belong. Paddy looked cross. Jonathan looked proud, Daniel drunk and arrogant. And she, Vicky, looked radiant. Happy, adored, standing in a crowd of people who all loved her, at least three of them romantically. The Golden Girl. She had this picture framed on her wall at home. The caption read: *Oxford, 2002*. This must be the rest of the slideshow from the night before.

Then it shifted – a whole montage of pictures. Black tie, sub fusc, swilling champagne, her hair badly cut but still shining, her clothes sometimes ill-fitting, skimpy, cheap-looking if not actually cheap. The cut-out tops and baggy jeans of the early 2000s. Her and Fiona. Her and Louise, her and Paddy. Her and Daniel, one of their first pictures as a couple, posing at another ball, this one Christmas of that year. Her dress navy taffeta. Jonathan and Fiona, Fiona in a red cheongsam, hair pinned up. The pictures whipped through the years. Vicky and Daniel's wedding, Jonathan and Fiona's, a baby Darcy, baby Toby and Gen, everyone so happy, everyone smiling, new cars, new houses, her parents, her and Jay, Jay winning an award in a tux, and another award, and another, Vicky getting her law degree . . . It was actually nice. A tribute to her life, such as might be pulled together for a fortieth birthday. She had a vague memory of Daniel up in the loft a few weeks ago, crashing about looking for old pictures – and yes, the WhatsApp thread had also mentioned making a slideshow, she remembered now.

'So it's just—'

Fiona made a noise in her throat. The image had shifted suddenly – it was a police mugshot. A woman, sullen-faced and pale. It was Vicky.

'Oh my God. That's – they took that when I was arrested for the . . . the man who died. The cyclist.'

Vicky didn't understand. Why would Daniel . . . Then the picture changed. A body on a wet road, covered by a coat. Where had that come from? Looked like someone's social media, and of course she'd never seen it from this angle because she'd been on her way to the police station by then and Tomasz was already dead.

'This is horrible!' Fiona rushed over, scrabbling for a remote. 'How do you turn it off?'

But the images rolled on. News reports of the company scandal. New shots of baby Lola that she'd never seen, again as if from Facebook. Industry shots of Jonathan's cameraman, some from award ceremonies, some more intimate, his wife, her pregnant swell. It was all of them. All of their crimes. All of their victims. With a sickening lurch, she even recognised Julia's mother in there.

'I can't turn it off!' Fiona was stabbing at various remotes, but there were at least five of them. The blinds went up with an electronic whirr. The lights came on and off. Music suddenly blared, making them both jump. 'Christ, what is this? I can't stop it!'

Finally, it came to a halt. On the screen was a montage of different people. From a baby to a woman in her seventies. A teenage girl, a toddler, a teenage boy. A twenty-something woman. A twenty-something man. A woman in her late thirties, perhaps. Vicky counted – ten images. All the people they had, between them, killed.

Then the title. Blood-red letters. *Happy birthday, Vicky and Jonathan!*

The final image was one she had not seen before either, and could not immediately place. A different teenage boy, tall and

265

handsome, squinting into the sun by a harbour. It was Tarne harbour, she realised. The photo looked old, from the nineties perhaps, given his clothes.

Fiona had given up and was staring at the screen, two different remotes in her hands, neither the right one. 'Who—'

'Is this the DVD from last night? In the machine?'

'I – I think so.'

'So who made it? Was it Paddy again?' She was going to kill him for all this. How dare he hurt her like this, scare her kids.

'No, no – there was a Google folder, we were all meant to put photos in for Daniel, and then he was going to get someone to make it. I guess he didn't look at the pictures before he sent it off?'

That was Daniel all over. Careless, making the least effort possible. 'So who did it? Think!'

Fiona was scrolling through her phone messages, looking in the secret birthday group. Vicky was also trying to remember what she'd read on Daniel's phone the night before. When he'd been lying beside her, warm and snoring, not cold and dead next door. 'It says . . . Oh my God.'

'What?'

'It was the owners. The people we hired it from. He asked them to – but I don't understand.'

But Vicky had figured it out, and suddenly she understood all of it. Why they were here, what this was all about, even. The true guilt she carried, that had brought her back here, to the place where it happened. Where she became, once and forever, a bad person.

'I think I know who's doing this,' she said.

That was when the bulbs overhead flickered and fused, blared madly so that she winced and shielded her eyes, and from upstairs she heard Darcy scream, and the lights went off.

Mhairi

The radio was even harder to understand this time, in the wind at the top of the small hill. 'What's that, Davey?'

'We checked with all crafts in the area like you said. Heard back from a cruise ship! The *Fastnet Rock* it's called.'

'And?'

'Get this, boss, they have this chef, Bobby Whatsit, on board, he's got a Michelin star, I saw him on that *Chef's Table*, you know on Netflix and—'

'*Davey.*'

'Right, yes. He was booked to go out to the island to cook for them. On the Saturday night.'

Mhairi could not fathom that – the depths of entitlement where you would even begin to think you could hire a famous chef to come and cook just for you. But if someone had visited the island on the Saturday night, that could explain where her missing guests were. Safe and sound on a cruise ship, perhaps. 'And it all went ahead?'

'Nah, wait till I tell you. Said they ran the credit card ahead of booking, and it flagged as no funds available.'

'What? Whose card was it?'

'Daniel Franks's.'

She pondered that. Daniel was a rich man, by all accounts. Made a fortune in the city. Three cars. A nanny, or at least until recently, according to his PA in London, and Mhairi was planning on pulling at that thread too once she got back to a reliable internet connection. 'So what, he was actually broke?'

'Aye. Looks like his accounts are all maxed out. His bank says he made some big payment a few months back, to a Miss Cody Bellario, and his work said he didn't get his bonus at work this year. Poor performance, excessive drinking, blah blah.'

'Weird. So why on earth would you book a private chef if you were broke?'

'Keep up appearances. Look the part, you know. For the 'gram.'

She sighed heavily. 'For the 'gram. Right, so, what you're saying is, the chef never made it over.'

'That's right. They'd have sailed into quite a situation if they did, wouldn't they. But no, they never left. There was a tender went over to Tarne that night, but nobody picked up any signals from the island.'

The chef and his team might have spared themselves by not going, but they would possibly also have saved some lives if they had. As it was, these people had been marooned out here for two nights, with no radio and no electricity, and at least three of them dead already. She could only imagine their panic. And panic was like a knife slipping between the ribs, gouging out a hole, pulling you apart until it all unravelled.

Amira

She couldn't see a thing. You thought you knew darkness, the faint gloom of the inner city, lit by street lamps and flashing signs, where you needed a blackout blind to even sleep, and confused birds sang all night long. But here it was – the real thing. The only light was the faint glow that filtered over the sea from the bigger island and mainland beyond, the high cold stars, and the distant twinkle of boats on the sea. She tried to slow her breathing.

Amira held up the torch, its light weak. 'Did it break? The generator?'

Paddy was stabbing at its control panel, holding his phone up, the beam of that fading too. He must be almost out of charge. 'I don't know. It seems to be dead.'

'Could it just be out of fuel? It runs on fuel, right?'

'Wake up, Amira!' he snapped. 'Someone is doing this.'

'You mean apart from you and Louise?'

'Yes! We didn't poison Rachel or steal the EpiPen, did we? Or sink the boat or turn the power off. Someone has brought us here. For revenge.'

'But I don't understand. Someone else thinks we killed all those people? How would they know?'

Again, the terrible distrust. He had started this, her husband. Had planned this horrible trick for his supposed best friends. How did she know he hadn't gone further? Maybe he included her as one of the guilty. After all, she had allowed the death of that little boy. She could have saved him, and she hadn't.

Paddy said, 'I've been trying to think. What if it's one of the cases, the people we killed? Someone who wants revenge on one of us – one of the families of the victims, I don't know. Anyone. And they've lured us here somehow to pick us off, and it's just a coincidence Louise and I decided to play the trick this weekend. Vicky said someone emailed her about the island, and the website didn't seem to exist. Weird, right?'

'But we didn't kill them. They were all just terrible, terrible accidents.'

He shrugged. 'Maybe people don't make the distinction. You cause a death, you may as well be a killer.'

She took that in. If that were true – and he didn't even know about Jonathan – maybe she was just as guilty as anyone here. 'Paddy, there's something I haven't—'

'Shhh!' He seized her arm. 'There it is again.'

The crunch of feet. In what sounded like heavy boots. Not a sheep or a seal. A person.

Amira tried not to breathe, but she couldn't help it, she was panting with fear now, sweat rolling down between her shoulders even though she was so cold she couldn't feel her hands, and she was shivering and whimpering, and then someone burst from the bushes towards them. Someone tall and bulky and breathing hard, shaking water off in droplets.

'You fucking bitch. You tried to kill me!'

It was Jonathan. Back from the depths, not drowned but wet through, and like a totally different person to the genial friend who always helped her out in group situations. She saw his eyes in the torchlight, and there was only rage.

Paddy stepped towards him as he advanced, hampered by his wet clothes. His voice sounded normal, though Amira could hear a telltale shake in it. 'Jay, man, it's good to see you, we thought the worst.'

'Oh, you did, did you?'

'Amira said she couldn't find you, but the boat was capsized and—'

Jonathan barked a laugh. His voice was hoarse, as if from shouting for help. 'Oh, she said that did she? Didn't tell you that she found me just fine, clinging on for dear life, but she pushed me into the water?'

'What?' Paddy whirled round to stare at her, and Amira was right back to that day in the police station, explaining over and over her decision to let a little boy stay in a house where he would be killed. The guilt that would never leave her.

'I – that's not what happened. He was trying to get on to my board, we would have both gone in. And I can't swim, you know that! I'd have drowned.'

'So you left *me* to drown? With only one arm?'

'But – Jonathan, I had no other choice! I was planning to get Paddy's board and go back for you, but you'd gone under. Or I thought you had. I didn't want to die too. I'm sorry.'

And I thought I was pregnant. The idea seemed ridiculous now.

'Amira, how could you lie about this?'

Paddy was looking at her as if he'd lost what little respect he had for her. As if he'd always thought her a little boring and slow, but at least like him a good person, a principled person, who'd chosen an important job over holidays in the Seychelles and a house in zone 2 and, oh, more rounds of the IVF they'd likely need to have a child. But now he saw her as she'd always feared she was. A hypocrite, a killer. A bad person.

Amira couldn't help but defend herself. 'You were the one who let him go when you knew the boat had a hole in it!'

'He wanted to go! Didn't you, Jay? The great boat expert?'

'Don't you call me *Jay*. I figured it out while I was stuck out there, clawing myself up on the rocks. You must be behind this. The note, and even Rachel – it was you who made the bloody cake! And you're the one most likely to have killed Dan – after we found Rachel, you came back to the house a good while after Vic. That's when you must have done it. It was you.'

Amira burbled, 'Well yes, the note, but not all of it, he didn't—'

Paddy shouted, 'For fuck's sake, Amira, he doesn't know!'

Jonathan took a step closer to Paddy. 'So I was right – you did this? It was all you?'

'No, no, that's not—'

'Oh, this makes perfect sense. I don't know why I didn't see it sooner. Weaselling round my sister all this time. You kept it up for years, didn't you? Doing your little law course to be with her. Daniel didn't care, he just found it funny that a runt like you thought he had a chance with her. Someone who never knows what wine glass to use and calls it the *toilet*. She wouldn't have spit on you, mate. So I guess you settled for this sad cow instead. And now you want revenge. I know you hated Dan. But why Rachel? You didn't even know her.'

Don't listen don't listen. But Amira could feel tears pricking her eyes at this tirade.

Paddy was shouting. 'I didn't do it! I just – we did the note thing. Louise and I. But I didn't kill anyone, I swear!'

'Louise too? Well yeah, that tracks. You two were obsessed with Vic, it's gross really. Pretending you're so happy to be saving the world and making fuck-all money, so you take it out on those of us who've succeeded. Worked hard.'

'Oh, that's rich. Did you work hard or did your dad sort it all for you? Find you an internship at a TV company, pull in favours? And it's perfectly true, you are all killers. You and Daniel and your precious sister. Guilty as any murderers. We all know about what happened on the mountain.'

'I didn't . . . Pete was a good mate, I was gutted about that. It was an accident. How fucking dare you.'

'But what about the first time, eh? What about Fergus McCann?'

Jonathan seemed to freeze at the name. Amira was lost. 'Who is that? The boy who drowned?'

Neither of them paid her any attention.

Jonathan was yelling. 'That was an accident! Christ, what is wrong with you? It's not like you've never had the same thing happen to you. That kid, the cliff?'

Paddy shouted, 'That wasn't my fault! He snuck out to see his friends, the staffing ratios were inadequate. You *chose* to take the boat out too far when you knew it wasn't safe. Just like you chose to go up that mountain in the wind. When you capsized today, it was down to your own arrogance. Always trying to prove yourself, always so fucking macho. Well, newsflash, Jay, your dad won't love you no matter what you do.'

Jonathan gave a grunt, like an enraged bear, and crouched in a swift movement. Amira couldn't see what he was reaching for – he didn't have a knife, surely? He'd been in the sea for hours, he couldn't have anything much on him. But it was a rock. He hefted it in his good hand, and swung it right at Paddy's head.

'Christ!' Paddy ducked, but not in time – he wasn't sporty, he didn't have those reflexes honed by years on the football pitch or tennis court – and it caught him beside the ear. Amira heard the crunch. Paddy cried out.

'Jesus! Stop it, Jay!'

'Why should I? You lured us out here to kill us!'

'No I didn't, I—'

'It's true, Jay,' Amira shouted. 'It must be someone else doing this. Paddy and Lou, they just wrote the note. And they had clippings of everything you – we – did. It was just a nasty joke. The kind of thing Daniel likes. Liked.'

'But people are dead! How do you explain that, eh? My girlfriend is *dead*.' Jonathan's voice cracked, and Amira saw that he must have cared for Rachel, even if he still loved Fiona deep down, even if she'd just been a trophy to him.

Holding his ear, blood pouring from it, Paddy mumbled, 'I don't know. I'm sorry about Rachel, I truly am, but that wasn't me. We just wanted to make you see the consequences of your actions.'

'Typical fucking self-righteousness. What about Dan?'

'I don't know. Maybe – look, I think there's someone on the island with us.'

'Convenient for you,' snapped Jonathan. He stooped for another rock, and Amira's stomach lurched. 'And where is your partner in crime now? Where is everyone? You've picked them off already?'

'Fiona and Vicky are at the house with the kids. They're all safe, I promise.'

'And Louise? Hiding out somewhere, waiting to strike?'

Paddy swallowed. 'She's dead, Jay.'

'What?'

'Vicky. Stabbed her.'

'What the fuck? You're lying.'

'It's true,' said Amira. 'She told me herself, and well – I saw her just after. She was covered in blood. She thought Louise was behind all this.'

Jonathan's voice was hoarse. 'Well, well, then – she was right. She was defending herself, her kids. She must have had no other choice.'

'You know,' said Paddy, slowly, 'for people who aren't kill-ers, there's certainly a lot of deaths around your family. Not just that baby, and your cameraman, that man Vicky hit, but Fergus McCann too. And your girlfriend. Some people might think there's a link.'

Jonathan stepped forward. 'What the hell are you saying?'

'Just that, if this all comes out, your reputation isn't going to survive it, is it? Cheating on your wife, and now your bimbo side-piece is dead too?'

'You fucking twat. Rachel had an allergic reaction! From a cake you made. How the hell could I have done that? And why?'

'You tell me. Or better yet, tell the press when they come knocking. You'll need us to vouch for you. We're not your sister or your wife or daughter. We can say you weren't involved. At least, not in Rachel's death.'

'You little prick. You've always been jealous of us, hanging about, glomming off my family. What was it your dad did, owned a potato farm? Jesus.'

'At least I worked for what I've got. And why would I be jeal-ous of someone who couldn't get into university at all, let alone Oxford?'

'You bastard. You and your pathetic fucking wife, leaving me to die. Who do you think you are? A bunch of nobodies, that's who. Can't even get her pregnant, the fat cow.'

That hit Amira, deep in her numb centre. It was what she'd always been afraid of, that people talked behind her back, thought her awkward and ugly and barren. But why was Paddy doing this? Why was he goading Jonathan? She didn't understand. Then she felt his hand grope for hers in the dark, squeeze it. He was trying to tell her something.

Paddy stepped forward. 'Come on then, big tough guy. I might be shorter but at least I've got two hands.'

With a snarl of rage, Jonathan lunged at him, rock in hand. But Paddy was ready, and set off running up the path.

'Go!' he shouted back to Amira. 'Get back to the house!'

And she saw that he had done this for her, to draw away the danger. She stood rooted to the spot for a few moments, until she was shocked out of it by a chill around her ankles. The tide was coming in. She had to move. Paddy had said go to the house, but she wasn't safe there either, not with Vicky and a kitchen full of knives. And Paddy had tried to protect her, so she would do the same for him.

So she did, following Jonathan up the hill. He was not fast, a large and lumbering man, probably still in shock from the cold water, maybe even hypothermia.

It was so dark. She could hardly see anything, only hear the swishes from Jonathan's waterproof trousers and the rasp of his breath, guiding her way over the rocky ground.

She panted over the field, catching her feet on stones and tussocks of moss and grass, barely any idea where she was going. The distant gleam of the sea, and she realised they were heading for the cliff where Louise had gone into the caves. Maybe Paddy was trying to get back down there, if the rope was still in place. Jonathan wouldn't be able to climb with his arm. Or maybe Paddy wanted to avoid the house with the kids, shield them from this violence.

Amira felt once again the hopelessness of an island. There was nowhere to go. There really was no way off, like the note had said. A yelp up ahead. Amira stopped, stumbled, and realised the cliff edge was much closer than she'd thought. Less than a metre away, so close she could feel the spongy moss under her boots. She moved back, heart racing. Her fear of heights as well as water was kicking in – why had she come here? She had known it was going to be horrible and she'd blindly trotted along with it, accepting their share of the astronomical hire fee even though she and Paddy had so much less money than the others, even though they'd got the worst room. She was pathetic, Jonathan was right. She'd spent years trying to make up for something that wasn't even her fault. People-pleasing and fawning over twats she didn't even like. Well, no more.

'Hey!' she shouted. 'I'm over here, dickhead.'

Movement up ahead. She could barely see, but it looked as if Paddy and Jonathan were by the cliff edge. That seemed like the same tree the rope had been tied to.

Amira panted. 'Look, you're right, Jonathan. I did leave you out there. I did think you were dead. So come on then. It's me you want.'

'Amira!' shouted Paddy, from the darkness. 'I told you to go.'

Yes, he had, but she was done listening to him or to anyone. She was going to face this herself, once and for all.

'Come on, Jonathan. You want to fight with a woman, is that it? Makes you feel big and tough? Well, I'm here. What's one more body on this island?'

He was breathing hard somewhere nearby. He wasn't well, clearly. He must have swallowed a ton of salt water. Maybe he wouldn't be much of a challenge. Would she finish him off, if she had a chance? She had done it once, after all.

Paddy, where was Paddy? She could barely keep track of what direction was what, in this pitch-black. She could hear no sound but Jonathan scrabbling towards her. He was muttering to himself. 'Fucking bitch . . . how dare you, how dare you . . . bitch, pricks . . .'

Where is Paddy?

He couldn't have gone over, she'd have heard the splash, wouldn't she? Maybe he'd climbed down the rope?

Amira screamed. Her foot had felt for the earth and found only air. Oh God. She was going to fall. She threw herself in the opposite direction, finding grass under her body, but her feet were hanging off into nothing, and oh God, the cliff was crumbling under her, the weak ground, and she was going, she'd never survive the fall and the rocks and water and—

Her flailing hands found a sturdy shrub, and it held, and she pulled herself up. She was weeping with fear. Where was Jonathan? Where was Paddy?

There. That large dark shape, that was Jonathan. He was peering over the cliff, maybe wondering as she was where Paddy had gone. And as the moon peeped out from the clouds, she saw him yank at the branch where the rope was tied, and crack it hard, leaning his whole strength against it. Amira screamed as it detached, pulled rapidly over the cliff, and vanished, taking the rope with it. Then the moon was gone again. But there had been no noise, no scream or crash. Maybe Paddy had got down already. Maybe he'd never climbed over at all.

Either way, Jonathan had heard her scream, and he was coming her way. 'Your turn, bitch.'

Amira ran. She ran for her life.

Vicky

The darkness was broken only by the glow from the log fire. Otherwise, the entire house, and entire island, were blacked out.

The children were crying upstairs. 'Mummy. Mummy!'

Darcy shouted from the head of the stairs. 'What happened?'

Vicky tried to sound calm, though she felt anything but. 'The power's off, darlings.'

A light glowed out – Fiona's phone. 'Is everyone OK?'

Vicky groped towards the stairs. 'Twinnies, stay still, you might fall.'

'I don't like it, Mummy!' howled Genevieve. 'It's scary!'

She felt her way up, step by step. 'I know it is. Come on, we have to be brave. Darce, where are you?'

'Here.' Her voice came from beside Vicky. 'I'm going down to look for the torch.'

'OK but let's all walk together. These stairs are really dangerous in the dark.'

She tried to calm the waver in her voice. They were safe, the doors were locked, the windows too. A small halo of light from the fire protected them, the darkness encroaching all around. Why had the power gone off just now, after that horrible slideshow? It couldn't be a coincidence, could it? She pictured the generator, the clunky box behind the boatshed. And who was down there? Paddy and Amira of course. No, most likely not a coincidence. They had probably shut it down, to scare her even more.

'Come on, is everyone here?' She felt for Toby's small hand, trusting in hers, and then Genevieve's. Safe. 'OK, let's go down. Step by step. That's right.'

Vicky led the twins down, very slowly, towards the sofa. Darcy and her mother went to the kitchen and started opening drawers, looking for candles or torches.

'Now stay away from the fire, alright? Keep still.' Vicky stood up, looked out the window. 'What is that out there?' she exclaimed. Her eye had been caught by something on the cliff. A small light moving about, extremely visible because everything else was pitch-black.

'Maybe it's . . . them.' Fiona spoke in a low voice.

Vicky wasn't sure how much Darcy had grasped about what was going on, about where Amira and Paddy were, that she'd banished them to sleep in the cold and damp shed. So why were they running about in the dark, if that was them? It looked like the light from a phone, or a torch. No, two lights. Moving around, casting crazy shadows. She remembered seeing Amira's phone upstairs, fruitlessly charging, so it wasn't hers down there. Whose was the second?

Fiona shivered. 'I don't like this. You're sure you checked the doors?'

'Yes, and put the dresser back over the trapdoor in the kitchen.' But the house was old and had weathered many storms through history. It had more secrets than Vicky had ever uncovered, and there could well be other tunnels, other hiding places. Someone could be in here with them.

'Oh my God, look!' Now the lights had moved, and seemed to be travelling faster, up along the brow of the hill. Towards the house. 'They're coming here!' shouted Fiona.

Vicky ran to the door, testing the lock. How sturdy was it? There'd never been any need for a lock out here, it was more symbolic than anything else. She would not let Paddy in (or whoever he was chasing, or whoever was chasing him, but she didn't want to think about that now). She would fight to her last breath before she let them over the threshold. Her eye fell on the block of knives, still missing one. The one she had plunged into Louise's stomach. Could she do that again? Kill a friend?

She knew the answer. Yes, she could do anything if she had to. And would.

Suddenly, the lights stopped, and then Vicky didn't understand what was happening for a moment. A bang so loud the windows rattled, and then an explosion of colour and light raining down.

Fiona gasped. 'The fireworks. For God's sake, someone's set off the bloody birthday fireworks.'

'What?' But of course. She had seen an email about fireworks in Daniel's inbox, but hadn't read it properly in her hurry to search every app on his phone. He hadn't actually ordered some, had he? How on earth had he got them over here?

Vicky returned to the sofa, looking for the kids again in the faint light. As a mother of twins, she was always counting in her head – one, two. Boy, girl. A matter of routine, ticking them off as safe. But now something was up. Because she could only see one now. She moved the blanket that was draped over the sofa, peering in the firelight.

'Gen, where's your brother?'

Genevieve was sucking her thumb, staring past her mother at the lights that filled the sky. Vicky saw them reflected in her eyes – yellow, red, purple. 'Don't know, Mummy.'

'Think, darling! He was just here. Where did he go?'

Stay calm, stay calm.

The front door was locked, she'd just checked it. He couldn't have gone far. She had only crossed the room for a moment to check the lock, and Fiona and Darcy were there in the kitchen rummaging, and a small boy could hardly have vanished from the room, even in the darkness, could he?

'He's scared of the bangs, Mummy.'

That was true. She remembered taking him to Battersea Park last Bonfire Night, and his terrified screams. Typical Daniel, to organise a birthday surprise that would only upset the kids. Some treat. And it cost a fortune. But she had to stop being angry with him, because he was dead, and she was alone. There was only her to protect their kids.

'So where did he go?'

'Don't know, Mummy. He's gone. Toby's gone.'

Vicky wheeled around. 'Toby. Toby! Fiona, he's not here!'

Finally, Fiona had noticed something was up. 'Where is he?'

'I don't know! He's got out of the room somehow.'

'But how? I didn't hear a thing.'

'Well, how could you, when you're crashing about like a herd of elephants? Stop that now and help me find him.'

Vicky ran to the pantry, then into Louise's room. Lifting the covers to peer under the bed, looking behind doors, in cupboards. Nothing. Nothing. Her son was missing.

'Upstairs! He must have gone back upstairs!' She ran up them again, two at a time, slipped at the top in her socks, almost lurched over. Righted herself, heart hammering. 'Toby. Toby!'

Throwing open doors, shining the faint light of her phone. Jonathan and Rachel's room, with her case still spilling out over the bed. Amira and Paddy's, signs of hurried packing everywhere. Fiona and Darcy's, nothing, nothing. The bathrooms. The hall cupboard with the hoover and extra pillows. Nothing. Finally, her own room, the twins' camp beds. Nothing under them, nothing in the wardrobe or en-suite. In one last desperate swoop she pulled back the cover of Toby's bed and stopped. No sign of the boy, but she did find a small pile of objects. Various bottles, expensive toiletries that she realised must have been Rachel's. Medicinal-looking, with glass pipettes, glinting in the light. And Toby was fond of playing doctor like Auntie Fiona.

All at once it fitted together in her mind. Toby liked to poke in people's things. The kids had been left alone while Daniel messed about with the hot tubs, no one supervising them. The toiletry bag must have fallen over in the bathroom *before* Rachel went upstairs. And there in the middle of the pile was what must have seemed like the coolest toy of all, like a real-life injector.

Rachel's EpiPen.

Mhairi

Exhausted and damp, Mhairi put her radio away. The battery was blinking low, and it was her only lifeline to the world. She turned to Arthur, who was hunched up against the light falling rain.

'Any idea why the power might be off? Seems like it's everywhere.' And it was already after three and she did not want to get caught out here in the dark, which would be in about an hour. 'How do they even get power out here – just the generator? No mains link-up?'

'Wind turbine, then generator and battery array for calm days.'

Mhairi didn't like to admit she wasn't the most au fait with machinery. 'And that works by . . .'

'Fuel up the generator for gaps in the wind supply, store charge in the batteries. Usually fine.'

'So it needs actual fuel to run?'

'Aye. Diesel, or propane.'

'But the turbine's not running.'

'No. Likely they turn it off for the winter, saves wear and tear.'

Mhairi thought about this. 'Expensive to run, aren't they, generators?'

'They are that.'

'You're not supposed to leave them full of fuel, are you, if they're not in use?'

'No indeed. Rusts the machinery.'

She looked up at the dome of the island, towards the only area she had yet to search. The nine-metre wind turbine, towering over them, in place of a light that had once guided ships, shattered the darkness, saved lives, brought men home. Standing still and silent, not turning despite the gale. If that wasn't on, the power would have switched to the generator, which would have been quickly exhausted. And if no one was supposed to be staying here over the winter, the fuel would not have been topped up. She had seen this happen once herself – on a remote cabin holiday booked by Callum, of course, not her speed at all. As the generator had surged then failed, all the lights had glowed intensely, and every appliance in the place had switched on at once, terrifying her, before blacking out. If that had happened here, to these paranoid and scared people who had lost three friends already, who knows what could have taken place. Terror. Carnage.

'Come on.' She began striding up the hill, feeling her legs chafe in the waterlogged fabric of her trousers. Arthur hesitated, then followed on. 'Let's check out this turbine.'

'Don't reckon guests can get in there, it wouldn't be safe.'

'But they were desperate, most likely. And maybe they wanted to look out to sea. Or survey the whole island.'

The stem of the wind turbine was rough up close, with peeling metallic paint and lichen. The small door had a rusted key. Mhairi turned it, feeling the heft of all that metal and machinery, but it went around. Inside was a very narrow space, not much wider than her body, dimly lit, shadows pressing from every corner, with a basic ladder running up one side. She looked up doubtfully – the top was very, very far above. Arthur shifted behind her.

'Not think you should wait for the team? The Forensics lads and that?'

She shot him a look. She was in charge here, after all. 'We've yet to find the other guests. Someone could be hurt up there. Look.' And indeed there were drops of blood, leading up to the ladder. A trail for Hansel and Gretel. And despite her fear of heights, her hatred of confined spaces, Mhairi followed it up.

Amira

Amira didn't understand what was happening. She'd been running up the hill, her breath tearing wet in her ears, no sound but the squelch of her feet on the boggy ground and the moan of the wind, when suddenly the world exploded. A fizzle and crack, then colours everywhere, electric green and crimson and bolts of white light so pure it hurt to look, filling the sky, banging and crashing, and at first she thought it was a bomb, but no, it wasn't that. It was fireworks. Of course. Daniel and his surprises – that was where he'd been all morning, with the mud on his boots and his secretive air. He had set up fireworks for Vicky, a gesture that was both thoughtful and thoughtless, because it would disturb the wildlife and probably scare the kids. She herself was not that keen on fireworks – another thing she was afraid of, Amira the wimp. It was one thing to watch a display from a safe distance, and another to be in the middle of it, surrounded by bangs and dazzled by lights.

God, it was so loud. In the flashes of colour, she saw crazy shadows, brief images of the house and the hill, the sheen of colour on the water. Vague impressions of two dark figures weaving in and out of the points of light. Jonathan – and that must mean Paddy was here too, not gone over the cliff. She staggered between them as if in a minefield. How did fireworks work – was there one central switch or had they been triggered by Jonathan or Paddy blundering through them? Amira caught her foot on something and screamed – no, it was just a stick, the firework on it burnt out already. This was crazy, she could lose a foot! She remembered those firework safety ads from the nineties. So she stood very still, and after what seemed like an endless amount of time, the bangs tapered off, a smell like gun smoke in the air, and it was then that she heard the screaming.

An animal in pure pain and rage. A human animal.

Was it Paddy? Had she lost him – could a firework kill a person? Maybe a flurry of a hundred of them could, because that's what seemed to be here. How had Daniel got a licence for this? He probably hadn't. Typical Daniel. She followed the sound of screaming, though it could be leading her into danger.

Vicky

Someone was screaming. When the noise of the fireworks – a brief and overwhelming display, a tumult that shook the house and set sheep baaing and birds squawking – had died down, Vicky could hear a different sound. She dropped the EpiPen back on the bed and ran down the stairs.

'What is that?'

Darcy, with younger hearing, cocked her ears. 'Someone's hurt.'

Vicky ran to the window, opened it to let the sound in, along with the cool night air. 'Oh God, it might be Toby! Could he have got out?'

Surely not. Surely he was in the house somewhere – hiding, scared but safe. Somewhere she had missed in her frantic searching. God, she was so afraid she couldn't think straight.

Fiona said, 'Vic, no, it's a man. Not a child. Listen.'

'So maybe someone got caught in the fireworks?' Paddy then. Did she care if he was hurt? She could hardly keep the door locked on an injured, bleeding person. A friend. 'Can fireworks hurt you – seriously hurt you?'

'Of course.' Fiona was up and peering out of the back window. 'I've seen people killed by them before, if they hit you in the body or head. I should go out to him. It must be Paddy who's hurt.'

She turned to Vicky and they weighed it up again, mutely. Their lives, the lives of their children, against decency, against friendship, against the oaths Fiona had sworn to preserve life. Vicky however had taken no such oath. 'I don't know if that's a good idea.'

'But he could be badly injured! There could be burns, or organ damage, or eye loss – God, I'm not set up to deal with any of this here, we've barely a medical kit!'

Did she care? Vicky was almost shocked at what she was discovering in herself, the depths of her steeliness. The same resolve that had allowed her to row the boat away from Fergus McCann – away from the drowning boy who would have pulled them under, only in the sea because of her – and bring herself and the others to safety and go on to live her life. To choose Daniel over Paddy, and over Louise, whatever that might have been, because he had not seen the worst in her, because that way it had some chance of staying buried, what she'd done that summer. To kill Tomasz Kazinsky and somehow live with herself after. So yes, she could and would refuse to aid Amira and Paddy, no matter how badly hurt they were.

Fiona said, 'What if Toby's out there? He could be injured. We have to find him at least.'

'He's in the house. He has to be.'

But where? She had searched the whole of the place, and she couldn't see a thing. He could hardly be in the attic or cellar. So maybe, somehow, he had gone outside. It would only take a turn of the key. Sure enough, she went to it now and somehow it was unlocked. She had wiggled the key moments ago to check it. She must have unlocked it by accident. Letting Toby out, to an island full of cliffs and danger and death.

Then Darcy exclaimed. 'Mum, I think that's *Dad* shouting!'

Amira

'Paddy!' she shouted. She had no idea where she was, or where anything was. She could barely see what way was up. It was so dark, endlessly dark, worse now the lights of the fireworks had faded. The screaming, the bellowing, was right on top of her now. 'Paddy!'

Someone was beside her. Hot breath on her face. A large body, lumbering, grunting with effort. 'He's not here, bitch.'

Jonathan. She could smell blood. He was injured, perhaps worse now, from the fireworks. Amira tried to run again, but slipped and slid on the ground.

'Please, I'm sorry you got hurt! I didn't mean for any of this to happen!'

'You and your fucking husband. Planning all this. Just jealous.' His hands lunged for her, grazed her arm, and she shied away.

'No! I didn't know anything about it, I swear.'

'Left me to *drown*.'

'I'm sorry! I had no choice.'

God, where could she run to? She stumbled over the hillside, catching her feet on hummocks of grass and holes in the ground. She was going to break an ankle. Jonathan was dragging behind her, and she could hear he was limping. He'd been hurt again. He couldn't chase her.

It was so dark she almost walked right into the wind turbine. Her hands grazed its rough metal sides, felt the little key in the door. You could climb those, couldn't you? He'd never be able to follow her, and maybe there was something up there she could use to signal for help. But it was so high, and she was so afraid.

A grunt behind her. He was close. And she was more afraid of him than of heights, so Amira threw open the little door and went inside the stem of the wind turbine.

Immediately, the noise of the wind died down. She put out her hands and felt that she was in a narrow tube, barely wider than her shoulders. Oh God. Claustrophobia. A small ladder built into one wall, the space lit by some faint light. All the way up at the top was a door, presumably so you could open it to get to the turbine if it needed to be fixed. Her breath sounded so loud in here. It was so small. What if she got trapped?

The door was rattling. Amira launched herself at the ladder, and began to claw her way up the side. Up, up, up. Foot hand, foot hand. She had always hated this, always been afraid of heights. Pathetic.

A hand! On her foot! Amira screamed and kicked, heard Jonathan slide behind her, bellow.

'You fucking *bitch*!'

How could he be climbing this? His arm was out of action, and he'd done something to his foot or leg too. But still he came. His thundering breath filling the space so she couldn't even hear her own panicked heart.

Up, up, up. Fifteen metres up. She was at the top now. A little door that she pushed open, finding herself on the top of it, the slightly rounded joint where the stem met the blades. The wind pushed her back. And then she looked down – God, so high – and his dark shape was there, filling her escape route.

'Where you gonna go now, Ammy? You're trapped.'

Vicky

The night air was cold on her face. Genevieve immediately started to whine, her small hand straining in Vicky's. 'Mummy, it's windy!'

It was indeed windy and freezing and rain sleeked across her face, but there was no choice. She wasn't leaving anyone behind in the house, it wasn't safe. She wasn't even sure she trusted Fiona now, after the revelation about her and Daniel. But they had to look for Toby, and get Jonathan to safety, if he was really out there. Protect him from Paddy and Amira, their murderous former friends. She wouldn't let them get their hands on her child. That was why she was holding a knife in her other hand, clutched tight.

'Be careful,' she warned Fiona and Darcy, who came behind her, shining their phones and the torch they'd used the night before, now lower on battery. 'There could still be fireworks that haven't gone off.'

'Dad!' shouted Darcy. 'Toby! Where are you?'

'Should we spread out?' said Fiona, unsure.

'I don't know if it's safe.' Someone, or more than one someone, was perhaps out there trying to kill them. 'Let's stick together.'

Moving slowly in the dark and the mud, they made slow progress up the hill. Vicky caught her foot on a firework stick, and exclaimed, but it was dead. 'Everyone be really careful. Watch the ground!'

'Dad. Dad!' Darcy yelled.

'*Jay!*' shouted Fiona, and Vicky could hear the desolation in her voice.

Vicky wasn't entirely sure it had been him screaming. How could he have crawled his way out of the sea? Unless Amira had lied about all of that. It struck her that this could be what was left of her family. Her husband gone, her brother maybe too. She would not lose Toby as well.

'Toby, baby!' she shouted. 'Come to Mummy! Where are you?'

A scream. Vicky jumped. 'What was that—'

'Came from above.'

'That was a woman, not Dad . . .'

Amira. Vicky could hear her voice now.

'Please, help me! Someone help me!'

She looked up, as Fiona shone the torch at the dark bulk of the wind turbine that had not been here when this island was theirs. All the way up to the top where the scream seemed to come from, and she could see two figures on the narrow platform at the top. And one was holding the other over the side.

Amira

She was blacking out with fear. Jonathan had her by the neck and was squeezing her with his one good hand, pushing her towards the edge of the platform, which was only perhaps a metre across and sloped at the sides. Clearly, you weren't meant to be up here without a harness of some kind. The ground was dizzying below her, the wind making the whole structure sway.

She screamed over it, trying to choke in air. 'Stop it! I'm going to fall, Jonathan!'

'I don't care. You tried to kill me! See how you like it.'

She could see his injured foot now, in the dim emergency lighting, and she had no idea how he'd climbed the ladder with it like that. Bloody and torn, his boot was in tatters and his flesh oozed from it. He must have stepped on a firework and been in utter agony, but rage seemed to have powered him on.

Now she was at the edge, her feet slipping and sliding as gravity began to take her.

'No. No!' she screamed. 'Please help me! Someone help me!'

Maybe Paddy would hear and come to her. Where was he? Maybe he was dead. Maybe she would soon be dead too. The wind whistled round her ears, and her head swam with the height, and this was it, her worst nightmare. She was going to fall. It would take seconds, and she would hit the ground and the pain would be unimaginable.

She struggled ineffectually with Jonathan, but he was too strong, too enraged. His face was so close to hers that his spit dribbled on to her as he crushed her neck, fingers digging in. God, he was large. She slapped at his hand, gouged it with her bitten nails. 'Let me go!' Nothing.

From down below, a voice, torn by the wind. 'Daddy! Stop it, Daddy.'

Amira turned her head an inch – the ground was so far away! – and saw Vicky, Fiona, and Darcy, plus one of the twins, all watching Jonathan try to kill her.

The moment of indecision was all she needed. As his grasp relaxed, she darted under his arm and stumbled back through the door to the relative safety of the metal tube. She shut the door behind her but it wouldn't hold him for a second, so she climbed back, down, down, down the ladder. Foot hand, foot hand. Shaking with the effort and with fear. As fast as she could, but terrified she'd slip in her wet muddy boots. Counting the steps, all forty of them, and then she put a foot on the ground and almost cried with relief. Solid ground. Back out into the freezing wind, though it had been so much worse up there. She was alive, but Jonathan was still coming, and now his entire family had appeared to take his side.

Mhairi

'Oh my God,' said Mhairi, stepping away from what she'd found in the middle of the litter of strange sticks, standing up like grave markers. A body smeared with blood, its foot mangled and pulpy, its head crumpled like a cardboard box. 'Who is it?' She had quickly abandoned her search inside the turbine, since it was clearly empty, if full of blood. Maybe from whoever this was lying here, dead just a few metres away from the door.

Arthur stooped over, grunted. 'It's a man, anyway.'

Whoever it was had been wearing waterproofs, and she could see an expensive watch, almost undamaged. 'What did this to his foot?' It looked like a bomb attack. She'd never worked on one, thank God, but had seen pictures in a gruesome terrorism briefing she'd had to sit through last year.

'Fireworks,' said Arthur. 'Can do a lot of damage if you stand on one. Kills wildlife all the time. Banned out here in fact. But that's what these wee sticks are.'

'Did you see anything, last night? Did fireworks go off?' She was on the wrong side of Tarne island to have noticed.

He nodded slowly. 'Aye, I reckon so. Late on. Close to nine or so. Didn't know where they were coming from. The boats let them off, you know, the cruise ships.'

It was a common enough sight, which would have raised no eyebrows on Tarne. The locals would simply have thought some ignorant tourists or incomers had set them off, scaring birds and seals and killing sheep from shock. But someone, one of the group, had stumbled into the fireworks and been blown up, as effectively as stepping on a landmine.

'Did it kill him? The explosion?'

Arthur peered forward. 'I reckon he fell over too and hit his head.' There was indeed a pool of blood around the body, seeped into the moss and grass. 'And come see this.'

A few paces away, another knife lay on the ground. No blood on this one, but she didn't touch it anyway.

Mhairi stood up. The light was already failing, and it would be dark within the hour. 'Arthur, I have to admit I'm stumped. I've no idea where the rest of them could be. We've searched every inch of the island.' Except for the caves, and she was pretty sure no one could be in there, with the rope fallen to the rocks. No, she had to face the fact that the rest of the group were no longer here. 'I'm thinking we should go back to Tarne. See if they've turned up.' There was nothing more she could do here.

Arthur grunted. 'You know, I used to ferry them over here sometimes in the old days. The Capemans, the twins and their mum and dad.'

'Oh? What were they like?' *Were*, she had said. She should have said *are*. At least until she knew different.

He thought about it. 'The dad was a nasty piece of work. Entitled, you know. Always underpaying, and him with a Rolex on his wrist. Pushed the boy hard, bullied him. He had something wrong with his arm, cerebral palsy I think they said it was, and the dad didn't like that, his boy not being able to play rugby and that. But the girl – well, she wasn't so bad. She wrote me a letter after I lost my own lad.'

Mhairi was trying to remember if she'd ever heard that Arthur had had a son who died. 'That was kind of her. I'm sorry, Arthur, I didn't know.'

'Aye.' He let out a big sigh. 'It was an accident. He was messing about in a boat, and he fell in, couldn't get out. Too cold, too rough. Happens all the time.'

'That's terrible.'

'No one's fault. Likely he was showing off, he was like that, no fear of anything. For a long time I looked for someone to blame, but the truth is, accidents will happen. We all bash up against each other and damage gets caused. That's just life. Isn't it?'

Mhairi tried to hide her surprise at this philosophical outburst. 'So you know why they lost the island? The Capemans?'

'Aye. Got into debt, they did, had to sell up. There were some who said locally they deserved it, blamed the girl's husband, said they were all a rotten bunch. But I think they did their best. The boy and girl. With parents like that.'

Mhairi nodded, unsure why he was telling her this now. 'Right.'

'Do you believe in revenge, Sergeant?'

'Hm?'

'You're police. You must come across some right bad people. Do you ever want to see them brought to justice? And I don't mean prison, that holiday-camp life. Real justice.'

Mhairi considered this. 'I do, yes. It's hard not to, when you see what people can do to each other. But as far as I can tell, revenge only makes things worse. You know what they say about digging two graves.'

'Aye. I do.'

'I'm sorry about your lad, Arthur.'

He nodded. 'He was a good boy. Wild, but a good boy. I didn't ever get the chance to tell him that.'

'I'm sure he knew.'

'Maybe.' He heaved a sigh, looking out to sea, perhaps to the spot where his son had drowned. 'I couldn't forgive, for a time. Kept tabs on the people who'd done it, even. Watched them thrive, when they didn't deserve it. Even thought I might – well. But, you know, life goes on. Wee kids get born and it's not their fault, is it? Life just goes on.'

Jesus, that was all she needed, her boatman having some kind of breakdown out here as well. 'Well, shall we get back to civilisation? It's almost dark.'

'Aye. Come on then.'

She cast a last look behind her at the silent, dark house, and the shadows lengthening over the land. There had been eight of them, and now four were dead, the rest missing. What on earth had happened on this island?

Vicky

Jonathan was alive. He was alive, despite her worst fears, but she couldn't let herself feel joy. She had told herself she didn't care what happened to Amira or Paddy, if they lived or died, and that she would be willing to kill them herself if she had to, but all the same she was profoundly shocked to witness her brother holding Amira by the neck and bending her over the edge of the wind turbine, as if trying to push her off. This was a side of him she'd never seen before. Violent, out of control.

Or had she? An image came to her of that day on the boat, Jonathan in the water, thrashing about, prying the cold white hands of the boy off his arm, lest he be dragged under. Fergus. Strange how she'd been able to put it almost entirely from her mind, but they had done that. They were guilty.

They were watching, frozen in shock, and Darcy called out to her father, which distracted him long enough for Amira to get away. Seconds later, she staggered out of the entrance to the wind turbine, hair wild, bruises all over her throat showing up under their torches.

'Oh, thank God! He's gone mad.'

Behind her, the sound of someone half-climbing, half-sliding down a ladder. Jonathan was coming.

Next thing Paddy ran panting up, limping and holding one hand in front of him. 'Amira, are you OK? I heard you scream.'

Vicky clutched the knife. 'What the hell's going on?' she said. Fiona shone the torch over them, making them blink.

Paddy winced. 'Your brother's been hunting us, that's what. He's trying to kill us. Then we stumbled into bloody Daniel's fireworks and I burned my hand.' She could see it was blackened, painful-looking.

'Daddy!' Darcy was sobbing as Jonathan emerged from the turbine. He looked terrible. Rolling-eyed, wet through, one foot bloodied and mangled, blood and mud smeared on his face. 'We thought you were dead, Daddy.'

He was panting. 'I might as well have been. Amira pushed me into the sea. Crushed my fingers with her paddle, look!'

Amira cried out. 'I had no choice! You were going to pull us both in and I can't swim.'

She had flat-out lied. Said he was already gone, and all this time he must have been floundering in the sea, alone. They could have found him hours ago! 'So you lied, Amira,' said Vicky, feeling rage seep into her blood again. 'You did find him. I don't know why I'm surprised. All you two have done is lie and lie and lie. For all I know you attacked Jonathan again just now. Tried to finish the job.'

'But you *saw* him. He was trying to push me off the top.' Could she really blame him? She'd been right not to trust Amira and Paddy. Vicky took a step back, pulled Genevieve close to her.

Fiona moved forward. 'Are you hurt, Jay? Can I—'

'Get away!' He gestured violently. 'I want to know what's going on and who's behind this.'

'But I would never—'

'You're pretty angry with me, aren't you? Scorned woman and all that.'

302

'For God's sake, Jay.' Even in the dark, Vicky could see that Fiona looked hurt. 'I would never do anything bad to you. You should know that.'

Vicky turned to her niece. 'Darcy. Take Genevieve and look everywhere for Toby. Stay away from the cliffs. Take the torch, go on.'

'But—'

'No arguments. Just go.' At least she could get the children away from whatever was simmering away here, what fresh violence might erupt any second. But where was Toby? He wouldn't go to the edge, would he? He would sit and wait to be found like she'd always told him? If he'd been badly frightened by the fireworks he could be anywhere. Please God let him be safe. Under a bed maybe and she'd just missed him, searching in the dark.

Darcy took the torch and Genevieve's hand, both of their lips trembling, and went off round the front of the house. Vicky could hear her calling Toby's name.

Darkness settled around them again. Paddy had the other torch, but its beam was faint, and she and Fiona had their phones. Precious little light to fight the blank expanse around them. She tried to marshal her thoughts. Her burning anger at Paddy, at Amira now too, and even Fiona, was not helping her to think clearly. 'Now this stops here,' she said. 'My son is missing and the power is off and we need to find him. Did you do that, Paddy?'

'No! Of course not. I thought Jay did.'

'Of course I didn't, you fucking idiot. Now what's going on here? Lou's dead? Is that true?'

Vicky swallowed hard. 'A lot has happened today, Jay. Paddy and Louise and Amira set us up. They wrote the note.'

'Not Amira,' said Paddy. 'And we didn't kill anyone, I swear it. We didn't touch the generator or take the EpiPen.'

'But Louise took the radio and gave it to Paddy,' said Amira, holding it up. 'Sorry. I have to be completely honest.'

303

Paddy winced. 'She just didn't want anyone using the radio until the note did its job. Until you all really thought about what you'd done, the deaths you'd caused. There was no point otherwise.'

'It's not working,' said Amira. 'Or there's no one on the other end, I don't know. But we can't raise anyone.'

Vicky sighed. What a catalogue of disasters this was. 'So it wasn't some bogeyman who took the radio, it was Louise. Let's work this out. If someone else is out here with us, we need to know, because we could all be in even more danger than we realise. Look, I think this might be something to do with what happened that summer. The boy who died.'

'The boy you killed, you mean,' said Paddy. 'You and your bloody brother.'

She swallowed again. 'Yes. The boy we killed. Fergus McCann.'

Amira

McCann. The name rang a bell, as it had when Paddy had said it earlier. 'And you said before that his father was a boatman? Which one?'

Vicky shrugged. She was holding a knife casually in her one hand, and Amira was watching it very closely. 'They all look the same to me. Sort of craggy, in dirty old coats.'

Paddy also shook his head. 'I must have known at the time, but I can't remember.'

'Was it Arthur?'

'Who?' Vicky looked blank again. Of course, why would she notice the little people who ferried her around, brought her food, cleaned her house, minded her children?

But Fiona remembered. 'The man who brought us over yesterday. His name was Arthur. Maybe it was McCann? It was on the booking email I think.'

'It was. It's our boatman,' Amira said shakily. 'The one who brought us over, who's meant to come back for us tomorrow. I think he was Fergus's father.'

In the torchlight, Paddy had turned the colour of heavy cream. 'Oh my God, that must be it. He's getting revenge. For us killing Fergus.'

Vicky snapped. 'It wasn't a killing, for God's sake! Just an accident.'

But the thing about accidents was that someone was nearly always responsible. Even if they didn't intend for it to happen.

Amira was putting it together. 'Vicky, I think it was him who sent you the email in the first place. He knew you owned the island, right? Or used to. And the price was almost too good to be true, you said. What if he lured you out here to punish you? And the rest of us are just . . . camouflage? Louise and Paddy's note was just, I don't know, some horrible coincidence?'

Vicky shuddered. 'I think it's true. The rest of the slideshow came on. It was all pictures of the people who died. Including Fergus. Did you do that, Paddy?'

'No! The others yes. I'll admit I didn't think of Fergus. I don't know why. We put them in the Google folder – well, Louise did. She said Daniel wouldn't even bother to look at them before making the slideshow and I guess she was right. So – someone else must have added the Fergus ones.'

There was a short silence. Then Vicky lunged towards Paddy, grabbing the front of his coat. Knife in the other hand. 'I bet you planned this together,' she hissed. 'All of you – Louise, and you, and this boatman. To bring us out here, and terrorise us, and kill us!'

Amira screamed. Paddy held up his hands. 'No. No! It was only the game, I swear it. I've never spoken to the boatman, except on Friday.'

'But how could he have known all this? That we'd play that stupid game, that Rachel was allergic, that Daniel would light the tubs? How could he tell? Is he watching us – listening to us? Is the whole place bugged?'

'I don't know. I don't *know*!' yelled Paddy. 'Please, put the knife down!'

Vicky was screaming now. 'And where is my son? Where the hell is my baby?'

Paddy sank to his knees, hands up in surrender. 'Vicky, I keep telling you. I do not know. I haven't even seen Toby, I didn't hurt anyone, I don't know why the power went out! It's not me doing all of this.'

It's true, Amira tried to say, but she was so afraid the words would hardly come out. And did she know that? Did she believe Paddy? Rachel's EpiPen had been in her washbag, she'd seen it herself that night, then a few hours later it was gone.

Jonathan grunted in rage. 'Bollocks it isn't. Look, I'm going to deal with this once and for all.'

And Amira began to scream again as he leaned over and grabbed the knife from Vicky.

Vicky

The knife glinted in the torchlight. Fiona shouted, 'Jonathan, please stop! You're going to hurt someone.'

'Someone's already hurt, in case you didn't notice. I could lose the foot! That's all I need, one arm and one foot. How will I get up the hills now? That's my career gone.'

'If you'd let me look at it—'

'We need to deal with these two first.' He pointed the knife at Paddy and Amira, who raised her arms, stumbling back.

'We didn't do any of this,' insisted Paddy. 'I swear to you, mate.'

'Mate? I'm not your fucking mate. Never was. Only stuck with you because my sister couldn't see what a weasel you are. You killed my fucking girlfriend.'

'Look, I think it could have been an accident. Rachel. She could have eaten the wrong thing.'

'Don't want to hear it. Just want you gone.'

Vicky had to tell him the truth. 'Jonathan! Listen to me. Toby took the EpiPen, OK? I found it in his bed. He . . . I'm sorry, he likes to go through people's things. It's how we found the clippings too. I suppose he thought it was cool, the pen. He has one like it in his toy doctor's bag.'

Jonathan sagged. Blinked. '*What?*'

'I'm so sorry, Jay. It's true.'

Her son had killed someone else. An innocent, unwitting killer. And it was her fault, wasn't it? That he had no manners, that he went through private bags, that he took things? They were both off the rails and it was her fault.

'But who poisoned Rachel in the first place then?' Jonathan stepped forward, towards Amira and Paddy. 'Who was it who made the cake, eh?'

Amira gurgled. Her feet slipped beneath her, and she cried out, caught at Paddy's arm. 'Please, no!'

'Stop it, Jonathan!' shouted Vicky. 'Look, Rachel wasn't even going to eat the cake to start with. It could have been an accident, it got contaminated somehow, I don't know. And Toby took the pen. The power just went out, maybe, if the fuel ran down. The turbine's not been moving since we got here so we've been eating diesel. The chef – I don't know, maybe Daniel screwed up the booking or something. And what about him – what about Daniel?' She looked round at them. Her friends, her family. 'Either one of you killed him, or someone is out here stalking us one by one. I think it's time to be honest, don't you? Does anyone know something? Paddy?'

'I . . .' He held up his hands. 'I don't know, I really don't. I would tell you if I did.'

'I don't believe you.' She moved towards him. 'Jonathan? Give me that.' She took the knife from him.

'No! Stop!' shouted Amira.

Fiona made a noise, half-sob, half-scream. 'Vicky, it was Lou. Darcy saw it all out the window. She . . . she wasn't sure what she'd seen, poor kid, she was distraught already over Rachel.'

'What? Tell me what she saw.'

'It was after she'd found Rachel – we left her at the house with the twins, remember, and I was downstairs lighting the fire. She said she saw Daniel outside at the tubs, bending over to check the water. Then I called her downstairs and she saw

309

Louise near the tubs. No Daniel. Louise was all wet. But she didn't think anything of it at the time.'

'She pushed him in?' Vicky couldn't believe this.

Paddy's voice was slow, from where he knelt on the ground still. 'I thought that's maybe what happened. But I didn't know. I was going to ask her but – I didn't get a chance.'

'But – why?'

'She was going on and on about how the note wasn't enough to get him back. That she wanted to play a really big trick on him, a nasty one. So I think maybe he fell in – he was pretty wasted this morning – or she pushed him and she put the lid on. But to play a trick. Not to . . . kill him.'

Vicky remembered it now too, Louise arriving wet and breathless at the beach as they'd launched the boat. Learning about Rachel's death, her shock and disbelief. Practically running back up the hill. 'It was her who found him. The first thing she did was go and take the lid off.' And her scream then, it could have been real. If she'd only meant to shut him there for a few minutes, to scare him.

Paddy said, 'I could see she was distraught. I tried to ask her but there wasn't time. She said to find her in the caves, but then . . .' Then Vicky had stabbed her.

'Why didn't he shout? Or climb out?'

'He was very drunk,' Fiona said, miserably. 'The heat might have overwhelmed him much faster than for someone else.'

'But why didn't you tell me?' she exclaimed. She'd spent all this time terrified that Paddy might come for her, or that there was some unknown stranger out here with them.

'Vic, you stabbed Louise! We didn't know what you'd do next! I had to keep Darcy safe.'

She recognised the looks on the faces of Paddy, Amira, even Fiona. Looked down at the knife in her hand. They were afraid of her. 'Christ,' she said, shakily. What a mess. Louise had killed her husband, perhaps by accident, and she had killed Louise.

'I'm so sorry,' said Fiona. 'Please – will you give me the knife? Or put it down?'

'Kill or be killed,' said Vicky slowly. 'Well, that's certainly come true, hasn't it.' And she believed them. She could see that people were terrified of her, that she was the real threat. With a deep exhale that turned into a scream, she threw the knife away from her so it landed somewhere off in the dark, on the bouncy ground. 'I just want this to be over. I want us off here, safe. Please, can we just stop all this?'

'And what about me?' said Jonathan, his voice hard and cold. 'Amira left me to die. I don't see why she should get away with it. Her and Paddy, who caused all this in the first place. I don't see any reason not to finish these two off.' He grabbed Amira again, tightening his hand round her neck, cutting off a strangled yelp. 'What do you say, you bitch? Into the sea, hold you under till you stop breathing. Or up to the cliffs again, push you off. We'll say you drowned, came off your paddleboard. Can't swim, so sad. Who's going to know the truth? After all, everyone else is dead, and we won't talk. We've always been close, the four of us. Vic, me, Fi, Danny. We'll avenge him. What do you say?'

Vicky said, 'Bit closer than you think, Jay. Or did you know Fiona slept with Daniel, while I was giving birth?'

'*What?*'

Fiona said nothing for a beat. 'I—'

'It's true,' said Paddy quickly. 'I'm sorry, Jay. Daniel boasted to me once, when he was drunk.'

Jonathan exploded, loosening his grip on Amira so she gasped in air. 'You slept with my brother-in-law? My best mate? Jesus Christ, Fiona. I thought you were the one person I could trust.'

She snapped, 'So I was just supposed to behave, while you slept with how many other women during our marriage? Dozens? Hundreds? I'm not blind, Jonathan. At least it was just one time for me.'

The rage seemed to have gone out of Jonathan, replaced by limp shock. 'I don't know what to say. You, of all people. I never thought you'd hurt me.'

'Well, I used to say the same about you, Jay. Then you left me, and our daughter, our family, for someone with the IQ of a paperclip.'

'But how could you do that to me – and to your best friend?'

Fiona scoffed. 'Some best friend. I've always just been a supporting character in Vicky's life. Even when my husband leaves me, does she ask how I am, or visit, or call? No she does not. She makes me come to this bloody island, with you and my replacement.'

Vicky snapped at her. 'This is hardly the time for your pathetic excuses. Look what's happening!' Amira was clearly terrified, eyes bulging, clawing at Jay's hand round her neck. Her knees sagged as he forced her down. 'This has gone quite far enough. Jay, let Amira go, she can't breathe.'

'Good! Look, I'm sick of all this. I've lost my career and my girlfriend, my reputation, my fucking foot! I'm not being blamed for anything else and I'm not dying here. We need to deal with these two. I don't trust them for one second.' He squeezed tighter, and Amira made a choking sound.

'Jay! Let her go!'

Jonathan ignored her. 'Come on. You two grab him, I'll finish her off.' Gesturing to Paddy, who stood frozen with terror, holding his injured hand like it didn't belong to him.

You will all either kill or be killed.

Vicky had killed. The prediction had come true, but only because they'd made it so. Only because of their lies and secrets and decades-long resentments. Perhaps someone really had lured them here in the first place, cut the power, made the slideshow, even caused some of the other strange happenings of the weekend, but really, whoever it was had not needed to lift a hand to harm any of the group. They'd done all this to themselves. Amira's face was purple in the torchlight. There wasn't much time left.

And then Vicky understood what had to happen, now that she had already lost her husband and her best friend, and three people were dead, and she was now watching Amira be strangled in front of her. What she had to do. The final truth she had to tell.

'Jonathan,' she called. 'Dad was going to leave me the island. Not you. Just me. That's why we lost it when Daniel went bankrupt – Dad had already made it over to us. I know you thought Dad just sold it to help us out, but that wasn't true, he never would have. He'd already given it to me to save on inheritance tax, so it had to go as part of the settlement with the family. When the . . . after the little girl died.'

'What? No, that's not true.'

'It is. He didn't want you to have this place, that's the truth.'

Jonathan looked like a bewildered child for a moment. 'But – *why?*'

'Any number of reasons. Wasn't too keen on you having a Chinese wife, was he? Didn't approve of you being in the papers. But it was more than that, Jay. Dad just didn't ever really love you. You know that, don't you? Deep down. He was ashamed of you. Of having a son who's disabled.'

She looked at Amira as she spoke, hoping someone could pick up on what she was doing, why she was being so cruel. And they did. The second Jonathan's grip loosened again, stunned by rage and loss, Amira slipped out. Then Paddy ran at him, pushing him hard, and he fell back, arms windmilling as he tried to stay up, and he landed on his back in the field of fireworks. And there was another loud bang, colours blinding her. Amira screamed, Fiona screamed. Someone else howled in a terrible pain, a sound like she had never heard before. Vicky closed her eyes, afraid of what she'd see when she opened them.

313

Mhairi

Mhairi had never felt so relieved to step down on to the solid stone dock of Tarne harbour. It might have been another island hundreds of miles from Glasgow, but it felt like a heaving metropolis after where she'd been.

Soon, there would be so much to do. Getting the bodies taken off, post-mortems arranged, evidence preserved, testimony given about what she'd touched and where Arthur had been, for elimination. Families to notify, press to brief. They would descend on Tarne, the vultures of the media, both social and mainstream. People would probably be hiring boats and trying to get out to the island to take pictures, so they'd need a permanent guard out there. It was going to cost a fortune, but she knew the interest would be enormous, a group of rich Oxford types and the bloody shambles they'd made of their weekend. She still had no motive, however. Could long-repressed simmering resentments, the kind that every friendship harbours deep down, lead to such carnage? She knew from bitter experience that they could.

Arthur was tying up the boat now, with rough practised hands. Mhairi stood for a moment looking back out to sea, the small island so innocuous. She couldn't face the scrum, not yet. Her eye was caught by the collection of small plaques set into the wall of the harbour. Names and dates of those who had gone out to sea and not come back. So many over the years. Familiar island names. John, Rory, Fergus. No one cared about a lost fisherman off a wind-swept island, but they'd care about the Mallacht massacre. God, she hoped they didn't start calling it that. She wished she'd had her roots done. If only she'd known she was going to be on TV. At least she was safe, and her little family safe too, at home with cartoons and toast. As she lumbered over to her car, ready to call her boss on the mainland and explain, Mhairi was grateful for her own life.

Then she saw Davey coming towards her across the harbour, radio aloft, hair plastered down with rain.

'Alright, boss? What did you find?'

'Four bodies. No sign of the rest.'

'Hmm. That's not good.'

'No. We're going to need a plan in place – we'll have to talk to the council and CalMac before we get inundated with press and rubberneckers. Find out anything?'

'Well, turns out there's been a death at the island before.' Davey nodded over, lowered his voice. 'Arthur's boy. You know he was killed out there? Drowned in a sailing accident. And the Capemans were involved, when they were kids.'

Mhairi looked over at Arthur, slowly gathering his ropes in his weather-beaten hands. She saw his daughter – Joan, was it? Something like that – walking across the harbour to greet him, striding in a padded gilet and rubber boots. Some kind of IT whizz, wasn't she, who'd made a fortune in London, then moved back to be with her dad on the island. Did a lot of work remotely still, they said. Mhairi remembered hearing the story now – the son who died, the wife who couldn't live with the grief either. So it was the Capemans he'd been talking about when he'd spoken of blame and revenge. Poor Arthur. She was glad he still had his daughter.

'I know, yes. Can't have been easy, ferrying them over there like that.'

Davey said, 'Before you ask, I've already checked his alibi, just to be on the safe side, and his boat was in dock all weekend, getting a tune-up. And loads of people saw him down the pub or in the shop and that. Pretty rock-solid.'

Mhairi was glad. She would have hated to have to arrest Arthur, her stoical companion in all that horror.

'Good work, Davey.' She saw him beam at the rare praise. 'Still lots to do though, so chop-chop.' As she spoke, his radio buzzed in his hand, unintelligible. 'You better get that.'

Davey listened, his face slowly changing from pleasure to puzzlement to shock. 'Aye, OK. Got it. Over. You're not going to believe this,' he said, pressing the off button.

'What?'

'I think we've found your missing guests.'

Amira

It was freezing on the boat, and smelled strongly of cod and blood, and the kindly, bear-like fishermen spoke with Scottish accents that were barely intelligible, but Amira could not have been happier to be on it had it been the *QE2*. She was safe. She had survived the island, where she'd been so certain she would die.

When Paddy had pushed Jonathan away from her, as hard as he could, and he'd fallen to the ground like rocks in a sack, setting off another flurry of fireworks right in their faces, there had been a moment of horrified silence after the smoke had cleared. Darcy had reappeared not long after her father hit the ground, carrying Toby on her hip and holding Genevieve with her free hand. Amira was trying to block out the memory of the disbelief on her young face.

'Dad. Dad? What's happened?'

It was Vicky who had taken over. Stepped forward, shielding her brother's body from view. 'Come on, darling. Let's go inside and we'll explain it all to you.'

Vicky and Fiona could have turned on Amira and Paddy then – he had finished the job she'd started in the water, and killed Jonathan – but no one did. As if they'd accepted it had to be done, that he might have killed them all in his blind range. Fiona had gone to him, quickly checked his pulse, come back and hugged Darcy tight. Blood on her face and jumper.

As soon as it was light, a pale and grey dawn, they'd waded and swum out to the capsized boat and pulled it in to shore. Vicky and Paddy had patched it up as best they could with some materials from the shed, Vicky trying hard to remember everything her father had taught her about boats. After many freezing, damp, chafing hours, they had got it afloat and piled everyone in. The twins and Darcy, not arguing this time, had been strapped up with what buoyancy aids they could find, and the little ones had mercifully fallen asleep despite the cold and wind. Darcy had been crying on and off all night, and Amira knew it would be a long time before she recovered from this, if ever.

With anyone who could taking a turn on the oar and the paddle that went with Amira's board, the precarious craft had bobbed along for what felt like hours in the expanse of black water, before a larger fishing boat had come into sight and picked them up. It had taken a long time to explain what had happened, the four dead bodies on the island and that they needed to be rescued, but eventually they had been allowed on. Stepping on to a more secure surface, Amira had experienced a deep burst of relief, so powerful it almost made her gasp.

Vicky was across the deck from her now, under a smelly blanket, a twin sleeping under each arm. She opened her eyes a crack – filthy blonde hair matted with blood – and gave Amira an appraising look. No warmth there, no liking, but maybe something that hadn't been in it before – a grudging respect? Anyway, Amira didn't care. She was never going to see these people again, just as soon as they got back to Tarne and everything was sorted out, if it even could be. The landmass of the bigger island was in their sights now, and they would soon be back to safety. Civilisation, police, order.

She had always seen herself as part of that – one of the people who came in when everything else had gone horribly wrong.

More than once she had scooped up children in her arms and taken them from danger to safety, or at least to the cold comfort of a foster family. A toddler covered in blood, whose mother had stabbed his father, spraying the child all over their Peppa Pig sleepsuit. A mute eight-year-old whose drug-dealing father had been peppered with bullets in their living room while watching Ant and Dec on the TV. She had seen some terrible things, had even been in fear for her life, but had never before been hunted. The memory of Jonathan chasing them over the island would never leave her.

Darcy was still weeping, a monotonous sobbing born of loss and relief. Fiona rocked her, kissing her head, murmuring words of comfort. Amira felt the ache as if from a long way away. She would maybe never have this, now. She heard herself say, 'I thought I was pregnant last week.'

Beside her, Paddy shifted uncomfortably, his hand strapped to his chest. One of the fishermen – the one with the large grey beard – had dressed his burns, but he would need to go to hospital as soon as they hit land. 'Oh?'

'I was late.'

'But we said . . .'

'I know. I lied.'

He said nothing. 'I lied to you too.'

'About so much.' She closed her eyes, trying to enjoy the fresh, albeit freezing, sea air on her face. She thought she might have frostbite in her left foot, which felt strangely burning and numb. What was going to happen now? Paddy had killed someone, technically, though if Vicky and Fiona told the truth, it might be seen as self-defence. Vicky had killed Louise and that was a shakier defence. Rachel was dead and no one knew why. Louise had probably killed Daniel. Maybe they would all go to prison. 'What do we do now, Paddy?'

Amira hadn't wanted to come on this trip, or any of the outings they'd taken with his friends over the years. The Group. And eventually he had come to see the truth of them too, their selfishness and blindness. At least his enthralment with Vicky was over. Did she even care now? She didn't know. All she could think about was a room with a hot bath, a cup of tea, and a door that locked. A soft bed. And would Paddy be there, the husband who had rejected her, refused to keep trying for a baby, idolised another woman for so long, forced her into these group holidays she hated, failed to stick up for her in front of his supposed friends, who had lied and manipulated and plotted? Set in motion these terrible events that had left four people dead?

Something cold touched her fingers. Paddy's good hand, gently extended. Amira didn't grasp it, but she didn't pull hers away, either.

Joan

She watched from the harbour wall as Mhairi Douglas disembarked from her father's boat. There had been talk all day among the fishermen, largely not out due to it being Sunday and a religious island still. About the group of southerners, all designer labels and loud voices, who'd gone over to the island and not come back. Where were they? She had been waiting nearby when her dad should have returned with them earlier. Instead, it was just him in the boat and he'd immediately got on to the emergency phone on the harbour wall. An hour later she'd seen Mhairi, the island sergeant, drive up with her hair unbrushed and a very grumpy expression, and her dad had set out again.

What was going on? It had been agony waiting. She'd rehearsed this moment in her head for months. As soon as the group had played their picture slideshow, they should have realised something was up, that their booking on the island was not real. Then they would likely have got on the radio, the twin of which Joan had in her glovebox. She helped her dad with the boat trips sometimes, though usually the owners didn't rent the place out in the winter. Her dad had wondered about that, but years of unquestionably obeying were ingrained in him. He had an email saying the island was rented and would he ferry them over, so he'd done it. As far as she knew, he had no idea his daughter was behind the whole thing, that she was 'Jane' from Scottish Cottage Rental, a fake email she'd set up that would be untraceable, bounced around the world by various re-routers.

Her plan had been to keep the radio switched off, leave them out there to stew. Then confront them when they returned today, after a nice long weekend of fear and suspicion, which was no more than they deserved.

Joan McCann had been keeping tabs on Vicky and Jonathan Capeman ever since they'd caused the death of her brother Fergus back in 2002. Joan had been off at university when it happened, and it had taken her almost two days to get back to Tarne, the worst of her life. Her mother had never recovered, and had walked into the sea herself five years later, so then Joan was back on Tarne for good, her life in London forgotten, her promising relationship with Stephanie ended, her career given up. It was then that she'd set up Google alerts for the Capemans, and had followed them all through the years. The cyclist Vicky had killed. The little girl who'd died because of the husband's dodgy company. The cameraman who'd died in the hills. And then Vicky Capeman's married name had popped up on a discussion forum for cottage rentals – she was looking for a place for her fortieth. Eight adults, three kids. It was the perfect opportunity to get them back here, and force them to think about what they'd done to Fergus, and to others. All she had to do was slip some pictures of her brother in among the photos they sent for the slideshow. Such privilege. Holidays, graduations, bottles of champagne in every shot. Joan hadn't bothered to look at them all, only burned it on to the DVD as asked. She'd just wanted some acknowledgement at least that they'd caused her brother's death. They had never been questioned about it, just fled back to London the next day, his drowning ruled accidental. Fergus swam like a seal. There must have been more to it, and she just wanted the Capemans to face up to it.

But she didn't understand where they were now. Had they not watched the slideshow? Had something else gone wrong? Why was the police officer going over? Joan was frantically trying to think if anything could link her to the incident. The booking wouldn't be traced to her, she'd covered her tracks well. The money would not have been paid out in the first place, as the account details she'd sent were fake. She'd bet, and been right, that Daniel Franks, the husband, was not the kind to point out such an error. God, it had been annoying fielding his questions. Could they have fireworks? Could they get a private chef to come? Was there really no Wi-Fi and if not could they get some installed? If the police ever got round to watching the DVD, they'd find the pictures. If only she could have done that remotely – but there was no Wi-Fi on the island, which was part of the appeal. The group would have been truly marooned out there. The only way off was the boat, the same one Fergus had drowned from. She had checked it when she went out during the week, to make the beds and prepare the house, set up the DVD. The boat had a small hole in it, she'd noticed, wear and tear from sitting out there for years, falling to bits. If they risked taking it out and it sank, well, that was a certain poetic justice, wasn't it?

The DVD was the only link to her. Had she actually committed a crime? Trespass – causing other people to trespass? Scaring people? Was any of it actually illegal? All the same, Joan was sweating. It was only supposed to scare them. Not hurt anyone. Just make them feel a fraction of what her family had felt, losing Fergus and no one even caring.

Her dad was walking towards her now. How to explain her presence? She got out of the car. 'Alright? I heard something went wrong.'

Her dad didn't meet her eyes. 'There's a lot went wrong.'

'Oh?'

'There's bodies, Joan.'

Her stomach clenched. 'What – what happened?'

'You know how it is with that rich lot. Tear themselves apart given half the chance. Seems they did it to each other.'

'You think that's what happened?' Her heart was hammering.

'Reckon they brought it on themselves, aye.' She felt something being slipped into the pocket of her gilet, and looked down. Saw the contours of something round and flat. A DVD.

'Dad . . .'

He was still looking out to sea, shading his eyes. 'There's a boat coming in now. Could be the rest of them. Terrible, terrible business it is. Still, nothing to do with us, lass. Is it?'

She gulped. Her fingers closed around the DVD, the only thing that could link her to any of this. 'No, Dad. Nothing at all.'

Fiona

She hadn't meant to do it. Of course she hadn't, she was a doctor, bound to save lives. But she had been pushed further than any woman should be.

It had started not long after Jonathan's cameraman died in the hills. It had changed something in him, and he'd begun staying out late, accepting every celebrity party he was invited to. As they lived outside of London, in Surrey, he often stayed over in a hotel, claiming he couldn't get back. Soon, that had morphed into the idea of getting a serviced flat to stay in mid-week. For work, he insisted. A man whose work involved being in the middle of nowhere, not in a penthouse apartment in Soho with a swimming pool and gym in the basement.

Fiona was busy. She had Darcy to look after, and she knew her daughter was very upset by the suicide of the girl in her class. Of course she was – what a horrible thing to happen, even if they hadn't especially been friends. Fiona was still angry Darcy had been named in the note the girl had left. No one person was ever responsible for someone else's choice to end a life, but the inquest had concluded that Darcy's rejection was one big factor in what had happened. She'd been doing her best to help Darcy work through the guilt, which she understood all too well from her own job.

Then there was her job. Covid had delivered a fatal body-blow to an already teetering health service, and she was now expected to carry twice the patient load as when she'd first started out as a GP. Telephone appointments, out-of-hours care. Jonathan kept telling her to move to the private sector, but she'd always resisted it, feeling there was something immoral in siphoning off the best care for the rich.

So perhaps she had taken her eye off the ball a little. She'd noticed he was staying up in London a lot, and was often drunk when at home, the whisky bottle level dropping precipitously. But she'd still been pole-axed with shock when he'd said he was leaving. Ninety per cent of her was anyway. She had known, in a sneaking awful way, that this day was always coming.

Her husband was handsome, famous, rich, and she was a forty-year-old woman who struggled to get into size fourteen dresses, still stretch-marked from Darcy's birth, and often too tired to do anything but collapse in front of reality TV. When they got together, she had been an Oxford medical student, a size eight with shiny dark hair down to her bum, and he'd been a drop-out, disabled, the black sheep beside his perfect blonde sister. Then there was the shadow of whatever had happened that summer they were nineteen. She'd known whatever it was had taken place on the island, but not what exactly.

Fiona had loved Jonathan since she was a teenager. She'd bargained, with herself and with him. If she let him go now, didn't make a fuss or give him a hard time, there was a good chance he'd realise he didn't like living in a bachelor flat with no furniture or pictures on the walls, ordering Deliveroo every night and missing his daughter grow up. She would lose some weight, smarten herself up, maybe go to Vicky's Botox provider, as her sister-in-law had hinted so many times she should, and win him back.

She wasn't expecting him to immediately – not six weeks after he left – tell her he had met someone else. Rachel. Instagram-famous, twenty-eight. And she knew what the accelerated timescale meant. He had met Rachel before he left – he had left *for* her, in fact. He'd had months to prepare for the separation, which was why he was fine and Fiona was barely holding it together enough to go to work and feed Darcy. She'd prescribed the wrong thing once or twice, but luckily the practice receptionist had caught her errors. It still haunted her that she'd missed Loretta Marsh's cancer at the start of her career.

Then this weekend. Jonathan's fortieth birthday, and Vicky's too. How cruel for her to have to go and see Jonathan with another woman by his side, a virtual stranger brought into their tight-knit group. Fiona had considered not going, but she didn't want to look churlish, and couldn't abandon her daughter to travel all the way to the west coast of Scotland with an inattentive father and some bimbo she'd only met once. So here she was. Fiona the good sport. Fiona the jolly-hockey-sticks prefect, the netball captain. Mother. Doctor.

And it was bitter, wasn't it, to watch him with her, around their friends, their little niece and nephew, even their daughter? Younger and slimmer and more glamorous, by about a million times, and Jonathan was still her husband. He still called her every day asking how to work the blender or who had the pension details.

Rachel was the interloper and yet all she did was put Fiona down, call her fat, go on and on about herself and whine about the Wi-Fi, and God! The number of people Fiona saw with real health issues, and there Rachel was, perfectly fine, whingeing about all her intolerances. And Fiona was just a little bit sick of being such a good sport that she could watch as her husband – yes, still her husband, no papers had been filed and no legal proceedings started or even discussed yet – went into his room with someone else, closed the door. That she could listen to them having noisy sex through the wooden walls, praying Darcy had her headphones in. No one could put up with such disrespect and callousness.

Jonathan wasn't a bad person – she'd never have stayed married to him all that time if this was his true personality. He was just shattered by the loss of Pete and his own guilt. He was having some kind of midlife crisis, and Fiona had been waiting for it to pass, hoping to stop him breaking things irretrievably. She just needed to get him away from Rachel and he'd come home, he'd go to therapy if she made it a condition of reconciliation, he'd be Darcy's dad and her sexy, successful, big-hearted husband. She'd hoped it might happen this weekend, with all the nostalgia and alcohol and his inevitable panic about turning forty. She'd be there to make him feel loved and safe. She had not expected he'd bring his fancy woman along, but then it was his birthday too. He would have wanted her there. But God, she was so bloody annoying, picking at the food, inventing spurious intolerances. Upsetting Darcy and Vicky and Amira and everyone.

The answer was clear – Rachel needed to go.

She hadn't planned it though. She was very clear about that, and would continue to be clear if and when the police should ask her about it. Although by now of course the plates had all been washed up and any evidence gone. Not on purpose. Just because she was tidy. And it wasn't as if she had brought the sesame oil with her in her handbag, that would be crazy. That would be murder. (Not to mention risky on the lining.) No, she had simply found the bottle in the well-stocked pantry of the house, and that evening, as Rachel went on and on about how she avoided sugar and really anyone who didn't just had to look at their body to know why they should, with pointed looks at Fiona, and picked over her meal for supposed allergens, Fiona had cracked.

So when she was tidying away Paddy's cake, and the slice Rachel hadn't eaten, she had drizzled a little something extra into the caramel syrup. It was just an angry outburst, no harm intended. She had put that bit back in the fridge, its plate covered in cling film, which Rachel had also objected to. *Isn't there any beeswax covering? I don't want to ingest a lot of parabens.*

She hadn't expected the woman to flounce back up from the beach and secretly scoff it in her room. And she certainly hadn't known Toby would steal the EpiPen. So was she really to blame? If Rachel's allergy was that serious, could she not have suffered an attack at any point?

Everyone else had been terrified when Rachel died, sure that the dire predictions of the note were coming true. But not Fiona. She had been terrified someone would know it was her. She had made sure to kick the plate under the bed – Rachel had left it on the floor, untidy as well as annoying – then take it away when no one was looking. She'd had the advantage of being the one who knelt down to try to give CPR, though it was useless. And there was everything still to play for. There'd been a moment between her and Jonathan the night before, a hug in the kitchen; and then again in the water, just the clear cold and her and him and their perfect daughter, when it had felt like the old days. Floating light in the sea, she had forgotten how much she hated her body, and reached for his arm to hold him up for a moment, and he'd let her, and he'd smiled at her, a sad smile, but a hopeful one too. She just had to get rid of Rachel, and look, she was gone.

She should own up now. It was too late for everything, and Jonathan had been lost to her anyway. She should admit that Rachel's death had been down to her, and not entirely intended. An accident. Though the police probably wouldn't see it that way. She'd be struck off, probably go to prison. Darcy would be left alone, especially now her father wasn't coming back from the island.

Fiona could not really take in that fact, but it had registered somewhere on the outskirts of her brain. Some part of her was doing calculations. Darcy was only fifteen. She'd go into the care system, and how would she survive that, a sheltered teenager who already blamed herself for the death of a classmate? Maybe Vicky would take her in. But would that be any better? Vicky was also on her own now. Wouldn't Darcy just become a glorified babysitter? Learn how to be thin and unhappy, like her aunt? No, Fiona owed it to her daughter not to confess to killing Rachel. After all, did it really make any difference now?

As Fiona watched the harbour of Tarne pull into sight – safety, salvation at last – she pulled her daughter tighter, kissed her on her shiny dark hair. It was all going to be OK.

BOOK CLUB QUESTIONS

1. *Truth Truth Lie* concerns a group holiday that's fraught with tension. Have you ever been on holiday with a large group and how did it compare to this one?

2. Amira has always felt like an outsider with 'the Group'. How much of this do you feel is down to people's behaviour towards her, and how much to her own feelings of insecurity?

3. Was Vicky wrong to marry Daniel, who had been unkind to so many of her close friends? Should she have been honest about what happened between her and Louise in the past, or did she have the right to keep it a secret?

4. All the guests on the island, even the children, are blamed for causing deaths in the past. To what extent do you think each of them is guilty?

5. Have you ever played the game 'Two Truths and a Lie', and if so did anything surprising happen?

6. To what extent is Joan McCann to blame for the events that unfold? What about Paddy and Louise?

7. Money is a flashpoint within the Group, with the richer members expecting the poorer to chip in for expensive activities. Discuss the etiquette around this and the morality of spending on luxuries when others are starving (as Louise points out).

8. Who was your favourite character, and who did you like least?

9. Of the four deaths that take place on the island, which killer was the most guilty, in your opinion?

10. Do you think it's fair that people in certain jobs, like social workers, doctors, and teachers, are often blamed for not preventing deaths they weren't responsible for?

ACKNOWLEDGEMENTS

I'd like to thank everyone who worked on the book, including Salma Begum, Gemma Wain, Ian Pindar, Victoria Oundjian, my agent Diana Beaumont, and my editor Victoria Haslam, who helped plot this twisted tale into being. Thank you to all my crime writer friends for their support, and to Dana for being an early reader – I hope your fortieth birthday trip turns out better than this one!

ABOUT THE AUTHOR

Photo © 2023 Philippa Gedge

Born in Northern Ireland, Claire published her first novel in 2012, and has followed it up with many others in the crime fiction genre and also in women's fiction (writing as Eva Woods). Writing thrillers for Thomas & Mercer, she has sold over a million books and has had several number-one bestsellers. She ran the UK's first MA in crime writing for five years, and regularly teaches and talks about writing. Her first non-fiction project, the true crime book *The Vanishing Triangle*, was released in 2021. She also writes scripts and has several original projects in development for TV, as well as having had four radio dramas broadcast. Several of her novels are also in development as television series. She lives in London and would love to hear from readers via the methods below!

Website and email via: www.clairemcgowan.co.uk
Twitter: @inkstainsclaire
Instagram: @clairemcgowanwriter
Facebook: www.facebook.com/ClaireMcGowanAuthor

Follow the Author on Amazon

If you enjoyed this book, follow Claire McGowan on Amazon to be notified when the author releases a new book!
To do this, please follow these instructions:

Desktop:

1) Search for the author's name on Amazon or in the Amazon App.
2) Click on the author's name to arrive on their Amazon page.
3) Click the 'Follow' button.

Mobile and Tablet:

1) Search for the author's name on Amazon or in the Amazon App.
2) Click on one of the author's books.
3) Click on the author's name to arrive on their Amazon page.
4) Click the 'Follow' button.

Kindle eReader and Kindle App:

If you enjoyed this book on a Kindle eReader or in the Kindle App, you will find the author 'Follow' button after the last page.